# SUMMER FUN

# SUMMER FUN
# JEANNE THORNTON

**SOHO**

Published by
Soho Press, Inc.
227 W 17th Street
New York, NY 10011

Library of Congress Cataloging-in-Publication Data

Names: Thornton, Jeanne, author.
Title: Summer fun / Jeanne Thornton.

ISBN 978-1-64129-238-2
eISBN 978-1-64129-239-9

Classification: LCC PS3620.H7837 S86 2021 | DDC 813/.6—dc23
LC record available at https://lccn.loc.gov/2021003845

Title design by Luke Bird
Album illustrations by Jeanne Thornton
Interior design by Janine Agro
Vector art by molotovcoketail/iStock

Printed in the United States of America

10 9 8 7 6 5 4 3 2 1

*For Wren, who was here through all this. In 2014 we almost adopted a rescue greyhound named Whisper; you would have known how to help this dog; I know it.*

*A children's song, have you listened as they played?*
*Their song is love, and the children know the way.*
—BRIAN WILSON AND VAN DYKE PARKS

*In Indian country here, there is a saying: it takes four*
*generations to heal one act of violence.*
—GLORIA STEINEM

# Author's Note

This is a totally fictional story, a tall tale. Any claims it makes about its characters—who are fictional, who are not real—should also be understood as totally fictional. Really: the act of projecting one's own context onto a myth does not make any truth-claims about the world or the characters in the myth, except maybe insofar as it would certainly be very unfair for one's life to assume the dimensions of myth outside of one's control, one's right to privacy, one's right to peace: for one's life to extend uncontrollably beyond the private so as to invite unfair mythic projection. It is hoped that anyone whose ghost hangs in that public firmament has long since grown used to being the subject of projection, that such people can exist in peace. This is because any projection is fundamentally false—fundamentally about the projector, not the vessel of projection—and any claims made in the name of such projection are therefore also fundamentally false, even if one hopes those claims are correctly understood as flattery.

Regardless: please accept this note as a magic cloak; drape it around yourself; be safe from anything I say, anything others hear. Be safe from all inference. This spell will not hurt you: I will pray for that.

# SUMMER FUN

# Discography

The Get Happies Love Drivin' (1962)

Burgers and Cokes, Gosh (1963)

Diner Girl (1964)

Everyone's Got a Car, Vol. 2 (1964)

Get Happies Haunted House (1965)

Right Now (1965)

Space-Girls (1966)

Greatest Hits, No Misses! (1966)

Psychic Attraction (single, 1966)

Summer Fun (unreleased)

Summer Fun Alive (1967)

Happy Mountain (1968)

Family (1968)

*Fourteen* (1969)

*Live Album No Joke* (1969)

*Another One* (1970)

*Fillin' Time* (1970)

*Here You Go* (1971)

*Broken Treaty* (1972)

*Greatest Hits Volume II* (1975)

*When Cars Could Fly: The Hits of the Get Happies* (1977)

*Greatest Hits Volume III* (1979)

*What If We Do This Forever* (1981)

*Psychic Attraction: The Great Hits of the Get Happies* (1983)

*Girls Need to Listen!: 15 Great Love Songs by the Get Happies* (1986)

*Drivin' to the Movies: The Get Happies Soundtrack Songbook* (1989)

*Suntime Funtime: Classic Get Happies 1962-1972* (1996)

*The Get Happies Say God Bless America to Our Musical Heritage* (1999)

*The Greatest Hits of the Get Happies* (2004)

*The Great Hits of the Get Happies* (2006)

*A Get Happies Christmas* (2007)

# Prologue

Dear B——,

Money, and lots of it, has been spent on cultivating this dog. That much is clear from the moment you bend aside the landscape bushes that line the front porch of your childhood home in Hawthorne, CA, revealing the hollow space where it's crawled to die. The dog is a gaunt shadow, a crescent moon built for racing, fur still smooth and groomed. At one time someone clearly loved this dog, brought it table scraps and brushed out any aerodynamic impurities that might lengthen its racing odds. You wonder if its owner misses it. One of its flanks is bruised, a crush of blood that blooms through the thin fur; one of its legs seems broken or on the point of breaking. It twitches, lying on its side, it whimpers; its big eyes look at you.

You crouch, both to get closer to the dog and to keep your head out of sight of the porch. You've gained a few inches in the weeks since your tenth birthday, 1953, and you need to make sure no one from your family catches sight of you. If your mom were alone, of course—or with your baby brother Adam, or less optimally with your middle brother Eddie—you'd be happy to ask her for help. Sometimes she is very clever about these things, and working together, you think you could help the dog without your father knowing about it. But this option isn't open to you now: your father has two very important business clients to dinner tonight, or maybe people whose business he's trying to win. Despite the many lengthy monologues he's given you, your mother, and your brothers over the past weeks on the subject, you're not altogether clear. All you know is that, having been introduced to the two men on their arrival, you're supposed to occupy yourself outside while your brothers sleep and parents eat.

Further, you're supposed to remain in range. At any time—your dad's informed you of this repeatedly, speaking in his insistent night-racoon scratch of a voice and putting his hand on your shoulder in a way that you feel guilty for feeling afraid of—he may need you to rush in to help him with his charm offensive. He may call on you to sing "Old Folks at Home," "Beautiful Dreamer," "You Are My Sunshine," one of your standards, to help him secure his investment of dinner in these men. If you're not here when he calls, he will notice; if he notices, he'll get anxious; when he gets anxious, trouble begins.

Sitting here under the bushes with this dog is courting trouble, not preventing it. Yet still you sit here, and with your eyes closed, you rest your hand on the greyhound's heart. The material components of caring come together easily, associatively, like the notes in a braid of harmony. You whisper to the shaking dog. And after a moment, you rest your face, as gently as you can, into the soft join between his powerful barrel of ribs and his lean front leg that terminates in a thick paw. He relaxes at your touch, heart beating. You imagine he closes his eyes as you close yours.

The earth is wet from rare morning rain that creeps into the hem of your short pants.

I'm gonna help you, you tell him. —You'll see.

AND YOU'RE IN LUCK: A few blocks away, at the corner of Mt. Vernon and Fairway, the boy you're seeking is home. Your cousin, Tom Happy, stands in the front yard of the house that his father and your mother's sister Marcella have recently moved in to. Tom is throwing a small pile of rocks, one at a time, at the trunk of a skinny oleander, staked in place to help it grow. Every time he chips the bark, he makes an animal hiss, cupping the sound with his hands like seashells until it sounds like cheers.

Hey Tom, you say, and he starts, embarrassed, and turns to you: blue mountain eyes, wheat-blond hair, jaw that will square up with time. He smiles, and it makes you nervous. Just a year or two before, his smile was easy, automatic; now it's more like he knows it's weird not to smile, as if someone has told him to practice it, just as you guess someone has told him to practice throwing rocks. Maybe you should also be practicing these things.

B——, he says. —How's it hangin' there, buddy?

You laugh, confused. —Hey Tom, you say. —I've got kinda a confidential situation over at my place, and I maybe need your help? Want to come over? It involves magic.

His eyes get wide; this is why you don't worry too much about his mean smile, because he always folds up after a minute in your company. Around you he grows innocent again.

You know magic? he asks. —No you don't.

I mean I don't know it *yet*, you say. —We have to learn it together.

You guess that he believes you, B——; you guess that he always will.

YOUR FAMILY DOESN'T GO TO church all that regularly; your father likes to tell you that he thinks people believe in God because there's something empty in them. But your Aunt Marcella insists that your mother and the rest of you accompany her on the big occasions, Christmas and Easter, the hall full of Methodist attention and your parents' smiles: your mother's polite, your father's smug, as if he and the priest have an understanding. You don't smile; your jaw hangs open, listening to the choir behind the priest, their voices swooping and knitting like seagulls—

*Lo! the sun's eclipse is over*

*Alleluia*

*Lo! he sets in blood no more—*

You try to put a nickel in the plate, but your dad puts his fingers on your wrist. *Be smart,* he mouths. So you hold the nickel tight—1944 its date, copper and manganese leaching into your fingerprints—and you listen to the seabird voices in the chords. You've already learned not to tell anyone else that you hear them.

TOM IS AT FIRST AFRAID to help you move the dog to the backyard shed—Oh jeez, it looks like a car hit him or something—but working between the two of you, you know you can manage it. The dog gazes up, suspended between you; either she lacks the energy to bite or she senses some good intention from you and lies still. In the shed, you lay her on a coiled blanket. The shed, though perilously close to the house's back door, is windowless save for a skylight covered in a moiré of leaves and dust, and its walls are lined with shelves that list ten degrees to either side, covered with all the belongings your father has not yet decided to throw away: bales of yellow newspapers, a short stack of Vocalion blues 78s he's spent some years collecting, a doctor's kit of uncertain provenance, a wooden frame without a picture in it, pitted from years of sea salt. It's all heaped in loose piles with chaotic borders: here, where no one looks, your father lets his careful control lapse. So it's here where you have to begin your work.

In a box, you find candles and long kitchen matches. With practice, you're able to light them and arrange them on either side of the arc of the whimpering dog. Tom knows the hymn just as well as you do; this gives you common magical ground. So you kneel beside him on the altar, let him sing the melody while you try to get your voice to roll to the back of your small palate, piping

it higher than it might otherwise go, sparkling mist over the top
of his words—

*Soar we now where Christ has led*—

The dog on the altar whines and twitches, its paws moving
in rhythm. Hanging over the altar is a beaten-up flag from your
dad's war-era work: one time you saw him drop it in the dirt, and
he declined to let it burn, so it isn't unpatriotic to use it this way.
And the breath of Charles Wesley is your breath: from your tail-
bone to your crown, you can feel yourself filling with something,
eerie electric blue. On impulse, you reach your hand toward Tom.
And if it was two years later, B———one year later, even six
months—Tom would stop singing at this moment, would draw
back his hand like a turtle into its shell. But you're young enough
now, untaught enough, and he doesn't laugh, just takes your hand
in reply. He grips it tightly; you feel safer, as if the fire in you can
arc now into him, too, a friendly circuit your skin makes. And you
kneel there together before the altar, singing life into the dying
greyhound.

And you really believe—and maybe Tom still does too—that if
you sing hard enough, you can reverse the effects of the car that
screamed into this dog from the LA streets.

But the name *B*—— bellows from beyond the corrugated tin
door. You and Tom have just enough time to let go of one another's hands before the door slams open, and your father is there.

PEOPLE ALWAYS TELL YOU THAT you and your father look
alike. They say this as if they mean it to be a compliment, and
maybe for another kid such as yourself, it really would be. But
you've always felt dread about the idea. You suppose that he's
handsome—tall, his tallness cheated a little by his eager forward
lean, hair the same mysterious middle territory between red and
brown as your own, its borders already retreating from testosterone, eyes intense and blue and rarely blinking. (This is a point

of difference you've always noted; you have your mother's eyes, apple and cinnamon.) He's wearing a suit and tie, its jacket generously tailored in tempo with the swift expansion of his courier business in the boom years since the war. He is flanked now by his dinner guests: a major in uniform and a lean, long-faced blond man who looks as if he designs rockets. Noticing the dog, your father leans forward, trying to shield them from the sight.

I don't understand, he growls, what you boys want to accomplish here.

Tom takes his chance and bolts, skirting the major's legs. You and your dying dog are both left alone under your father's stare. You have embarrassed him in front of men who are important to him. His breath smells like spice and water, abstinent. He is massive, drawing you into his anxious gravity like the earth itself.

YOUR MOTHER, ARRIVING WITH YOUR brother Eddie in tow, works quickly to calm the situation. She's good at this: she draws out an icebox pie she's kept in reserve, and she brings the two guests inside so that you and the man swollen before you can have a *father-son chat*. Your father gives her a grateful nod. She smiles back at him, and then, looking at you, nervously twists her lips. Her eyes are as afraid as your own, but you know she's not without sympathy for you. You're grateful for her sympathy; it always makes what your father does to you a little easier to bear. It's bad enough most of the time, when you're pretty sure you haven't done anything wrong. How much worse will it be now when you have?

She departs, one last look in your direction, leading Eddie by the hand. The major and the rocketeer follow, their eyes on your mother. Eddie stares back at you; he knows enough by now to pity you.

You're alone in the shed with your father. He begins to speak, to scratch.

I need you, B——, to explain just what it is you were doing,

he says. —It's very important I understand your intentions here. And B———it's very important to me, B———, that you never tell me a lie.

You look up at him. Right now he is calm, but it's critical that you assess, as precisely as you can, the other places to which his mood might go. What other moods has he had today? How much protection can you expect from the company that has just left the house? You know, you always know, that there's a very limited time in which to perform this analysis; he's watching you, and if he becomes too aware that you're working out a safe answer, his anger will double. He's reaching the end of his patience now, you can see; his thick arms cross over his equator; his face behind his glasses glows red. His hand is twitching.

Me and Tom were trying to use magic to save the life of a dog, you say quickly, your eyes closed. —We'll never do it again, honest.

Whatever analyses he's performing at this moment, as you fight not to cry—it makes him nervous if you cry, and situations get worse—they are inscrutable to you. But he looks, suddenly, at the dog beneath the American flag. You watch, trying not to shudder or reveal anything else, waiting for him to shout. Instead, he chuckles.

Do you know what the only skill that matters in this world is? he asks. (You exhale; if he's lapsing into his didactic mode, you're safe for a while.) —The one skill ninety-nine percent of the men you'll meet in your future career completely lack?

You don't need to answer most of the questions he asks you. You've learned that by now, although it's dangerous not to answer if he expects you to. But this question seems safe not to answer, you judge, and you're right.

Initiative, he proclaims. —Most of the men you'll meet lack initiative, B———. They're lazy, blind, weak; they just want you to help them. *Help me. Help me.* —He affects a wheedling, feminine voice. —Yet you saw this problem, and without asking anyone's advice, you elected to solve it. Initiative.

You stare at him, like Snow White offered the apple, unsure whether to take it. —I was worried, you begin.

What worried you, he demands.

I dunno, you say quickly.

You do know, he says. —Or you wouldn't have said it.

You've really screwed up now. —I dunno, you say again, but then correct yourself. —I guess I was worried you'd maybe hit me. —You laugh, hoping to neutralize this.

His face flinches, so slightly you're not sure anyone else would've noticed. Your heart leaps; you've made a mistake; you eye the exits. He carefully lowers himself to one knee, his face even with your face.

I want you to listen to me, he says. —Are you listening?

You nod; you have to, before he'll continue.

I would never hit my sons, he says. —That's extremely important to me. That's a point of principle. A point of principle is something you don't deviate from.

He seems to be waiting for you to respond. You nod quickly.

I'm not the kind of man to hit my sons, he explains. —I'm disappointed that you don't know that about me.

For a moment, he seems to move inward, nodding to himself, as if some scab has just torn off the skin of the universe and caught him up in an eddy of old, slow blood. But he shakes it off; he recovers. He looks at you, assessing you. You make yourself smile back at him.

Come on, he says. —The guests can wait. My son is more important. I'm going to help you save this dog.

Slowly, he turns from wall to wall, frowning as he reviews his possessions. The dog's eyes gaze warmly at you; his breathing has slowed down. You never got to finish your song; your father will hear you if you try to do it now.

He turns from the wall, a flashlight in one fist, the doctor's bag in the other.

We'll have to get in there and suture up the damage, he announces. —I'm going to need you to hold very tightly, B——. This breed seems kind, but they can bite your whole face into nothing like *that*. —He snaps, the dog flinches.

Your breath is coming very short. The dog's eyes are looking at you; she whimpers as your dad touches her. You smile at her.

Your father has taken out a scalpel, which he wipes off with his handkerchief. —To a clear-eyed man, he's saying, —it's all just a matter of moving carefully, step by step, through a problem. Hold his neck tight. —His eyes are wide, ecstatic even. Decisions are being made.

And you can interrupt him, B——. You can stop your father. You can knock the scalpel out of his hand; you can argue with him; you can cover the dog's body with your own. Why don't you do that?

It doesn't matter that you've already learned that nothing he says is worth much of anything. You think about that—how his kindness is worth nothing, how his anger is worth nothing, how clearly and logically you know both of those things—as you hold the dog down. You take initiative, as he said you would. He was kind, and if you cross him, he'll stop being kind. So you smile at her, you whisper for her not to be afraid. And your father sets to work restoring an expensive possession to a good and salable state.

I WOULD LOVE TO FINISH this letter to you in a less bummerific fashion, B——, but I'm in such a bad mood right now. I can hear the neighbors yelling at each other through the trailer door, loud enough that I swear their voices are echoing all the way out against the walls of the butte. Human voices are bad enough without echoes, and I'm so, so, so sick of never getting to be alone.

Love, Gala

# PART ONE

# September 1, 2009

Dear B——,

With this letter, a sorcery has come upon you. Your will is not your own. You will listen to what I have to say to you. You have no choice.

Here is what is going to happen to you. One day, you are going to grow up. You and your cousin Tom Happy will form a band. Your brothers will join you in this band; a neighbor will too. The band will be successful beyond what you or anyone considered possible. You will work extremely hard, and through that work you will produce albums that people will continue to listen to fifty years after their release.

(It's your record, *Space-Girls*, that I'm playing in my trailer out here. All electric light in here is extinguished: instead, three candles with lush pictures of saints and bilingual prayers slowly melt their way into the metal of my stove, my bare feet scratching against the fiberglass carpet, outside all the desert dark beyond the blue glow of the neighbors' trailer windows, and it's your record I put on when I prepare what I'm preparing.)

Something will happen to you in the course of producing these albums. A crisis will come upon you, a cruel shroud that will settle over your eyes and mouth, that will silence you for years. You are still silent, now, as I write you this letter. But don't worry, okay? Because soon you won't have to be.

Soon, your band, the Get Happies, will reunite for a world tour. Soon you will release the album on which your career foundered back in 1967, forty-two years ago. You will release the album, and it will be perfect; it will be better than the rest of us—listening in with our illegal bootleg MP3s, our encyclopedic knowledge of tape edit tricks of the 1960s—will believe possible. It will initiate a world revolution in music. Your reemergence will initiate another world revolution altogether.

Believe me, B——, that this is going to happen. I'm going to make it happen.

YOU SHOULD KNOW, BEFORE WE get too far together, that I am not actually going to tell you anything about my life story at all. I was born in the early 1980s. I grew up in an affluent Texas suburb. I am a white transgender American woman. This is most of what you need to know.

THE MAGIC RITUAL I'M PERFORMING to ensure that your band will reunite is of course constricted by the cramped space in which I've had to install my altar. It's wedged between the plaid built-in couch against the south wall of the trailer and the fold-down kitchen table and benches on the north such that there's maybe a foot and a half of clearance on two key sides. The altar itself is a Doc Marten box that I've decorated with a black cloth and a diorama of your band made from paint and a bunch of Goodwill-scavenged G.I. Joes, each standing in a magically appropriate position. I did a bunch of drawings of cool magic robes for myself in my sketchbook—tiger print, diaphanous butt-crack lace, gigantic Misfits logo across the front for graphic design reasons— but fabric stores are tricky to come by out here, and let's just say my sewing skills are *very much not the equal* of my music appreciation skills, B——. So instead of robes I have a Mascara Masque T-shirt I keep as clean as I can in the stack washer plugged into the mains out back and a skirt with long vines and leaves growing out of the navel of it, a cellulose anchor that roots me to the earth.

Until I actually *did* it so that I could *write* you about it, B——, I was scared for weeks to do this ritual. I felt like my cramped living conditions were maybe too dire for magic, that the way I live is not up to code where the spirit world is concerned. Yet is scary occult ritual only for the rich, the rigorous and prepared? So I did it. I invoked the prayers, drew the pentagrams, connected the circles, adored the archangels: to the east, your baby brother Adam with his bad mustache and bass, its neck doubling as conductor's baton for the army of backup musicians he has invited to share the stage. To the south, your other brother Eddie, long blond hair hanging about his ears as he sweats and smolders over the crash cymbal. Behind me to the west, Charley B, no relation, guitar strings liquefying along with guitar face as his notes arc and bend and texture, his affable eyes. And to the north, your cousin Tom stiffly gyrating on the microphone in his late-seventies garb of buckskin and feathers while his blue eyes count the asses in seats. All of you are gigantic—the biggest things I can imagine—and you are at the center, B——, choosing the chords on the piano, the pioneer on this magical path, the one in whose footsteps I have to follow if I'm going to get out of this desert place. To summon enough transformative energy to fill the box canyon of fissures and departures my life has become. To become a real person, just like you became, and just like you'll become again.

*We have to become friends right away.*

We will become friends, too. Once this ritual is complete, on the night your concert tour circles through Albuquerque, as it must, as is necessary to connect with the moping sixty-somethings who now make up your fan base, I will be in the crowd. I will shine up at you, in all of my glamours both psychic and mundane. And you will look down at me from behind your piano. You will know me, B——, because I know you. Because I am devoting a great deal of time and furious ink and missed hangouts with my pal Ronda—who is maybe not a pal, but we are both trans and we both live in the middle of nowhere so we are forced to be pals—in order to know you.

You will reach over the stage with your long arm—you are as tall as me; older but with a strength I know does not diminish—and you will lift me up to join you. I will have eyes only for you. I will not look at Tom Happy, who stands on the stage with you, capering at the corner of the stage, mic clutched close to his chest like a saint-bone crucifix. You will pass me a guitar, which I am totally learning to play.

THIS WAS MY PRAYER, B——. And I prayed for it a long time, as long as I could, the 99-cent candle burning a ring into my stove surface, until I started to feel stupid and the needle at the end of *Space-Girls* had run out. So I dispelled the circle, snuffed the candle, sat on the toilet in the plastic bathroom with the damp hanging laundry all around me, icy from the wall AC, brushing my face like submarine leaves. I put on my bike shorts, tank, denim skirt, and sports-strap glasses, took a can of gross raspberry malt liquor from the mini-fridge, and went around back, outside the east wall of the trailer where the bedroom is, where I sat on the stool, plugged my Goodwill guitar into the Thunderbird portable amp I keep out there, and practiced your songs as quietly as I could in ultraviolet twilight—"Suntime Funtine," "Auction Block Rock," "God's a Girl"—until the neighbors in the next trailer shouted, and I stopped. The neighbors are maybe nice people when they don't remember I'm here; for now I try to stay on their good side, out of sight.

Sometimes I go out at night to smoke cigarettes behind the

trailer. I sit on a small pallet where the owner of the park has stacked crates of old spray paint, rivets and screws from long-ago-lost machine shop hardware, motorcycle tires in different states of sun-bleach and disrepair. I can see the stars over the mountains through my cloud of smoke, and I think about the moon and the constellations and the fact that you're seeing the same moon. It bothers me that I can know that about you and that you don't know that about me.

I DREAM SOMETIMES, TOO. LAST night, before I started this letter to you, after doing three Tarot readings and throwing up once in preparation for this ritual I'm about to enact, I had an intense dream. You don't mind me telling you about my dreams, do you? I promise it'll just be this once.

I dreamed of a cis woman. One of her eyes was red and one was gray, and her hair was made of purple flames, and she wore silver studs in her face. She was riding a lion, naked but for a pair of Doc Martens, and her shoulders were covered in blood, and she was laughing. I was tied to one of the paws of her lion with what looked like coaxial cable, lashed around my ankle. She was calling me to follow her, her and her lion, and we galloped together into a vast city—like the city I came here from—sick with green smoke, silver towers, red dead sky, and Tom Happy's nasal voice echoing from every open window, singing that steel drum song about islands. And I think the apocalypse cis woman and I had sex or something, B——? I don't know; sex is something I find hard to imagine, even in dreams? All I know is that I woke up alone, the mechanical sunburst of my alarm clock telling me it was just before dawn—and I spent an hour wondering whether or not I should kill myself—and then I started this letter to you. Because I am proactive in response to despair. Because we all have to be.

*Don't back down from that wave.*

o   o   o

I'M ALSO SORRY THIS LETTER is coming in later than I'd planned. You can blame Ronda. I met Ronda soon after moving out here and getting the job at the hostel, which I guess I should describe to you for context. I guess take a deep breath before you read this next part, and maybe get out some notebook paper and pencils or something to make a map for later reference, or just to doodle with until I get through with the boring description stuff and start talking about you again, and about what great close and personal friends we are going to be very soon.

So the hostel I work at is just south of Elephant Butte, NM (pronounced *beaut*, like short for beauty; I was thinking it too, though.) The town is called Truth or Consequences, after a game show. As I understand it, one night the citizens of whatever-the-town-was-named-before were squatting in their shacks, heating up canned stews in iron pots, bandannas knotted over their faces against the desert winds—I don't know what they were doing—when the voice of the show's host Ralph Edwards came over the wires, all *I Am That I Am*. A million dollars: that's what he promised to any town willing to change its name to help promote his show. Most towns passed; the citizens of T or C cashed their check and repainted their post office. Now all they have left is the name, which makes the town sound—agreeably, I think—like the site of a mass cattle rustler hanging. They also have a statue of Ralph Edwards in the park. Every year until his death, Ralph Edwards flew to the town that had given up its name to honor him. He threw them a party and he told jokes. Truth or Consequences was all he had left.

I work at a hot spring close to Ralph Edwards Park, like a half a mile from my trailer. It's called the Dream-Catcher Hot Springs Hostel, and it's right on the Rio Grande: a few dark-stained dormitories with screen doors and coffee cans full of sand and cigarette butts, cabins, a small office, a gravel-and-opuntia yard with picnic tables cracked by long sun. There's also a dock at the back assembled out of some rusty steel bars and wooden slats. Ropes trail from the support struts near the dock ladder, tracing out ley lines of current in the mountain-cooled river. You're supposed to climb down the ladder, wrap your legs in the ropes, and let go, spread your arms cruciform in the water while the rope and the river play tug-of-war with you until of course the ropes break and you end up a day later in Juarez. And sometimes you can see the black shadows of gigantic river fish next to the trailing rope, schooling beneath you like asteroids.

Ronda showed up today at the office while I was playing *Doom II*: a five-nine transsexual woman with hair knotted in a high ponytail, shoulders broader than mine with a weird sun poncho hanging from her wrists, neon pink lipstick, skirt too tight, platform wedges totally inappropriate for crossing thin sand. I'd played through this map several times before, so it didn't take too much time, maybe a minute and a half or something, to finish up and save my game before I swiveled my chair to meet her.

Oh hey, I said. —I've been meaning to call you.

I always want very badly to be believed when I say things like this. I had no idea, from her face, if she believed me or not, but at least she didn't say anything about it, just took her sandy wedge off of the door frame and planted it, flipping her ponytail at me like a graduation tassel.

I've got today off, she said. —You want to do the baths with me?

I'm working, I said immediately, and as immediately regretted it. —I mean, I've got stuff to do this afternoon.

Ronda seemed unsurprised at this, but she'd evidently expected it: her hand slipped into her purse and drew out a ten-dollar bill. —That's cool, she said. —I'm gonna do the baths anyway, if that's okay?

This is a tactic that Ronda figured out would work at some

point: if she offered to pay to use the baths, I couldn't really turn her away by being too busy with work. If you make yourself into a customer, you and your needs become unassailable. It is a horrible trick.

I could see the sad setting in behind her eyes, like a spiny, stumbling millipede, something I was not confident in my ability to handle effectively. And she'd put her money away before I'd even told her I'd join her.

THE HOT SPRINGS OVERLOOK THE river. There are three sets of them, some encased in bath enclosures along the sand and scrub grass of the banks, some open to the sun. To get to the baths, you must walk out under the night sky and down the stone steps to the hidden natural basin among the scrub trees by the riverbank. You can soak by the rushing river, the blue mountain nights and their paint-spatter constellations; you can lean your elbows on the stone ledge scuffed smooth with years of other elbows, stare over the surface of the river as fog ferries out of the mountains and dream about something other than yourself and your problems. Or at least it would be nice, to do that.

When I quit pretending to work and went to join Ronda, she was already in the tub, leaning out and looking at the river. Her bikini was mismatched: its top red and high gloss, its bottom a complicated construction of two layers, one transparent and one opaque, with some kind of fluid thinly trapped between them, along with little cutout fish shapes; when the suit squeezed, the fish swam. For the moment, the fish were still. I took my sandals off and slid my feet in with her.

What's up, I asked.

Not much, she said. —Hanging. I've been sad, so I wanted to come over here. See the sun. It helps when I'm sad, you know?

Girls grow in the sun, I said.

She didn't answer. I moved my feet against each other until

all the sand had washed free from them and they were smoother than they'd been. In silence, half my mind worked to gauge just how sad Ronda was, the other half thought about how I had been a lousy friend to her. I hadn't made an effort to see her; I had to make amends. The best way to make amends, I think, is to give someone the thing that you'd want to receive yourself.

It's really interesting about that song, I said. —You know it was recorded at the *Summer Fun* sessions, right? But the weird thing—and this becomes clear when you check out bootleg sessions from earlier Get Happies albums like *Right Now*, or even further back—is that the bass line is that same walking thing done throughout. And it's tied to a lot of different songs with sun elements. So that bass line is kind of a sigil, right?

Ronda was looking at me in a way that I knew meant I should stop talking. We sat there for a while, soaking in the springs, in silence.

Is something wrong? I finally asked. —Do you want to like, talk about it?

No, she said, after another moment; she said it letting out a sigh. —It just sucks being trans.

It totally sucks being trans, I agreed.

So we talked about *this* topic instead of about sigils; *this* topic is usually what we talked about. How do I even communicate to you what it's like to have these conversations with this other trans woman? The encounter: a mundane setup, an interaction on the street, at a job, at a store. A statement, utterly insensitive, cruel, destructive. And then the eternal debate: did the person mean to do it? Did it happen because one or the other of us was trans, or just because we were deficient in some other way? Were we being too sensitive? Were we? It's not that we're being too sensitive? Aren't we?

I know what the right answer is when I'm speaking to Ronda: no, you're not too sensitive. No, they meant to do it. No, it was totally because you were trans, and it's totally fucked up that it happened that way. Again: you do for someone what you would want to have done for you. I want someone to do this for me: to tell me that *no, everyone was really against you all along.* If someone stands up for me, then I can continue to believe, without guilt, that I'm complicit after all. A friend does this for you.

This is what she came to me, I guess, to get. The specific culprit this time was her sister-in-law, a specific argument they were having about Ronda's half-brother, who has problems, and who lives in Ronda's trailer with her. (I don't even want to get into Ronda's family stuff right now; trust me, you do not want to know.) Ronda's sister-in-law misgendered Ronda not once, not twice, but thrice during a conversation about some specific assistance program that Ronda's half-brother was or needed to be applying for. Being misgendered is par for the course; what we were trying to tease out today was some kind of correlation as to *when* Ronda was being misgendered, specifically: like did it happen more often when Ronda's sister-in-law was upset with her and her reluctance to include her legal name rather than just the initial R on key government documents, or did it happen more often when her sister-in-law was relatively pleased with Ronda, telling Ronda's brother a nice story about the last time they had gone shopping together, or about the foods they might eat at the forthcoming big family Thanksgiving? If you added up the absolute number of misused pronouns you got one interpretation; if you factored in more qualitative concerns, like tone of voice or whatever, you got another interpretation. This is what's so fascinating about these conversations: there is a mystery to them! It's sort of like talking about God, and as frustrating. But by trying to answer questions you can't answer, you sort of construct a creed with one another, harrow it just a little deeper into your skin.

The whole time we had this conversation Ronda floated, just her head and neck protruding, cooking, while I sat on the step, my ankles and feet trailing in her waters, my body getting cold.

I don't know why they hate us the way they do, she said. —I mean, why? Why is it they hate us so much? What exactly is it that they like—despise?

I sat uncomfortably. —I mean, I don't know that they *hate* us, I said. —It's just—we're weird to them. I mean, it makes sense? And they're incurious, and they're entitled? But I mean—they don't *hate* us.

Ronda floated. —Well, *I* hate us, she said, eyes relaxed.

I FIRST MET RONDA WHEN she came into town to buy drugs. She and her Lenin-looking dealer came by the baths to unwind afterward, and he'd pointed me out to her: *Hey, there's someone like you here, doll.* If I had been in Ronda's place, I'd never have spoken to anyone pointed out to me like that. But Ronda came right up.

Do you smoke? she asked.

I gestured to the American Spirit I was chaining, and she shook her head. —Oh, I said. —No.

That's a shame, she said. —I like your glasses.

I felt then the complicated emotion that I feel whenever I encounter another trans person out here in the wilds of 2009. The complicated emotion started with a question: did this new girl even like, read me as trans? Why should I even care if she did? But I *totally* cared if she did: I felt, while she was looking at me, as if I existed, was possible in a way I didn't even realize I'd missed from the city, and no matter how many times I encounter other trans women moving through my life like little paper lanterns in the shipping lanes, reading the fat kanji painted across their surfaces that promise Meaning like nothing else: I will always forget how much I miss that feeling of being seen. I will learn to ache for it all over again, each time one of us vanishes. That was how it felt in the beginning with Ronda, for me.

I'M GONNA MAKE SOME STEW for myself for dinner tonight, Ronda said, toweling off. —You wanna come by? We can keep working on beating that *Mystic Knights 3* save file we started that one time.

I'm doing something tonight, I told her. Which is true, B———: I'm writing this letter to you. I didn't tell her what I was doing, though, and she didn't seem surprised that I was begging off. She just nodded, toweled off, put up her hair and draped her weird poncho over her shoulders, and went off in her truck, skirt and wedges hanging from her hands and feet sugaring with earth. And I felt lighter as I watched her truck get small, vanish behind tire dust, as if I was getting off work for the day: the time for being present with a friend was over at last.

I HAVE THIS ROUTINE IN the baths, B———. You so want to hear about my bath routine.

I lock the door; I set the towels by the edge of the tub. I pace the edges of the tub two, three times, like an animal trampling a bed; I check the lock. There are three walls in the baths: three to block out the rest of the hostel, the fourth open to the river. By day, in the 102-degree light, you can see the red hill rise out of the desert on the opposite side. Staring it down, I let my braid out, hair falling over the soft white strip of defoliation on my forehead, always cool to the touch like fat on sizzling bacon. My tank top today is a bunch of braves riding out of a sepia mist, DEFENDING THE HOMELAND SINCE 1492; I try not to think, as I remove it, about how my stomach and hips don't connect where my brain tells me they should. I do the bra thing; I unlace my combat boots, unzip the skirt and shuck off the bike shorts, fold and set them aside. I make myself stand up, drop all optical defenses, and get into the water as I watch the hill across the way. Nothing has been built there; no one lives there but lizards and wind.

Sperm production requires a certain temperature: your body in heat adjusts itself to hit the sweet spot; everything expands. The best part of the springs at hot noon is that between the water and the sunlight, you cook yourself into stunned submission; you let the anchor hooks of consciousness detach, get into that dreaming place that ritual of any kind is meant to reach. So I cook, and I think, until it's time to get out—I stand, visible, dripping—I blink in confusion, gather my clothes. There's wind from the mountain—water scours from my skin—what if the canyons of myself were shaped differently, what if I were cis, what if I were rich? Then those dreams blow away too, an offering to the gross desert. And only one dream remains: wondering just how we will meet, B——, just what we will say, just what you will see in me. Just what you will give me of myself at last.

Love, Gala

# September 3, 2009

Dear B——,

The painting that hung on the wall of your mother Susan's child-hood bedroom shook every time your grandparents fought. Susan could see it from her bed: ten years old and piled in chessboard afghans, cloth doll lost among the fevered tangles of her limbs. She kept her eyes fixed on the painting, tried to breathe, tried to let her mind float, like she was trying to get over hiccups. If she could banish every thought, her mother wouldn't scream any-more—wordless ragged screams that went on until her breath ran out—and her father wouldn't pound his fist on his desk as if he were trying to pound her mother to nothing, as if her mother wasn't already nothing—and the painting wouldn't vibrate. But Susan must have failed, because it did.

Her father had a very stressful job: *we rebuilt the whole city,* he would say to her when she asked him what he did, where their money came from. At first, she thought he'd personally rebuilt it—he was tall and broad, qualities that would one day seep into you and your brothers—but then she learned that he meant the loans and investments he'd brokered had paid other people to rebuild it. It still seemed impressive: like he'd clapped his foot, and gold rose out of the land to serve him. He'd promised Susan's mother that if she tied her life to his, if she came west with him to California, to this city that the earth had flattened out—*the perfect opportunity Nature created*, he'd say, *find something broken down to nothing and build it up again*—he would always take care of her. He reminded her of this promise often. He hadn't signed up for what she became.

Susan couldn't remember a time before her mother's silences, although she knew there must have been one. Her mother never spoke, never met eyes, glided from room to room in silence while servants went ahead of her, accomplishing whatever she needed to accomplish. Her illness felt regal: queen following drones. Sometimes Susan would be reading on the couch, noodling on the piano, and she'd find her shoulders growing cold and still. And she'd turn to find her mother there, watching her. Sometimes she ducked away from her mother's stare, and sometimes she tried to meet it. But her mother could stare like no one else—a level, smoldering stare, almost vibrating in its intensity, reading your mind—and Susan could never match it for long.

Her mother had decorated the house, continued to decorate it: moved furniture in the night, hung and took down artwork, so that Susan would wake up and enter the living room and for a moment believe herself transported to another house altogether. The paintings her mother hung always fascinated Susan. Paint itself fascinated her: Venetian stone, pulverized and suspended in linseed, pigments layered too thickly to grasp the meaning of right away: value and hue resolved into figures, then dissolved into value and hue again. You could watch for the moment of change without quite catching it. Later in life— in the house in Hawthorne, her sons moved away, alone in her world that you can not see—Susan would, when unobserved, drag herself to the porch steps, sit slumped with her back to her house, and stare at the leaves of the trees across the sidewalk:

she focused and unfocused her eyes, trying to turn them into paint and back.

The overwhelming quality oil paint had, like overdubbed recordings: a sound so large and complicated you can forget yourself within it. You can hide.

HER MOTHER WAS THE ONE who'd chosen the painting in Susan's room; Susan was sure of that. The painting was a kind of Bloomsbury production in blue and gray, a woman in the middle distance who gazed at a young man bent over a desk and scribbling at papers. The woman looked at the man, steadied herself against the door frame as she watched him. It was a bizarre selection for a child's bedroom. And it was a mystery: like a panel in a newspaper comic sliced free of context, a secret narrative gift that floated to Susan from her mother's castle in the moon.

Her mother was a goddess of the sky. Her father was a god of the world. Susan was nothing, hiding in her room while they clashed and the picture frame shook. Her father had rebuilt the city from the earthquake: maybe he was the only thing holding it together now. Maybe her mother could scream so loud that her father would disappear, and all the demons of the earth would run loose.

If her parents were gods, how was she supposed to take care of them?

SHE FELT ALMOST SILLY THE first time she prayed to the painting. Just the barest whisper—*please stop shaking, if you stop shaking, I will do whatever you say; I will give you whatever I have*—so low no one could hear it, if anyone was even listening to her. But the painting kept shaking—they kept fighting, below—so she whispered it again, louder.

Any ritual action, repeated, becomes stronger: every time a band rehearses, it becomes tighter; every time a hit song is played on the radio, the magic embedded within its harmonies soaks that much more intensely into the weave of the world. So the second time Susan prayed, her parents stopped. Below, she could hear her mother sob, her father speaking lower than she could understand. She stared at the painting. Still, it stared back.

*Thank you*, she whispered, honoring the bargain she must have made.

SHE CONTINUED TO PRAY, GROWING louder and more confident, and the words of her prayers began to lift away from the earth of mere prose, gained melodies and directions. She sang her prayers whenever her parents fought, sang them sometimes even when they were quiet, insurance against the next fight. She added motions; she marked out the four quarters of her room, circled from one to another: painting, oil lamp, flower in pitcher of water, window facing north over the slow and rising hills. She sent up her prayer in each place. She traced designs in the air: this design was her mother, this one was her father. Be at peace, she begged. Be at peace. Be merciful; be loved.

She thought, one night long after the sun was down and the moon was full and high, unable to sleep and pacing the quarters in her nightshirt: my mother went insane. Now I'm praying to a painting. Does that mean that what happened to her is happening to me, too? Does madness transmit by blood, just like hair color, like height? Sin passes from generation to generation: the work of each generation, then, is to renew the generation that will come after it. The child is the father of the man. The maiden gives birth to the mother, to the crone. So am I going to go insane too? Will my children?

THE DISEASE TOOK HER THREE days later: kneeling in prayer, she tried to get up and found her legs full of needles, her head fogging to gray when she tried to stand. A servant found her unconscious; doctors were summoned. No one told her what the doctors told her father; she was sure it was one of the terrifying diseases with the short names: polio, dropsy, scarlet fever; moontouch, whisp, alkali muddle. She was sure they expected the disease either to cripple her or kill her, or both. She stretched across the bed, not expecting to get up from it again. Her father sat at the foot of the bed, speechless, looking over her and silent. He wasn't hitting anything; the painting was still. Susan couldn't see his eyes.

I made a bargain, she thought, staring at the ceiling of the room where she'd given prayer. A bargain was made.

HER FATHER WITHDREW HER FROM school, had the servants bring her books to read when she could. When she got tired of reading—alone, the house a harmonic soup of creaks and sounds and drafts, advance honor guard of spirits gathering in the hallways just outside her bedroom—Susan stared at the image through a red mist of death fever. She stared at the man from the painting. He was the woman's lover; for the first time she realized that. These were lovers, tied together. He was pale, you got the sense tall if he unbent himself from his chair, plum-red lips the only warm color in the whole composition so that everything pulled your eye straight to him. There was some awful demon in the papers on his desk that was his and his alone. And the woman's job, like a beam of moonlight, was to lead him out the window to freedom.

Susan imagined taking the woman's hand, and together they could walk deeper into the image, deeper into the hallway, where the woman would show Susan her life. Plants she was potting, watching grow into monsters. A dog she'd raised. Rumpled bedsheets heated by a warming pan. Notes written to herself in a journal, in secret. A whole hidden life, a consolation.

SHE SPECULATED ABOUT WHAT THE instant of death might

feel like. It would hurt for a moment, as if a scab as large as her body was tearing away. Her weightless soul would slide out of the bed and fall feet first into the frame of the picture, her nightgown billowing around her legs from the movement of air as if she was wading into a lake. She imagined her soul floating through starscapes, clouds of fleshy, pale angels opening their mouths and letting protopsychedelic waves of rainbow paint gush like thought balloons from their lips. At last she would disappear into a dark, dying star, rise through a column of pure light, and appear from the inkwell on the man in the painting's desk like a tubercular Tinkerbell. She would slowly grow, slowly grow pale, silently walk to the back of the office where she would tap the woman in the painting on the shoulder. They would look at one another a moment, nod, not speak. And then they would trade places: Susan would assume the woman's position watching the man, stuck together in linseed and pigment for eternity.

ONE NIGHT SHE WOKE UP to find her mother watching her, silent in the corner of the room, at the door between the painting and the lamp. She couldn't see her mother's eyes either, only feel them. Somehow she knew her mother was looking at the things she'd drawn invisibly in the air.

Her mouth was becoming more and more difficult to move, but she did so then, began to sing the prayers she'd devised with whatever breath she could muster. Her mother heard her.

THE NEXT DAY, THE PAINTING was gone. In its place hung an oversaturated pastel of a girl with honey locks, striped leggings, and dreamy eyes, swinging in the dead center of a gilt oval frame. Susan stared at it. She tried, again, to still all of her thoughts—to be very quiet until the hiccups stopped—and to her surprise, she found she could do it.

She began to improve; she could get out of bed now, sometimes.

She kept this secret: waited until all sound of the family's presence in the rest of the house had stilled, and then she had to creep out of bed and down the hallway, heat clicking wetly from radiators, silent ghost moving through the same halls her mother was elsewhere, haunting.

Finally she found the painting. It now hung opposite a credenza with candles and a small dish for visitors' cards, empty, a cabinet full of hunting rifles on loan from her uncle flanking it. Susan stood and stared at it. She moved her mouth, praying, but the prayers no longer worked; she could no longer remember their tune. And eventually she got scared her mother would find her, and she hastened back to bed on dying legs.

LATE FLU CARRIED HER MOTHER away the next year. Her father found a new bride—younger, compliant—and the house stopped changing, and Susan never prayed again, forgot her songs. Much of the incident disappeared, its contours warping and collapsing in on one another like candle wax every time the flame of her memory sparked. Repetition changed the memory's contours, too: made it stranger, more magical than it had probably been. Whatever had actually happened to her remained buried beneath waves of overdub.

But she still remembered one clear moment. She woke up to find that the man in the painting had turned to her. He had looked at her, his eyes at once like her father's and like her own. And she knew suddenly that there was a violence in the world—an old sin that was propagating forward in time like a cresting wave—and that her life was being claimed in service against it, to ride it, to help it break. She had no choice.

She thought: *one day, marriage will happen to me.*

Love, Gala

# September 4, 2009

Dear B——,

I was in the hot springs again today before my shift, hunkered down beneath the waterline with my brain smoking so that when I closed my eyes the trillion-candlepower sun made the capillaries under my eyelids stand out like cave paintings. The rattle of bottles came from the yard—the owner talking low, an early run for coffee filters gone foul—my shoulders were tight where the sun steamed the water from them.

I was thinking about my shift—the amount of money I could expect to make from it; the impossibility of ever using that money to change my life, fundamentally, from what it was right now—when I saw the figure walking on the side of the hill just across the river.

I slumped back beneath the water, cool air on my cheeks where they stuck out of the warm. The figure had a wide-swinging, high-stepping gait, like a kid trying to splash every puddle in the rain-soaked sidewalk. They were wearing a hoodie; I instinctively respected this basic indifference to clothes that matched the weather. It was hard to make out more details than this, which had an obvious reciprocal meaning: there was no way that any figure over there could make out details about my body, either, here in the stew.

So I started to relax, which is when the figure held up the big digital camera from their side, pointed it at the hostel, and turned on the red light that I swear I could see glinting like Martian war-radiation from all the way across the Rio Grande: the red light that meant *record*. I ducked, held my head underwater until my blood churned through my ears like bubbles of cabin air from sunken ships.

When I surfaced, the figure was still present, their camera still out, the red light still on. As nearly as I could tell, the lens was pointed at the second, natural baths at this point, currently empty and awaiting the cleaning that I had yet to clock in to do. Flickers from the pink hands, fingers on the tight/wide angle selector. They were walking, careful where they put their feet even with their eyes in the viewfinder. They were walking in the other direction.

The figure's face beneath the hood was obscured, their shoulders vibrating. And then wind on the hood: sucrose purple hair. A blast of sunlight bouncing off ears that seemed made mostly of metal and plastic. Lipstick radiant, cartoon pink against the brick-red hill, the dead gray brush, her cold gray eyes. The cis woman I had seen destroying the world in my dreams was suddenly filming weird rocks on the hill across the river from my place of employment.

Alarmed, I turned to face the back wall of the bath. But I kicked, in turning—subliminal betrayal; the body cannot be trusted—and sent up a splash. When I turned back again to see whether the dream figure had noticed, her camera was trained directly on me. My eyes met her eyes—one red and electronic, one a color I could not yet see. Was she still recording? The tan skin of my forehead breached the water, wind drying out the space between my eyes. A thought forced its way in: the image of myself rising out of the water, letting her see more of me, shoulders, chest. The thought was mortifying, sent me further down.

Beneath the water, I sat stewing, eyes open and stinging from the mineral particulate moving around me: tiny stones that blended with the water, that remained on my skin like armor, like dust, and above me I imagined her camera light sweeping over me like the ray of a red sun. But when I surfaced, her camera was at her side and her back was to me: she was clambering down the hillside to the north, likely bound for the bridge just north of Ralph Edwards Park that I knew would bring her back to my side of the Rio Grande. And I began to worry.

SETTING THE COFFEE ON THE chair mat and sitting on the floor with the BACK SOON sign up on the door, I went through the Private Customer Files until I found her. The implausible name on her photocopied California driver's license was CARO-LINE WORMWOOD. Caroline Wormwood was officially 5'6" with HAZ eyes, and she was born September 11, 1987. The picture was terrible: ghost-pale turtlish face, large wide nose, sleepy eyes, freckles and acne jumbled together. Her hair color was listed as BLU, and I scrutinized the black and white photocopy, trying to figure out if this had been clear from the original picture. Did they actually let you do that in a driver's license?

Other facts about Caroline Wormwood gleaned from the files: she'd paid for her stay in cash, at the lowest rung of the hostel's sliding scale. Two weeks paid up in advance, with no intended departure date listed. The vehicle listing was left blank. She was staying in the women's dorm.

AFTER CLEANING THE SHED, IT was close to time for the townies and guests to roll in for their soaks, so I swept the bath area, tightened the pipes, and turned on the system before running to the corner store for a pack of American Spirits and an amethyst crystal. The morning was still burning off, and I shivered as I sat on the steps of the second baths, feet in the water and ashing in a coffee can, rubbing my fancy new crystal around the filter with my smoking hand. Across the river, the shadows burned off the hills, and the steam rose from the surface of the springs.

An older couple was the first to show up, just in for the night en route to Salida, Colorado: a lithe bodyworker wearing sunglasses and a big Horned God pendant, her husband's gold-pigmented beard slowly fading to lead. Caroline Wormwood followed: I shivered again as I saw her approach. She'd ditched the hoodie and the video camera and was bare-legged, torso and shoulders shrouded in an olive army jacket with the words PVT WINO stitched over the breast pocket, her kneecaps baggy and her calves goose-pimpled pink in the cool morning air. She'd painted her toes in glittery spiderwebs that curled against the leather of her Tivas. She gave me a sleepy smile—did she recognize me? Can you fail to recognize someone whose body you've recorded?—and her row of earrings sparkled and winked. Her swimsuit underneath her army jacket, unzipped, was a droopy two-piece, purple too, made of some dull-metal looking material. She tossed her coat on the deck and got into the hottest water, the purple hill of her head looming over the stone edge of the bath, black roots now visible, running vertical like shadowy claws about to make off with her skull. And I felt the feeling I get from cis women: the mixed fear/envy feeling, like toxoplasmosis, maybe.

Hi, she said suddenly, not looking at me.

Hi, I said, unsure of the etiquette in the situation. *Hi, Caroline Wormwood, do you maybe have film of my body? Can you maybe destroy it while I watch you?*

I feel like I'm boiling away, she said first. —Like I'm gonna turn into soup.

I can probably find some carrots and onions, I said.

She laughed, although I couldn't tell whether it was earnest or the laugh cis people give when they relate successfully with a trans woman: the *oh you are human!* laugh.

Come in with me, she urged. —We can be soup together?

I don't soak in public so much, I said, face level: how does one pretend to be normal? How does one pretend one has not had a strange eschatological dream about the person one is talking to?

Caroline studied me. —I'm Caroline, she said. —Listen, are you the one I filmed earlier?

I flushed and lit another cigarette. —Maybe, I mumbled.

Oh, it's cool, she said, as if I had apologized. —I was just up filming the hills—I didn't know anyone was going to be in the bath that early. I just film. It's pretty neutral what I'm filming. I didn't mean you any harm. —She bobbed under for a moment and then rose up. I tried not to see her eyes flickering toward my skirt; I tried not to adjust my posture.

She asked me my name. —Gala, I said.

Gala, like a party? she asked, and I shook my head. —Too bad, she said. —And your preferred pronouns are *she* and *her*, right?

My preferred pronouns are *you* and *fuck*, I said, kicking my feet out of the water and splashing her in the face. Which was not totally professional, but at least I didn't actually dump the coffee can full of butts and ashes into her water when I bent down to get my cigarettes and stalked to the fence to smoke one, and then another. Then I went back to the water, where she was still floating there, quietly. She looked up at me as I approached again.

I'm sorry for offending you, she said, smiling. —Is it bad to ask pronouns?

I think you mean I'm sorry for offending *fuck* you, I said. —I explained about my preferred pronouns already.

Her smile twisted into a different smile. —What's your problem?

Nothing, I said immediately, suddenly conscious that I was an employee of this place. —I'm sorry. I'm working; it's early. It's fine. —She was still looking at me strangely, so I added: —My pronouns are she and her.

We sat in silence for a while, and in the end I felt stupid for complaining, guilty for having been mean.

I'm Caroline, she finally said, as an olive branch. —Mine are she and her, too.

Cool, I said. —Twinsies.

She laughed. —Are you going to be around tonight?

No, I said to her, grateful that she'd resumed the conversation. —I'm going to go home and summon demons.

Can I watch? she asked.

I tilted my head at her: why would she say that? —I mean, I'm around most other nights, I said.

She nodded, and she submerged for a moment. I watched her swim for a while, trying to decide whether it'd be okay to ask her to delete the film she'd taken of me, if this was an okay boundary to establish between us. Something about my inability to just come out and say this—*hey, maybe you could take the naked film of me on your camera and make it not on your camera!*—made me angry, in part because I wasn't sure anymore whether I wanted her to delete it. I slid my feet like a mermaid's tail into the bath with her. Essential oils leached into the hem of my skirt, and Caroline surfaced, smiling.

What do you ask the demons for when you summon them? she asked. —Whatever they're paying you, I'll double it.

I stared at her—steam and sulfur rising around the sugar-bright hair that hung like a violet shroud at her neck—and I believed her.

Love, Gala

# September 5, 2009

Dear B——,

Questioning your impulses is where the trouble begins; this might be your family's creed. Your grandfather never stopped to question whether driving an ancient black steel Ford through the mountains was a viable method of emigrating to California or not. He simply did it, all the way from some terrible all-American town in Kansas, like Superman, except his only power was that drought and eerie heat had combined to kill his crops with super-speed. So he moved his family west. Your father remembers the headlights like the eyes of a dim insect expelled from its hive, your grandmother and your unknown, theoretical uncles asleep beside him on the board. Your dad only tells you about it once, maybe twice in your memory. It's not a place he wants to visit often.

EVERYONE LIVED TOGETHER ON THE beach—temporarily, your grandfather assured everyone, until he was on his feet, until the dream could start to move beneath them. Your dad tells you about the sensation of waking up hacking ocean grit out of his nostrils—his skin desiccated, bruised, the monotony of blue-black waves with enough power to splinter bones that taunt him every few seconds with their seductive roar, striking around his feet like an angry cat sinking the tips of her fangs a few cells into your skin to remind you that she is wild.

Your dad and his dad and your grandmother and some of the uncles that he never speaks about all slept in a tent, really a sheet of canvas riveted to the roof and stretched off the side of the same Ford that had brought everyone here, its black paint now slowly staining white from salt and sun. Nothing shut out the roar. Your dad tried to build dirtheap sand towers that wouldn't fall down, but they did. Who needed the ocean? Glowering, he thought that.

Every morning but Sunday, a truck pulled up the dune road that ran beside the boardwalk. Your grandfather climbed onto its running board, and he and all the other heads of beach families went to the groves to pick oranges. He came back late at night with money and liquor, singing, and the family would gather around the fire for bread and hunks of blackened potatoes floating in broth, and to sing with him.

Your dad liked it when your grandfather sang. He tried to do it too. He found out quickly that he had no power to carry a tune. Instead he beat the sand with his feet, echoing the rhythm of the death waves.

*He don't plant taters*, he sang. *He don't plant cotton.*

THE NEXT MORNING YOUR GRANDFATHER woke your father in the dark.

Today, he announced.

There was no choice. They got dressed in the dark, gulped a cup of coffee each from the pot on the still-dying coals, and made their way shivering up the road to where the truck would arrive. Your father half expected one of the other laborers to recognize the ring of purple bruise around the lower orbit of his left eye, maybe deduce the link between your grandfather's ring and the red nick carved into his own skin. He didn't try to hide any of it, even turned to make the wound more obvious in the predawn gloom. But none of them cared, even if all of them probably noticed. It wasn't unusual.

As they sat together on the back of the truck, your granddad held your father around the shoulders to protect him from flying loose.

There was one long break for sandwiches—your grandma had packed some kind of fish-and-lard salad—and there were a few shorter breaks for coffee, at least formally. But there were also ten million tiny halts, passings of the bottle, your granddad singing. Your father hated these breaks. If the adults wouldn't screw around, he reasoned, everyone could be done so much faster. The bosses might even reward them for being fast, though being fast and skillful was its own reward. His arms would barely move, but what were his arms? Weak, useless, babies, disgusting. The more he moved them, the more they hurt; he kept moving them.

He tried to work through the second formal coffee break to make up for the others' slack until a drinking friend of your grandfather's came up to him. The man was as large around as he was tall, like a top, eyes forlorn above his blond stubble, his red roasted cheeks.

Stop making us look bad, he said to your father, and things will go easier for you.

Your father tried, as best as he could with his teen rhetorical skills, to explain that he had no intention of stopping, that if the other workers felt this made them look bad, that was their own business to resolve. The worker punched your dad hard in the stomach, throwing all the wind out of him, and your granddad was the first to laugh and encourage the other old men to pile on top of him. He sat out the next hour, aching and whimpering and trying to recover enough to stand up, to *want* to stand up, and the boss, furious, wanted to dock him the hour's pay, but your granddad furiously talked him out of it.

He's *my* son, he blustered. —It's his *first day*. You be *good* to him.

And again he kept his arm around your father's shoulders on the truck ride home, the other workers sighing and singing and hooting in slow sunset relaxation all around them.

As he lay there on the sand, your father imagined owning a newsstand. He'd sell different papers, magazines, comic books; he'd fill out purchase orders and take shipments and negotiate the rent down with the landlord; he'd let the dimes and dollars accrue until he could buy a second newsstand, smaller but on a better intersection. Eventually he would have newsstands around the globe, at which point he'd begin purchasing newspapers themselves. He'd publish stories in them about how he and his family had once needed to sleep on the beach, how they had to go without food, how sometimes he looked at people in clean clothes walking up and down sidewalks and how he'd want to lie down and let them walk over him as he slowly liquefied in the sun, drizzling into dank asphalt cracks. But he had saved his family from all of that, and everyone who read his articles would know it. The president would read his articles. There would be a statue of your father erected by the seashore, staring out at the waves. In the bottom crook of his eye he'd acknowledge the ocean, its secrets, which only powerful forces like your father and the ocean knew. He'd forgive them. They couldn't touch him anymore.

*We love you,* he imagined the president saying to his statue. He shook it off, feeling furious at having had a thought like that.

THAT NIGHT, YOUR GRANDFATHER RETURNED. Your father watched his family, squatting on the dunes while they cooked around the fire that night and your grandfather drank and sang. When he thought they wouldn't notice, he walked further along the dunes, skirting the ocean.

He watched them eating the food his grandfather had earned,

the food even now in his stomach, building his adult body. He thought about where the truck might take him tomorrow, how much stronger he might become. He thought, and he thought, and he tried to hold on to his dream: that one day, everyone could see just how good he could make things, just how well he could love them.

Love, Gala

# September 6, 2009

Dear B——,

Here is your gossip update: when I was closing the office for the evening, there Caroline Wormwood was again, leaning against the wooden column that held up the front of the porch.

Can I help you, I asked. —Are you here to get me fired?

Sure, if you don't do what I say, she said happily. —I want to interview you for a project I'm doing. Tonight, maybe? Or no, you're summoning demons tonight. Tomorrow night?

Why do you want to interview me? I asked carefully. —I was mean to you earlier.

Forget about earlier, she said. —Earlier doesn't exist! No, it's just this project I'm doing. I interview people I meet as I travel for my movies—I make movies, weird movies. It's casual. Come on, dinner and an interview. Wear something nice.

She wasn't mad at me for having stood up to her about my pronouns, B——: I supposed I owed her something. And she was looking at me in a strange way that I didn't understand. What was it? Did she just want to interview a transsexual or something? One must be very careful not to misread what was happening.

Dinner and an interview, I repeated. —Okay, I can do dinner and an interview. Tomorrow night.

Wear something nice, she repeated, putting a finger at the corner of her lip.


I OWN A CELL PHONE, but I leave it on its charger in the trailer for most of the day as protection. Tonight after work it was full of missed calls from Ronda. I took an hour to clean the kitchen and start drawing a bath before I called her back.

You never answer your phone, she said.

Yeah, sorry, it's got bad reception out here, I said. —Sorry I missed your eleven calls. What's up?

She told me the details of a recent slight by her sister-in-law while I put away dishes, dug through my cache of ancient bath products, and watched an avocado-and-cream bath bomb slowly dissolve against the rosacea-beige plastic of the tub. —Uh huh, I said to her, trying to take off my bike shorts and tank without making obvious taking-off-clothes sounds into the phone receiver. —Wow. That sucks. Uh huh. That's terrible.

Are you doing anything tonight? she asked, suddenly. —Do you want to meet up or something? I can buy you a drink.

I can't tonight, I said on instinct.

So tomorrow night? she pressed. —It really pisses me off, and I don't know—I just wanted to talk to someone about it.

Oh shit, I would tomorrow night for sure, but I can't, I said. —I have a date! Or I mean, an interview date.

Her whole tone shifted; Ronda loves dates. —Yeah? she asked brightly. —Who do you have a date with? Boy or girl?

Girl, obviously, ew, I said. —She's a guest at the hostel. She wants to interview me for this video project she's doing. I don't know how much longer she's going to be here.

Video project? Ronda asked. —Like about transsexuals, like wow, imagine transsexuals?

She's traveling, I explained. —She's making a movie in every town she visits. Just whatever she feels like filming. I'm someone she feels like filming, I added.

How do you know it's a date, she demanded.

She said to wear something nice, I said. —Do you think she was fucking with me or something? Like saying I don't know how to dress, because I'm trans?

Probably she was fucking with you, Ronda said. —Tell me more?

She kept asking questions about the situation, drilling down on my responses: how had we met? What did the concept of a date mean to me, relative to the concept of a meeting? What were the other signals that this was a date? What did I like about her? I tried to answer as best as I could, surreptitiously undoing my braids, stripping down to my bathing suit, and, in a yogic coup, managing to slither without sound into the bath while still holding the phone.

So wait, Ronda said finally. —Just to be sure, this is a cis girl we're talking about?

I lay in the water, second bath of the day; the water had grown colder since we'd begun talking, and I inched my toes to the faucet to try to heat it. —I mean, odds are good.

That's a bad situation, Ronda said. — I don't think I'd ever date a cis girl.

You're straight, I said. —You *a priori* wouldn't date any girls.

Yeah, well, especially not cis ones, she said. —*A priori* or any other kind.

I thought about that, water echoes and the smell of avocado around me.

You sure I can't come over? she asked again, suddenly. —I could help you pick out an outfit for your thing.

Oh, I said, trying hard not to splash in alarm. —I can't. I've got to work early, and I'm, you know, I've got to get ready for the date.

Ronda was silent for a while.

I dreamed about her, I explained. —Before I met her.

*I summoned her,* I wanted to tell Ronda, but that was something crazy to think.

So what do you want to do on your date with your dream cis girl, Ronda finally asked.

She's not my dream cis girl, I said, suddenly angry. —God, it's probably not even a date. She's going to be asking me a bunch of questions about my life. I want to ask her a bunch of questions about her life, too.

How nice for her, Ronda said.

AFTER GETTING OFF THE PHONE, I tossed it into the bedroom, away from the reach of water damage, cranked up the hot faucet with my toes, and settled my phone hand, grown cold, into the warm. I lay there for some time, thinking about the crappy family situation Ronda had told me about: her sister-in-law who was against her, her brother who didn't stand up for her, her other brother who wanted to die. It was hard to sympathize with her when she didn't just get out of the situation: disappear, go to a city or something, all these surely easy things to do. Ronda was a different kind of person than me; she could do a great job in the city, around people who were more her kind. I had not done well there.

My cis dream girl: this is what Ronda had said to me. It was wrong to resent Ronda for having said this. So instead, I fantasized about helping Ronda. Maybe the interview with Caroline would somehow play on TV, and someone from a rich place would send me a check for it. I'd give half the money to Ronda for a train ticket and wave goodbye to her from an Amtrak station until she got to somewhere she could be happy. Maybe you would see the interview too, B——, would see it and see me. And the fantasy slowly shifted from Ronda to center instead on what our friendship might become, and I floated for a long time working through it before I got out, shivering, the water grown blank and cold.

Love, Gala

# September 7, 2009

Dear B——,

Public school had worked, as had the WPA and the clearly impending Second World War, and your father had risen from the beach. By 1940, he'd put together a small moving business called Prometheus Movers, basically a truck he was half owner of along with a Hollywood extra named Lock Cable, probably for career reasons. To your dad, Lock had two virtues: he was good looking, and he was egoless enough to allow your dad to paint a logo of him as a Greek god holding a torch on the side of Lock's truck and to claim eighty percent of the profits while making Lock pay for eighty percent of the gas.

Yeah but see thing is it's my truck, Lock once protested.

Your dad sighed a world-weary sigh, a sigh he'd practiced as an eighteenth birthday present to himself. —I'm doing the heavy lifting here, Lock, he said. —That's what I do. I move things from where they are to other places, where they aren't yet. From what is—what isn't. That's Prometheus. That's the essence of business.

But it's my truck and I shouldn't pay for it is the thing, Lock said.

What's a body without a brain? your dad asked. —A *skeleton*. What's a pickup truck without a *business plan?*

Still, your dad kept his word about payment, and as long as Lock kept up his end of talking to anyone your dad wanted him to talk to until they agreed to let your dad handle everything they owned, even twenty percent of the take was essentially free money. And Bill was likable enough. It was the way he was big without seeming to know he was big—physically large, stooping through doorways, but often prefacing arguments with people who owed him money with a soft *Before you think of hitting me, let me explain something*, the way his hands shook with preemptive indignation in the act of filling out an invoice, the way worry lines had already, at eighteen, cracked across his face. It all made Lock feel like protecting him. And if protecting Bill meant giving him free use of his truck and letting him scream at Lock whenever a client deserted them—*we're going backward*, he'd scream, *backward is not growing*—then that's just what Lock was going to do. From each according to his ability, et cetera: it was friendship, he figured.

LOCK LIKED TO GO WITH a woman named Marcella Tellebore, known in better parts of the county for being a card, someone who owned plenty of board games. Marcella—Marcie, to Lock—was planning a games night. In part, she told Lock, she wanted to find someone for her housemate: her cousin, Susan, only recently moved in.

She's a really special girl, Marcella argued. —She had a whole year of college before she—well, she decided it wasn't for her. That's the kind of girl she is—really independent, really sensitive. So if you know anyone solid. Stable.

Lock immediately thought of Bill. Bill was solid—he never spent any money—and he was always able to control his anger when it counted. Plus the guy never seemed to go out with anyone, walked hunched over through the streets from chronic back pain, biting his lip when he stood in lines or waited at traffic lights. The introduction would be a favor to both of them.

THEY MET FOR MONOPOLY IN the apartment Marcella and Susan shared, the liquor bottles all polished on a shining silver tray, the floral curtains blowing soft in the window-mounted fan that interrupted the bright green expanse of wall. Lock picked the top hat as his playing piece. Marcie picked the tiny dog. Susan—skinny, twenty, eyes big but set off by sleepless purple circles—picked the boot. When she moved it she made it skip on its toes. Bill watched her wrist move as she danced her boot down the board.

I don't care which token you give me, Bill said. —Whichever token I start with, I'll build into such a moneymaker that it'll be the token everyone wants to start with next time.

A confident man, Marcella said.

Some people will think it's a lucky token, Bill said. —But the rest of us know that there's no such thing as luck.

He's a real philosopher, Lock said nervously.

Susan looked at him, her eyes level, as your dad blindfolded himself with one hand, fished in the tiny token pile, and pulled out his choice: the steam press. He squinted at it and nodded slowly, as if he'd found the coin in the fairy cake. He winked at Susan. She continued to stare, fascinated, repelled.

FORTY MINUTES INTO THE GAME, Lock and Marcie, flirting hard, were both distracted enough to forget to bid on properties they landed on, allowing Bill to pick them up at auction.

You can't keep doing that, Lock protested the third time it happened. —It's not even a rule.

It doesn't really seem sporting, laughed Marcie, hands adjusting Lock's collar. Susan sat studying the boot between her fingers.

Anything's sporting as long as you don't cheat, Bill said. —And I'm not cheating. Now let's talk about Oriental Avenue.

I own Oriental Avenue, Susan said.

I know that, Bill said. —You're going to sell it to me.

Why would I do that? Susan asked.

Because I'm going to offer you $800 for it, Bill said. —That's cold, hard cash on the table, right now. The value of the property on the card is nothing. Folks'd have to land on it 135 times or more before you'd see such money again. Ridiculous. Never happen. You're not even factoring the taxes on it. I'm doing you a favor.

No, you aren't, Susan said.

Sue, snapped Marcella. —Don't be a spoilsport. Take the money! This gentleman is being very generous in offering it to you.

Susan turned to Marcella—*if I do that, he'll win,* she wanted to say—and Marcella was looking at her like a senior nun looked at a tiresome novitiate, and Susan realized her cousin understood the stakes of the game, and how little they mattered. She felt so stupid; social things had been going on again; again, she'd failed to understand.

Slowly, she returned her gaze to Bill. —I want $900, she said.

Bill smiled and offered his hand for Susan to shake, the money neatly counted within it. She put the deed in hers. They exchanged theatrically. His smile dropped the moment he took the deed, which surprised her. Didn't he realize she was letting him win? Was she failing to play the real game well, too?

Lock was talking about all the wonderful things he'd use his wad of Monopoly money to buy for Marcie—roses, emeralds, a silver-plated limousine and her own tiled bathhouse. He arched the bills in his fingers and released them, letting them spatter in her face like CMYK rain while she laughed. Susan watched them, biting lead cosmetics off her lips. Bill had organized his portfolio of deeds by color and was constructing a crabbed spreadsheet on a pad of his company stationery. She let the Chance cards coast her around the board, paying her rent to stay in Bill's growing green and red slums, keeping silent when Bill took the dice for an extra turn between the increasingly occupied couple on the couch, the column of black numbers on the memo pad getting darker and longer as he went, his own wad of bills neatly tucked beneath the edge of the board. When Lock and Marcie stopped being able to pay rent, he forgave the cash in favor of property deeds. When they ran out of deeds to give him—when he owned, in fact, every property—he smiled and told them not to worry about it, to treat the owed rent as a loan. Sometimes he'd loan them extra hundreds to keep them on their feet. Susan stopped skipping her boot when it was her turn, tried to shuffle it forward among the long alleys of green, choking houses that bloomed all around her playing piece. Lock and Marcie were spending more and more time looking at each other; the board had lost their interest.

At last, Lock landed square on Oriental Avenue with hotel.

$550, said Bill. —I'll add it to your debit account?

No, that's fine, Lock said. You win.

Bill's face twisted. —That's unacceptable, he said.

Marcie, her neck flushed, exhaled and adjusted her ankles. Lock sat on the couch beside her, blinking at the board.

What do you mean, it's unacceptable? he said. —I'm bankrupt. The game's over. You win.

We're very tired, Marcie said quickly.

The game's not over until you pay back your debts to me, Bill said. —Or until I finish building on all the properties.

Bill, we're *so* tired, Marcie said. —And you're *so* much better at this game than we are. And I'd love to plan a rematch with you, if—

I'm not better at the game, Bill said. —You're not honoring

your debts to me. You're trying to quit before it's your time to quit.

Do you really want to make us wait until all your little hotels are on the board? Marcie cooed. —I don't think that would be very fun.

You don't have to speak to me as if I'm an infant, said Bill. —I'm not an infant. I want us to play by the rules. An infant can't understand rules.

But you were cheating, interrupted Susan, without thinking about it.

Bill turned to her. His eyes, suddenly, were flat, blank like the backs of mirrors. She could watch the apple in his throat moving, swallowing. How still he could sit, she thought, and then he stood up and kicked the table from beneath, snapping one of its carved legs off, scattering all his deeds and hotels and houses and dollars onto the carpet.

LOCK EVENTUALLY GOT MARCIE TO stop shouting at Bill, strong-armed her into the kitchen to make a cup of tea. Susan could hear them from the crook in the wall into which she'd melted at the start of trouble. She listened: their voices quietly rising and falling. She stared at the ruin on the carpet, Bill laboring to clean it, muttering to himself as he organized deeds by color, houses with houses, hotels with hotels.

Are you okay? she asked Bill, when he seemed calm.

Bill looked at her, his eyes vibrating but dry.

You don't have to pity me, he said. —I reject your pity.

That's fine, she said, quickly. —You can do that if you want to.

He stopped cleaning and looked at her. She studied him back.

I guess I made a real mess of things, he said in a very quiet voice.

She found herself biting her lip, feeling the thin, sick vein in it run just below the ridges of her tooth.

o   o   o

LATER, IN HER ROOM AFTER the guests had gone, she pried
her heel from the back of her shoe. Inside was a smaller shoe,
made of pewter, its spur poking into a callus on her heel. She
hadn't even been able to feel its irritation. She spread out on her
bed, her party dress hanging between the hems of her stockings,
thinking of his face in the moment she had gotten on her knees to
help him collect his money, how the luxury real estate had lined
her fingers like a red nest as she handed them to him in a heap.
And how grateful he could look, she thought, how at peace.

Love, Gala

# September 8, 2009

Dear B——,

The interior of the women's dorm, where Caroline planned to conduct our interview after our dinner of pancakes and eggs, didn't look any different from the other dorms—big circle of couches, beanbags, butterfly chairs and fold-ups clustered around a rain-damaged coffee table stacked with newspapers, issues of *New Mexico Highway* and *High Times*, the odd *New Yorker* with the local library's address written on the subscription label. There was a TV-VCR combo unit on a little metal shelf, piles of old VHS tapes in dog-eared white cardstock sleeves arranged in teetering stacks, titles of movies and shows written in ballpoint spiderwebs on the spines: *Point Break*, *Charlie Rose/Russell Means*, *Walk through Yellowstone 8/88*, *Sacred Yabyum Energy*, *Doris St Kitts Vacation*. There was a bookshelf, romances plus Poul Anderson, Spider Robinson, Lewis Shiner, Paul Quarrington, Philip Dick, Alistair Bantam, the inevitable Castañeda, Lame Deer, Black Elk. There was a communal food shelf laden with bread, yeast, canned vegetables, a massive Ziploc bag of probably oregano, a fridge full of old yogurt and Tecate and sauces, a freezer packed with ancient gray steaks awaiting the Last Judgment and the New Life to come.

Caroline had on an interview outfit: kelly green cords, purple smoking jacket, chartreuse polo shirt; she glowed among the dust and adobe, clasped her hands together in a politician's cheer. The camera she perpetually carried was now mounted on a tripod with only two of its original legs; the third had been amputated below the knee and replaced with what looked like a splintered mop handle. She set everything up, jockeying her apparatus into place while I sat frozen on the greasy couch. At last she got it working—the red light winked open—and she hustled over to sit at the far end of the couch, where she straightened her spine and crossed one corduroy leg over the other with a zip, smiling the breakfast mascot smile of a born interviewer.

Okay, she said smoothly. —Try to be as natural as you can be. Try not to edit yourself. And—energy! Energy! Energy! Go!

She pointed at me, and I sat staring directly into the camera.

What would be the most useful thing for me to talk about, I asked nervously.

Everything is useful! she said. —Are you anxious? Talk about your anxiety?

Okay, I'm anxious, I said. —Talking about how I'm anxious. I think my voice sounds bad and I maybe look bad. I would like not to be interviewed anymore.

She looked disappointed, so I got it together.

I could talk about the Get Happies, I said. —I'm good at talking about them.

Who are they? she asked.

I stared at her. —Are you joking? The Get Happies. The band.

She made a face, pulled at her collar. —What do they sound like?

There is something unsettling about someone asking you a question like that, B——: *Food? Tell me more! I've heard mixed reviews about that one!*

What do you mean, what do they sound like? I asked. —They

sound like the Get Happies. I think George Bush sang with them one time. They're the most American possible sound.

Are they like—hip-hop or jazz or something? Caroline asked. —I don't know very much about hip-hop and jazz.

I hate this, I said.

She leaned forward. —Talk about that hate, she said.

I crossed and recrossed my legs, my cheeks hot from the devil starlight of the camera's red bulb. —What's even the purpose of this interview?

To get to *know people*, she said. —I mean, to know you.

That's the thing I want least, I said. —Let's just talk about the Get Happies? To really know me, you have to get to know the Get Happies.

Okay, so who are the Get Happies? she asked.

I thought. —There's B——, I said. —B——'s brothers, Adam and Eddie. There's the weird guy, Charley Brushfire. There's Tom Happy.

Did they name the band after him, she asked.

No, it's a coincidence, I said. —He's the low voice, and sometimes the lyricist. He wrote all the songs about like, rape culture and male gaze and pom-poms and material acquisition. Everyone hates him; it's safe to hate him.

See, that's very interesting to me, because, said Caroline. —Take Los Paranoias—from like, the same time period, right? Like the 1980s?

The sixties, I said.

Whatever, Caroline said. —They have that whole song where Nigel tells that girl there'll be nowhere for her to hide if she ever betrays them, that even her family can't protect her because he's her family now. But everyone loves Los Paranoias. Why does everyone hate Tom Happy?

Then I don't know, I said. —I don't know why I love the stupid Get Happies. I guess I'm *myself stupid*.

Don't call yourself stupid, she said sharply, and suddenly I felt something: on instinct, I sat up straighter, adjusted my feet against the dorm floor. She looked at me through the camera, its red eye moving over me while she adjusted some knobs, keeping me in focus.

What should I call myself, I asked. —I mean, what should I talk about?

Tell me a true fact about yourself, she said.

A true fact about myself, I said. And I don't know why I said what I said next, B——, which was this: —I guess I did a magic ritual to meet B—— from the Get Happies. And I think that's what made you appear.

This was a totally insane thing to say. Caroline heard me say it. She nodded slowly, adjusting her knobs, but her eye no longer in the viewfinder: she was looking at me now without technical mediation.

Tell me more, she said, her voice a little softer and slower. —You believe that you made me appear with a magic ritual? And I'm supposed to bring you to meet this person I don't know anything about?

I nodded; I wanted to say *I know it sounds stupid*. But she'd told me not to call myself stupid. I couldn't stop imagining what my own body must look like in her lens. I hope I looked hot, maybe, passable, like a real girl.

I've never been summoned before, she said. —Tell me more about this summoning. Tell me more about myself. What else was I supposed to do?

You can do whatever you want, I said nervously.

You said you summoned demons, she said. —Do you think of me as a demon?

Did I? —No, I said.

I'm not supposed to be murdered, she said, wiping her hands on her slacks. —Some kind of demon you sacrifice to music.

No, I yelped.

Sensitive about murder? she challenged. —A murderer would certainly be sensitive about that.

I'm not a murderer, I pleaded. —Please forget I said the weird thing I said.

But I can't, she said. —I'm extremely interested in interviewing you about the weird thing you said. Please tell me more about your experiences with summoning. Is this something a lot of people here do? Can you teach me how to summon people? How many people do each of us get to summon?

Did she mean to ask whether all transsexuals know how to summon people through magic, B——? I didn't know what to tell her, but fortunately she had gotten interested in the topic of magical summoning, and soon it was mostly her talking, telling me all the things she might do with it—the moviemaking effects she might achieve, the economic systems she might destroy, the old friends she might see again. If she was talking, if I was invisible, I was safe: I remained safe. She never actually asked me, B——, why I was so intent on meeting you. I think it was just a given that I would be.

CAROLINE TELLING ME ABOUT HER plans for magic phased into Caroline telling me about her movies, and we ended up watching one of these on her fat old laptop that trailed cords and wires, thick as a slice of garlic bread propped on the coffee table. It took some time for her to set the computer up, untangling plastic spaghetti as she frowned and drummed her fingers at load screens and progress bars.

In her movie, a girl foreign correspondent, played by Caroline with a baseball cap and a windbreaker, shivered by the side of a suburban street, a microphone made out of a flashlight and balled aluminum foil six inches left of her mouth. Horrible electronic music played as she rolled her eyes back toward her forehead, slackened her jaw, opened her mouth to release a tide of severed arms from different action figures and what I guess were watered down SpaghettiOs dyed neon purple.

This was from my action figure phase, she said. —There are actually a lot of these. They get surprising.

Do you pretend to vomit in all of them, I asked.

Not in all of them, she said, fondly. —They were a phase of mine.

SHE SUGGESTED WE TAKE A walk to the river and the baths.

We can go in maybe, she said. —You work here, right?

I don't have anything to swim in, I said.

Good thing I already recorded you, then, she said. —Just give me a second.

She went to the sink to brush her teeth. I sat on the edge of the slashed up cutting surface by the fridge and watched her, terrified I was misreading this whole situation. She looked at me out of the corner of her eyes, rotated the toothbrush to sand plaque from her teeth in a goofy striptease kind of way. She spit.

Could you like feel my forehead, she asked. —I can't decide if I have a fever or not.

I felt it; she closed her eyes. She felt sebaceous, like fried food.

WE WENT OUT INTO THE night, out to the yard where abandoned ashtrays slid like ghost ships over the picnic tables in the wind, past the abandoned adobe pits of the baths that I'd have to scrub and fill and facilitate in the morning, down to the geothermal pool on the banks of the river. Steam came off it, a rock bowl containing reflected alphabet soup stars. We were close enough to the office to hear the telephone ringing.

Shit, I said. —It'll be a second, okay?

She scowled, angry that I was answering the phone. But if I didn't answer it, who would? The desert was my garden to tend, and somehow I knew it would be Ronda on the other end of the line.

I'm in trouble, she said. —Can you come help me?

I sat on the rolling office chair—*this fucking bitch*—and prepared to be a good listener and ally to my sister.

UM, SO I HAVE A surprise for you, I said, clasping my hands. —My friend Ronda decided to get trashed at a bar in Elephant Butte, and some guys are being terrible to her, and she's worried they're waiting for her in the parking lot, okay? So I was *thinking* that maybe we could go and rescue her!

Are you serious, Caroline said.

Yeah, I said, brightly. —Do you want to come help me with her?

She considered. —Let me get my camera, she finally said.

WE BORROWED MY BOSS'S CAR—HE keeps a spare set of keys in the office—and headed to Elephant Butte, me driving, Caroline filming, radio playing Foreigner. The real estate in Elephant Butte is cheap because the customer base is low, so Ronda's favorite bar uses a ton of space to serve almost no people: two stages, long tables topped with black vinyl, huge yard with tall milk jugs for ashing into, all for the benefit of a kid who worked at the grocery store, an older guy in a ball cap, and the twerpy-looking owner of one of the souvenir shops. The three of them clustered near the single draft hose and shot us nasty looks as we passed. The rear wall of the place almost disappeared into the draw distance, only three or four beer advertisement swirls of neon revealing how far back we'd have to walk to get to the gross bathrooms. Caroline loved it, made arcs around the ill-lit space, while the locals watched her. Ronda was sitting at a table alone, trashed and updating her eyeshadow.

You brought an entourage, she said, looking at Caroline in her coat and neon shirt making epicycles around the beer neon back stage.

I thought you were in *serious trouble*, I said.

I braced myself for escalation, but Ronda was too tired. She let me shoulder her weight, carried her spike heels in one hand. The softness of trans women against your body: like house cats crossed with lynxes, trophy pets of some demented breeder who turned us out feral. I began to lead her out the front door.

Are you going to pay her tab? the bartender asked. (Its tab, I thought I heard the grocery store kid mutter.)

Before I could think of how to resolve this, Caroline quickly crossed to him and propped her elbows on the bar. —How much? she asked.

The bartender openly stared at her chest. —Seventy bucks, he said, and Caroline took a hundred dollar bill out of her wallet, which seemed full of them, and gave a small salute. The other patrons whistled and laughed as Caroline smiled, picked up her camera, filmed them appreciating her as she backed out.

No one was waiting for Ronda in the parking lot; there were just mountains we couldn't see beyond.

RONDA LIVES IN A CRAPPY trailer park on the north side of Elephant Butte, on the way out of town toward the reservoir, which I mention because the logistics of getting out to her place: two transsexuals, both alike in dignity except Ronda was trashed, plus a queer filmmaker, two cars between us. In the end, we chose to leave my boss's car at the bar for me to bike out to get tomorrow, and Ronda, Caroline, and I bundled into Ronda's busted old station wagon to take her home. She slumped in her front passenger seat, tracing figure eights with her nails, bitten through and dangling a fringe of dark violet polish, while Caroline recorded the back of my skull.

Ronda owned terrible CDs: overproduced nineties chanteuses, weird holiday compilations and best-of career retrospectives, discs she'd bought for the one hit at the front of the track list. The one listenable CD was a 1980s pop-psych group, their jangly textures coruscating around us. There was a late-80s Get Happies CD stuffed in there as well, B——; I let it lie on the floorboard.

From the back seat, I could feel Caroline's camera. Was letting her film me and Ronda even ethical? I didn't know, but letting her do it was the path of least resistance, so maybe it counted as self-care.

Ronda stopped scraping at the window and rolled onto her back, let the seat drop so she was lying down, eyes heavily closed. She looked like a carved sarcophagus; she looked pretty.

Everything sucks for us, she said. —You're lucky you don't date guys.

You might meet a good guy, I said vaguely.

I didn't tonight, she said, opening her eyes a crack before wincing and closing them again.

The law of induction, though, I said.

I never know what you're fucking saying, she said.

So I got silent and drove through the dark, and after a moment Ronda kept talking. She talked about the kinds of guys she was interested in and proved why none of them could ever, mathematically, be interested in her, or in any trans woman. And I kept praying that she would give up and stop talking. Stop talking about this, because I didn't know what to say anymore without feeling stupid in the attempt to say it. And eventually my prayer was answered: we left the lights of the town proper behind, driving red gravel roads toward the reservoir in the darkness, and Ronda stopped.

I wish I had a rear projection screen, Caroline announced after a minute of quiet. —It's hard to see anything outside of the car. Maybe I could just like, layer in another background in Final Cut or something?

What are you even talking about, Ronda groaned, her eyes closed.

Oh, my documentary, Caroline said, swinging her camera

from the nothing outside the car toward Ronda, steeped in 1980s dream-pop, within it. —Want to do an interview? You can talk about anything you want.

Ronda sat up slightly. —Are you filming me? You can't film me.

But you'll be famous, Caroline said.

I don't want to be famous, Ronda said. —I want like—two pots of coffee and a hot dog.

Where do you expect us to be able to buy a hot dog? I asked, driving, not turning or threatening to turn.

You can always buy a hot dog, she grumped.

Exactly where? I asked.

She sat for a moment, silent and angry, before pushing the lens of Caroline's camera, still pointed at her, toward me. —Film this bitch, she said, and she propped the seat all the way up and hunched within it, like a covetous crone queen.

RONDA'S TRAILER HAD LONG AGO lost its wheels and engine, but she (or, presumably, her dad, who she'd told me bits and pieces about and who had a gusto for unorthodox home modifications) had compensated for that by painting the steps cherry red and propping three giant lean-tos of wood, concrete, corrugated tin, and zip-up plastic sheeting against the sides. In the full moon's light, they glistened like IV sacks. Caroline, brightening, got out of the car and began to circle the trailer in slow reverse panorama, filming, but I made her get back in.

Hey come on, I said. —You can't like—film their life, okay? It's creepy.

Why are you so lame? she asked. —Come on, when are we going to be in a situation like this again? This place is incredible. Like the ET house.

Just please stop filming, I pleaded, getting in front of her lens.

She scowled. —You're totally bougie, she said. —You're the bougiest bouge that ever bouged. Have any of your bougie friends ever told you that before? At your like barbecues or movie nights or trips to Williams Sonoma or whatever you do?

I don't go to Williams Sonoma, I said, tired. —I just please want you to stop for a while.

And she did; thank God, and I led Ronda out of the car. She'd sobered up some from the argument, and it wasn't as hard to lead her as it had been. She leaned on me, some, as she walked across the sand and gravel.

Your trailer's really neat, I said to her as we walked.

That's right; you've never been out here before, she said. —Well. You should come out sometime. —She turned to look at me. —You should come to Thanksgiving with me, she said. —Me and my whole family—my brother'll be in town, my sister-in-law. It'll be amazing. I want you there with me.

This sounded like a nightmare. —Yeah, I'll see if I can, I said.

You always see if you can, she said, and she swung her other arm around my neck, almost hanging from me like the branch of a tree. —Don't wait to see if you can. Just say yes, sometimes. Okay?

I decided not to answer, hoping she was too drunk to realize I hadn't.

We got her door open—the space behind it was dark, the wood paneling of the trailer seeming hostile and uneven within the black, and I thought I could smell something like old bacon fat against the cold. And I suddenly hated the idea of leaving her here in this place. But she didn't hesitate: she walked in, her shoes in her hands, her bare feet stepping over the old wood and painted nails of the porch, against the bug-spotted linoleum within. She yawned in the doorway and covered her mouth with a fist. And I told myself I was respecting her by leaving her here alone.

We're taking your car back to T or C, I said. —I'll bring it by in the morning, okay?

If you feel like it, she said. —Say goodnight to your little girl-friend for me.

WOW, YOUR FRIEND IS KIND of, Caroline began, once we were back in Ronda's car.

Negative, I finished. —Yeah, she's a real Dahlia Downer. A real Slit-Your-Wrists Sally.

Are most trans women like that? she asked. —I mean, not you, obviously.

I took a moment to savor this. —We're not all negative, no, I said. —Maybe some of us? Maybe the straight ones. Straight as in ones who like men, I clarified, before she asked.

Which you don't, Caroline said, and I smiled and nodded, and she shifted an inch closer to me from Ronda's passenger seat. We continued to drive along the river toward Truth or Consequences and home.

The hot dog footage was gold, though, Caroline finally said. —I can't wait to fold that in.

And I knew what I was supposed to say: *You didn't have permission to film my friend.* But I didn't say anything; I didn't want to become like Ronda in her eyes. Nothing good could come of that.

THE DREAM-CATCHER, WHEN WE PULLED Ronda's car into the parking lot, looked exhausted, a washed-up river rodent who'd tried to drag itself back into the water, who'd failed.

So, Caroline Wormwood asked, lounging with her legs curled up under herself in my friend's passenger seat, her blindfolded camera resting on the dash. —Where were we?

I looked at her and thought about how nice it would feel to be in my own trailer, my own porch with its plants. Even if Caroline was a sprite or demon I'd somehow summoned, she looked like another human, and tonight I think I was done with that kind of thing.

I should get home, I said.

Her face turned into a cartoon pout. —I don't like that answer, she said. —Are you working here tomorrow?

Always, I said.

Did I say something wrong, she said, and her voice was different. And suddenly I felt ashamed: I hadn't realized that I had the capacity to hurt her. Why hadn't I realized that?

It's fine, I said. —You didn't say anything wrong. Thank you for interviewing me about—about weird things I believe.

Her smile came back, immediate and open. —Good, then I'll see you tomorrow, she said. And she let her hand spring out to grab my shoulder, sank her nails into it like a falcon capturing a possum; I froze, all my sense neurons suddenly moving to register her hand on me. —Whether you want that, or not, she added, and she cackled.

I walked back to get my bike, the impression of her nails in my skin still stinging: did I want to see her tomorrow, B——? I didn't know—I felt weird about the fact that apparently I didn't have a choice, other than to call in from work—I felt, at twenty-six years, so old—and I kept thinking of what Ronda had said to me. Just say yes, sometimes. And then one of the songs you wrote started to play in my head, and I reached the bike racks, and I turned around and walked back.

And the song you wrote was even playing, B——, when I reached the women's dorm: "Psychic Attraction," its eerie organ breakdown, spooky group harmonies between theremin cadenzas, soft vocal wail from your brother Adam. A deep sea sponge brought up to land and drenched anew in salt water, alveoli of a former smoker blooming and bursting with the first nicotine hit: the same way I feel when I hear any Get Happies song. The same way I felt when Caroline opened the door and draped herself across the doorway in a chartreuse tank top and boxer-briefs with a rainbow waistband and a pirate skull design.

I knew my powers were too vast for you to resist, she said, yawning. —What's up?

I thought you didn't know who the Get Happies were, I said, stupidly.

What are you talking about, she said.

You're playing this song, I clarified. —It's a Get Happies song. It's one of the most famous songs ever recorded.

No it isn't, she said, and I stared at her. —I mean, it's maybe famous? I hear it a lot. But it's not by this band you like.

I'm unsure of how to continue talking to you, I said after a moment.

This is my mix CD of songs my grandmother wrote, she said.

I looked at her. And suddenly, I knew who she was—as you do now as well, B——. And suddenly I knew that evil magic—the kind you use to force the reemergence of a prominent musical genius by way of conjured cis women—is totally real. And remembering the advice Ronda had given me, I stepped into her doorway, the better to hear your baby brother sing.

Love, Gala

# PART TWO

# September 11, 2009

Dear B——,

Caroline did her best to outrun her money. There's a house she likes to talk about, one of the first places she ran to, in Seattle, by the beach. It's one of those places on stilts right by the water, years of waves etching out grooves in the dark wood like a saw made of salt and sea acid. The day she moved in, her lover, the one who'd brought her there, gave her the turtle-shaped necklace she always wore.

It's America, her lover told her. —Like the *Indian* name for America.

Wearing the turtle on her chest, she and some queer kids jacked a rowboat from the beach. She had film of it: all of them, her lover among them, laughing as they hauled it pallbearer style across the sand leaving barefoot tracks. They lashed it to one of the stilts of the house and dreamed of fixing it up: *the first rowboat in our armada,* Caroline crowed. But there was an eight-ball sized hole in the hull, and though attempts to fix it arced from hopeless to surprising Rube Goldberg competence, the damage was too great. Once something begins to crack, it's hard to save it from its own weight and pressure. Caroline thought about this while she worked on the rowboat; she thought about it while she and her lover lay in a cold, salty bed together, not speaking or sleeping, facing one hundred eighty degrees from each other, a film rule she'd learned never to break.

On the bus east from there, Pacific dreams at her back, she remembered the view from upstairs: gazing at the dead smoke sea, the gulls through picture windows stained with the nose prints of cats.

CAROLINE CAME FROM CALIFORNIA TOO, B——. She'd settled in a nation of money that mellowed like cheese wheels as new fortunes enjoyed the process of becoming old ones: redwood neighborhoods, dream cottages with lavender paint and gabled roofs, geometric bird feeders and wind chimes hanging from never-trimmed trees in the yard, political bumper stickers on the mailboxes (THE LESSER OF TWO EVILS IS STILL EVIL), thick fences. Daily in her return from school, she passed the smoke store and the vegan pizza parlor, crossed El Camino fat with traffic to and from outposts along the smiling, metastasizing Silicon Valley; she made sure to look both ways down the four-lane road and to wait for the white walking man to chirp before she crossed. She avoided the dead strip malls, depopulated like empty bee-hives after the swarm had eaten all the honey and moved on; she walked through the empty pharmacy parking lots of the good strip malls—gourmet food emporia, coffee houses, restaurants that specialized in Greek food, Mongolian, fusion barbecue, and the Japanese import store that had the melon gum her dad had taught her to love, and she continued down the narrow sidewalk blowing melon bubbles shipped to her by invisible hands.

The schools were well endowed, and everyone read books. It was important to care about things other than money. Her father beamed that message into her by osmosis; everyone's father above a certain income level did. She absorbed it.

And it wasn't like they were *rich* rich. The kids at her school were becoming *rich* rich: someone's dad would set up a good portal site or banner company, and Caroline would go from playing Super Nintendo on CRTs at townhouses, apartments, and modest ranch-styles to memorizing gate codes and walking through ever vaster gray marble kitchens with ever healthier snacks. Her own address steadily refused to change, the perimeter of her own walls and fence steadily refused to increase. She could accept that. Her *rich* friends read the same books, too, so they tried not to be jerks about their money. Everyone got along. Who cared if your neighbors had new cars every year and your family had to content itself with the same old one? It worked, didn't it?

Your mother died, her dad explained to her, whenever she asked him why he was raising her alone. She could never decide if it made it easier or harder that he didn't keep any photos of her around.

Whenever her father was between QA contracts, she'd find him there when she got home. He'd hang around and wait for her while he dusted the living room or put flea powder on the carpet. He'd sweep her up in a hug and they'd play Mario Kart, Street Fighter, Mortal Kombat together. He'd play Johnny Cage, and she'd play the girls.

More often, though, he'd have a contract to work on, and so she'd come in to the strange dust and silence of the house at afternoon, alone. She'd make herself a sandwich in the kitchen from the economy-sized tubs of peanut butter and the vinyl spatula with flowers traced on the white handle, and she'd watch TV shows that featured moms waiting at home for kids who complained, until she learned to turn them off in favor of cable horror repeats.

She was into movies and shows. Friday nights it was a ritual for her and her dad to hit the movie rental place in Sunnyvale and pick out VHS tapes, two for her and one for her dad. He'd never get around to watching his; she'd tear through hers by Sunday afternoon and be jonesing for more all through the weekdays. Gradually she figured out that it was better to pick movies that would hold up to second, third viewings during the week: canonical classics (your Star Warses, your Raiders, your Aladdins), inscrutable non-Disney cartoons from mysterious foreign places, recondite *Python and Fawlty* episodes, *Stan & Ollie*, etc. They were something other than where she lived, something more exciting than the peace and harmony surrounding her. She wanted to bring that world closer to her world somehow, minimizing the drought times between trips to the rental shop: she memorized the names of background bounty hunters on the *Executor* and the number of shots Marion Raven could knock back, tried and usually failed to engage her dad in The Argument Sketch, thought about where Sulu and Chekov went during the strange times when mystery extras filled the navigation and helm spots.

ON THE DAY HER MONEY first found her—her tenth birthday, the year 1997—her dad was between QA contracts, and so here he was, lying on the couch with a fat *Infinite Jest* and its two bookmarks on his chest, his prehensile toes manipulating the dials of a box fan. He was good looking, I've always assumed from the way Caroline talked about him: shaggy hair, a shaggy beard, surf-salt blond and stained both white with age and dark with UV radiation years after he'd hit the beach, T-shirt stretched over a barrel chest and jeans hacked into shorts, no logos on either, permanent squint behind spectacles made necessary by difficult fiction.

One of Caroline's key jobs in the house was to collect the mail from the row of boxes at the gate of the townhouse complex, to balance the envelopes in her arms as she punched the four-digit combo into the electric lock. Checks went to her dad directly;

obvious junk to the trash; bills and contracts to his desk; infrequent letters to the coffee table where they could be reviewed over takeout dinner. The letters were getting more infrequent since they'd claimed their hundred free hours of Internet, of which Caroline burned up her fifty in sending brightly colored emoticons and brilliant jokes to her school friends (Q: *What's the last thing that goes through a bug's mind when it hits the windshield? A: its buttttttt.*) Caroline almost never got letters herself: she'd persuaded a classmate—a girl who by all reports was going to end up as a senator who'd speak passionately in defense of biodiversity—to try keeping up a correspondence with her, which lasted for one letter each, and once a year her paternal grandparents sent her (and not her dad) a terse photocopied Xmas letter with the same $20 gift card to Circuit City attached.

So the khaki envelope with its weird Montana postmark and her name—CAROLINE WORMWOOD—computer-printed on it caught her and her sorting algorithm by surprise.

Her dad watching her, she got over her fear and opened it. Inside was a check in her name for $1000, even. It was attached to a track-fed carbon of a statement that broke down units sold per quarter, total publishing figures on each, percentage of sales owing to an entity called *Dahlia S.* The $1000 itself had then been neatly deducted from Dahlia S's percentage and cross-referenced to what Caroline would later memorize as her own Social Security number. *Birthday initiation*, read the memo line on the check. Something about the form—the faded purple dots like rivets that spelled out her name, which clearly a computer now knew—made her uneasy.

It's money, her dad said. —It looks to be *your* money.

I don't want computer money, she said nervously. —Can we send it back?

I don't think the computer *wants* us to do that, her dad said, making his voice spooky.

Who's Dahlia, Caroline asked after a minute.

Her dad quickly went to the kitchen, where he soaked a wash-cloth in steaming water and lay it like a pastry crust across his face, massaging the fruits of his eyes beneath.

Dahlia is your mom, he finally said, and he went into his office for a full fifteen minutes, sweet smoke emerging from beneath his door.

She stared at the bank statement, the dead RGB guns of the television aimed at her, and she tried to imagine what her mother must look like. Silicon chrome molded into cyberhips and bosom, liquid silver arms that reached out to feed money like oatmeal into her mouth.

SHE'D NEVER IMAGINED HERSELF AS the kind of girl who had a thousand dollars to spend. VHS tapes were like $20 each; she started writing down a list of fifty movies she wouldn't mind owning. Her dad convinced her to get a video camera instead. —It's smart to be on the right side of production, he said.

They went to the Circuit City together to pick it out. She loved the Circuit City anyway, loved to walk the aisles when her dad would bring her there to upgrade his modem from 28.8 to 56k or buff his RAM or whatever. The cameras in the AV aisle were all neatly mounted and security-tagged in ascending order from cheapest to fanciest. This was the shape of a life, she figured, a straight-arrow vector from cheapest to most expensive. She wondered what age she'd be when she reached each new purchasing level. In *Star Trek*, you start as an ensign, you end as an admiral.

Her dad helped her hook it to the TV the first time. Returning from the bathroom, she rounded the corner into the family room and stopped: the camera eye focused down the hall with its red wink at her, and her own tiny form filled the glass. She was in the world of the TV. She moved her arms and watched her arms move, opened and closed her mouth, while her father watched.

o  o  o

SHE FILMED HERSELF READING STORIES to her stuffed animals and playing herself back. She took the camera with her on (rare) outings to the beach or the zoo, filmed herself talking through the answers to her homework, one night took the camera under the covers with her—its red light flickering beneath the blankets like a cave—and filmed herself falling asleep. She watched the tape later in secret, watched with a feeling of awe as her face slowly lost consciousness on the screen.

There was some essential difference between the movies you could rent from the shop in Sunnyvale and the movies she made herself in her bedroom or townhouse courtyard. Uncomfortably lit, colors weird, sound barely audible beneath ambient fans or A/C, actors who laughed through their lines. And just the way all of her shots went *on* so long, just the unprofessional coffee cups, stacks of magazines, stray ballpoints and crumby dishes in the background of shots, every difference that separated experience lived from experience professionally designed. Her goal, she also realized early on, had to be to erase that difference. That's what good means: concealing your tracks.

Her means of becoming a pro, she decided, would be special effects. She and a sleepover friend, hopped up on sugar, devised a complex shot that'd depict a young woman on the ground waving a wide goodbye to an off-blasting spaceship from the perspective of the spaceship, basically by using a rope tied around the camera's midsection and a steady hand, and it *would* have worked, Caroline knew, had stuff like angular momentum and human panic not existed. Her dad helped her sweep up the glass and metal and was gentle with her, comforted her when she shouted at herself about how stupid she'd been.

She started hoarding her allowance and trying to pick up baby-sitting jobs, which were harder to get when she explained that she needed the money to replace an expensive camera that she'd dropped off a building. Losing the power to record depressed her:

suddenly there was a wall between her and real life that only more money than she had could help her scale.

She marked the days down on her calendar until she'd have enough cash scraped together to replace the machine—a month and ten days, she figured, after her eleventh birthday. But on that birthday, another envelope came in her name from Dahlia S: her mother, the computer. It was another $1000 check, *BIRTHDAY* on the memo line.

I didn't need it, though, she told her dad in the car to Circuit City. —I almost had the money. Why was I even saving it?

It's a good habit to save money, her dad said. —People have told me that.

Her new camera was better than her old one and cheaper, because that was what it meant to live in the greatest country in the world. She kept filming, sat in English class writing titles in her notebook for a career's worth of movies that she'd make, doodled posters in the margins. She divided this future career into phases: her *early works* (she'd make three of these, the second of which would be an understandable mishap and the third of which would represent a *striking early maturity*), her *mature subject matter*, her *later experimental work*, and finally a kind of *summation*— a single work, an aleph through which all the previous films, or maybe her *whole life*, might be viewed. She knew she'd finally become capable of her aleph when she was fifty, sixty, however long it took. She wrote the titles of these movies backward to make it take longer to finish the list.

*One day I will be a movie director*, she affirmed to an English class questionnaire about Discovering One's Talents. *It is my main dream.*

IT OCCURRED TO HER, OCCASIONALLY, that she had no way of really knowing whether the cycle of her birthdays would continue—whether the money would keep coming or not. But on the afternoon of her twelfth birthday, when she'd made it back from the middle school, the envelope was there like always, its computer type now as dependable a part of the holiday as pumpkins were to Halloween and shopping mall Muzak to Christmas. She decided on a miniDV—why cheat your future?—and she picked her camera proudly from the middle shelf.

FOR HER THIRTEENTH BIRTHDAY, PART of her money went to upgrading her editing setup, another, larger part to paying a guy in a cluttered storefront in Oakland to transfer some of her favorite miniDV productions to legit DVDs, the rest to supplies and props for a blood-soaked conclusion to a series that she anticipated would take the rest of the year to film, one structured around the idea of a murderer who stalked her childhood Barbies according to a major arcana schema. Her dad gave up on trying to follow what she was doing, and she mostly gave up on telling him about it.

She decided to invite only her closest two friends to her thirteenth birthday party. Only Senator Brill came. They spent the sleepover evening watching DVDs of Caroline's movies, Caroline narrating the circumstances of composition, until Senator Brill excused herself to go to the bathroom, took the cordless phone with her, and disappeared for over an hour. Caroline slept on the floor and let her ailing friend take the bed: Senator Brill snored in her retainer, facing the wall, Caroline looking up at her. The moonlight came through ancient Colorforms she'd forgotten to unstick, transforming her friend's face like stained glass.

Her entries to festivals started to get rejected around the same time that she learned, via confession by one of the Senator's and her mutual buddies, that Senator Brill had been letting people know, reluctantly, that Caroline had made a pass at her on her birthday, and that she didn't like outing her really close friend in this way, but that it was really important for anyone who knew the both of them to know that Caroline was maybe a lesbian, which was *totally fine* and of course Senator Brill supported her in her sexual preference, but people should maybe know that before inviting her over to their houses, just FYI. Caroline listened to the mutual buddy tell her this, apologizing profusely to her—oh god I'm *sorry* I'm *so sorry* you must *totally hate me* I'm sorry for *ruining everything*. She told the buddy it was fine, and she found an old lunch sack in her backpack to help the buddy stop hyperventilating. And she wondered why Senator Brill had decided to do this, whether it was a decision she'd like sat down and planned out: to convert secret facts about her friend into social currency. How did someone plan something like that?

She watched the video she'd shown Senator Brill that birthday night over and over on the little two-VCR and CRT setup in her room, kept scanning the footage forward and backward for signs of errors and flaws, something she had done that might've explained what the Senator had done. But there wasn't any failure that she could see. She sank, biting her lip, into the comforter she and her father had tie-dyed together one afternoon, its rainbow sides pooching up around her like a hot-blooded bivalve, and she thought: *Either the universe is crazy, or I'm crazy. It can't be both.* It didn't occur to her that it could be neither, what neither might mean.

HER FOURTEENTH BIRTHDAY WAS THE gift that kept on giving, in terms of awful suck. The imagery was shown on channel after channel in indecent repetition—she thought the buildings looked like candles melting down; was she an evil monster for thinking that—and her teachers, who'd long since stopped mandating that the class stand for the pledge to the flag, suddenly got all pious and resolute, leading the class in proud singsong. Everyone became so *serious*: Senator Brill assembled a protest march mostly of fellow Honor Society kids down the C Hallway, and then, after the administration had stopped the march and given her a first-ever detention for organizing it, she showed up at school in a T-shirt with *DICK AND BUSH ARE SCREWING AFGHANISTAN* Sharpied on it, a piece of duct tape printed with peace signs over her mouth. A teacher tore the tape off and sent her to the office.

Caroline joined the Honor Society and then dropped out of it; what was the point; all of them were liars pretending to care about leadership when they clearly only cared about college acceptances. She was confident that this wasn't honor. She'd stopped making movies, felt ashamed about it, felt ashamed about everything. And her shame opened to her like a door in the air.

ON HER FIFTEENTH BIRTHDAY SHE tore up the check. She lay on the floor of her bedroom, the tie-dye fallen around her, library books stacked on her stomach, the first stones of a burial cairn. She'd charged her camera and held it above herself, dangled it like an infant mobile, its red eye open. I'm not going to be what they are, she prayed to the lens.

SHE STARTED GOING TO A queer youth group in Oakland, took buses to it so her dad wouldn't know where she was going, hooked up with a girlfriend who was curious about her movies and who lived with her divorced mom, also gay. Her girlfriend and her mom worked in the same restaurant—Caroline's eyes shone when she heard about that—and they got Caroline a job there too. She met other queer kids, went to queer shows, swam in a vast queer world, one that she knew would never vote for someone like Senator Brill. (There were trans women in her world, I'm sure of it, two or three at least, sputtering like trick candles before disappearing in the swell of more highly valued queers.) Her sixteenth birthday came; she cashed the check and donated the money via anonymous envelope to help save a punk house in the Mission that had fallen into arrears. The country got worse. She got her heart broken. She filmed cops at demonstrations from a safe distance; she tried not to get arrested; she didn't want people to see her dad come pick her up. She made allegorical movies for house shows, electric backdrops that melted and shifted behind bands. She taped weddings and submitted invoices; she saved percentages of every invoice that came in (on time, as they always did) toward college; she wrote papers for high school classes on a lover's typewriter with her head resting on the lover's thighs. And she lay on the ground on the banks of Lake Merritt one afternoon, reading a book alone, and she rolled onto her stomach in the grass and put her arms, wiry from restaurant work, flat against the earth, and she pushed and lifted her body up with what she knew had to be all her own effort. She pushed up again, liking the feeling of doing it.

SHE KNEW IT SHOULDN'T HAVE bothered her as it did when, on her seventeenth birthday, the money never came. It's not as if she'd wanted this money. She resented this money, wanted to destroy it, have it be as if it had never been. She hadn't enjoyed it for at least three birthdays now, and she'd spent most of the weeks leading up to this one thinking of socially responsible ways to dispose of it. She'd come up with a good plan, she thought, half to a needle share program and half to a fund for housing queer youth. She'd felt really good about this plan, and now the money had failed to come.

The dread finally lifted, though, when she went to the mailbox one evening to find out whether the zines she'd ordered from an Olympia distro had come in or not. Instead she found an envelope with her name on it, a slash for a return address, and a stamp, B——, with you and your brothers' faces on it. You were standing in a cluster of two-dimensional palm trees, every one of you incongruously playing a guitar.

*Caroline—*
*Meet me at Sal Angel's on El Camino at eight p.m. this Friday.*
*We'll discuss your future situation. Happy birthday.*

*Dahlia Slinks*

The letter ended with a signature that was essentially a forty-five degree line, its terminus puncturing the page like a Univac stylus into a punch card. Caroline's zines had also arrived. She held them by the bindings in one hand, her mother's letter in the other. She hefted them, compared their weight.

IN RECENT YEARS, HER CLOTHING style had drifted toward that of her fellow queer kids, which was partly a conscious choice and partly just due to the inevitable clothes-swapping involved in dating within your gender and size range. She hadn't ever picked out anything she guessed was appropriate for meeting one's long-lost mother, and she felt a little stupid about that at the same time as she felt stupid for wanting to wear something to impress her. She took her girlfriend to the thrift store and picked up a khaki dress with a beaded belt, which worn with Docs she guessed would read as queer without being undaughterly, unseemly. How did one be daughterly? This was something she didn't know.

THOUGH UPON ARRIVING AT SAL Angel's—first hiding in the long semisuburban alleyway behind the restaurant for ten minutes spanning 7:55 and 8:05, hyperventilating—she decided she needn't have bothered with trying to be ambiguous about queerness, since Dahlia Slinks—her mother, Dahlia Slinks—was the gayest woman she had maybe ever seen. Caroline had no idea how she could tell her mother was gay—her tailored pinstripe and creepy Mexican-painter slicked-jet spitcurl certainly weren't *not*, nor was the red handkerchief in her breast pocket or the way she wore sunglasses indoors, but neither were these things in and of themselves sufficient. It was more the whole aura of her: she vibrated faster than anyone else at Sal Angel's, like she was a suspended shriek and all she had to do was let herself move and the diner would shatter like glass. Caroline watched, heart cracking open at a fault line she'd forgotten about, as her mother spread through the restaurant like green fog, its tendrils meeting Caroline in her khaki dress at the door; she smiled and the fog seemed to form a finger beckoning her daughter in.

Between them, unique to their booth, was a little glass vase containing a cut white rose. Every customer's head, it seemed to Caroline, was angled toward them, their tongues lolling red like submissive wolves.

You can keep the flower, her mother said. —I bought it for you. —She reached out to the open collar of Caroline's dress, adjusted it; her short red nails were embalmed in lacquer. —This is lovely, she said. —I see you didn't inherit my hair. I was hoping you'd darken over time.

They ordered: cucumber salad with vinegar but not oil for Dahlia; a hamburger with onions and fries for Caroline. She ate it as they talked, big annelid ribbons of onion dragging grease smears against her lips that she tried to keep clear with the cloth napkin. Dahlia took a bottle of organic shiraz out of her purse, gave the waitress a $50 bill, and asked for two glasses.

I guess you'll have some questions for me before we get down to business, Dahlia said as they drank. —I'm happy to answer any question you'd like to ask.

Caroline breathed into her glass, fogging it, feeling the fog evaporate against her lips.

It's hard to think of only one, she said.

Dahlia laughed; Caroline laughed as well.

Okay, Caroline asked. —Where have you been?

Dahlia spread her arms slowly, like she was wearing some

cloak on which the backdrop of the world had been projected. —
Everywhere she said. —Traveling the world. Too much to tell you.

Cool, Caroline said. —Why didn't you take me with you is, I
guess, my next question?

Dahlia smiled; she had clearly been prepared for this as well.
—People make their choices in life, she said. —I chose not to be
tied down. That's not something I'll do you the disservice of pretending to apologize for. I don't feel guilty about it. But—but oh
honey—may I call you that?

Free country, said Caroline, looking down.

When I look at you, honey, Dahlia said, resting her thin chin in
her lacquered hand, —I can't help but wish things could've been
different than they are. Do you forgive me?

Caroline stared, coming to understand two facts: she didn't like
this person at all, and this person knew that.

Okay, she said flatly. —Sure. Why not.

Good, said Dahlia. —So that's settled. Now tell me everything
about you, about your friends, about your life. I want to know all
of it. What did you spend the money I sent you on?

Caroline looked at the rose stem, the slick vegetable necrosis
beginning to form at the site of the cut. —I forget, she said. —No,
wait, Dad put it away for me. For college. A college education.

Dahlia looked at her, finally took her sunglasses off. Her eyes
had little feathers of tiny wrinkles surrounding them, from a
distance fading out to a soft, powdery shadow, eyes shelved by
mascara slices as thick as wax.

Well, she said finally. —That was superfluous, as I think
you'll see.

I changed my mind, said Caroline, folding her arms. —You
can't actually call me honey.

Beneath the branches of the rose, there was a little cellar of
garlic salt; she shook some of it on her fries, picked one up,
chomped it with her eyes locked on her mother's.

Okay, Caroline, said Dahlia. —Then I guess we're done chatting, and we can move on to business. Happy seventeenth birthday.

She drew a thick baby-blue folder out of her bag and handed it to Caroline. Within it was a thick stack of paper, its cover sheet reading: *For the benefit of CAROLINE WORMWOOD.* The rest of the pages were spreadsheets as dense as Enochian tablets, meant to show the full derivation of the sum at the bottom of the cover sheet. If Caroline started to receive this sum today, she calculated, it might last until, as best as she could determine, the end of her life.

Dahlia looked at her, eyes never seeming to blink, and Caroline imagined the green fog solidifying around her, an invisible hand at the scruff of her neck lifting her slowly out of her shitty Sal Angel's booth.

Take your time, said Dahlia. —Read it all. You're becoming wealthy. Many people find this disorienting.

Caroline looked at the folder, imagined the wine spilling over the pages and staining them in blooms of red.

How did this happen, she asked finally.

The trust was founded by my mother—your grandmother, Dahlia said. —She came into some money, which she left in trust to me. And I used it for a long time. And because I used it *wisely*— as you'll have to learn to do, Caroline—I've developed it to the point where I no longer *depend* on it. So I made plans, seven years ago, to pass it on to you—to get you used to it, little by little. To prepare your way. And here's your way.

Caroline kept looking at the money.

Why haven't I ever met my grandmother? she asked. —Is she dead?

I don't know, said Dahlia, folding and unfolding the batwings of her spectacles. Caroline watched the folder, imagining it snapping shut like a mousetrap on her fingers.

What do you mean, you used it wisely? she asked. —Did you invest in military contractors or something?

*Actually*, it comes from a core of investments in technology growth stocks and sustainable green enterprises, Dahlia said. —With healthy leveraging into traditional growth stocks and debt futures as a hedge against shifts in the market. And I do angel investments in woman-owned businesses, though that doesn't make it grow so much. So no, Caroline, to the extent that anyone can *not* invest in military contractors and stay solvent, I *don't* invest in military contractors. —She indicated the folder. —*This* money, if you want to know, comes from songwriting. This is very pure money you're turning up your nose at.

Songwriting? Caroline asked.

Publishing royalties, Dahlia clarified. —The portion of money due a songwriter whenever he—or she, in the present case—gets a song performed, sold, printed for retail sale, or licensed for subsidiary rights distribution. There are endless applications.

Caroline tried to assimilate this: her grandmother, publishing money, royalty, like a queen. —What songs did she write? she asked.

Dahlia pointed at the ceiling. After a moment, Caroline realized she was pointing at the circular speaker panel, which was exuding music: the kind of well-eroded American background music, polished like rocks in a riverbed, that your ears spend years learning to treat as silence. But here it surrounded her: the Get Happies, B——, you and your brothers singing harmonies on the breakdown from "But You Aren't" (first released on *Space-Girls,* Valley Forge Records, 1966) with voices that skip and weave like trout over the rapid white surface.

Did she write more songs? Caroline asked, after the song had finished. —Do you remember her writing songs?

Dahlia sat back—she really was like a vampire, Caroline thought, so tense at every moment that it was as if she had rigor mortis. Yet now, for the first time in Caroline's sight, the death chemicals relaxed; Dahlia slouched, slackened her mouth; a gap appeared between the back of her neck and the lapel of her power suit. These were stories she usually told to people she barely knew, constructions of her past that functioned like armor over her thin necrotic skin—and now she was telling those stories for the first time to someone to whom they had some relevance, some relation. Caroline felt sure that her mother was enjoying it, though she wasn't sure her mother knew that. She wasn't sure her mother was used to naming feelings she had.

I remember her performing it more than writing it, Dahlia said. —I remember her playing it for all of us in the common room. We lived in kind of a, what you'd call a commune. —She paused, made eye contact. —There were a whole lot of us in this commune, somewhere in Oregon. This was—I mean, we moved around—but it was somewhere it rained. All women, and some boys, living somewhere it rained. And she rarely ever played, you understand. But maybe the kids were fighting, or there was an argument among the women, or the septic cistern was backing up again, or the electric bill was due and everyone thought everyone else had paid it, or someone had said something racist or patriarchal or colonialist or just bitchy to whoever was in *power* and there had to be a *tribunal* to root out *counterrevolutionary elements*, my God—have you ever read Nabokov, *Invitation to a Beheading*? I recommend it to you. If you've *ever* thought of joining some kind of social justice group, Caroline, let me tell you right now that you'd be a fool to do it, because take it from me, I have shoveled enough hippie shit—and I mean that both as a metaphor and very, very literally—to last *both* our lifetimes. That is *not* the way for intelligent people to live.

Caroline imagined her mother kicking her friends from the queer community until they died. —You were telling me about Grandma's guitar playing, she said.

Dahlia took a deep breath. —Your grandmother played songs like I've never heard, she said. —I don't know how to explain them. There was one about rabbits looking for shelter from the rain. There was one about angels who didn't know what it meant to be in love. One about the moon; one about a girl with a scar on her face and a hook for a hand. Maybe these were all the same song. I don't remember anymore, and she never let anyone record her. She never let anyone write her songs down.

The genial DJ shouted something over the PA, tried to get everyone to buy something, a distant sound like wind bottle-whistling over the mouth of a grave.

What happened to her, Caroline asked finally.

Dahlia stiffened again. —She vanished, she said. —She left a note and took the car and disappeared. Maybe she died. This was in 1980, as I recall. Do you have other painful questions for me? I'd be elated to answer them.

Her eyes, hypnotic, burned red in the diner light.

That's fine, Caroline finally said.

She's not credited, you know, Dahlia said after a moment. —For the songs she wrote while she was young. Pretty typical. Except someone's actually sending her the money for these uncredited songs. That isn't typical.

Why would they still be sending this money, Caroline asked, —If she—your mother—is dead, or, or vanished.

Because she didn't want it, Dahlia said. —She made the arrangements to have it devolve to me. It was more complicated than that—there were a lot of people on that commune, even as late as 1980—but it ended up with me. A consolation prize, I guess, for not having a mother around.

What a funny coincidence, Caroline said.

Her mother scowled at this, but continued. —I went with your father because I thought I could maybe not be—what I am, she said. —I don't know. Break the cycle. And he seemed nice—he seemed stable—a computer science student, a nice family, well read, cynical, very mean when he wanted to be. I valued meanness. —She smirked. —And then he turned out to have no *right* to meanness. He was just as depressing as all the rest of them.

She seemed as if she was about to enlarge on this, but she looked at Caroline and checked herself. She looked flustered, a little.

I'm sorry my father and I were *depressing*, Caroline said.

And I'm sorry you're angry and that you've decided to misunderstand everything I've said, Dalia said. —And then, in an immediate key change: —I didn't abandon you. I didn't. Not in the same way. I watched you, as best as I could. I worked hard for you. I tried to put this together for you so you could do whatever you wanted to do in life. And I'm here, aren't I, to give it to you? I'm here. —She put her fingertips on the folder, slid it toward Caroline. —Here I am.

Caroline looked down at the folder from where she floated, suspended in the green fog and the river of music that issued from the speaker, uncertain of which direction she should now swim.

I don't want this, she said at last.

Dahlia smiled. —I didn't either, at first, she said. —I got used to it.

No, you aren't listening, Caroline said. —I don't want this. This isn't me. I don't want it to be. Keep it. Give it to someone else. Throw it down the well.

Dahlia curled her lip over her lupine tooth. —It doesn't work that way, she said.

HER MOTHER KEPT TALKING TO her then, giving her advice about what to invest in, what not to, how much she should withdraw at a time to leave fluidity in the system, to sustain it. Caroline sat, breathing, looking at the cut rose breathing the still water provided for it, how someone had worked hard to keep it alive—given it every nutrient that they thought it needed—and how hungry it must have been for something besides water, some worm excrement or ancient snail shell or vitamin soil, something only flowers can feel the lack of.

You're wrong, she said, —but I don't know why.

Her mother seemed to soften. For a moment, Caroline imagined what it might be like for her mother to reach across the diner table, to touch her forehead.

What're you afraid of? she asked.

Caroline thought. —I don't want to be separate from them, she finally said. She didn't specify who *them* was: she pictured a swim of faces, each different in some way from her own, their expressions hard to read.

Dahlia sighed. —I would like to believe that your friends, if they really are your friends, could be happy with you suddenly being wealthy. That they wouldn't be petty enough to resent this. That you have enough moral character, my daughter, not to be changed by the experience of having enough money not to *worry* in life. That they understand that *you* having money makes *them* more able to succeed, precisely *because* you have more money. You'll understand that, at some point.

She kept talking, and Caroline wondered if she owed money an apology.

AND THAT WOULD HAVE BEEN it. After some more tense efforts at chat, ultimately bilaterally abandoned, Dahlia took the ticket to the front desk, seeming amused by the custom, while Caroline looked at the folder on the table. She finally took it; her mother would just find a way to get it to her otherwise if she didn't. It was easier to take it just for now, to find room to breathe.

They walked together to the door. Caroline told herself to be mature, to keep walking in step with this woman who said she was her mother, whom Caroline guessed she believed. They stood in the twilight, gaslit shadows of the neon SAL ANGEL'S sign on their faces. Dahlia offered Caroline a ride home; Caroline declined. She stepped forward and let her mother put her arms around her waist, tentatively, like she was picking up some dangerous animal, and she let her own body fill with unnameable, silent heat.

Then her mother spoke again.

She told everyone that she would disappear one day, she said, and her voice seemed faster, like air escaping a staked balloon. —That she'd change her name, drive off, leave everything behind, vanish. She *always* said this, *always*, I *always* remember her saying it. She said she'd become good at disappearing. But—you're sure you never met her, aren't you? She never came to you, did she?

Caroline jerked back, and her mother dropped her arms to her side and bit her lip.

I'm sorry, she said. —That wasn't helpful for you to hear.

Caroline stood there, dumbly watching Dahlia, somehow wanting to hug her, to keep her standing. But there was no way that she knew to express that idea. Dahlia watched her too, wary, like she was flattening her ears. The diner sign buzzed; the music inside continued, far away and hard to hear.

LATER, AT HOME, SHE FOUND her father on the futon in his office, typing a long screed into a LiveJournal query window with complex prog oscillating from the speakers. She brought him to the coffee table, where he sat on the couch and squinted at the blue folder. She crouched on the floor opposite, balancing on the balls of her feet.

Did you know that this was going to happen? she asked.

He typed three blank spaces into the query window; he erased them, one by one.

I knew she was sending you part of the money, he said. —She told me she'd planned to do that. I didn't know she was going to send all of it.

Caroline slumped on her side. —I don't get any of this, she said. If this woman—Grandma—wrote these songs with this like famous rock star, why was she living in some horrible commune in the first place? She could've afforded something amazing, couldn't she?

Refusal is a big part of the American tradition, her father said. —In a way, it's definitional. A nation of refusal to engage. —He noticed his daughter's rolling eyes. —I also don't think she had the money the whole time, he said.

But the song came out in 1960-whatever, Caroline said.

There's the thing, and there's the value the world places on the thing, said her dad. —It's an important distinction. The band who recorded these—their music is, well, ubiquitous now. But in the 1970s, they were—let's say, not what I remember about popular music. It wasn't until Reagan used that song in the campaign commercial that the world tour happened, the greatest hits packages. I imagine the money took your grandmother somewhat by surprise. —He cleared his throat. —She was an interesting woman, your grandmother. Your mother talked about her a great deal.

Caroline waited for him to expand on this; he didn't.

I could burn this money every month, she finally said. —Then I could find other sources of money, and burn them down too. Let's make a list on the computer of all the possible sources of money we can burn down.

Have you considered film school, her father said cautiously.

She felt like crying, and yet she felt like only disgusting people would cry in this situation; she felt sick, greasy, saturated, incontinent, as if she'd been force-fed sugar and butter, creamed far beyond her capacity to digest.

So she stopped refusing her money. It was even exciting not to refuse it, she decided, once she brought herself around to it: researching the schools she might want to attend, making decisions about them. She edited her old films into a worthy admissions portfolio, spent time filming new things. She quit her job at the restaurant to focus on her grades. Her teachers began to praise her, and if her old queer friends began to fall away, maybe they weren't such good friends after all. She thought, often, about things her mother had told her, the hour and change they'd spent together magnifying and swelling in her memory to fill all the seventeen, eighteen years they'd missed. She'd been balancing on one foot all of her life and hadn't realized it.

She wrote an application essay about the pain of growing up without her mother and the joy and elation at meeting her again.

On the strength of this, she got in to the school of her choice, an arts-heavy private university in a strange Southern city. She graduated high school, and she came out of the housing lottery with a double dorm, hoped her roommate was hot. She bought a used car—loaded her things—said goodbye to her dad—drove across the country, West to East. Wild rock mountains and rain-shadow deserts, and then smooth driving on smooth-paved roads, telephone wires, gas stations and rest stops and fast food wherever, whenever she wanted them. This part of the country was long adapted for human habitation, and she had enough money to buy whatever food she wanted on the way. In New Mexico, she stopped at a Native-run gas station, where she fingered a necklace in the shape of a turtle shell on a leather cord.

She walked into her dorm room to find Senator Brill there, alphabetizing her books.

Oh, hello! said Senator Brill, crossing her arms. —What a small world, yeah!

AFTER NERVOUS TALK—HOW COULD they not have *known*, what a weird administrative quirk—Caroline retreated to the bathroom. She sat on the toilet and studied the labels of cream rinses and hair products. And the childhood photo of Senator Brill faced

her: the senator and some forty Honor Society pals on a middle
school trip to New York City to attend a UN session, all of them
kneeling in Times Square in black dresses and awkward suits.

This was life: Senator Brill, or someone like her. Someone who
got to make decisions about issues other than the ones that immediately touched her, whose decisions were rarely, if ever, canceled
out. Someone whose children would do better than she did herself. And here they were together, beyond the gates inheritance
had opened for them: Caroline, the prodigal daughter returned at
last to God, smoke and fat rising from the blue folder she would
carry for the rest of her life.

SHE TOLD ME THAT STORY, B——, while both of us lay
under the blanket in the dorm, her turn to roast next to the space
heater, me gathering whatever heat I could.

Senator Brill would've just graduated a couple of months ago,
she said. —I hope she did okay. I hope she had good internships.

The wind was high outside, and I lay there, the sad butter-
scotch-melting-on-ice-cream post-makeout blend of dysphoria
(vulnerability and trust and low-grade alarm at the closeness of
our bodies, like a smoke detector going off two trailers away), Caroline with her arms over her head and tufts of pit hair uncurling,
her turtle necklace crawling between her breasts.

What'd you do with the used car, I asked.

I don't even remember, she said. —It was two, three years ago
now. Hopefully someone cool took it. —She shivered. —I called
my dad before I left school, she said. —I call him sometimes.

I didn't ask her about her mom. We looked at the ceiling, listened to the rain. *So you're pretending not to have money basically*
is what I wanted to say to her, but I didn't. What she was doing
was important in a way that went beyond pretending, I guessed,
and exactly who was I to judge her for what she was doing? I tried
to decide exactly who I was to do that.

Do you still have the money? I asked.

She sighed. —I don't like that question, she said. —It'd be like the surgery question for you.

I went under the blankets, but she flipped the sheet back from my face, and I hissed at her like a cat. —What? she asked. —I'm sorry; was that shitty? That was shitty.

No it's cool, I said. —I'm sorry for being complicit in anti-wealth bigotry.

Hey, I'm sorry, she pleaded. —Hey. I'm sorry. I'm sorry. Please let me tell you I'm sorry?

I looked at her, propped up on her palms, the turtle's beak pointing to the mattress like a divining rod, fuchsia hair hanging in her face. She looked distraught at the idea that she'd caused anyone harm: the mournful eyes of a Godzilla stomping a city flat.

I'm sorry, I said. —You don't have to be. I was being awful.

She settled down on the bed.

It still comes, she said. —I mean theoretically it does. I tore up the checks when she tried sending them to me monthly; I tore up the statements. I try not to get them at all; I try to be on the move whenever my birthday comes around. Sometimes the post office gets them to me; most of the time they don't. I don't know. —Her eyes got faraway, like she was describing a comet she'd seen one time, an evil star. —It must be out there, somewhere. Gathering in some account, swelling with interest like a blackhead. It's terrible. I try not to think about it. —She shivered. —Are you getting enough heat? Am I hogging it? Here.

She clambered over me like a giant spider, unblocking the coils, and I thought about the money she tore up, and I thought about Ronda in her trailer, alone.

So I've told you all about myself, Caroline said. —Why don't we ever talk about you? What's your story?

I rolled away, the blanket tight around me, and eventually she gave up on pursuing this question, instead stretched out by the heater, limbs extended in yoga lunge.

How much is it a month out here, she asked. —I've been meaning to slow down. And you know a lot about this band, right? It's basically my family history. I think I should stick with you a while. I could edit wedding videos or make brochures or all kinds of different things. I could totally pay my share.

*My family history.* It hung there, like a ladder dangling before me, one she was extending. I could almost feel it, still thinking about Ronda with part of my mind. We're transsexuals: this is what I was thinking. Chances for transsexuals to change their situation do not come around all the time.

So come on, Caroline said. —So what can you tell me?

Love, Gala

# September 13, 2009

Dear B——,

America is the kind of place where you can become whatever you want to become, your dad likes to announce whenever he buys a birthday gift for himself. That is, as long as you've got the grit.

Do you have the grit, B——? he asks. —Eddie? Adam? Any of you? Only me?

None of you ever knows how to answer him, but he doesn't expect you to. Just asking the question of his three sons is his birthday gift to himself. So he asks it, again and again he asks it, while you stretch your hand out the window of your father's flying car and feel the wind coming up on it, bending it back like a sail, wherever your wrist wants to take you. Imagine yourself as your hand, surfing somewhere he is not.

Your dad buys birthday gifts for himself whenever he feels he's earned them, more than just once a year. The lack of any real date of birth makes this sort of justifiable. The flying Impala your dad bought for himself just this past May 1959, B——, was a monster: blue turquoise like a lightning bolt, its hood distended and pregnant with raw horsepower, chromed hoverstripes and gravity-brakes and tailfins capable of hurling the car into high

Martian orbit, taking with it your dad, you, and your brothers—Eddie now eleven, Adam now eight, you now fifteen, three boys spread shoulder to shoulder across the back seat. Normally your mom rides shotgun with your dad, but she's home today, her place ceremonially vacant. Her seat in front of you crushes your long legs. Adam hums a song in the middle; Eddie presses the side of his face wetly against the window he's forbidden to open. Your father's opening his wallet, pulling nickels and pennies he wants to be rid of from the zippered coin pocket.

*Summertiiiime,* your brother Eddie sings, in tune with Adam's humming. You tense: you know your father is in a talkative mood. This won't go unremarked.

Edward, your dad says. —You're how old now? Eleven, twelve years old, right, tough guy? I was twelve years old when your grandfather took me out to the groves. Up before sunrise. Slashing your hands on branches. Sun burning your scalp so hard your brains cook like poached eggs. There's your summertime. That's what the song refers to. I know all about *summertime,* tough guy.

Your father has told you this story before, many times. The memory is like a drain in the shower floor of his life: every experience will eventually slide into it. When you were as young as Eddie, you remember feeling sad that he had to go through all of that. You try to keep your face blank, now, unnoticed.

It'd be illegal for me to make you work today like that, your dad muses. —The government would put me in jail for doing to you what was done to me. Remember that.

Sorry, sir, Adam tells him, beside you. You cringe—your baby brother hasn't yet learned not to volunteer—even as you're grateful. For now, your dad's attention has fallen on another target: your hand can float out the window, free, as the flying car glides to a halt, no part of it in contact with the asphalt.

Sitting on a dented patio chair beneath the shade of the Arkanon station is your cousin Tom Happy, the sun turning the edges of his hair white and his face tan and lean. He looks like an angel who does extra roles in Westerns. His face is wet with heat that seems not to have touched his collar or his armpits, like the sweat's collecting in a secret amniotic plastic sheath under his brown work jumpsuit. Seeing the Impala park, he gets up, adjusts himself, and breaks into a brisk, tip-generating jog. He doesn't even falter when he recognizes your father in the driver's seat.

Fill her up for you, Uncle Bill? he asks gamely. He winks at you, crushed in the backseat.

Tom, says your dad. —I didn't know you were working here.

Just for the summer, Tom smiles. —Found a sweetheart deal on a used Lincoln floater and my dad's willing to help me out with the payments. But I've got to pay him back.

Eddie pipes up: —You gotta fix it up and everything?

Eddie, your dad warns.

It's not so tough, Tom smiles. —You got a part here; it's got three hoses coming off it. Those hoses gotta connect to something. Real formula.

You can hear your father's smile crackle and spark.

Then I'm holding you to a higher standard, smart guy, he announces. —I need her filled up, Tom. I need the oil changed. The car's floating a little lopsided. Incompetence at the factory. You see how it is, working a place now yourself, how that kind of thing can happen. To correct it I'll need you to beef up the left hover pistons, leave the right alone.

Sure, Uncle Bill, no problem, Tom says.

Make sure no oil's spilled, Bill says. —It'll etch the paint. This is a brand new car. One day you'll appreciate what that means, Tom. I have faith in you. Every drop of oil I find, and I'm going to look, I'll deduct a sum from your fee. You'll have to make up the difference to your boss out of your own pocket. You understand?

Understood, Tom replies.

Your dad studies his face. You and your brothers have been so studied. You keep staring, always fascinated to see this investigation from outside. At once you hope your dad will do something drastic—spring from the car, start screaming at Tom, shove the dipstick in his face and flick drops of oil on his uniform—something that will prove, once and for all and in public, just who he is. Something that will exonerate you.

And when your dad gets out, you grip the plush backseat, your hands tense enough to tear the fabric; you squeeze harder and hope it tears. But your dad takes his pack of Winstons with him and walks to a pillar that holds up the center of the station, some five feet from the pump, where he leans and taps the pack against his wrist. Tom, engaged with the gravity converters, looks as if he might say something when your dad strikes match after match against the pump, but either Tom decides that your dad must know better or that the world would be better off were he to be consumed in a burst of flaming compressed petroleum, and he bends back to work.

You watch his hands move as he works, a task that mystifies you. If he connects the wrong hose the engine will fail. There's no getting around a failure like that.

Why's he going out there to smoke anyhow, you say to your brothers. —Usually he smokes in here so that we all gotta cough.

Cause it's a new car, dingus, Eddie says.

He emphasizes the point by leaning across Adam to punch your shoulder. Your youngest brother begins to cry. You grab your shoulder and roll your eyes back in your head until they're white.

My arm, you wail. —My racchus nerve. You punched me right in my racchus nerve. My whole arm's dying.

There's no racchus nerve, Eddie shouts. —Shut up, B——.

We just learned about it, you say. —They only tell you about the racchus when you get into high school. You'd go crazy with fear if you knew it existed before.

Adam stops crying, starts giggling, and Eddie's scowl softens as he tries to figure out whether you're putting him on, and you sit there, B——: elder sibling, sun at the center holding the system together while your dad smokes next to a gas pump.

Before leaving, your father performs his inspection: kicks the hoverstripes, runs his fingers over the still-warm engine block, opens the gas cap and bends to sniff its bouquet. Tom stays admirably stonefaced throughout the process, beyond a brief moment when he meets your eyes, then winks and rolls his own. You feel a little better. Someone else sees how your dad is and has elected to say nothing. There's a kind of peace for you in this.

HOW MUCH DO I WANT to say, B——, about this phase of your life, at home with your father and brothers? How much does it even exist for you as a linear narrative anymore, rather than a periodic one: a clock, its hands circling until the moment you turn eighteen and it becomes safe to leave? But not periodic in the sense of *regular*: your father's emotions cresting in traumatic moments, in syncopation, an irregular metronome that ticks when it wants. You work hard, don't you, to adapt yourself to it, to hear its rhythm so that you will know when to tense yourself, to brace yourself. In later years, you will tell interviewers that you are not a genius: you are just a hardworking person.

HERE'S ANOTHER MOMENT: —COME INTO my office a minute, he says to you.

You're alone this time; he's forced you to work for him for the summer; your brothers are not present. So you follow him out of the sweltering warehouse of Prometheus Parcel and through the secretarial pool to his office. The walls here are pincushioned with tacks bearing tiny reminders, in some cases affirmations, and there's a small liquor cart filled with seltzer bottles, an ancient record player with a stack of jazz and blues 78s and 33s, and a solid walnut desk with a folding chair behind it, a throw pillow on its seat. The room smells uric beneath a haze of ancient smoke.

Your dad shuts the door behind you. —My desk, he says. Sit down at it.

You look at him with alarm. His temples are twitching. To explain this moment, you must have committed a crime; you race through your memories to figure out what it is, come up with a suggestion you made earlier. You'd said something about the messengers, you think, a way you thought they could be smoother. You thought you could help him.

I'm sorry, you say, preemptively. —I realize now that what I said wasn't a good idea.

B——, he says. —Sit down.

You'll only make things worse if you delay. He sits down after you, keeping some ten inches away from you the whole time. He looks at you, soft for a moment, and then he slams his palms against the desk surface.

So you think you can run my business, he screams. —So you want to be me, tough guy! All right! Let's see how hot you are at being me! Where's my paycheck! What hours am I working next week! Why's this box dented! Why aren't the taxes paid on time! When's the new typewriter ribbon supply coming in! Every hour! Every day! Choking you! Killing you! Killing you!

You hold your breath. There's a certain rhythm you can swallow in, you've learned, that helps prevent tears from escaping, though you can still feel their burn. Finally, your dad, reeling and red in the face, picks up an ashtray with Apache designs on it and stiffly ratchets his body to a sitting position on the carpet. Wheezing, he takes a cigarette from his shirt pocket and lights it.

Stop crying, he says, smoke billowing around his face, and your tears dry up at his voice. —I don't trust those messengers to come back here. I trust you.

THAT NIGHT YOU'RE EXHAUSTED, CAN'T even play the piano, fall into bed ready for it to repeat the next day. You lie there in your bottom bunk, Adam floating somewhere above you. Eddie, on his bed, is turned toward the wall. Your dad makes you keep the place neat; the floor is totally bare of clothes, comics, toys, anything; the walls are bare of picture hooks that might have spoiled the paint. Except for your bodies in the beds, there's no clear-cut sign that any human kids live here at all.

There's a big photo on your dresser of your dad and mom on their wedding day. Your dad likes the three of you to keep it in here. Your mom looks different in the picture: her face is skinnier and her eyes are open wider, as if she's just waking up. Your dad is mostly glaring, tight smile on his face. Often you or one of your brothers puts the photo face down while you're asleep.

Tonight you just fold your pillow under to prop up your head so that you can stare at it unrestricted. There's moon from the window washing over the glass, and you can see your dad's eyes glisten at you. Your mother's eyes stare up straight at the lunar light.

No one comes through the door. Eddie, encased in blankets, stares at the wall. You have no idea if he's sleeping. He isn't moving; you feel strange about him when he isn't moving.

Adam, above you and invisible through the mattress, begins the song.

*Come down, come down from your ivory tower*
*Let love come into your heart.*

His voice, still high, soars somewhere along the melody line, like you taught him to do. He sings softly at first, trying to fly under the range of your dad's hearing, as you've also taught him.

You drop in just below him. He keeps the melody, and you let your voice drag it away where appropriate. *I love you, ooh ooh ooh ooh . . .* At last your middle brother's voice knots in, taking the space just below you. You lie in bed that night, singing "Ivory Tower" with Eddie and Adam until they drop off and only you remain. And you wish there were angels above you, B——, each silently driving clouds like cars with cirrus tires, long microphones

that dangle from celestial piano wire just brushing your lips. They
will use their angel technology to record you, which means you will
never disappear in your sleep.

YOU PRACTICE PLAYING A LOT now when you get home,
the moment you get in the door to the moment you get to sleep.
Even beyond that: you practice on the bus home, in the car while
your dad's telling you about the world and how he sees all of it
fitting together, while you sit in the folding chair in the black hole
lobby where the sun turns the room into a forge that smelts your
time down into slag, nickels, and dimes. You try out different
keys, chords, patterns, everything in your head. It's like staring at
a Magic Eye poster: the same elements, first static, then picture.

You imagine the kind of girl who'd listen to you play the piano:
she curls on your living room sofa with a tall glass of hot choco-
late before her, and at the sound of the music, her hands squeeze
tighter; the marshmallows melt. Imagining the warmth of the
cup, the itch of the blanket, your mind shuts down. You think of
girls often, but the thoughts always seem to short themselves out.
You're not sure why.

Once you think of a whole song on the bus: theme, variations,
everything, ghost voices floating over it. You try to keep it in your
brain until your next chance to sneak out to the shed and record
yourself singing the parts. But sometime in your sleep it gets mud-
dled up with the music that plays in your dreams always now,
and you've got no way to sort everything out when you wake
up, and it's gone. You're sad about it for a day before you realize
it doesn't matter. There's music all the time, now, like a crack's
formed in a dam, like a dry river is starting to fill. A river can
never run dry twice; you're fifteen; you know that.

ANOTHER MEMORY, ANOTHER TIME IN his office: four
sheets of paper stapled to four carbons. The sheets of paper are

stained, folded, creased, crumpled, all like they've spent weeks in different back pockets of different jeans. The carbons are immaculate.

I tried to select a sample from each week you've worked here, your dad explains. —To give a full survey of the problem. I could have picked several more examples. At least two per week.

Okay, you say. There's a chair you could theoretically sit in, but you know better than to do anything but stand at attention.

The top sheets are the original packing receipts, your dad continues. —The carbons are copies of the return paperwork I've had to do in order to refund the money of the people who sent these packages. Do you know why I had to do that? Because these people felt *cheated*, B——.

He has a record playing, mostly solo piano. You listen to it in the back of your head, your mind untangling keys as the song changes, the sound of the needle scratching and the ambient studio noise of the next cut rising. Just what did the studio that produced this ambient noise look like? You balance it against the sound of your Wollensak recordings in the shed, its metal walls. What are this studio's walls made of?

B——, your dad snaps. —I'm waiting for your explanation.

I—I put all the right slips with the right packages, you stammer. —I swear.

You're saying I refunded money I shouldn't have, your dad says sharply.

No, well, no, you say. —I mean, suppose the messengers got mixed up? I mean they take a lot of packages around, and it can get confusing—

He drags on his cigarette. The piano player is doing something joyous with the keys. When your father speaks again, he sounds hoarse, tired.

What is the mark of a man, B——? he asks.

You know his answer to this. —Never complain, and never explain, you say.

It's easy to remember, harder to live by, isn't it? he says. —I give you a D for your job performance, B——. But for shifting blame, instead of owning up to it like a man—for that, I give you an F.

Oh no, you say.

He squints at you. —Feel good about that F, do you? About being an F person?

He continues to talk, and you work hard not to cry. This is a matter of slowing down your breath, swallowing your spit, trying to feel cold, black weeds growing through your thighs and feet and into the ground. It occurs to you that you could hit your father. You're the same height; you're far younger than him. You could do it right now.

But you don't: you don't want to hurt him, you don't want to hurt anyone. Instead you think about the music on his record player, the velvet hammers smashing wires taut to the point of snapping, but instead they sound like water falling. You can follow them, let them collect on your skin, let them wash around you until your fury osmoses out through your pores and the water absorbs everything until nothing remains. It's just you and the tape rolling in your head. Your dad's studio noise and nothing more.

He folds the packing slips and carbons into quarters, tears them once lengthwise, and slides them into the trash.

You need to be careful, he says suddenly, something in him cracking open. —You're too young to understand how precarious things are. Do you realize how quickly everything can fall apart, how quickly we could all be on the streets, without a home, without a business? Have you ever thought about how anyone could survive without a home or a business? —His eyes are shot with red. —Have you, B——?

YOU LEAVE HIS OFFICE AND go into the bathroom. You stare at the mirror: every day you are getting older and the skin above your lip is getting darker. It is possible, you realize, that girls will think you handsome. An acid reflux of guilt splashes like turpentine across the walls of your stomach, and you make a fist and punch yourself in the cheekbone with it. It's hard to find the right angle, and it sinks into the fat of your cheek, barely hurts.

You feel stupid at having done this, flush with shame. And you try to remember what he said, exactly, whether there's any reason outside of yourself to have done what you've done. But you can't remember. Suppose you had recorded him, you suddenly think: then you wouldn't have to remember; you would know.

YOU THINK OUR LIVES ARE funny? your father shouts, another time, this time at dinner. —That me having to waste a whole day going to Sacramento to pry some documents out of the hands of that pencil-mustached queer in the district office so you can poke around this meal I provided you with, you think that's all done for your amusement?

Yes, says Eddie, and then he ducks as your father picks up a highball glass and throws it at his head. It misses, shatters against the wall of the dining room behind him.

Eddie starts to laugh. Adam pales. Your mother presses her arms against the table. You can see her mouthing words—*Let's try to calm down*—but no sound comes out; it never does.

You say nothing either, B——: in these situations, whoever draws your father's attention becomes his target. Which is why you feel all the air suck out of the room in the moment that Eddie points to you.

He did it, he says. —B——! He's the one who imitated you first! I was just imitating *him!*

Your father's neck snaps straight; his eyes are upon you. There are two more glasses within his reach: your mother's, Adam's. Your eyes flicker back and forth between each of them and your father's face.

Is what he's saying true, B——? your father asks.

And now you look at Eddie. You don't even know if what your brother is accusing you of is true or not; you know that it doesn't matter whether it is or not. You know that the correct response, of course, is to deny it. You'll be punished as well—your father will ensure that there's some pretext for punishing you, make no mistake. But he won't do so with the same certainty: he'll weaken. True, it wouldn't be noble to hide behind your little brother for something you're actually guilty of, but in this moment, nobility is clearly a sucker's play.

You study Eddie's eyes to make a prediction about what he'll do. Will he be more noble than you were? How deep does his love for you go? You look at him, but you know that you have the same father as him. His eyes look back at you and show you he knows the same. Neither of you is looking at the shards of glass on the carpet.

It's true, you say immediately. —I did it.

Your father's whole body turns to you, an insane comet that blots out all sun. He looks down at you. If you look back, you can kind of neutralize the fear in yourself, B——, like you're at the cold center of a flame.

I don't hit my children, he finally says. —I want you all to remember that. That is a thing that I pride myself on never doing.

He brings himself taller when he says that. But you are taller than him now, you suddenly realize. You feel a flush of shame at this and you're not sure why.

Your father draws close to your face.

I don't deserve your disrespect, he whispers. His breath smells dead beneath the ketchup rind of the meatloaf stuck behind his teeth.

IN THE BATHROOM, YOUR FINGERNAILS digging into the meat of your fists, you raise your fist again, trace the path through the air to your cheek. It's easier the second time, like you've made a recording with your body, like familiar grooves of a hit single that you can play whenever you want.

YOU GO TO THE PIANO, cheek hot. Your fingers, when they uncurl from your fists, feel slow, like squid feelers, like girls' hands. When you place them on the keys you can feel the weight of the hammers resisting the pressure, bending your fingers back. You play a note and it's the wrong note. And your veins are suddenly full of slow liquid garbage; you slam your fingerprints into the keys, send them rising and falling through a furious progression of chords and scales, chromatically creeping up the octave and the higher octave until they hit some angry saturation point and boil over into a whirlpool of seething whitecap bubbles. And like a rubber band that's snapped, your spine goes slack; you relax into a tense shuffle beat, a simmering progression that loops, that repeats.

Like you're swinging a hammer in a circle, you try to get control of your progression, keep your fingers taut, keep playing, breathing. Your shoulders wrench up the octave, down the octave; you keep playing. At last you're at a still place, your emotions calm. You don't need to look at the keyboard. You don't need to look at the room. You close your eyes and stretch your fingers to the chords where you know you need to begin.

It's a strange game: you know the chords, the path the song has to take. Now you just have to find a way to keep weaving the string of melody through each of them, around each of them, in turn. As long as you keep moving from chord to chord, every note will be right. You should have thought of it before. You think of how stupid you are as you play, just you and the piano keys and the living room and the bench beneath you like a raft on a rain-swollen river capped with diamonds, the kite string of melody stretching from your fingers. You keep playing until the melody has nowhere else to go; you let your fingers lift off; you let the kite sail into the sky.

You turn to find your father watching you. He stiffens when you meet his eyes, and you drop your own eyes, hoping to spare him whatever's hurting him.

SO OFTEN HE'S WATCHING YOU: sometimes your mother or your brothers, but most often you. You represent something to him, you think: his oldest son, his heir, someone who will be responsible for taking what he did and doing more. It's comfortable, in a way: you have a place in the world in his eyes, a shape he's drawing out for you to fill, something he would like to give himself. But he can't give himself anything. Instead, he will give it to you.

You will let him watch you, you think. Until one day your time with him will run out—you'll get taller, you'll get older, you'll get married maybe to some girl who will not hurt you, some date on a calendar will pass and you'll be able to leave the house he built for himself, away from the beach. You'll wave goodbye, get in your own hovercar and fly away, never speak to him again: you'll never have to be seen by anyone but yourself. You can't even imagine what that will be like: how good it will be, for once, to rest.

But part of you hopes there are angels still watching you, B——: watching you and recording, little chrome Wollensak vocal mics hanging from their scepters to catch every word you say, every thought you form, every a capella chord you braid together in your head to drown out his voice. Part of you hopes angels are recording: if they are, then one day, when you and your father are both up in the heaven he doesn't believe in, he will finally see everything you do to protect him. And he will be kind.

Love, Gala

# September 15, 2009

Dear B——,

It was well into the afternoon before I made the trek out to Ronda's horrible trailer to return her car. By day, it looked better: sparkling car parts gathered in overturned box lids, gas cans, an empty computer case full of cables tied together with another cable, a whole lawn mower someone had been reassembling, loose screws gathered in a tomato sauce can with half its label gone, a full Dickens Village Christmas set with perpetual sparkling snow even in ninety-degree shade. It was still trash, but well-organized.

Her brother—Dino, I remember she told me his name was—was on the porch when I pulled up, propped on a swivel chair and mummy-wrapped in a scarf, knit cap, and sweats. There was a cigarette becoming ash in his hand. He squinted at me, eyes red around the edges with a spray of busted capillaries like dark cabbage roots left to blacken in the sun.

Hi, he said stiffly. —She's inside.

Great, I said. —I'm Gala, by the way. How'd you know I was here for your sister?

He nodded and didn't respond. I set my boot up on the first step of the porch, like a surveyor digging in.

What a gorgeous day, I said. —Isn't it a gorgeous day? Doesn't it make you want to just run around?

He didn't respond to this either, and I waited, trying to guess how he was going to smoke his cigarette through his scarf, but he made no move. So instead I walked to the door of the trailer, folding my sunglasses into the prow of my tank top as the jetsetters might do.

The trailer door opened immediately on Ronda's bathroom, whose door hung ten degrees out of true on its hinge, but which was otherwise clean and stocked with a stained glass window's worth of nuclear fluorescent bath products. To the right was a dark space full of kitchen machines, what looked like a bed, and a dimly glimpsed Xmas tree with its lights extinguished; a sour medical smell frosted with bacon fat emanated from it. The sound of Nintendo came from the door to the left, which was ajar, and I knocked for a moment before entering.

Ronda's room was a canopy of hanging camisoles in every autumn color, plus sky blues and death-mushroom teen fuchsia. The back room linoleum was crushed solid with other fallen clothes as well, forming a dense forest floor. Dominating one end was a beanbag chair and dresser that looked as if it'd been split with an axe and carefully reassembled with carpenter's glue, its drawers vomiting bras. A fat TV/VCR combo unit connected to an NES formed its centerpiece. The other end of the room was a bunk bed, metal storage shelves beneath it laden with makeup, greasy tools, more NES cartridges, a couple of fantasy novels, and a lava lamp whose colors had long ago bleached out.

On top of the bunk bed, wedged between the mattress and the ceiling, was Ronda. A garrote wire connected the NES to her hands like an umbilical cord soaked in black oil. She looked over at me, unsurprised, from beneath a pink comforter printed with fleshy oysters. She hadn't changed out of her sleeping crop top, but she'd already applied some combo of cleanser and razors to her face, and she'd put her hair up. That impressed me.

Hey I brought back your car, I announced, dropping her keys on top of the NES.

Oh cool, thank you, she said flatly, continuing to play. On the screen, a blond cartoon paladin jumped and hacked through a series of bland maroon-and-gray castle hallways.

Is that *Legend of Philippe Clash*? I asked.

Yeah, said Ronda. —I haven't beaten it in a while, so I was gonna spend the morning beating it. It's a thing to do.

Another thing to do is drive me back to the hostel, I reminded her.

She nodded, keeping her eyes on the screen, and she continued to play her game. She was surprisingly good at it. I'd never been good at impossible, Nintendo-hard games like this one. My speed was always RPGs: as long as you kept turning them on and sitting in front of them for a finite space of time, steady, indelible progress would be your reward. But platform games required you to develop grace. Ronda had that: her cartoon paladin's horrible fixed-arc jump would drop with perfect timing to flank a skeleton throwing spears, and she never missed a hurdle in the horse racing part that everyone hated. I wondered how often she played this game, alone, to have such grace.

I heard you talking to my brother out there, she said. —You haven't met him before, right?

No, I said. —He seemed nice?

For the first time today, her expression changed; she laughed, her eyes remaining on the screen. —That's like, a sentence no one has ever said before about him, she said. —I mean, I take that back. He is nice. He's a sweetheart. I just can't deal with him right now. I told him to stay the fuck out for at least an hour. I told him to make himself useful. Was he being useful?

I considered this question. —He was reducing the number of cigarettes in the world, and they're bad for you.

She looked at me, and then she paused her game and threw the shellfish comforter off. She was wearing a black thong with a thick strap and what looked like rhinestone studs.

If you wanna talk, come talk in the shower, she said.

It felt half a dare—*so are we friends? Are you sure? How far are you going to follow me?*—and half-classic, no-boundaries trans girl bullshit—*look at this body, I worked hard for it*. In either case, I followed her in, sat on the tiny toilet while she got undressed behind the curtain and started the water, filling the small space with approximations of cherry blossom and sandalwood smells. There were hair ties in rainbow colors in the medicine cabinet; I sat cat's-cradling them in my fingers, stretching and slackening them like a heart valve, while she worked.

I'm just sick of him, is the thing, she said. —I just worry.

What do you worry about? I asked.

Then the water came down unaccompanied by voices for a while—she had decided not to answer my question, I guessed—and I continued to flex and distort the rainbow ties in my fingers: now they seemed a tunnel, now a spiderweb.

That girl from the other night, Ronda asked finally. —Is she your girlfriend now or something?

What, no, I said. —I mean, we made out? I mean I guess I don't know where it's going.

Making out doesn't mean anything, Ronda said.

But she said she wanted to stay out here a while, I said.

What the fuck? Ronda asked. —Why would she do that? She's been here for like—not even two weeks, right? No one wants to live out here.

I wanted to live out here, I argued. —I don't know. Maybe she thinks it's cool out here. Maybe she thinks I'm cool.

Again, the water came down. —She's cis, right? Ronda finally asked.

I mean, yes, I said. —I mean we'd established that.

No, *you* established that, Ronda said. —So what'd y'all do? Tell me.

I flinched, a kind of third-order doom dysphoria coming over me: I didn't want to talk about anything physical with Caroline with Ronda; I felt like Ronda was acting unfeminine—ergo, *trans*—by wanting to talk about it with me; yet I felt also this was what real—ergo, *cis*—women must do with one another in response to hookups with other women, and Ronda, being a better trans woman than I was, knew that and I didn't. I hated other trans women; I hated being around us, like a radio you could never turn off, like having to be awake and not asleep.

That's personal, I said.

I'm sorry, she said, flatly and immediately, a robot shorting out.

No, I'm sorry, I said after a moment. —I just—it was a lot.

After a pause, she asked: —So what, are you like all gay now? Gay and in love?

I didn't answer, let it linger until she seemed to drop the question, or any pretense at conversation, and eventually the water turned off.

Could you hand me a towel maybe, she said.

Stomping on her stupid linoleum, I handed a striped towel to the hand she extended over the shower curtain. She shut the water off, dripped, wrapped herself up, and opened the curtain; she was tall, and the stripes barely covered her. She pulled a second towel from the rack and wrapped it around her hair, and then she started to make the day's second application of cleanser to her face. I suddenly felt really uncomfortable there in her bathroom, and I think she knew it, because she didn't say anything to clarify what was appropriate: where I should be, whether I should stay. So I went out to the front room to wait for her to take me home.

Ronda's brother had moved in to the dark body of the trailer, lying on the couch. Sheets and blankets had been stapled over every window, leaving only glowing, fuzzy rectangles of fabric.

You know if Ronda has anything going to the post office today? he asked. —Because I can go to the post office for her. You know, if she needs that, or anything else.

His bloodshot eyes, in the dark, looked weirdly kidlike, hopeful. —No, sorry, I said.

He nodded. —Hey, I got a question, he asked. Are you—like Ronda?

I looked at him. —That's right, I said.

That's cool with me, he said.

I appreciate that, I said, folding my arms and narrowing my eyes.

Yeah, he said. —She needs to know someone like her.

I didn't know how to respond to that, and we stood there awkwardly until Ronda came out. She was wearing a tight black dress with white polka dots, her ponytailed hair wrapped in all of the rainbow elastic, lips painted nuclear tanager and ears bearing multiple tiers of gold-and-birthstone rings. She didn't look at her brother as we left.

He wanted to know about the post office, I said to her in the car, tires throwing stones against the windshield in cracks. —Do you like—do a lot of mailing?

Yeah, I sell stuff online sometimes, she said. —He helps me out. A lot of people around here have a lot of stuff they don't need anymore, and sometimes we can flip it.

That's why there's all the weird stuff around your house, I said. —I get it.

She fell silent. —So I tell you all kinds of stuff about me, she said suddenly. —And I still don't know shit about you. Tell me something about yourself. Like, where are you from even? Tell me that.

I'm not from anywhere, I said after a long, delaying laugh. —It's not important. I don't know what to say about it.

Everyone's from somewhere, she said.

It's not anywhere special, I said. —It's not real. It's too *nice.*

I wish I lived somewhere nice, she said.

Ashamed, I looked out the window at the trailers and houses scattered through the sand, and she played her psychedelica CD and continued to drive.

Love, Gala

# September 17, 2009

Dear B——,

There's one girl out there for you, your father tells you. —Some people call her a soulmate. It's your first task in this life to be worthy of that soulmate. To be able to provide financially for her. Do you understand?

Yes sir, you say.

It's your second task to find her, he says.

Yes sir, you say. Your mother listens to this conversation from the next room, feigning sleep, a book tented over her eyes.

He continues to give you advice, at first about women but quickly modulating into business: you get the sense the two fields of endeavor have the same meaning, designing a life around oneself. It's 1962, and for three, four summers now, you've worked for your father at Prometheus Parcel. He's never promoted you, but neither has he fired you. He has some sense of you as a *working man*, a status he's extended to you like a line of credit. You are good at self-starting, at knowing how to stay out of his way: he likes to tell you that.

I need to grow you as a leader, B——, he says. —Eddie's coming up behind you, and Adam after him. I need you in a position to help groom them, too. Then they'll rise as you're rising.

He is building something from the three of you, a sigil to bind your lives.

THERE'S A DREAM YOU HAVE on the night of the conversation about women. You're walking, befuddled, goofy-footed, through living rooms with walls painted aquamarine, avocado, magenta, each color DuraLux fresh, overstuffed couches in each room, fanned stacks of *National Geographic, Playboy, Life, Time*, bookshelves lined with identical green spines and nothing on their page, a mobile on the ceiling twirling like a turbine. And the living rooms have windows that look into other living rooms, mysteriously sunlit when you aren't in them, the promised high tide marks of golden rays dappling through the doorframes, and someone is baking a peach custard pie in a kitchen you can't see. But you can hear music: the needle spreading dry brush ink over cartoon images of Doris Day, Edith Piaf, Chet Baker doing Gershwin, unreal voices that sing as you trip and scuff your feet on beige carpets-of-the-future—

A girl sings along. What does she look like? Is she in her bedroom? Her skirt sweeps with her as her feet accelerate from vanity to desk to bedcovers to door, hem snaps back in time to the implicit backbeat—maybe she's arranging her souvenirs; she's been to the beach, to the county fair, beneath the bleachers. And she sits at her desk, her head in her hand with her eyes open, she leans back on her chair; she sings along with the record, clears her head; music is in her, lets her float away somewhere wholesome, somewhere good, and what does her bedroom look like? Doilies on a night table? Four poster in walnut with carved angels? Record jackets, plates with leftover staling crusts, mayonnaise long since turned, glasses of milk now evaporated, secret stash of Virginia Slims tucked into the base of a drawer of stockings and slips? How does she live there? What is it like to exist there when no maleness is present to exterminate its purity, like a photon you can only measure by destroying? The sarcophagus of a pharaoh queen, its enchanted air sealed away from the likes of you, and a big brass key on a white lace ribbon dangles from her desk—

Basically, *oh shit B*——, your dream self had better find that room pronto, while she's still singing, before the hypno-spiral groove on the record runs out—you speed up your pace—race from living room to living room, clumsy, worthless, trip over throw rugs, smash your knee on hassocks, get your head caught in the dangling bead cord of the ceiling fan, aw, *gee*—the smell of peach custard is getting stronger—the music is getting louder— her voice, never scuffed with puberty, gets brighter—everything gets brighter—the colors of the walls bleach out—you are so close to her bedroom B—— you can taste the air of it—

And you wake up in the bedroom you still share with Eddie and Adam, the reek of balled socks and the silhouettes of old baseball trophies in the windowsill and green sunspots flashing over your eyes as they adjust to the dark. And you wonder if this is what your father was trying to explain to you.

YOU WERE STILL IN HIGH school when you started walking at night: around junior year, after dinners when your father held court, yelled at your mother for her passivity or your little brother for his secrecy or your middle brother for his crimes. He never yells much at you specifically these days, which is either a function of your working for him for some years now or your relative height. You don't know whether he knows you sneak out to walk at night, uncontrolled. You hope he finds out and the anxiety of it rips him up, and then you hate yourself for hoping that. When you hate yourself like that, a good trick is to take your finger and twist it as far as you can without breaking it. If you hurt yourself, you get scared, and you calm down. It's vital to stay calm. It's vital to leave the house because the house is where you die.

The first time you sneak out, you take a quick terrified loop around the block, head hunched into your shoulders and eyes crazy, and you stare into the window of every car that zooms toward you, imagining your father's face behind the wheel, ready to take you back home. But the more you walk the streets of Hawthorne, the safer they feel, like you're a crab crawling on an unfamiliar beach, bringing more and more of your own smell with you each time you visit. And soon you can even sit on the curb to rest without worrying that someone might see you. You can lie down on the asphalt, wondering if a car will fly into you, not minding if it does. It's peaceful, like you're in space, freefalling through stardust. This is how adults feel: numb and awake. And the little victory of the escape means something, a heavy metal thing you can slip into your pocket.

WHERE DO YOU GO, B——, when you wander the neighborhood at night? Down the identical grid streets, noticing the details only suburban kids know as elves know forests: the pinwheel garden in one yard, the shoes neatly lined under the porch rocker of another, the forgotten doghouse with a name painted in gold, the rustle of trees, the quiet rivers of rain that disappear down storm drains. You pace at the bus stop, watching four lanes of fat steel cars shift and glide, then across the street, across the highway. Sometimes kids from high school are in the cars, belching football songs or racing; sometimes they recognize you and wave and invite you to join them. You wave back; you say you have other plans. You think about things you did with those kids, how they remember them, how you remember them; you wish you had recordings, so you knew what really happened, so your own perspective didn't corrupt it.

Some nights you walk miles, watch the neighborhoods give way to shipyards, construction companies, vacant lots destined for future capitalization. And then you come to beaches. You hop the seawall and walk past trash heaps of picnic plates and cairns

of spare rib bones, somewhere under the black sky the move-
ments of crabs, dead rays drifting in the surf. If you could hold
your breath you could walk west to Hawaii, your country's last
star, your ankles sinking into the cold muck of ocean trenches,
balancing one foot in front of the other against undertow and
riptides and strange lantern fish, and if you miss one step the
undertow drags you out and away, and the harder you struggle,
the faster you disappear.

Tonight, your dream of the infinite apartment still swimming
around you, you don't think you should go to the ocean alone.

TOM HAPPY STILL LIVES AT the corner of Mt. Vernon and
Fairway. You haven't spoken to him since last summer, when he
worked briefly at a soda fountain on your walk home from Prometheus Parcel, and he told you his story of his financial ruin at
the hands of a succession of girlfriends.

They were takers, he'd said. —Whereas me, I understand how
to make money grow. —He looked anxious that you believe this
about him. Something about the memory of his anxious face is
what brings you to his house this night. You want to see someone,
tonight, who's a little bit afraid of you.

YOU KNOCK ON TOM'S SCREEN door, holding your windbreaker together with your hands in the pockets and the Wollensak
recorder you bought last summer with your Prometheus Parcel
wages under your arm, the succulent containers on the porch
dreaming slow dreams while you shift your weight from foot to
foot and make the porch boards creak. The kitchen lights flip on,
the door cracks, and here's Tom Happy, his sandy hair sticking up
behind his ears. A plaid Pendleton shirt hangs open on his skinny
frame. Here on his porch, he looks like a dog trained to bite throats.

My *goodness*, Tom says. —What're you doing here? It's not
like you to come visiting.

Hey, you say. —Nothin' much. I was wondering if we could talk, and uh, if I could record it, so I can listen to the recording when I don't feel normal, you know?

He looks at you, B——: your hunched shoulders equalize your height.

Sure, B——, he says. —*Mi casa su casa*, always.

You've been to his place before, of course; at least once a year like clockwork your mom somehow arranges with your dad to let her bring you and your brothers by. But tonight, the order of your aunt Marcella's house is broken: pillows from the couch are strewn over the floor, wine-stained glasses rest on the teakwood table, a belt, black leather, hangs at the end of the bannister. Tom rubs his head and leads you into the kitchen, pours you both tall glasses of water and twists his fingers against his bony temples. His eyes are two stove burners on low.

So what's on your mind? he asks. —You're interested in recording *me*, huh? Come to hear the secret of my great success? —He laughs, peevishly.

You look at your water glass. —Sure, you say. —Do you have anything stronger?

It's after midnight, he says. —Which means it's before noon.

Forget it, you say. —I don't want to be trouble.

I'm kidding, Tom says.

From a locked liquor cabinet in the next room—the key already in its lock, already half turned—he draws a bottle of gin. You drink, let the juniper reek settle in your nose.

You can tell me anything, B——, Tom says. —You know that. Thick as thieves! So what's on your mind?

Nothing, you say. —Nothing—I just, you know, I had to get my head on straight. I'll be fine in a minute. Then we can record.

Tom swallows his water and sits forward in his chair some, hands on his knees. You draw up your shoulders, trying to lift your collar farther up your neck.

I dunno, you say. —It's stupid. I had a creepy dream about girls.

Doesn't sound so creepy to me, he hoots. —Now haven't you ever had those before, B——? Hasn't your dad taught you anything about the birds and the bees?

You flush; you have made a mistake in talking about your dreams. —I guess he, uh, made me go on a date the other day, you say. —Does that count?

Tom stops laughing. Again he lets his hands clasp, one fist working into his palm as if he's crushing a leaf.

Listen, B——, he says. —Friendly advice. Fuck that old man, okay? He's just a nasty piece of work. My mom and I—let's just say we don't always see eye to eye, you understand. But she hates him and always has, and there I agree with her 100 percent.

You feel yourself relax: there was a reason you came here.

Listen, now I'm serious, Tom continues. —You're not a kid anymore. None of us are. You should be thinking about moving out on your own, getting your own job instead of that creepy package company.

Aw, he'd never let me do that, you interrupt.

What do you mean, *let you*? Tom snaps. —You just *do* it! I'd do it myself if it weren't for this precarious financial situation in which I'm finding myself of late—

He details some recent reversals in his career, now advanced to a diner attendant at Sal's Famous, while you try to pay attention to what another person is saying and mostly succeed. You don't mean to be rude. It's not as if you're uninterested; Tom's good at finding ways to apply the lessons he's learned from his stories of tip-stiffing surfers and ministers fussy about their coffee preferences to your own situation. It's just that it's a lot of work to guess whether people are thinking bad thoughts about you or not. When they tell you stories, you can be sure they aren't; people don't tell important things to people they hate or want to hurt. So it's a time you can let your brain relax: you can find some ease with yourself, elsewhere. You like your cousin, you think.

And then he takes the ease away: —We could even go into business together, he suggests.

The music in your head has been churning as he talks; now you can feel it shift into a minor key. And you might have gotten up, made your excuses, probably followed a completely different course in your life, had you not heard the second set of footsteps on the stairs, felt the softer air that moves into the kitchen in advance of the yawning girl, like medieval cupids bearing trumpets. A long plaid bathrobe shifts open and shut over her tall leg as she walks across the linoleum.

Tom? she asks. —You never came back to bed.

Tom puts his water glass to his mouth. She notices you staring at her leg, quickly adjusts her robe.

There was sort of an emergency, sweetheart, he says. —SOS. Men at work.

You flush. She smiles at you, leans over Tom, ruffles his hair and plants a kiss on the pinprick bald spot nestled at the crown of his curls.

Introduce me, she asks.

Look who's giving the orders, Tom says. —All right. B——, this is Anna Lee. Anna Lee, this is my cousin B——. B—— was having some trouble sleeping, so he washed up on our shores. That's just the kind of buddies we are.

Hello, you say.

Hi, B——, she says. She yawns, shakes the yawn out of herself, lets her eyes flutter open. Her eyes are purple and brown; they are huge, draining eyes. —Are you thirsty or anything? Do you need something to eat?

We've taken care of the thirst angle, Tom says.

I'd, uh, have something to eat, if it's not too much trouble, you say.

Then I'll see what's in the icebox, she replies.

You force yourself not to watch her walk away. A knife is drawn from a block; a latch is undone; a jar is set on the table.

That's my mom's best bathrobe, Tom calls after her, giving you a sidelong glance. —Don't get any mayo on it, right?

I won't, she calls.

You stare at Tom. —Gee, it seems strange that Aunt Marcella would let your friend use her robe, even if she is sleeping over.

Tom looks at you, trying to assess whether you're actually this naïve, or whether you're fucking with him (as we say in the future). You let him assess you in silence.

Listen, B——, he says finally. —Keep quiet about this, all right? Don't queer this whole thing for me.

I'm not queering anything, you say, eyes level. The breadbox opens; the breadbox closes; a knife is scraped over toast. —So did you make love with her?

Tom leans back in his chair, picks up the rest of his gin and water, knocks it back as if he's ascended a spectacular peak.

That's one way to describe it, sure, he says, worldly-wise.

Did she cry? you ask. —What kinds of things did she say?

He squints. —It's not that articulate a situation, he explains.

You suddenly feel stupid, unsure of why you were curious about what Tom's girlfriend said in the first place.

I mean you know from experience, Tom says carefully. —Don't you?

You look down at the floor, and Tom leans his chair forward. He looks at you with real concern.

You're not serious, he says, looking at you as if he can't believe this: that hair, that height, those sad eyes.

I mean I dunno, you say. —Like I don't know—like how do you know that a girl's really interested in you, like that she really wants to do that?

Tom taps on the table, his excitement battling his desire to keep this quiet, just between you. —That's where you're messing up, he says eagerly. —That's the whole fly in your particular ointment. It's not your job to figure out whether a girl's interested in you. It's your job to *make* her interested in you. Listen, here's what you do. You get yourself invited over to a girl's house. That's the first step. You figure out some pretext for that; there are a million; if you can't, just invite yourself. Then you get alone with her. Then you just look into her eyes. You look at them until she asks you what's wrong.

He demonstrates this on you; you feel a little electronic shiver. —What next? you ask.

Then you say something insulting to her, he says. —Not, you know, real overtly insulting. Just maybe you ask her if she's lost weight since last you saw her, or you talk about how you just wanted a moment with her where she shuts up. Just get her kinda off her guard. Then, while she's off balance, try to figure out a way to touch her.

He's still staring into your eyes; you laugh, uncertain of the correct response.

It's like with one hand, you offer her the stick, he continues eagerly. —Then you slip her the carrot. —He laughs happily. —You get the idea, right? You wouldn't believe how often it works. —He gestures at the kitchen, where Anna Lee is working to feed you. —Exhibit A for the prosecution, he giggles.

Wow, you say.

He's watching you still, strangely intent, and then he clears his throat. —You gonna try it yourself, now? he asks, voice soft. —You can practice on her, on Anna Lee. That is, if you let me get mad and throw you out afterward.

You look up at him, and he winces, seals his chest with his arms.

I don't know, you say. —I think maybe it's better to you know, find a girl who you don't have to hypnotize?

He nods. —And Cuba could overthrow the Castros all by their lonesome, too, he says.

ANNA LEE RETURNS, BRINGING A sandwich for you and a sandwich for Tom, a glass of water for herself.

So, Tom's friend B——, she asks. —What brings you here so late at night?

You remember wanting to record Tom, to create a tool to restore a sense of normality for yourself whenever you need it, but this idea no longer appeals to you; he is not helping you to feel normal. —I don't know, you say. —I was walking.

Tom jerks his thumb at you. —He was having dreams about girls.

Really? asks Anna Lee. —Could you tell me about them? I'm taking a class on psychology at El Camino. Maybe I could analyze your dream and figure out what's disturbing you.

This oughta be good, Tom stage whispers to you, and Anna Lee smiles harder.

They're kinda personal, you say. —You're in college?

Uh huh, says Anna Lee. —C'mon, I won't make fun of you.

Trusting this, you tell her about the maze of living rooms— the colors on the walls—the music rising from unseen record speakers—the girl's voice singing along.

Interesting, says Anna Lee, frowning and nodding slightly. —What music was playing?

Uh, I dunno, you say. —A song I can't figure out.

How does it go? she asks.

What do you care how it goes, Tom asks.

Don't be mean, Anna Lee says, curling her lip at him. —If it's stuck in his head, I'm sure it's important. Come on, B——, you can't hum it?

Of course he can hum it, Tom says; he smiles at you. —He can hum *anything*.

And as your cousin says this, you suddenly feel you can meet Anna Lee's eyes.

THE PIANO, AN UPRIGHT, IS concealed in your aunt's sewing room. The top of it strains under neatly stacked skeins of yarn (arranged primaries first, secondaries after, white and black and brown flanking to North, South, West), and the wall hangs with cross stitches, dogs and crosses and Bless This Houses and clouds over ponds, none of them complete. There are stacks of magazines bound with twine on all the shelves.

You sit on the bench while Tom guards the door and Anna Lee sits on your aunt's desk, ankles crossed, between two vegetable-shaped pincushions. Anna Lee smiles at you, and simultaneously you feel two things: (1) if you play this song for her, she will be your friend, and (2) it's wrong for you to be friends with her when she's dating someone who is, structurally, a more appropriate friend. These feelings confuse you, and you respond by shutting them off. Instead, you rest your hands on the keys, close your eyes, and play the song from your dream.

When you're done, she opens her eyes and looks at you. —That's wonderful, she says. —What was that?

Tom's gas-flame eyes are turned on you, turned up. —I've never heard that song before, he says. —Where'd you hear that?

You shrug. —Maybe I made it up? you ask.

Nobody makes up songs like that, Tom scowls.

Maybe someone else made it up, then, you say, widening your eyes to make them mysterious. They laugh; this means you're safe.

INEVITABLY, THEY ASK YOU TO play some more, and lacking any other songs you've invented, you go through your repertoire of whatever you remember. Christmas stuff, Ivory Tower, Gershwin, the Diadems, a couple of Four Freshman things, Chuck

Berry. Different stuff, dumb stuff. At last, Anna Lee requests "Teach Me Tiger."

Aw, c'mon, he doesn't want to play that, Tom groans.

I love that song, Anna Lee says, leaning forward. —You can play it, B——, can't you? I can sing the words if you're uncomfortable.

No, it's cool, you say, and you begin to play before Tom can stop you. *Wah-wah-wah-wah-wah*, you sing, and then, self-conscious, you stop. Tom, by the door, looks uncomfortable.

I guess I'd better get home and get to sleep, you say after a time.

Sure, says Anna Lee, her voice slurred, and you turn. She's looking at Tom. After a moment, he notices and returns her look.

Yeah, B——, you better get home, he says.

On your way out the door, he winks. —Come over and play again sometime, he says.

Sure, yeah, you say, wondering if he means it. And then he closes the door, and you're alone on the porch, and you wonder why you feel quite this alone. Why you wish you had been invited to stay too. It's not until you've crossed all the lawns to your house, until you're back home in bed with the your Wollensak recorder safely stashed atop the upright piano, that you realize you've forgotten to record anything that will help you.

*Wah-wah-wah-wah-wah*, you whisper to the dark bedroom, and in the shadows the bodies of your brothers stir.

Love, Gala

# September 20, 2009

Dear B——,

Greek amphitheaters were designed for two purposes: to slaughter
livestock and to amplify sound. Music and the occult have traveled
together ever since: acoustic recording was originally developed to
allow Thomas Edison to perceive the dead. A studio console is the
altar; voices pass from the void of the east into the wand of the microphone. Studios are ritual chambers (c.f., Gold Star, Western, Sunset.)

Now my trailer had become a ritual chamber also: a desecrated
one, all my action figures of you and your brothers pried up to
make room for Caroline's tripod. It lowered in the corner as I did
my research, her bag of red velvets crumpled on the counter next
to a wide pan still crusted with eggs, fried cheese, mystery grit.
(She had come to the trailer the night before and brought over
a frozen microwave meal, assuming I had a microwave; we tried
defrosting it in the pan; she had lain on the mattress in the back
bedroom of the trailer, pressing her bare arms against my pilled
comforter, smile on her face.)

My research had a ritual purpose: to find Caroline's grandmother. Or: the mother of Caroline's mother. Or: the subject of
many fevered biographical false trails. Or: your former wife.

o   o   o

I THINK WE CAN EVEN do it, I explained to her, out in the baths again with the wind chillier than it had been. —I've read everything about the Get Happies there is to read; I've listened to every weird bootleg interview. But you have information that isn't in those interviews—your history, the bank records. There must be some way to put them together.

She perched on a stone step, knees drawn into her chest, bowstring of her spine softened and stretching in the water. —You want to summon my grandmother, too, she said.

I want to *find* her, I clarified. —With you, I mean.

Why? she asked, after a moment.

I didn't understand this question. —Any number of reasons, I said. —Solving a mystery no one's ever solved before? A really dramatic ending to your interviews? Family connection?

She closed her eyes and nodded, kept still in the water. It was the other side of her I had started to see over the past days, since the night of the interview: the dreamy, silent substrate of the energy that went into her interviews and recordings, the albumen that fed the chirping bird. I didn't like to disturb this part of her— honestly, I related to it—but it also frightened me.

Is something wrong, I ventured after I thought enough time had gone by.

No, she said, eyes still closed. —I don't know. It's weird to think of this band of yours as somehow my family. I don't even know them.

I hear that, I said. —But you *could* know them.

It's weird to hear you talk about my family, she said.

Why, I asked.

She didn't answer this, kept dreaming. I told myself this was okay; I kept silences too. I'd come to this place in the desert too looking for silence. Ronda's question to me only a few days ago: *why would she do that? No one wants to live out here.* In my fantasy, it was six months from now, we had gone to meet her grandmother and to meet you, B——, and returned; we lived in adjoining trailers, as she'd said once she wanted to do—had she not said that? Had I imagined that?—and we lived in silence. I knocked on her aluminum door, heard no response but quail calls and highway exhaust, yet was not afraid. And she could feel the same with me, I promised myself, when she knocked: we would not have the power to hurt each other anymore. We would plant a tree in the sand between us, its roots moving down, turning the liquid earth solid. It was important not to allow myself to think too much about these fantasies: it was important not to be openly weird with the cis woman I had used ritual magic to summon.

I'm not even saying that we'll find her, I said. —I'm saying, *if* we find her. Then?

If you find her, Caroline said. —I don't know what I'd do.

It's your long-lost grandmother, I said, laughing a little. —This is easy.

She opened her eyes; again, those red streaks in her irises that the sun brought out. —What do you mean, this is easy? she said. —Why does this matter so much to you? Who *are* you?

I flinched, and she stood up. I started to follow, but she turned to look at me again, and I felt a wave of psychic force push from her forehead, keeping me connected to my stone step. Water rolling off her, she rose from the bath and walked to the fence, and then, looking back at me, she went further away. I kept my eyes down at my own legs blurring beneath the sulfurous surface. When I looked up again, she was standing on the dock, the Rio Grande moving beneath her. Her arms were out at her sides, and I think she was looking at the hill where I'd first seen her, and the sky above it was brilliant blue. Her camera was somewhere else: I had no idea what she was seeing, what she was thinking. Her mouth was moving, saying something I couldn't read.

I watched her for a while, and then I went back to looking at my own legs, thinking about what she'd said: *who are you?* A few nights before, her hand had moved over those legs, which for months I had shaved for no one, which no one ever touched. My thoughts moved over that, circling faster and faster like a dragonfly over a fen, until the water's surface moved again, and her own legs were sitting next to me, her body half in the water and half out. I'm sorry, I said reflexively. Then I met her eyes. Her lips were twisted, her expression mean. She slid all the way into the geothermal pool and swam to its opposite side, propped herself against the rock; she stared back. Steam was rising more than ever from the surface of the water: the air was getting cold.

THE QUESTION OF YOUR WIFE, B——, is one of the weird little biographical eddies in the broader Get Happies story. Each Get Happies stakeholder—fans, biographers, music critics—gives her different amounts of emphasis. The exciting thing about your band, beyond its power to make those of us who sit in low-lit trailers in New Mexico feel less alone with our choices, is its ability to support a multiplicity of biographical interpretations. A biographer might emphasize Eddie and how he ended up. Another might emphasize Tom; still another might emphasize Adam; still another your father. One might even emphasize your mother. The biographer reveals herself in the telling, but any telling of the legend is fine. Repetition of any permutations will increase its power; repetition of any distortions will do so even more.

But when your wife exits the narrative, as she will, few biographers seem concerned with where she goes. Few people are even aware of her as a solid human person: there are some early photos of the two of you together; a *house proud* image of her sitting in the home studio you share while you lean at the mixing console, in command. There's a photo of her winking at the camera from backstage; there's some speculation that her voice is one of those etched into the background of the much-maligned 1965

Halloween party album. Her name is known; her family background is known. Her motives for departure—even the date of
her departure—are not.

This has always been one of my roads to you: the Sorrowful
Mystery that I contemplate to work myself up whenever I listen
to *Summer Fun*. And now, facing the question of how to reach
Caroline—down whose roads the future waited—I had to solve it.

CAROLINE STAYED AT THE DORM, leaving the night open
for the real work. A ritual chamber is a recording studio: I burned
sandalwood in mine, draped it with the dismembered guts of a
plastic Get Happies cassette tape, a 1980s EP bought at one of the
thrift stores for a quarter. On the CD player, "Psychic Attraction"
played on infinite repeat, the theremin sliding in and out of existence. Who wrote the words your brother was whispering? How
could I find her? And I stared past the control board into the dark
eastern space of the trailer, and I checked the levels, and I waited
for something out there to speak, that I might begin to record.
That we can find the new sound at last.

The phone began ringing in the bedroom, its awful electronic
bleat. *Ronda*, said the caller info.

Go away, I said to the phone as I set it back down. —Go away.

The phone kept ringing, fat candy wasp buzzing against the
formica surface.

Go away, Ronda, I said, louder. —I need you to go away.
Please, go away. Please.

The phone stopped ringing. It rested for a moment; I breathed;
the candle flame flickered both without me and within my chest.
A rhythm guitar played from the speaker; a lonely harmony whistled. And the phone started to ring again, B——, and I willed my
friend to go away, to please understand that she was safe where
she was, where I was not.

Love, Gala

# September 21, 2009

Dear B——,

Excuse me, interrupts the teenager, and you look up from your
burger. —You're famous, right?

The teenager is wearing capris, a long-sleeved blouse, her tall
hair trussed up with a ribbon. Every step she takes toward you
feels somehow like she's fighting the clothes she's in, some kind
of werewolf imperfectly masquerading as human. Her eyes are
fixed on yours, her arms crossed, her stance wide. She makes you
afraid.

No, I'm not famous, you say. —I mean, we work hard.

She narrows her eyes. —You've got that radio single about the
hovercar race, she says. —And you played at the drive-in contest.
You and your band won it, right?

Oh, well, we were featured, you say. —They paid us to play it.
So we weren't really in competition.

That just means you won the competition before it even started,
she said.

You find yourself laughing at this, but cautiously: it sounds like
a compliment, but it doesn't feel like one. Why is this girl talking
to you, B——? This is something that happens to you sometimes,

now, since your father has started to organize small gigs for you, your brothers, and your cousin Tom to perform the songs you and Tom have started to write, at Tom's insistence. You should study better how to handle it. But you're grateful: the obligation of speaking to girls first has gone away. Now you can just focus on what's good in those interactions without the need for emotional risks.

So what'd you think of the other bands, she asks. —Did you have any favorites? Did any of them stand out?

Uh, I liked all of them, you say. —They all worked hard. —You squint at her then, trying to work out whether this was the correct response. She looks back at you, as if she's waiting for something. From a booth, two other teenagers are peering back at you: one tall and gaunt, her bouffant crown of blond hair making her taller still; the other shorter, the line of her nose surprisingly close to your fan's own (a sister?) The girl speaking to you notices you looking at them. She steps slightly closer.

Want to come say hi to my friends? she asks. —They'd love to meet a famous person.

She can't keep a straight face while she says it, breaks into a smirk: one that reminds you of your father's. This is what makes you stand up to accept her invitation, picking up your cheeseburger and bearing it before you, like an offering, as you join them.

YOUR FAN'S NAME IS MONA Slinks. She makes introductions: her sister, Sherry, the tall girl, Wendy. Wendy blushes behind freckles. You blush as well, uncertain why.

Your name's B——, isn't it? asks Sherry. —You're tall. You're even taller than Wendy.

I don't know how tall anyone is relative to anyone else, you say. Mona bares her teeth.

Like an inch or two taller, Sherry says. —Wendy's a giantess!

And you're just a *giant ass*, Mona says; Sherry laughs. But Wendy turns up her smile.

The waiter comes, and Mona orders a clean ashtray and half a tomato for herself, disco fries for the table. She points to you.

He'll take the check, she says. —He's famous.

Then she lights a cigarette from her pack and holds it in place, the ash growing, while she eats a tomato slice with the other hand.

Not into your burger? Mona asks you after a moment. —Want a cig to go with it?

No thanks, you say.

Afraid you're gonna scar your little pink lungs? She snickers; you blush. —I wouldn't want to do that. You've got a very pretty falsetto.

When Mona laughs, the laughter collects like raw pearls in the oyster shell of her thin nostrils, and then each one drops in shrill nasal HAs, like jewelry breaking.

Mona, scolds Sherry, —you're going to give poor B—— a *complex*. —She turns to you and smiles in apology. —Your voice isn't pretty at all. It's very muscular, very big and strong.

You laugh nervously, and Mona snorts, then coughs, then blows a chunk of tomato onto a napkin that she wads up in front of her. You watch, enraptured. Wendy blushes and looks at you apologetically; you're not sure why.

AFTER A SAFE PAUSE, MONA'S friends start to ask you questions about the music business, whether or not it's exciting, and you answer as best as you can while Mona smokes and presides.

It isn't that much, you say. —We know some songs and people ask us to play at parties. My dad wants to take us on a tour this summer, once my brothers are out of school. Some different cities up and down the coast.

But you have a record, Mona says. —That's what the host said at the drive-in show we saw you at.

Oh, well, sure, you say. —My dad heard us playing and, I dunno. He thought he could sell us. —You feel something tighten in your chest when you say this; suppress it; the girls will think you're weird if you feel.

How do you get a record, though? Mona asks. —Who do you have to ask? Do you have to pay for it? Is there a way to arrange it so that you pay on the back end instead of the front?

You don't want to admit that you don't know these answers: your dad is taking care of all of it. —I mean, you need a song first, you say, remembering to laugh: sometimes Tom does that, laughs to show girls that he is at ease.

Mona has lots of songs, Sherry says. —We played a couple of them at the drive-in. Did you like them?

You flush and turn to Mona, who's smiling, her eyes narrowing in satisfaction. She rests her arm on the edge of the booth behind you.

Don't worry about it, she says. —We enjoyed playing with you. We're the Pin Up Dollies, if you don't remember our name.

She goes on to talk about her band: her ideas for songs, the arc of albums she intends to write, her opinions about the male producers who *control the industry*, John Black Zero (who recorded the Diadems record you love, you elect not to mention) being the most diabolical example. She speaks for a long time, sometimes punctuating herself with little jabs of eye contact, literal jabs of her finger, *you understand?* While she talks, the others finish their food: Wendy hastily, as if at any moment she'll be interrupted again, Mona's sister very precisely, tiny bites that move around the circumference of her burger, leaving only a final core bite of meat and cheese at the end in a great burger crescendo. And you try to remember, B——: there was a girl band there, wasn't there, guitar, bass, and drums, their music angry, loud, the guitarist screaming at the MC when he tried to cut their power and remove them from the stage. You liked the idea of a girl band, you thought: you remembered

Tom and Eddie trying to think of which one they would prefer to fuck. You remember thinking you should train yourself to ask those questions: the more known you are, the greater scrutiny you'll fall under, and someone might notice if you don't join in.

Mona's still talking to you about her band. —We're really good, she's saying, —and we'd be perfect as your opening act, you know, if you want to introduce us to your dad, and—

And suddenly an older woman is standing at the booth, a finger folded into a paperback book to mark her place.

Is everything all right, girls? she asks, looking not at them but at you with a wide smile. —Who's your *friend*?

Go away, Mona snarls, and Sherry giggles. Wendy looks at you with apology in her eyes. Is this Mona's mother? You're startled at this concept.

Uh, my name is B——, ma'am, you say. —It's a real honor to meet you.

What a polite young man, Mona's mother replies. —I think your young man is very nice, Mona.

He's not a young man, Mona says, which makes you start for a moment. —He's a potential *business partner.* Would you go back and read your book, please? Would you leave us alone?

*Mona*, Sherry says. Wendy' eyes are lowered, now. The fact that you are substantially older than these girls—two years? three?— occurs to you, and you worry, but Mona's mother doesn't seem to mind your sitting there with her daughters and their friend. She beams at you. You're the solution to something.

It's truly a pleasure to meet you, B——, she says, and she departs to her paperback and her tea. She's sitting in a booth not far away, and from time to time you can see her peeping over at you, feel her writing you into a story she's telling herself. Half of you wants to stand up and rush over to her—*it isn't true; everything you think is wrong*—and half of you, listening to your father's advice, listening to Tom's, insists you stay put.

o   o   o

MONA'S MOTHER OFFERS TO GIVE you a ride home from the diner as compensation for buying a meal for her daughters and their friend. You glance at your Impala (once your father's, now yours, an early inheritance) floating in its parking space, you glance at Mona, and then you say yes. And like that you're in a sedan with the three members of the Pin-Up Dollies, bound again for Hawthorne. Mrs. Slinks insists that you ride in the front seat, tall as you are; Mona is displaced to the rear, crushing Wendy in the middle between herself and her sister.

Just say the word if you're uncomfortable in any way, B——, Mrs. Slinks says to you, anxiously.

The word, Mona growls, but her mother ignores her.

After that, no one speaks; Mrs. Slinks hums along to a Liberace concert that's on the radio; you listen along, imagining it with voices. You're convinced the girls are all staring at you.

Uh, Mona, what's your favorite dessert? you finally ask.

She pulls a cigarette out of her purse, lights it, holds it up.

When I was a girl, we didn't have our dessert in the car, Mrs. Slinks says.

Times are changing, Mona says.

AT SOME POINT IT BECOMES clear that Mrs. Slinks intends to bring you home with Mona and Sherry.

For a quick snack, she says. —He's clearly a hungry young man. And your father would love to meet him.

You're not sure if Mona notices the way you suddenly hang your head; you feel even guiltier, realizing that you want her to. But Mona's suddenly leaning forward, alarmed by something else.

Wendy and I were hanging out tonight, though, she says. —We were doing homework. You said you just wanted us to go out for a quick bite.

And we got a quick bite, says Mrs. Slinks. —Courtesy of your young man! And we should bring him over to our house, to thank him. You should spend some time together.

We're going to spend lots of time together, Mona insists. —As his band's opening act. As business partners. —No one responds to this, though, and she sits back. —Bring Wendy along as well. Wendy loves coming over. C'mon, let's not split up this party.

Wendy wants to go home, I'm sure, Mrs. Slinks says, and Wendy doesn't dispute.

I'll pick up my books from you at school, Mona, she says. Her voice is higher than you'd expected: this makes you realize she hasn't spoken all evening. She has only looked at Mona, and at you.

Mona opens her mouth to rebut, but then closes it and lights another cigarette. You look back at her, wanting to apologize, although this time you're not sure for what, but she looks out the window, away from you. She looks like she's thinking very hard about something. Once she notices you looking back at her.

What, she says, and you turn away.

On reaching Wendy's house, Wendy stands on the sidewalk as Mona blows a kiss goodbye and rolls up the window. She stares through the windshield, waving as the car glides away, visible first through the front window, and then the rear windows, and then she is gone. Mona ashes on the floor of the back seat where her feet had been.

AT THE SLINKS HOUSE YOU'RE served macaroons and almonds in a dish. Mr. Slinks is a tall, stout man who works in aerospace somewhere down the highway, and he cracks your fingers in his handshake. Mona smokes, curled in an armchair at the outer edge of the coffee table, her denim-wrapped legs pulled under her. Here, away from the diner, Mona keeps quiet.

Just off the living room there's a staircase. Family photos hang along the railing of it, tobacco clouds at the corners of their frames. The staircase, you are certain, is the one from your dream.

In your stomach, the macaroon filling churns against the gravy fries, and Sherry tells her father about your virtues, gazing the whole time at her sister.

MR. SLINKS INSISTS YOU COME to see his garage, his *other pride and joy*, he asserts, gesturing toward his daughters, half of whom roll their eyes. The Slinks garage smells like oil and aging paint thinner; the work area is immaculate, free of sawdust and stains. A C-clamp on the edge of the bench has dug a quarter-inch into the pine wood. You have no sense that any work has ever been done here.

I have a real nice book collection out here, B——, Mr. Slinks announces. —You a book lover, B——?

Gee, some, you say.

Everything in moderation, he replies. He pulls a glossy magazine from between two volumes of Winston Churchill's war memoirs and hands the magazine to you. It opens easily to a photo of a naked woman sitting on the deck of a yacht.

Any interest in this? Mr. Slinks asks.

She looks sad, you say.

Huh, says Mr. Slinks, taking the magazine back and inspecting the eyes of the woman in the picture. —That's fine.

He replaces the magazine and gestures at different things around the garage, pretty much at random. You feel embarrassed and low.

So this is everything, he says. —Books. Cars. I don't get out here as much as I should. Very busy. The curse of Cain. You're a young man. You probably have all kinds of energy that I'll never have anymore. Never waste it.

He squats down and takes a rifle from the drawer beneath

the workbench. Putting it to his shoulder, he sights the door to the kitchen, and then he pivots in place until he's brought the barrel to a degree short of your face. Politely, he brings the gun down, its line of fire tracing your body like a watchman's warm flashlight.

Brilliant craftsmanship, he says. —Winchester. Home defense. Do you own guns?

I've never seen a gun, you say. —It's pretty intense.

Fortunately I haven't needed it yet, he says. —Hold it. Take it out for a spin.

You take the gun and copy his position, shouldering the rifle and pointing it at the garage door. It's hard to focus your eyes in the right way to see clearly through the sight.

How's it feel? he asks. —Feels powerful?

Kinda, you say.

Give me back the gun, he commands, and you obey. He holds the gun in front of him in both hands. —It's very important to experience that feeling at least once in your life, he says distantly. —You should experience it as often as you can.

He lets the gun stock balance against his foot, the barrel pointing roughly toward his face, as he takes a cigarette from a box on the workbench and lights it.

Which of my daughters do you find more attractive? he asks. —Mona or Sherry?

Oh, gee, you say. —I'm not sure I could you know judge them based on just that kind of—

Of course you can, Mr. Slinks laughs. —Come on. Quit being afraid of me. I'm their father. I'm asking you. You're a red-blooded young man. I know you have feelings in this regard. I've got a right to know their nature.

You take a breath and look at your feet.

Mona, you say after a minute.

Mona. —Mr. Slinks nods. —She knows how to take care of

herself, that one. Nothing but trouble. It would take an extremely strong man to handle her. Are you up to that challenge, B——?

I think it'd be interesting to be in a band with her, but her band is for girls, you say. —So I can't be in it.

He frowns and smokes, thinking. Then he nods and begins to put the gun away.

I approve of you, he announces. —You're strange around the edges. But I work in engineering, and eccentricity is not a problem for me. You have my blessing to court Mona, tentatively. But I want you to remember everything we've discussed today. I also want you to start seriously considering the question of your income and your future. Do you understand? Do you agree?

Yes, sir, you say.

Smoke? he asks.

No, sir, you say.

Good man, he says. —Let's rejoin the women.

ON YOUR RETURN, THE LIVING room is silent. Mona, in the corner, is smoking with her eyes turned inward. Sherry reads a movie magazine. Mrs. Slinks sits with her hands folded, smiling. When you return from the basement, she cranks to life.

It's time for us to go to bed, Mr. Slinks announces. —Leave the children to be children. B——.

He motions you closer, and then he takes your hand and crushes your fingers a second time. You bite your lip; you must not show emotion at physical pain.

I've enjoyed meeting you, he says. —Please don't let me down.

He and his wife walk to the back of the house, flip off the light in the hallway as they go. You stand beside the door to the kitchen a while, and then you sit on the couch next to Sherry. As soon as you sit down, she stands up.

I think I'm going to bed too, she announces. —Mona, that means there's room over here on the couch, with B——.

I'm good here, Mona says.

Mona, says Sherry.

Mona shoots her sister a dirty look. Then she stands up and walks across the room, as smoothly and elegantly as possible. She stands in front of you, her hands on her hips; you arc your neck back hard to look her in the eyes.

Do you want me to sit on the couch with you? she asks sharply.

Uh, if you want to, it's okay, you say.

See? Mona says to her sister. —He doesn't want me to.

She goes into the kitchen; cabinet doors begin to open and close; she clicks her raspy throat at the cat. Sherry shakes her head and looks at you.

B——, I hope we see a lot more of you, all right? she says. —You seem like a really solid kind of guy. And you know we're all worried about Mona.

Is she okay? you ask.

She will be, I think, Sherry says, looking at you.

ON RETURNING, MONA FINISHES HER cigarette and leans across to the case on the table, takes another, and lights it. After a moment of smoking, she looks at you.

Move over, she says.

You do so, and she sits down next to you, leaning against the opposite armrest, a canyon of air between.

I'm sorry about my sister, she says.

Gee, why? you ask. —She seemed really nice.

Mona snorts, drawing on her cigarette. —Sherry's not nice, she says. —She's *worried* about me.

What's she worried about? you ask.

My future, she says, but you can tell somehow that this is a falsehood, B——: there is a more specific concern in play. —I don't know. That I'll end up living on Skid Row, out of a box. That I won't have any future to speak of.

You frown at your legs. —I guess I worry about that too, you say.

She straightens up, looks you in the face. —Do you?

All the time, you say. —I guess it wouldn't be so bad. I mean, I guess I could live out on the street if I needed to. I'd get by.

You wouldn't miss people, she says.

What people? you ask.

*What people*, she says, imitating your voice. —I don't know. Your band?

You're unsure of how to answer this, whether this is a trick question: what does she want you to say? That you'll miss your brothers and cousin? What is it that people miss about other people? Now her whole body is turned to face you, curled up with her back against the armrest, watching.

I mean, I don't think I'd miss people either, she says after a while.

Sure, you say, relieved that you agree on something. —It's nice when people go away.

She laughs, delighted, and then you both lapse into silence. She stubs out her cigarette and lights another, and you breathe her secondhand air. What's she thinking? Your own thoughts, independent of her, seem to have stopped. Suddenly you're compelled by the idea that everything outside this living room has disappeared: Mona's family, your family. You find yourself liking the idea of that, as if the room is a snow globe that surrounds you both, a protection. A melody forms, aeolian snow flakes; you and your brothers' voices rising to catch them on your tongues.

She knows what you're expected to do, you realize: what Tom and your father expect you to do. She's waiting for you to try it. The air is thick, as if you're breathing syrup instead of oxygen; she looks tired, already tired of waiting for this. And seeing that, you know you can't do it. You are an infant; you are worse than an infant: a girl, and you've missed your chance and Tom Happy will never respect you ever again. You exhale, a pearl diver washed up exhausted on the beach, white lungs at the limit of their endurance.

Leaning over, Mona takes two cigarettes from the case, lights them both, and offers you one.

You seem like you're getting a cold or something, she explains. —It's best to knock out the bacteria early, I've found.

You take the cigarette from her. Its filter is covered in lipstick. You roll it back and forth on your lower lip, wondering if the stain rubs off in a way that you'll have to take the time to erase.

SHE INVITES YOU UP TO her room to listen to records with her. She climbs the stairs and you follow, up the dark carpeted hall. You imagine the song from your dream suddenly playing, almost tangible somewhere outside of your skull. She makes you wait outside the door for a moment; you can hear drawers open, close. Then she cracks the door: into the dark hallway spills brilliant light.

Her bedroom has two nails pounded into its pink walls, just wide enough for a guitar neck to hang. There's a desk piled with textbooks, stationery in all colors, a fountain pen. No clutter on the floor. Norman Rockwell prints on the walls, a wide calendar. A candy apple red alarm clock. A shelf lined with carnival prizes: stuffed bears, ducks, cats, straw hats. Each of them has been damaged somehow. A photo of Marilyn Monroe by a vanity mirror laden with compacts, cracked brushes, lipsticks and blushes made out of raw poison lead. A mobile hanging over a bed with pale pink sheets. A window, shut to the street. And a record player with a stack of 45s and LPs—her own record player, in her room. You marvel at that a little. She closes the door behind you, takes a glass ashtray from the desk, goes to sit on the bed. There's a backpack full of books there; she sets it aside.

Wendy's, she explains. —We were studying earlier. Or she was studying—I was cheating off of her. —She laughs a different laugh than usual; it is fond.

Gee, uh, won't your parents care that I'm up here, you whisper.

Of course they know you're up here, she whispers back. —I'm doing them such a favor right now. Sit down—you always make me nervous. You never *sit*.

The only place to sit is the bed, so you sit on the floor, at her feet. She laughs, lights her next cigarette.

Do you like these walls? she asks after a few drags.

They're okay, you say.

One day I'm going to have black walls, she muses. —Black sheets, black clothes, windows painted black. It's the color that absorbs all the other colors. It's the color with the most energy.

That sounds scary, you say.

You'd prefer white, she announces. And then, looking at the smoke: —You know, I don't want to be with anybody. So we understand one another. I want to turn into an old hag immediately. I'm sixteen; I want to jump straight to seventy-five, and then I'd just stay seventy-five forever. I'd have joint pains and I'd pack my hips in mud to feel good again.

Oh, you say, considering this: what does she mean, she doesn't want to marry anyone? Everyone is supposed to marry someone.

She watches you for a moment, tapping her cigarette in the ashtray. Then she folds her feet up underneath her on the bed, scoots herself back to rest on the pillow. She wants to lie down, you think, to rest, but she doesn't have that power because you're here. You distort everything with your presence; you should leave; you don't.

Do you want to listen to a record, Mona asks suddenly.

It's late to do that, isn't it? you say. —I mean, won't your parents wake up?

She makes a disgusted face, again like your father. —It's a very long record—multiple records, she says, ignoring your question. —It's about the devil. Wendy and I are into it; it's something I want our music to do. We can sit here and listen to it here in my room, you on the floor, and me up here. If that's what you want.

Okay, you say, nodding.

What do you want? she asks.

You don't know the answer to that question, and you need to think of it. So you just stare into the negative space formed by your folded knees.

I don't know, you say after a while.

She nods, almost, leaning back on her pillow. —Okay.

What do you want me to do? you ask her.

I think you should go home, she says.

You don't move, and after a while she stands up and stubs her cigarette, taps her foot. You count the ticks of the alarm clock. Finally you get to your feet, pulling yourself up with your hands on the mattress. You push against it, pink sheets, pink springs; you feel it push back against you.

And when she turns her back for a moment to empty her ashtray into the tiny trash can, you grab a lead lipstick from her dresser and put it in your pocket.

Good night, she says to you downstairs, on the porch. —Thanks for hiring us as your opening band.

Uh, thank you, you say. And, in a panic, clutching the stolen thing: —Gee, I had a really nice time. I think maybe we could see a movie, if you wanted.

Her mouth twists to one side, a kind of laugh spreading like an internal bleed beneath her skin.

That sounds really nice, she says, and then she shoves the door shut with both hands, as if she's sealing a tomb.

The Impala you left floating in the lot of Sal's Famous looks weak as you approach it, hours of walking later, painted in laughter and date-night light.

Love, Gala

# PART THREE

THE GET HAPPIES
right now!
VF-712 - IN STEREO

# October 5, 2009

Dear B——,

Now it's 1964, and your father likes to call you at night. He's
been doing this since you moved out of the house last year, after
the concert fees you were earning made you begin to wonder
why you stayed in a room you shared with two brothers, in a
house you shared with him. He calls you every night, sometimes
more than once a night. Sometimes you don't pick up, let his
ring shake the interior of your skull, disharmonize with what
you're playing on the piano you bought yourself until he either
stops calling or he doesn't, curls up to rest at the mouth of your
cave. And sometimes you break down and answer. After all, he
isn't merely your father; he's your manager. There will be costs
for betraying him.

Hey dad, sorry, you tell him. —We had a really big show last
night, a sell-out, so you know, I was asleep later than I'd planned
to be. So it took me a while to get to the phone. —You laugh;
if he's detected any malice in what you've said, your laugh, like
sprinkled salt, will dispel it.

I wouldn't let your head swell, your dad grumps. —Three years
in a business; that's still a flash in the pan from where I'm sitting.

The question is, will anyone be playing your records in fifty years. That's the trophy we want to put in our case, B———.

We'll try harder, you say, as automatically as you'd laughed.

The ostensible subject of his call is money. As your manager, he's the one who releases your pay to you. He seems to enjoy it, as if he's administering a communion: something that transforms. You've long stopped counting exactly how much you are worth; it's enough, and you have to trust him with the details of it. Honestly, most of the time you don't mind: the more your father talks about the importance of retaining publishing rights, the importance of local radio and of solid contractual relationships to bind family members in harmony, the intricacies of revenue splits between management (him) and talent (you), the less you want to care about it. The record company is a higher power; they'll ensure your money gets to you in the end, whether he wants it to or not.

It surprised you, still, that he tried to insist that you remain at home: dinner table lectures about the virtues of early thrift, about how he and your grandfather didn't even have a home once—lived on the beach; didn't you know that about him? But he listens when you tell him you can't work there as easily as you'll be able to work in your own place. —The hits might stop coming, you warn.

You leave the childhood home one morning, some clothes in a duffel bag and your record collection in a milk crate. Your mother, Eddie, and Adam come out on the porch to watch you; your father claims he has to work. But you like to believe that he's peering from behind the curtain of his den, hurting as he watches you leave; you insist on this belief.

THE PIANO YOU BOUGHT YOURSELF with the money from your first national tour is the one very nice thing you own, although you like the rest of your choices: a row of plants lining the window, some having survived the first year and others that you think look just as interesting dead; record sleeves stapled to the wall to cover one whole section of the kitchen with physical music; a red plaid couch built, enigmatically, into a corner molding; a net that hangs from the ceiling and contains carved wooden sea life; tall candles depicting frightening saints; a balcony-mounted birthday telescope Eddie gave you that is certainly stolen; a card table that holds a coffee can with all your silverware in it. The kitchen has a sliding door that opens onto a deceased zucchini garden beneath one window, and in the distance you can hear bikes in the canyon, and the bed has no frame, just a mattress you cover in lime green and white.

You're mostly alone in this house. You like that, having four secret walls to yourself; you like walking in as little as an undershirt and boxers from one room of the place to another, lying on the unmade bed with your arms spread wide around you; you like filling up the tub and soaking for hours as you think of melodies and sometimes plunge your head under, bubbling air out your nose. You can feel your short red-brown hair ripple like an anemone about your skull and imagine what the melodies might sound like if you were drowning. There's space here to be still, to relax in silence, just you and the voices you arrange: an indoor silence at last, a kind you've never had. You must work to deserve it: you must protect this power to be alone whenever you want.

YOUR BUDDY HARRY COROT, YOUR dad is saying to you on the phone. —Your great friend over at Valley Forge Records who doesn't return his phone calls. He's not returning my phone calls. I need you to get him to do that, B——. It's very urgent.

Gosh, what do you need to tell Harry, you ask, knowing that this, like all questions, will antagonize him.

I'm your manager, B——, he growls. —You pay me so that you don't need to know that. Just please don't give me more problems. Just please do what I've asked you, for once.

Maybe it'd help if I tell Harry what you need, you say. —I mean, I'm the one that sees him all the time, not you.

There is silence on the line, and you bite your lip, hoping he yells.

Do you want to take a shot at me, B——? your dad finally asks, quietly. —We can do that, if that's what you need to do right now. If you think you've got enough grit to stand behind what you say.

I don't need to take a shot at you, you say, keeping your voice calm.

I think you might need to do that, buddy, your dad says. —That's what I think. Now that you think everybody loves you. Now that you've got a fancy place all to yourself in Hollywood, the place you bought with the money I work so hard to make sure you get.

What time did you call Harry, Dad, you ask.

Do you realize how quickly everything can be taken away from you, your dad continues, no longer actually talking to you. He cracks his knuckles, sending a nauseating celery crunch through the line. —So fast you won't even know it's coming. So fast you won't even have time to remember what success looks like. When you believe you're finally safe—that's the most precarious time. No one will love you then, B——, or even hate you. You'll just disappear.

I'll call Harry, you tell him. —As soon as I get off the line with you, okay?

Your dad sighs.—I'm not your enemy, he says. —I hope you know it hurts me that you need me to be.

I have to go write songs now, you say, and you hang up before he can say anything more. As soon as he's no longer on the line, you unplug the phone and you sit down, swallowing so as not to throw up, reviewing what you said to him and how: the times you raised your voice, whether you hurt him by raising it.

o   o   o

SOMETIMES, TO AVOID YOUR MANAGER'S calls, you sleep over at the Slinks house. Mona's parents are okay with this— you've been dating now two years; you are rich—as is Mona, who doesn't like sleeping alone.

I don't have good dreams, she tells you, the first time she asks for one of your chaste dates not to end. You know that Wendy used to stay over to protect her from them; you know that Wendy hasn't done that for some time now.

Tonight, the wooden wind chimes you bought for Mrs. Slinks with royalty loot from the *Diner Girl* LP are still hanging by the kitchen door, and you carefully retrieve the key taped to the back side of the clapper, let yourself in, and mix some of the strawberry ice cream from the freezer with milk and malt flour to form a shake you serve yourself in a chipped teal golfer's mug, sip on as you climb the dark stairs to Mona's room. You don't need the light; your feet remember the way.

Mona is already asleep. Her room's arranged neatly for her, the laundry all in its hamper, the outsize desk tidied (or anyway a big blank spot cleared from the center of it, hands sweeping all her notebooks and makeup vials and Kleenex boxes to the periphery like she's some powerful anti-magnet), the records all in their boxes except the one still on the needle, tonight "I Love You Baby" by the Diadems, produced by John Black Zero. One red candle flickers on the bookcase full of notebooks that she has filled. You snuff the candle, drink your milkshake, and take your khakis and striped, reeking performing shirt off. At first you never knew where to put it—on the floor is unacceptable, in her hamper is unacceptable; your horrible androgen sweat will invade and corrupt everything she owns. You've settled for folding it on the cot Mona's parents have installed in the room, by way of keeping up appearances, and taking it with you when you come and go. Slowly you've been training yourself to imagine that her belongings won't crack when you look at them.

When Mona sleeps, tossing and kicking her legs like a lazy whirlwind, she takes up basically the whole twin bed. You start by kneeling by her bedside, head pillowed on your folded arms and watching her growl and turn. Sometimes you have to fall asleep like this, and you wake up with your neck pulsing in pain. More usually there is some kind of opening, a moment when she's turned away and teetering on the edge of the mattress; at these moments you can hoist yourself into the space she's abandoned and lie very still. This way if she rolls back into you, it will be because she wants to touch you.

You always fall asleep fast next to her if she stays asleep, but you like it better on the nights when she rolls into you and wakes up. Tonight she wakes up.

Hey, she mutters, coiling around your arm. —You smell awful.

YOU AND MONA DO NOT have sex when you sleep over; you never have. She assures you she wants you to stay there. It took you a month of doing this before you finally believed this was for reasons beyond the fact of her parents knowing that you're doing that, of this protecting her from something: your presence blocking worse presences. So you lie beside her, emitting death rays at her while you sleep.

Early on, following a horror movie date during the time when she still mostly wanted to talk to you about music business questions you couldn't easily answer, you experimented with kissing. Her lips, the first time, were like atomic warhead candies: first you must kiss off their sour nicotine coating, next the sweetness underneath dissolves in your jaws. And then it was like she was a plug reversed in an outlet: a spark came off her, and her hands pushed your shoulders away.

It didn't work, she said. —It never works. I thought for sure I could get it to work with you.

What didn't work, you say, trying to keep your voice cold and flat, invulnerable. But she turns away, and you don't press her on the question.

You assume, after this, that you won't ever hear from her again. She calls you the next week and invites you to her house. You sit in the living room, her family beaming at her and you together, and then you go up to her room to talk about records, sitting far apart.

IT WASN'T DIFFICULT TO GET your father to agree to let the Pin Up Dollies open for you during your early concerts: this is because you didn't ask him, or the other members of your band, before you booked them. But your brothers and cousin didn't complain. Eddie and Tom were content enough to leer at the girls from backstage, and the novel presence of girls and instruments brought in additional male fans, haunted-eyed teens and twenty-somethings who are very quiet as Mona screams and slashes her guitar strings at them from the stage. In later years, your audience will shift to being primarily men of your generation, quietly radiant in their memories of their youth with you, B——. Early on, it's the girls who come to see you. The girls do not like Mona's musical ideas—there is something mortifying about what she does, almost a contagion; the women in your audience instinctively shy from it, not wanting guilt by association—but they like yours enough not to stay away. It works to everyone's advantage, especially given that your father has to pay them less than he would any other backing band, something he's careful to insist you not tell Mona. You keep your word to him: harmony is important; everyone should continue to get what they want out of this. He and the band draw the line at inviting the Pin Up Dollies on tour, but Mona's fine with this.

I have zero interest in spending time gliding around the country in a horrible van with your cousin and father, she says. —Even for success. Sorry.

It's cool, you say, which is true.

There are other ways she wants to push for success. She pulls together enough cash to buy studio time for a single: like your father, she knows that the single is the first step in the growth of any new band. She asks you to produce it, and you spend a solid two weeks on the project. You never get to arrange female harmonies, and you like the lyrics Mona writes much more than Tom's couplets about hovercar racing bravado, enjoy finding strange instruments to weave around them, the challenge of blending Mona's rasp without sweetening it. But she rejects the final mix you offer her.

You changed everything, she explains. —You took off the guitar track altogether! There are *cellos*. There are people singing in the background that I don't even know.

Yeah, the girl group sound, you say, enthusiastically. —It's a single, you know? There's the hook you try to give people, so they stay close long enough to hear the rest of it that they ordinarily wouldn't want to hear. And that leads you to the next single, and the album, and then the rest.

It sounds nothing like me, she says angrily, and you don't know what to tell her. No one gets to sound like who they are; that isn't how success operates.

TO TAKE THE LITTLE LADY *off their bill statements:* this is what Tom Happy has told you, many times, that the Slinks family is expecting of you.

Why else would they be letting you sleep over and fuck her, he asks you. —Why else would that be happening? Under their own roof when her dad owns a gun, my goodness. They want you to cross that line. Use your head. Use a rubber. I know a place in Mexico. They do good, discreet work. Say the word and we can make this happen, cousin. We can sanitize the whole thing.

He looks at you as if he is giving you a salute. You don't correct key assumptions he's made.

o  o  o

IN BED BESIDE HER, YOU feel the crackle of mysterious female energy around her like fireflies. You wish her fireflies would circle around you, too, that your fireflies could breed with her fireflies producing thousands of tiny fireflies with blended color fireworks in their wings. Instead you feel like lightning is going to shoot out of her and burn you to a pair of white eyeballs sitting atop a pile of black ash. You imagine her fingers sinking into you and you do not know why, try to eliminate the image.

You can feel the electric inch between you as if you're trying to hold two halves of a magnet apart. You don't know how she experiences that inch.

I'M SORRY, SHE SAYS TO you once, out of a silence. —I really am. I'm defective.

It's okay, you say to the door.

You can feel a hot, wet circle of breath against you that cools in the breeze from the ceiling fan.

You don't hate me, right, she says softly, drifting. —You don't want to leave. You don't think I'm defective and broken. This is okay.

Of course, you say.

You're sweet, she murmurs, and she drills the top of her head against you. Fireflies are pushing through your skin. She isn't broken, you know; you are. But you can try with your music, so you can try for this too, work hard to reassure her almost as well as Wendy did: second best. There are no illusions about what you can each give, so this is the best connection either of you can imagine. You feel grateful for it.

When she falls asleep, you get out of bed, cross the hall, and masturbate into the toilet with its cranberry-colored seat cover, your horrible body jerking with stabbing pains. Impacted ejaculate finally tears loose of your vesicles like defective Velcro, and you are awful, here on the linoleum, covered with filth that reeks like urine, like the beach, like the sea. Then you clean up as best as you can with scented tissues. If you were her you would not need to clean anything; you would be eternally clean.

In the morning you find the door of the bedroom open, Mona already gone to her record store job, her mother whistling as she empties the teenagers' lipstick butts from the ashtrays. You roll in her bed a while before you get up to dig through the drawer for the clothes you left here some days ago. Mona's mother or sister or anyway someone washed them for you, and here they are, folded and smelling as clean as her blouses. Someone has already whisked your reeking clothes from last night away to be made new.

HARRY COROT, YOUR A&R MAN at Valley Forge Records and the bane of your father's life, is somehow present to apologize for his house on the cliffside as soon as you and Mona arrive at the party he's invited you to, parking your Impala behind better cars. You're wearing a T-shirt and suit pants because it doesn't matter what you wear, and you think pinstripes are cute. Mona is wearing a dress her mother bought her last year in hopes (her mother's) that you'd ask her to the prom.

It's temporary, Harry says. —I mean it's a nice piece of space on a nice piece of land, no question. But I think we can do better on a few things. A lot of old fixtures that we'd want to take out and replace. A lot of restoration. The pool backs up; salt gets into the lines; it's something to do with the way the house is piping through the ocean. It's terrible. But I'm boring you. I'm really sorry. I'm terrible.

A toilet flushes somewhere above the foyer, which is painted a creepy custardy Italian yellow and lined with old French furniture that Mona drops her scarf on. She smiles down at Harry, as if she's daring him to pick it up, and Harry smiles back at her, eyes glittering like an albino rat's behind ashtray-thick spectacles. On the wall, copies of gold records hang in the place of paintings. You're delighted to see one of yours, *Everyone's Got a Car*, just above a small table between two chairs, in the space where a mirror might go.

And who might this be? Harry asks, looking at Mona.

Oh, right, you begin. —Harry, this is my uh, Mona Slinks. Mona, this is Harry Corot, my A&R guy at Valley Forge Records.

Charmed, she says. —I'm sure B——'s mentioned me to you before?

Sure I have, you say to Harry, earnestly. —Mona's band opens for us when we're playing here in LA. The Pin Up Dollies.

We're up and coming, she says to him, smiling so as to show him her teeth: from knowing her, B——, you know that she is trying to put him off guard, hoping this will get her an opportunity to pitch her music to him. In your pocket, you cross your fingers for her.

A girlfriend who plays guitar, Harry says. —Of course that's the sort you'd pick. I'm fascinated by all of this. Let's get some drinks and go downstairs.

He's distracted for a moment by another arrival, and Mona kicks your foot, drawing your attention, then whispers in your ear: —He was staring at my fingers.

You're confused. —Why?

A ring, she explains.

You glance at your own fingers on instinct, as if a ring has materialized there. —I didn't even notice.

It'd be disgusting if you told him I was your wife, she says, giggling.

Aw, I wouldn't want to give anyone the wrong idea, you say.

Why not give people the wrong idea? she says. —People lie about who they are all the time.

I don't know; I think I'm pretty honest, you say, as if you're throwing salt over your shoulder.

Mona grunts. —So am I, she says. —I'm perfectly scrupulously honest all the time. Can't you tell?

You look at her nervously, and on instinct you take your hand out of your pocket, flex your fingers, take hers. Her bitten-short nails dig into the flesh on the lunar side of your knuckles, and you let go.

You know better, she warns.

HARRY TAKES YOU BOTH TO get drinks, tall mimosas blooming with slices of unseasonal strawberry that glow neon red as you descend the stairs, as if you are torchbearers for a louche cult. At the center of the barroom with its brick fireplace, Oriental rug, and black German grand piano, there's a tiny knot of people arranged in a half circle around the couch. A shortish man sits there, his uncombed hair hanging monk-like around the outer orbit of his head. Everyone in the circle is talking to him and laughing with suspicious frequency. He doesn't speak, only nods. He's drinking a glass of something like water that he sips as he listens, and when the glass gets empty he hands it off to a tall, smiling man with a pompadour and a gentle green sweater who runs every time to refill it from a pitcher full of lemons and replace the glass in the short, silent man's hand. A horrible vibration is emanating from this man, and your neck cranes to watch him as Harry leads you outside. But his neck never moves; he sips and does not notice you, and your strawberry mimosas glow pink and orange against the blue evening view of the black ocean, background to Harry Corot's deck, where many people are standing and chatting around an empty swimming pool.

A girlfriend who plays guitar, Harry muses. —So do you two play duets together sometimes? I smell an angle here.

B—— doesn't really have anything to do with my music, Mona says.

They're really good, you say, and she glowers at you.

We've got a ton of material, she says. —At least three singles, by my count, and an album to follow it up. I'd want to produce my own stuff—I'm cheap. If you've got any interest—

So *here* you all are, Harry says, speaking to a knot of women he seems to know from somewhere unrelated to music, women with coppery tans and plenty of jewelry. He is good at making introductions between this knot and you and Mona without either of you—or you, anyway—knowing he's doing it, minimizing the shock of your name.

You're the boy who writes those songs about hamburgers and cars, says one of the women. —My little sister loves those songs.

That's fascinating, Harry says. —Real market research happens around this pool. We should sell *shares* in this pool, it's so much the secret of our success. A *talent pool*. How old is your little sister? Where does she go to school? Mona here might know her.

The women turn to her. —You're still in school? one asks, her eyes seeming to puff full with sugar.

Until I run away, Mona says, and they laugh; she doesn't.

SOMEHOW HARRY EXTRACTS YOU FROM the conversation, conducts you via social pressures and tides you don't understand to another part of the deck, where you can't see Mona's panicked, furious eyes looking for you from among the art women.

She's a real spitfire, your little lady, Harry says. —So you're waiting to make an honest woman out of her when she crosses the stage for her diploma?

She isn't actually in high school anymore, you say. —She works at a record store, and also as a musician.

Harry has a way of laughing that communicates both that he appreciates you and that he is a clement judge. —Let me guess, a girl group, he says. —*I'll cry if I want to*. I can hear it. Desperate for people to look at them. They don't play their own instruments, of course. The whole John Black Zero template.

He points somewhere inside the house, toward the knot of people, and you remember the tiny man sipping his water, the record on Mona's turntable.

John Black Zero is here? you ask. —He has his own label, I thought.

It's a good idea to invite him to things, Harry says, sipping his mimosa. —Listen, I'll do you a favor. Get a tape of the little missus and her band. Tell her you gave it to me, and I listened to it, and I said no, all right?

You clear your throat, something your mother does when a person says something impolite, but may not realize they've overstepped. —But that wouldn't be true, you remind him.

We need a lot more people like you, Harry says wistfully, tapping his mimosa stem against the metal balcony as if it's a pencil. It's a sharp metal tap—you appreciate its sharpness.

She does play her own instruments, you say. —She plays guitar, and her sister plays drums, and her friend Wendy plays bass. You should sign them.

Harry says nothing, just looks out over his balcony at the water below—there are lights, the bright star of a warning buoy somewhere far out—and you fall quiet. He wants to change the subject, you tell yourself, this is what the silence means. It's okay: you think you've made your point; if not, there will be plenty of time to make it again later. There will be years.

B——, Harry says, and you flinch. —It hurts me to have to ask you this. But are you happy with Valley Forge Records? Are you happy with me, personally? Is there anything we're doing with respect to your career that's made you angry, or upset with us? Anything that would cause any hostility?

His tone decrescendos as he speaks; his whole face is different, all love drained from it. At first you don't understand this, like a puppy who's been kicked. Then you get scared. From across the deck, you can hear Mona raising her voice; you can hear the art women laughing at her. You start to laugh, too, voice high and paralyzed.

I dunno, you say. —I don't—I'm not angry?

So what's this about with the album, then? he asks.

You imagine your apartment dissolving around you, people able to see through its walls like a fish in glass. —Uh, is it not good? We can make another one.

Harry cocks his head slightly. —The album is fine, he says. —You telling your father—or, I'm sorry, your *manager*—to pull it from production because you don't think you tried your best on it is less fine. I don't like to spoil the party with this kind of thing, but there might be legal consequences. I know I shouldn't be speaking to you directly about that. —He cocks his head back in the other direction. —You didn't know about this. Is that what I'm hearing?

You're still looking at the deck, the earlier call with your father in your head. The memory of his voice in your ears suddenly scrapes, grates, and you think of one of your songs to drown it out. And then the song isn't enough: you stomp your foot hard against the boards of the deck. For a moment, you imagine that you're kicking a hole through it, that you'll fall through, die against the rocks on the beach. But money has made this deck solid.

You really didn't know, Harry says.

That is accurate, you say quietly.

I'm sorry, he says. —I wouldn't have even brought it up. So many problems with this manager you've got.

What you're about to say hangs before your consciousness like a rich pastry on a plate, like liquor and pills; you know it's wrong—it is what wrong means—it is irresistible.

Yeah, he's not our manager anymore, you say.

Harry smiles at you like aloe vera on a burn.

You're sure, he says. —It's up to you. Whatever you want to do is the right thing to do.

I'm sure, you say, filling yourself up on his words, how good they make you feel. —He's out. He's history.

That's a smart choice, I think, he says. —I was really hurt, B——. I was worried you *hated* me.

You flush. —Of course not, you say. —How could you even think that? We're really making it thanks to you. I mean obviously you're doing better. I mean this is a real neat house and all. But I mean you guys work real hard.

He waves his hand, dismissing this. —Right, he says. —I should have trusted you, genius that you are. So I'll forget the conversation with your father ever happened. And I'll look forward to finishing up the master tapes for a release next month. I've got faith in you. You're a producer. You're a solid citizen, B——.

I mean as long as I can keep making records, you frown. —Like as long as people aren't just pretending to like them.

He looks at you, and then he takes off his glasses, steps forward, and gives you a gigantic embrace, his head coming up to your chest, his glasses forming the clasp of the meat bracelet of his arms around you. You stand perfectly still. He steps back, puts his glasses on, and claps you on the shoulder.

I want to introduce you to John Black Zero, he says. —Come inside.

JOHN BLACK ZERO IS STILL on the couch where you left him, his glass of water still full, a half circle of people still holding court around him. Now, inbound to him through the asteroids in his orbit, Harry brushing people aside for you, you feel the uncomfortable black hole gravity emanating from him: half your height, the Cuban heels of his black shoes dimpling the carpet. His eyes are tiny cinnamon-black spirals floating in a hollow of white above, white below, burst sleepless veins of pink staining their coronas. His entire suit is black, and his hair shifts like serpents. His eyes move over you like a petroleum slick on the surface of a still ocean. Then they slide to Harry.

How are you, Harry, he says. He has kind of a lisping child's voice, sing-song, as if he's trying to wheedle sweets. His breath smells like lemon and sarcophagi.

Mr. Zero, Harry says. —This is B——. I'm sure you've heard of him—one of our rising stars over at Valley Forge, with the Get Happies. Their latest single came this close to knocking your latest out of the Number One spot. But we'll getcha next time.

He has a way of making this sound ridiculous and boastful at once as he says it, disarmingly so, and the narrow putti lips of John Black Zero twist into a smile.

I mean, I figure there's room enough for both of us, Mr. Zero, though, you say helpfully.

His smile remains, though his eyes get hard: their irises seem to spiral like waterspouts, and you can feel the hull of your ego creak. Some of the people around you laugh tentatively; Harry is one of them. You suddenly feel as if he's standing farther away from you. On terrified instinct you extend your hand to John Black Zero. He doesn't take it.

Uh, congratulations on the gold record for "I Love You, Baby," you say, slowly retracting your hand and pretending to scratch your temple. —One record producer to another.

I love you, John Black Zero whispers.

I'm sorry, you say, your voice suddenly shrieking north into falsetto.

I love you, Zero says. —I love you, baby. Wagnerian. That's what I was trying to achieve. The roar and the anger and the passion. Like a tornado in your heart. Destroying everything in you that resists that feeling. That's what the kids need. Most of the kids don't understand that about me.

You swear his eyes are turning into awful glowing spirals. Your smile is gone. No one speaks all around you.

You're a nice kid, too, he finally says, sadly. He tips his water glass back, pours the rest down his throat, and offers the glass to you. —This is empty, he says.

You take the glass because it is unsafe not to. You walk past the black piano to the jar of water, ice, and lemons on the bar, where you fill the glass. You return it to him. No one has joined the half circle around the couch and no one has left. No one is talking. Harry Corot is trying to laugh, but there is no sound.

B——, he chokes out finally, —ha ha, you didn't have to get his water; Mr. Zero's just pulling your leg, you know, professional joke among professionals, ha ha—

Confused, you stop and look to Harry for guidance—should you drink the water yourself? Pour it back into the jar? But John Black Zero takes the glass from your hand anyway, leaning forward suddenly like a nimbus cloud spreading its tendrils. He takes a sip of the water, makes a face, and sniffs.

Peeeee-yew, he drawls. —This is the *worst* water I've *ever* tasted. —He turns his eyes back to you. —It *stinks*, he says. —And no one really knows how *bad* it stinks except you and me, B——.

Carefully, he pours the glass into the half-full ashtray on the end table, careful not to spill, so that all the cigarette butts float like canoes on an ashy sea. Not a drop gets on the wood. He hands you the glass again.

The sink in the kitchen upstairs comes from outside, he says. —It's *fresher.*

You take the glass and run. John Black Zero snickers on the couch behind you. Harry is saying something that makes him laugh louder, snot sucking into his long, dry nose.

YOU CLIMB UPSTAIRS TO THE front door, and then, feeling Zero's radiation at your back, you climb higher, to what, despite the weird organizational plan of the house, you are comfortable calling the second floor. There are three doors here; one of them, at the end of the hall, is obviously a bathroom. From somewhere far below you can hear Harry's voice—*B*———, *has anyone seen B*———? You step into the bathroom, close the door, and hold it braced shut for a few seconds until you realize that there's no need to do this. No one will follow you for a while.

So you sit on the closed seat of the toilet in the dark. Someone on the other side of the wall, in one of the other rooms, is listening to jazz music. Its beat thrums through the plaster from the vibrations of the hi-fi. You slump to one side, lean your head against the plaster, allow them to shake you.

After a while, you stand up. You flush the toilet, to cover your tracks, you guess. You wash your hands.

From the hall, the music is louder, emerging from behind a door cracked an inch, gold light creeping over the carpet. You lean against the doorjamb a moment, trying to hear better, but your klutzy foot knocks softly against the door and sets it moving, widening the triangle of lamplight over the hallway carpet. You step back like spilled milk is about to enclose your loafers.

Inside the room, there's a woman lying on a wide sleigh bed, the covers rumpled and only half tucked in. As soon as the door swings open she sits up; before, she was spread cruciform over the covers, long wrists and fingers hanging from long arms that jut from a white blouse unbuttoned two from the top, black skirt hanging loosely between her knees. Quickly she pulls one knee up and props herself on her elbows, looking at you. Her hair's done up in the ruins of a French twist, now squashed against the pillow with odd strings of hair escaping; one black heel hangs off one long toe; her feet hang off the end of the bed at the ankle. Another heel, discarded, lies next to a wadded mass of nude-colored hose on the carpet. A massive mahogany-framed mirror hangs on the wall, duplicating her, revealing you in the doorway with your eyes on her. Dave Brubeck rondos spiral in invisible odd time through the heavy herbal air of the room.

Can I help you? she asks sharply. Something about the way she speaks makes you wonder if she has a cold. She coughs, seeming to confirm it.

Uh, my dad likes this album, you say.

She narrows her eyes and doesn't at first respond. In the mirror you can see her shift, trying to bring her legs more closely together, to hunch her shoulders forward to deemphasize her unbuttoned chest, to do all this without your noticing her doing it. In the mirror you look like a big, stupid predator animal. You can watch your own face droop at this. Her face slowly softens.

If you're looking for Harry, he's downstairs, she says. —He was supposed to tell everyone not to come upstairs during the party. That I wasn't up to being disturbed today.

He uh may have, you say. —Gosh, I'm sorry. I was kinda trying to avoid Harry is the only reason I'm up here.

Why are you trying to avoid Harry? she asks, eyebrow raising. —Did you steal something of ours?

Oh no, of course not, you say. —I don't even know if I have pockets on these pants. Uh, I guess I do.

She waits.

No, uh, I was just feeling sad, you say. —Someone was talking to me, and, and it was kind of a bad experience. I'm sorry. I'll go be sad by the pool maybe, if that's okay, ma'am.

Was it John Black Zero? she asks. —Who created this bad experience.

Uh, yes ma'am, you say.

She growls and flips her head; two wayward strings of French twist fly up and fall back to the nape of her neck. —He's complete feculence, she says, softening. —I told Harry not to invite him. The way he talks to women, also. Be lucky you're not in my position.

Yeah, you say miserably.

She blinks at you. Her duplicate in the mirror studies your miserable predator's reflection. Both of her lean forward.

I'm hiding up here from the party, she says. —Do you want to hide up here with me for a while? If you do, come in and close the door.

You smile, trying to bury your face in your chest; she smiles back at you as you close the door. She flips her legs up under herself, perching next to the pillow like a happy cat, and she pats a space on the coverlet next to her. You sit down and she extends her hand to you, like you are negotiating a contract all of a sudden.

I'm Lana, she says. —Harry's girlfriend. It's a real pleasure to meet you.

Sitting on the covers together, suddenly she seems as tall as you are. It's jarring; you're not used to looking into anyone's eyes without bending your head.

B——, you say, taking the fingers of her hand. She giggles.

B——, Lana says. —You're that kid who writes all those songs about cars and burgers and things. Harry talks a lot about you. You must write songs all the time.

Uh, yes, that's true, you say. —I mean you've gotta write songs all the time to, to stay competitive in this industry. It's uh, a grit thing.

What a little soldier, she says, and she scoots back to sit on the pillow, holding her knees tight to her chest. Her skirt pools up under her. —I really like that song you do. That diner girl song. Harry played that for me when he was first talking about signing you up. Such a pretty melody. I'm not so crazy about the words. It's curious you know about Dave Brubeck. You're a kid. I guess I wasn't a kid so long ago.

You squint at her; she doesn't seem that much older than you, or Harry. It's hard to figure out her age.

It's mostly my dad that likes Brubeck, you say. —He likes

Brubeck a lot. He doesn't think that much about what we do. But he works hard, you know.

Oh, you're as good as Brubeck any day, she smiles. —Just at different things, probably.

You wonder if you're supposed to be attracted to her. You are, you guess. You know this is what anyone would think of what's happening, you alone in a room with her. A boy and a girl. You write songs about exactly this all the time. And here she is leaning in.

B——. —She smiles. —Have you ever listened to Brubeck on reefer, B——?

You flush. —Uh, no, you say.

Do you want to? she asks. Her eyebrows raise half an inch when she asks it.

Uh, my dad wouldn't like it, you say after a moment.

She laughs, putting a hand over her mouth.

I mean I'll try it, you say quickly.

She smiles; both of her smile, her and her reflection, at both of you, the mahogany frame of the mirror binding you both.

All right, she says, slowly and happily.

She stretches and curls around the pillow to reach the front drawer of an end table. Inside, there's a little wooden box shaped like a book: *Great Digested Works of French Romanticism.* Inside there's a bag of drugs, a Zippo, rolling papers. She perches, sets the box between her knees, and begins to assemble a joint.

I love turning new people on, she chirps. —I love feeling like Satan, Mephistophelia. You don't know what you've been missing. Sometimes, cooped up here alone when Harry's on trips, you know, it's all that gets me through. Harry introduced me to it. He picked some up for us one time, on a trip to Mexico to see some distributor. It was the first year we were together. He got it from some Indian reservation. Did you know there were Indians down there in Mexico, too? I never knew that. You always think of them as so American.

She finishes rolling, lies back against the pillow, and slides her stash box aside with her foot as she lights the joint. She inhales; she holds; she releases with a sigh. Soon she sits up and hands the drug to you, moving closer. She shows you how to smoke it.

Sometimes you think of your anxiety as a mosquito, gliding through the space in your brain, stopping sometimes to press its needle in and feed. As the smoke hits, you imagine the wings scorching, curling like leaves on a bonfire. It explodes in a tiny blot of blood.

You sit, legs folded, beside her while she stretches on the pillow, and you pass the joint back and forth between you.

How does it feel? she asks you. —You feel better?

Her words sound as if they're bubbling up from the surface of a black lake that you're suddenly aware has always surrounded you. How is it that you haven't seen it before now?

I think so, you say. —I feel, uh, different, anyway.

Lana laughs, and it makes you want to laugh with her. And you do.

Do you like singing? she asks. —Of course you do. God, what am I saying. You're like—a boy wonder. Of course you know how to sing.

I'm not a boy wonder, you say. —I just work hard, is all.

Just wonderful, then, she says, and she scoots back against the headboard, bringing her lungs straight and opening her mouth. —Harry can't sing at all. It's like he has no equipment for it. I have to do all the singing for both of us.

Jazz music is circling the heavy beige space, five to four, your heart speeding up to catch it, and your brain feels like a stiff paper napkin with rich tendrils of ink soaking in, turning everything colors. She's singing along, softly. You frown. Everything about the way she's singing is wrong. It makes you start to laugh.

You can't sing like that, you say. —It's getting all swallowed up by your throat. It's terrible.

She frowns and closes her mouth.

I'm singing fine, she says. —This is how I sing.

You have to sing more from here, you say, indicating your chest.

I am singing from there, she says.

No you aren't. —You laugh. —I had to teach all my brothers this same stuff. It's like you want your voice to go a certain way but you can't just make it. You gotta like, let it ride out from the back of your throat, like you're riding a horse and you can just kinda lay the reins left or right once it's up to speed—

You have no idea if you're making sense, and you're aware— sinking back into the black lake around you, insects chirping louder and louder—that Lana has slumped back against the headboard, neck slack, the end of her joint loose from her mouth. Some smooth iridescent gate has slammed shut over her eyes.

I'd like to be alone now, she says abruptly, sounding tired. —I think you should go back to the party.

And she is very tall, you suddenly realize, checked out and leaning against the headboard, now coughing with her long arms hanging from wide shoulders like the wings of some great, transformed swan.

The possibility that's now occurring to you, B——: you can not unsee it, you can not unhear it. The lamplight triangle is swinging wider and wider as a door is opening in your mind.

You watch the crack spread across her face as she recognizes what you're seeing. She's afraid, you realize; she must be so, so afraid. The door in your mind is opening onto the worst possibility in the world. You imagine a cloud of smoke emerging from your ears, accumulated green smoke like a screen onto which your thoughts can project. You want to wave your hands through it, disperse it to atoms so your thoughts can't be seen; fascinated, you don't, watching them form.

She doesn't see them. Agitated, she stands, circles the bed, and leans against the door to block it. She crosses her arms. You imagine the weight of her against the door. You imagine all the walls coming apart.

Listen, she says, her thin voice snapping like a whip's cord from the rear of her throat. —I don't know what ideas you have about me, and I don't want to know about them. But right now, you need to understand that your whole career depends on Harry, and Harry's whole career depends on how seriously people take him. So before you think about saying *shit all* to anyone, you'd better think about how it's gonna make *you* sound if you—

Her voice is striking through the mildew mist of green droplets that suddenly fills your nostrils, the terrible image like a Fantasia devil forming from bats. Her voice rages like waves, and you're a small wet rock anchored only to a great dark spire that disappears into icy ocean trenches in the absolute blackness just beneath you, and here on the surface the wind of Lana's voice—*everything you might say, we'll deny it, it's not like you'd be the first to try.* Raindrops are dragging across your face so hard they leave gouges. Something is bleeding from beneath your skin. You're crying.

Lana sees this, and she stops for a moment. She looks down at you. She can see your projected thoughts, or maybe she can't see them. You don't care what she can see. The cold iceberg rising in you; you can't avoid announcing its presence, coming up through the surface of the ocean where you're drifting.

I w-wouldn't say anything, you say.

That's right, Lana says.

I, I don't think it's wrong, you say. —I don't think there's anything wrong at all—

Are you okay? Lana suddenly asks, and the room is full of sunlight, and the iceberg that had been rising inside you begins to melt. Boy, how it melts. It melts into a whole new ocean, clean water floating on the surface of the one you'd swam in before, which you suddenly realize was poisonous rainbow gasoline. And you are very warm and you are very numb and you are very, very afraid.

You can feel Lana staring down at you, creases in her forehead yawning and closing like deep sea vents as she watches you cry.

After some time, she puts her hand on the doorknob—I'll be right back, she's careful to say—and she opens the door, disappears into the hallway, runs water in the other room. She returns with a glass of water. You take it and drink it. Water has a taste, you realize, wide and oblique, like you're chewing on a diamond.

Do you feel better? she asks you after half the glass is gone.

Yes, you say earnestly. —Yes, thank you, I'm sorry for—

Some of the tension drains from her shoulders when you speak this time; you can feel its seismic echo in the mattress springs. She sits on the bed and kicks her feet, like she's a little girl dangling them over the edge of her mother's bed, but her legs are too long. She scuffs the carpet.

I meant this, she says. —You don't know anything. It's important—I don't want to lose what I have. I can't lose it. I can't even imagine life without it. Don't even say anything to Harry. Do you understand?

Yes, ma'am, you say, floating.

I mean of course Harry knows, she says quickly. —Of course. And Harry's known me for a long time. But Harry shouldn't know that you know what you don't know. If you know it. I don't know what he'd do. —She scuffs her feet on the carpet again like skis over snow. —Oh, if you have questions, she begins, and then she stops, waits.

You look into the glass. *So can you—? Do you have—? Do you and Harry—? Did you ever like girls? If you did used to like girls was it hard to switch to liking boys? Did you have to? If someone like you liked girls were they maybe not like you at all?*

You end up asking nothing. She lies back, exhales, grabs handfuls of covers to hold herself still.

Are you feeling okay, she asks. —Her voice rises like thick oil-smoke from behind you. You're loath to turn and look back at her because if you do you may never leave alive.

I should go back to the party, you say.

No, don't, she says dreamily, and she rolls on her side, an inch from you. —Stay and talk to me. I don't talk to many people.

The two of you sit in the mirror together.

I was in the service, did you know that? she asks. —I have shrapnel in my belly. All my babies died before I was born. —She giggles, coughs on stray resin in the rear of her throat, and makes the thumb and forefinger of each hand into an L. Her blouse hiked up, she squares off a section of skin. —Right here, she continues. —You can't feel it. You're not my boyfriend.

You laugh, unsure why; you are becoming terrified.

I can still feel it, she says. —Cold, and like an itch you can't scratch. I didn't want to put things off anymore, after. So I went to Paris where they said things were changing. I settled my affairs and disappeared, and then I reappeared again. There's a story that's like it: a sword tossed into a lake and the Lady of the Lake tosses it out again, golden. And Harry caught me.

You are wondering: *how does someone disappear?*

Harry sees me, she's saying. —Do you understand how important that is, for someone to see you? That's so important for you to understand. —She looks carefully at you. —You like Harry, don't you? I want you to like Harry.

Uh, I do like Harry, you say, louder than you'd planned, and as you say it you stand up. —Uh, and uh I should get back to the party now—uh so I'm going to go—thank you for, for talking to me, and for the drugs and everything.

She has stopped talking, started looking at the floor.

Okay, she says finally, as if she is used to saying goodbyes to young people like you.

Really, you say, uh, thanks for talking to me—

Really okay, she says, and she looks in the mirror at herself.

You feel like you want to apologize somehow for what you've done, in leaving, but you can't think of a way to do it that isn't essentially *staying.* So you stand there, just out of the frame, not looking at your own reflection, while she watches hers.

AND THIS IS HOW YOU'RE standing when the doorknob responds to some poltergeist desperation of yours and turns, opens. Harry is standing there, hand on the knob. He stares at you and Lana.

Oh, hello, Harry, you say, putting on a smile.

B——, he says, —I was just looking for you, and I couldn't find you, so I thought I'd check in on my girlfriend. And here I find you, with my girlfriend. B——, this is Lana; Lana, this is B——. It's a pleasure to introduce you.

You watch as his glance goes across the border of the bed to Lana. You keep your face dumb and smiling.

We've been talking, Lana says. —He's very charming. I was telling him how wonderful you are. Ask him. —She flops on the bed across the space you vacated when you stood, scratching one leg with the other foot.

It's true, you say.

We were also smoking grass, Lana explains.

Harry raises an eye at you, and then passes you to lean over Lana, one hand on either side of her face. He lowers himself to kiss her mouth. You can hear it when her eyelashes click shut. Then he turns to you to study your face. You guess that he's looking for signs of jealousy or discomfort. You don't think there are any. He runs his tongue over his teeth, wets them, smiles afresh.

John Black Zero's left for the evening, he says. —I wanted to tell you this. And, ah, I thought we could meet some people who're— substantially less individual than he is. Yet no less important. If you're willing.

Sure, let's go, you say.

Lana is lying on the bed, arms folded over the shrapnel inside of her, smiling at you like a recumbent punctuation mark, smiling at Harry who brings the ocean and the sun.

It was really wonderful meeting you, B——, she elaborates. She leans to shake your hand and when you do, she presses something into it, a warm soft tube of paper, pre-folded, sealed with her spit.

It was really neat meeting you, you say, eyeing Harry on the side. —Really, you've got no idea. Uh, the grass is really great.

Play ball, then, she says.

And you have one second before you turn to follow Harry out to memorize her features—the blur—unitary eyes, lazy scuffling feet. And then you are in the hallway with Harry, the sounds of the record company party beginning to steep in your ears, the smell of pot fading under the crack of light beneath the closed door. And we both know, B——, that you will never see Lana again.

SHE TURN YOU ON IN there? Harry asks. —The grass, I mean? That's what we say.

Uh kinda, you reply, pocketing the joint she gave you. He studies you carefully again, and you try to keep fresh guilt from your face.

I didn't know you were a grass man, he finally says. —That's excellent. We'll use that.

So you descend the stairs to the pool again with him, B——, stopping for dregs of liquor in the kitchen among the schmoozers. He doesn't talk about Lana the way you talked about Mona earlier; he frowns, purses his lip, pauses more than usual when he speaks. Lana's wish comes true: you do think of them together, and you like him better, B——. You do.

Uh so I can get the new album done in a month, you say later, interrupting something he's saying about a producer you'd enjoy. —I promise, Harry, okay? I'll make that happen, no matter what.

He smiles without surprise and claps you on the shoulder.

That's my hitmaker, he says. —Oh, and speaking of which—

He leads you into a small den, a desk that looks virtually unused. There are photos of Harry hanging on the wall, shaking hands with different musicians you know; there are photos of Harry in Paris in uniform; there are no photos of Lana at all. You guess that she took some of the photos; you wonder whether there are photos that Harry didn't hang. Harry opens a ledger, pulls an envelope out with your name on it, hands it over. You open it: a royalty check for more money than before.

I thought I'd give that to you personally, he says. —Avoid the trouble we had last time with your father and the stop order and reissuance and all those nightmares. But I guess that won't be a problem anymore, will it?

Suddenly you flush. —Listen, Harry—what I was saying earlier, about firing my dad—I was kidding.

He looks at you. —You're not serious, he says.

Yes, you say, suddenly afraid. —I mean, yes, I was kidding just now, when I said that. —And then you fold up the check and put it in the pocket of your pinstripe pants.

Good, Harry says, touching you again on the shoulder, softly now. —Good riddance to him. So let me show you off a little. I'll introduce you to some of the distribution guys, the radio relationships people, they're really swell guys. Plenty of 'em have swell wives, too.

You are leaving the house for the patio; many of the swell wives are crowded up to the railing, far from you. One of them sees you and trots over, earrings tinkling in the hot night wind.

There's a girl out on the rocks, she announces.

How'd it happen, Harry demands. —That's an expensive railing—

You're already jogging past the chaises and potted palms at the far end of the deck, where people are watching the slim figure in her borrowed party dress pick her way across the stones. Every so often she stops, sends up a flare of hot red from her lighter, and continues moving, nicotine clouds rising toward the headlights coursing around the cliffside road above her.

There's a gap between the railing and the rock face that you're still slender enough to squeeze through. Once you're actually on the stone, it doesn't seem as sheer; stringcourses of dead salt grass a foot wide give you places to step as you move out, sometimes on all fours, sometimes hanging like a spider over steeper angles, the beach sands some fifteen, twenty feet down, Harry shouting from the balcony for someone to bring you back; you are valuable. And you're terrified, black ocean below you smashing and the last salt spittle of its anger moving like rough mist over your skin. But finally you make it to the griddle of stone where Mona sits, her knees and shins torn up and the seams split down the sides of her dress. Her hair is wet and stiff as she shelters her cigarette.

Hi, she says, breath drunk. —You climb pretty good for an old guy.

I'm sorry I left you alone so long, you fret. —I was talking to Harry's girlfriend up in their bedroom.

Mona laughs and drags on the cigarette.

You're so wonderful, she says brightly. —You should leave me for Harry's girlfriend. I think the two of you will be very happy together, and you can bring her over for dinner any time.

Her flint strikes and doesn't catch. Voices from the party are still shouting out to you.

Uh, so did you have a good time at the party, you ask.

You know filmstrips in biology class where even if pack animals make all the right noises or challenges or whatever, they can maybe still not be the right kind of pack animals, rest-of-the-pack-wise? she asks. —I told one of them I wanted to wrestle her. What kind of person does that?

Her voice is close to breaking. She looks down at her cigarette and sets it on the griddle of rock. Mist beads on the burning
cherry and puts it out. You sit on the rock and stretch your shoulders against the damp.

I want to die, she says, looking at the ocean.

Don't say that, you say quickly.

She turns to look at you. —Why? she asks.

You try to think of the answers other people who are more real
than you might have for this question. —I don't know, you finally
admit.

She leans back and flicks the filter of the extinguished cigarette
down to break on the sand.

I don't know either, she says. —We're better than other people,
aren't we?

You watch her, your lip stinging with salt water. She studies
you, drunken defenses taut in the muscles of her cheeks, eyes soft
like an animal trainer.

I mean I think other people are okay, you finally say.

Some time later, she says, —You know the first time we met?
When my *mother* invited you to my house? I didn't even like you.
—She looks you in the eyes. —I thought if I talked to you, I could
*charm* you. I thought I could get my band an opening slot with
your band. That was the most important thing to me in the world.
—She laughs. —My band, she says with contempt. —God, I was
a *child*.

What she's told you should hurt you, you think. Instead you
feel a strange peace from it: what she wants from you is much
simpler than you'd thought. It's only later, alone, that the other
side of this will occur to you: that her telling you that this is
what she first wanted from you may indicate that there are other
things she wants from you now. And that what Lana told you is
operating in you, too: that you are becoming more solid every
moment: that these things together mean you have more power to

hurt people than you could have ever thought you had. But these are thoughts for later, B——; for now, appreciate what you've heard, here above the beach, its clouds.

Gee, you say, keeping your voice soft. —Thank you for telling me that. No fooling, really.

She looks at you for a minute as if you're an alien. Then she stands, wobbling, and gets on all fours, moving down toward the incline.

I want to find a way down, she says. —Let's go back down.

She begins to work her way down the shale, loose threads freeing themselves from her torn seams, slowly descending toward the packed wet sand and the waves. You look back at the smear of faces far off at Harry Corot's railing, the revolving lights of police cars beginning to arrive. You begin moving down the cliff too, following Mona. You must ignore other paths that seem to appear. If you step where she steps, you think, you will not fall, will reach the beach safely, a place where you can crawl under a rock in the rain.

Love, Gala

# October 20, 2009

Dear B——,

I didn't expect Caroline even to want to go with me to Las Cruces to collect my blue pills: an errand to a doctor's office in a desert city an hour south of our own desert city, a border town swarming with ICE agents and manufactured housing dealers. But she was elated to go, bounded into my boss's truck with her camera in her arms, even offered to drive when I was still stuck on hold with the doctor's office to confirm that my prescription was there. This made me blush. I'd been driving for such a long time, and the idea that I didn't have to do it for once was one of the most romantic things I'd heard. The incredible luxury of not driving: you could read a book! You could look at scenery! You could talk to the person next to you, or ignore them altogether, fall asleep, close your eyes, and wake up in the place you'd decided to go. I handed her my boss's keys (their chain a waterproof tag with his address, a well-matted rabbit's foot, a unicursal hexagram), and we crunched across the gravel as she turned the truck sharply toward the town's main street, bound for the highway access, not looking at the road as she dug in my boss's center console for CDs. He had *American Beauty*, some stuff by Gregg Allman and Bauhaus, an Olivier Messiaen double CD set, and something called *Eight Lamas From Drepung.* She selected this last one and cranked it, all windows rolled down, while I remained on hold with the clinic. She'd taped her camera down to the dashboard, the red-eyed mermaid on our prow: it slurped in power from the cigarette lighter umbilicus like a preteen from a milkshake.

We'd been driving nearly an hour, almost to Radium Springs, when the endocrinologist's office phone finally picked up.

Hello, said an uncertain voice on the other end.

Oh hi, I said, trying to ratchet my own voice as high into my head as it could go. —My name's Gala, and I'm coming in to pick up a prescription today?

What? asked the voice, hoarse and baritone.

Gala, I said. —I have a prescription that I'm supposed to pick up today, from your office, in Las Cruces? And my friend and I are almost there, and, you know, we wanted to make sure it was ready.

There was a silence.

Yeah, said the voice. —Could you—maybe come another time?

I punched my thigh stiffly, trying not to let it be audible on the phone. —It's a lot better if I can like, pick it up today? I said. —I mean it should be ready, right?

Um, said the voice. —My dad—he took the day off, is the thing.

I hung up. —Oh my God, I said. —They never fucking got my prescription ready. They just never did it. Why do they just never do it?

You know what I just realized? said Caroline. —We don't actually have to go back.

I stared at her. —Yeah, I guess that's technically true, I said. —We have absolute freedom of will in this world. Seriously, what am I going to do? I've got like a week of hormones left, and you'd think that'd be enough time to take care of things, but you'd also think that if they said the prescription would be ready today, it actually—

No, seriously, think about it, she said. —We don't actually have to bring this truck back. My grandmother's in Montana somewhere, probably, right? That's where all her bank statements used to come from. It's as good a lead as any. We could leave for there, today. How far could we get? I mean, pretty far, right?

I opened my mouth to laugh, but couldn't manage this. —Don't even joke, I said. —We can't go to Montana. This isn't our truck.

We could look for her once we're up there, she said. —Montana hotel party! And I could buy the truck from your boss—I mean, send him a check once we're there. What's stopping us? —She turned to me, bouncing in her seat with excitement. —Seriously, whatever we don't have, we can get. Like which way are we going, south, right? So we'd have to go west into Arizona instead, and we can pick up more clothes in Tuscon I guess, on the way, and then start working our way north. We can see the vortexes in Sedona, and maybe the Nevada boron mine. Super simple. What's even stopping us?

I stared at her behind the wheel: the slow realization that she was serious, the camera at the prow pulling us forward like a red-eyed stallion whose flanks she was lashing.

I don't know, I said, my voice again rising. —Moral decency?

She laughed, and I followed suit slightly later.

No, but I have all my stuff in my trailer, I continued. —I can't go without my stuff. I have my letters, and my CDs, and—we can't just replace everything.

It's not as hard as you would think to live without anything, Caroline philosophized.

Come on, I begged.

I mean, maybe this is what you need, she said. —You wanted to go with me to see my grandmother, right? So let's go now. This is how I want to do it. It's a compromise.

I'm not going to let you just steal my boss's truck, I said.

Try and stop me, she said, cackling.

And I don't know what happened, the road moving so fast, the distance from T or C increasing, the uncertainty as to where I would get my meds, memories of the city, memories of *your father*, B——, suddenly looking at me, suddenly asking me if I was stupid or something—

*Turn around*, I screamed.

She didn't. —Calm the fuck down, she said, her face closed off. —For a like, MTF transgender person, you're pretty conservative. Can I just say that?

Please turn the truck around, I said, my voice now very low, marbled with imminent panic.

Without saying anything else, she turned up the eight lamas from Drepung as loud as they could go—their groaning harmonies oozed over the red sand, echoed from the distant rock walls, the oddly philosophical road sign that read *GUSTY WINDS MAY EXIST*—but finally, she lurched the car onto the shoulder of I-25. I started breathing again as she rolled off the shoulder into the dirt, tires throwing up scrub grass and ruddy dust as we jounced from side to side and the camera recorded and the eight lamas throat-sang until we'd crossed the road altogether, until we were on the other side of the interstate, again driving toward the hostel and home.

There, she said. —Now we're going north. A more direct route to Montana.

Okay, thanks, I said, quietly. —T or C is exit seventy-five. So that's where we're getting off. Exit seventy-five.

No problem, she said, and she continued to drive for a few miles, while the lamas chanted, until she abruptly reached over and slapped the volume knob to turn them off.

Are you calmer now, she asked. —I mean, are you okay? That came out wrong.

I'm fine, I said.

I would've paid for the truck, she said. —I mean, more than it was worth to him. I wasn't just going to steal it.

That's nice of you, I said.

But it would've felt good to believe we'd stolen it, she said. —You know, just for a moment. More alive than you get to feel sitting in a trailer and working at a hostel for months and months. That's sort of like feeling dead, in my opinion.

Okay, I said.

I used to feel dead, she said. —I don't want to feel it ever again. I want to teach you not to feel that way, either.

I didn't say anything.

I would have stopped, she said. —Before we got too far. I would have.

After another silence, she turned the lamas back on, and we drove for a few more miles while I thought about whether I felt dead or not, what it would be like to feel different than I feel. I hadn't moved for a while, I realized: I rolled the window down and leaned one arm against the open window, as far out of this truck as I could get it, letting the sun tan me. After a while, my heart rate got back to normal, and my thoughts drifted back toward the more sedate problem of being about to run out of hormones in the middle of the Southwest with no clear plan. That's what I was thinking about when we came upon another sign—FUTURE SITE OF THE NEW MEXICO SPACEPORT—and Caroline, seeing it, first signaled and then abruptly veered off the highway onto a cracked county road, intermittent asphalt stretching east into endless undead fields of grass and desert stones.

Compromise, she said.

AS A CHILD WHO LOVED space, I loved to imagine spaceports as Yes album covers with organic scallop crystals growing out of the earth. Yet the spaceport they're building just south of

T or C looks like some giant dropped a plate out of the clouds, threw scads of dirt in all directions in the effort to pick it up, then left it to rot and crack in the sand. That's what it looks like from the air, at least, from dithered-to-heck 256-color photos of it on the office computer. From the rolled-down windows of the truck, parked on the snake-infested shoulder of terrible county roads, it just looked like a mess, accented by aluminum box-style construction portables that threw searing griddle sunlight at you as you approached them. Work had been resumed recently: a rough circle of tall rebar spires jutted from the concrete, awaiting the installation of financial offices, control rooms, vending machines; the long space of a runway had been marked in spray paint over stone. The spires were gated off by a stripe of yellow CAUTION tape, only fifty percent of which was attached to anything. Big stacks of mirrored glass sat shrink-wrapped in puckered plastic on the unrefined sand beside.

Without a word, Caroline removed her camera from the dashboard, replaced the battery, and began to walk toward the site, her red eye recording. I slumped in the passenger seat—what if I didn't follow her? I didn't want to follow her; what if I just did what I wanted to do—but then of course I followed her.

Tiny pebbles and discarded snake fangs lodged themselves between my sandals, toenails, and flesh as we moved toward the concrete circle. Our shadows got long over the cellulite pockmarks of the earth, warped red and rippling. What were we even crossing: would this become a parking lot? How long before sewage ran off into the Rio Grande, before new aerospace factories sprang up like death caps? How long before only the wealthy and the *space* wealthy would be left? These were my thoughts as we crossed the border between civilian territory and FAA-approved construction site: one moment we were compliant with the law, the next we were not. Caroline stood in the center of the space, slowly circling it with her camera, vacuuming up every illegal sight.

Look at this, she marveled, filming a temporary shed loaded with suits of conquistador armor molded in what looked like brass that someone had gone over with a rough sponge and grimy, aging paint. After scouting for a moment, she set the camera on the flat top of a fluorescent orange barrel and picked up two of the helms.

Behold, Sir Bedivere, 'tis yon damsel of the desert, she said in a plummy British voice. —What news yon damseleth of Camelot?

You don't conjugate *damsel* in Middle English, I said.

Why is this even here? she asked happily. —Is America conquering the moon?

I don't know, I said nervously. —Maybe it's some fundraiser, like *the history of exploration*. Who knows why it's here.

History of exploration, like us, Caroline said. She turned the camera to me. —Put on the armor, come on, she said. —For the shot!

I put my hand over my face. —Please don't film me here, I said. —Please let's maybe go? Please let's maybe not get arrested here?

She didn't lower the camera. —Usually you *love* being filmed, she said.

That's *really false* and I would *really like to go*, I said.

Finally, the camera slept; she lowered it and glared at me. But she made no move to leave, and we stood there, trespassing on federal property, watching each other. She looked at me carefully, as if I were a falcon she was training and she had to decide whether I needed to have the hood draped over my eyes or whether I needed to be allowed space to sulk. I felt dumb and bad, a sullen boy next to her, the depressing lead of a romantic comedy before he learned to Embrace Laughter.

Come sit down, she said, and she walked over to the side of the concrete slab and sat, her feet hanging down toward the dirt, with the scorpions. I hesitated until she looked up at me impatiently, and I lowered myself to join her. We sat, side by side, the camera sitting between us.

After a while, she asked: —Why do you get to win all the time?

What do you mean? I said.

You were the one who made me think about my family again, she said. —I asked you not to make me do that, but you did it anyway. That's why I wanted to come here.

I stared at her. —That doesn't make sense, I said.

Don't tell me I don't make sense, she continued. —Because again, I said like—okay, if you were going to make me do something I didn't originally want to do, I should get to do it in the *way* I wanted to do it, right? But again, you got your way, and I didn't. So I just wanted to get something that I wanted, like coming to a cool spaceport and filming it.

We could go to jail, I said.

So we go to *jail*, she said. —So what? We get out in a day or two. It's an adventure.

But I mean—we wouldn't go to the same jail, I said.

Why wouldn't we go to the same jail, she said, blinking. —Is this because I have more money than you, or—

I'd go to a men's jail, I explained.

Her eyes widened, and then narrowed again.

That doesn't have anything to do with anything, she said.

I opened my mouth, and then I closed it. And then I turned and looked out at the country road—almost no cars, a truck once, a motorcycle twice, way out past the radial Nazca lines that some creeping outsize Spirograph had combed into flat sand, leveling the place for construction. Feeling shitty about myself, I elected to also feel shitty about the spaceport. Who needed a spaceport? Did we have active commercial interests in space? The only people who were concerned about whether or not America and New Mexico had a working spaceport were people who'd watched a lot of *Star Trek*, people who had a lot of time to spare believing that the existential threat of Imminent Asteroid Disaster was not only a more important thing to use as much money as possible to fight than general poverty, climate collapse, etc., etc., but that a large enough amount of money *could* fight it: this incredible faith that if you collected enough money in one spot, it might coalesce into a terrible green-gloved hand big enough to flick away the rocks or comets God flung at us. All of us stuffed together in this world, bodies resting on top of bodies surrounded by sweat, stink, breathing, all so the ones on the top could see *possibilities*. They could see ground to build on, occult workings far greater than anything I could come up with, all here on inexpensive and stolen land.

Remember when I said I could buy a trailer here, Caroline said, breaking the silence.

I looked at her. —Yes, I said warily.

I'm sorry I said that, she said. —It put a lot of pressure on everything.

Wow, I said. —Apology accepted.

Good, she said. And then her face grew soft, and she smiled. —Actually I think you should sell your trailer here, she said. —I think we've all been here long enough.

After another moment, she leaned toward me, her body covering the camera like a great bridge, and she leaned her head against my shoulder. The October wind had gotten cold, and we sat there like that for a while, and I kept scanning the road in terror that the police might appear at any moment, might squint at me, slowly ask *Let me see your ID* with eyes on my chest. But if I moved, she would go away, so I made myself remain.

I THINK SHE FELT GUILTY, so she ended up taking me to a Sal Angel's just north of T or C for dinner.

Order whatever you want, she said to me. —Grandma's buying.

Whenever someone tells me to order whatever I want, I'm compelled to find something at the exact median price level on the menu, which fortunately turned out to be an omelet platter that

I liked anyway. Caroline had four different appetizers, and she grazed from each of them: she'd brought her camera in, and she was reviewing footage as we sat together and outside the sun slowly went down, turning the desert first pink, then blue, then black.

There was a church group there, a whole van's worth in matching shirts, out of some grim West Texas town (Sanderson, Odessa, Lajitas?) Their hands were joined and heads bowed as the fleshy leader, red-faced and buzz-cut, muttered a prayer over their burgers and eggs. None of them had been looking at us, I noted; had I come here alone, they would definitely have been looking at me, and maybe one of the kids might've even come over to me, pressed a tract into my hand. But even as queer as Caroline clearly was, together we somehow neutralized out. Just a femme and a butch, just a boy and a girl.

It could always be like this, I thought. We could travel across America together, just like this, eating hash browns coated in crystal butter, the cis woman and me, seeking you out. You could even come with us one day, B——, all of us invisible, all of us singing harmonies along with Eight Lamas from Drepung out the rolled-down windows of a stolen truck: you high, Caroline medium, me low.

Hey, I said. —I'm sorry I was a downer when we broke into the spaceport.

We've moved on, she said.

I met her eyes for as long as I could before I looked down at my plate and finished the food I'd been given. It could always be like this. I should not be so judgmental about this. This would not be so bad.

Love, Gala

# October 31, 2009

Dear B——,

Alone one afternoon, you go to the public library to look up the story Lana mentioned: the Lady of the Lake. In the story, a knight throws a sword into the water. A long, smooth hand wreathed in wet, smelly ivy rises from the silver mirror surface, catches that sword, drags it under the water where she and the serpents and the crocodiles are. And there she makes it into a new thing. And when she emerges from the lake with this new thing, you must take what she offers. You will never again see what you threw away. You think about this story a lot, B——, alone eating French fries on the couch with the TV going and no one to stop you from doing that. Perhaps no one to stop you at all.

TOM HAPPY'S NEW HOUSE—TO WHICH he insists you and Mona travel, one Saturday, for a housewarming party—is in Brentwood, on a lot rebuilt from scratch following the big fire. The house looks washed out, haloed in the gray of a rare overcast sky; the lawn is clipped recruit-short, the new trees in the yard wrapped tight by wires like staked heretics, windows polished to vacancy. When you knock, Mona in tow, it takes Tom zero time to answer, as if he's been perched at the outer edge of the staircase you can see just over the right shoulder of his clean white button-down. Other party guests do not appear to be in evidence.

B——, he says. —Mona. So glad you could make it. C'mon in. Let me show you around.

His foyer is extremely white, matte paint brushed over every surface, photos of palm trees and hula girls hanging at intervals. Just visible beyond the foyer are three exits: one leads to a dining table and credenza laden with wedding china; one to a living room with French doors open onto Italian loveseats; one to a room with a file drawer, empty bookcases, an empty desk blotter with a pen still capped in its set.

Beginnings of a little art collection, he says, indicating the photos. —You know—get a little money, you start developing a few, you know, *droits de seigneurs*.

Cool, you say. —So are we the first to get here or something?

Tom laughs, a little embarrassed, as if he is trying to bluff his way into a safe of gemstones. —Hold on there, Craig Breedlove! There's plenty more house to see. There's the upstairs, and the pool. You ever think guys like us would end up with pools?

Excuse me, Mona says, and she gives you a dirty look as she walks toward the white foyer, vanishes into one of its illusion crevices. You panic; you feel still more alone with Tom, who is standing close enough for you to smell juniper and halitosis.

You know, you've never had me over to your place, B——, he tells you.

When are the other guys getting here, you ask quickly. —See the thing is, I've got these charts I've gotta fix up for the session people for tomorrow?

Tom's eyes immediately grow sad; his face, defying that sincerity, twists into a mock pout. —You're gonna clear out of my housewarming party? You can't take one lousy day just to hang out with your best friend? You wound me, sir.

See that's why I wanted to know when the other guys were getting here, you say. —So I can hang out with all of us for a little while before I've gotta split. Because I've got stuff to do for all of us, you know?

You find yourself talking faster and faster; sometimes Tom likes to fight back when you tell him how things will be, and if you talk faster he's more likely to give in early and let you do whatever you need to do to feel okay. But he doesn't look as if he's about to fight back: he looks, instead, at his wall-to-wall carpet.

I mean, if you've got to go instead of hanging out with me, he says.

Aw, c'mon, you begin.

No, it's cool, Tom says, and he looks up at you; he starts to grind his teeth a little, a gesture you recognize as prophylaxis against crying.

I'm really sorry, you say, suddenly really feeling it. —Uh, maybe we could stay for a little while. Sorry, I'm just tired. But we can stay a little while. That's okay, Tom.

Sure, he says, nodding very quickly. —A little while, sure, that's fine. Let's have a nice day, you, me. The women. Let's eat some food, let's catch up for a little while. Then you go home and relax, so you'll knock it out of the park at this session or whatever tomorrow. Like you always do.

You can feel his hand on your shoulder; resist the urge to flinch until he removes it. —Come on, I'll give you the grand tour. We'll see if we can't find the little lady. Place is so goshdarn big we can't find one another half the time.

En route to the little lady, you find Mona studying the grass skirt of one of the hula girls in the photo. Both of you fall into step behind Tom, fanning out like beta dogs in his wake while he leads you through the rooms. A quick stop in the disused den, a longer sojourn through the living room (complete, you now see, with fat cabinet TV, fully stocked bar, and more Hawaii photos, including a massive one over the fireplace of a smiling woman with a surfboard, her curves Technicolorized a supersaturated bronze.) In the kitchen he indicates, one by one, the places where his wife Barbara prepares different meals. The tour of the upstairs doesn't take quite as long, mostly because there's nothing in most of the bedrooms upstairs: bare carpet hooks, lonely windows gazing at asphalt.

Future expansion of the family, Tom chuckles. —Sure, it looks pretty fallow now, but in nine months, we're definitely gonna have need of this space. And nine months from then—look out! I figure it don't hurt none to be prepared in advance, you know, once we get the assembly line all up and running. —He turns to look at Mona. —You ever thought of having kids, B——?

I think I would hurt them, you say immediately.

You better get moving on that action, Tom says. —He who plants the apple seed in the springs shall enjoy the fruits of the fall.

Are you calling me fertile dirt? Mona asks.

Tom laughs. —I like this one, B——, he says. —Got a little bit of pepper in you, don't you, sugar? That's good. Seasoning.

You're a piece of human dog shit, Mona says.

Tom smiles and rubs his hands together. —But you can't deny I'm doing something right, he says.

Working for your cousin, yes, Mona says.

Tom's face loses its smile, and you look at a spot on the wall and try to find the spell that turns you invisible. Mona doesn't look to you to back her up; you have been together too long for her to expect that, and anyway she's the stronger one. Everyone must know that.

We're a team, Tom finally says.

THE LAST STOP ON THE tour is the master bedroom. The door is closed. When Tom tries to turn the knob, someone on the other side grabs it, holds it in place.

You can't come in here, Barbara's voice says.

We can't come *in* here? Tom repeats. —Oh my goodness, why not?

I'm changing, Tom, she says. —For the pool. Since B—— and Mona are over.

What're you changing *into*? Tom asks. —A *butterfly*?

A bathing suit, she says, sounding tired.

He rolls his eyes for your benefit. —It's going to rain today, sweetheart, he says.

B——, Mona, I really think you might like the pool, Barbara continues.

We didn't bring bathing suits, you say.

Exactly, Tom says. —They didn't bring bathing suits. Why don't you put your clothes back on and come down? We want to see your smiling face.

She is quiet for a while. —Sure, I'll be down, she says.

That's better, Tom says, again rolling his eyes.

THE POOL, ITS STILL SURFACE untroubled by wind or sunshine, stretches across the better part of the backyard, a bisecting stripe of tiles its only ornament, a wide navy ribbon of shining stone. The place is flanked by a small shed, a copse of trees with a probably ornamental birdhouse, a sundial, and a small set of patio furniture topped by an ashtray, its center scorched and flaking but otherwise clean. When she sees the ashtray, Mona dives in her purse for her pack.

Not much to see today without old Mister Sunshine up there, Tom says. —Kind of a little cabana over there for equipment. My little patch of woods back there, whole Thoreau thing. And the deck up here, for quiet conversation. Or *swimming*.

Swimming seemed like an okay idea, you say cautiously.

You don't have to make excuses for her, he grouses. —She's got no common sense most of the time. None of 'em do. Present company excepted, of course.

He turns to Mona magnanimously as he says this, then stops at the sight of the cigarette at her lips. —Smoking!

You can't have one, Mona says.

Now how did an angel like you pick up such a horrible habit, Tom says, crossing his arms. —Curdles all your workings.

Mona, uh, she can do what she wants, you mutter.

Don't tell me what I can do, Mona says. She sits down at the table, puffing.

Tom shakes his head at you. —It's your life, he says. —It's your decision. And hey—speaking of decisions—cocktails. What do you want? I'll fix up a little something for the four of us.

Vodka Manhattan, Mona says.

Do you happen to be twenty-one? Tom says.

No, but I know how to make the drink, she says. —So I'll make it for myself if you won't.

You can decide what drink I should have, you say to Tom.

Tom holds up his hands in mock surrender and saunters into the house.

Let's leave, Mona says.

We can't leave, you say. —He's bringing drinks.

She holds up the cigarette again. —Do you think, if I threw this at the right angle, that I could burn his house down?

Gee, I don't know so much about geometry, you say.

Let's find out, she says, cocking her arm back, but before she can let the cigarette go, Barbara Happy has joined you both on the deck, her lean movie-extra figure draped in a white bikini printed with bright teal stars, two tiny moles printed on her shoulders. Her eyes go to Mona's cigarette, hungrily.

Hi, I'm so sorry about before, she says, gliding over. —You must've been mortified.

Not so much, says Mona. Her eyes are fixed on Barbara's moles.

Barbara laughs uncertainly and crosses her arms. —Could I get just the tiniest drag of that? she asks.

Be my guest, Mona says, taking the filter end from her lips and presenting it to Barbara. You're curious; she seems to have forgotten the whole idea of burning Tom's house down. Barbara takes it, taps the place where Mona's spit and lipstick remain, and puts it in her mouth.

Thank you so much, she says. —What Tom doesn't know, right? —She winks at you. —Don't tell him, she says.

We'll both be good, Mona says, patting your hand.

Barbara smiles, thin ropes of smoke rolling out of her nostrils. —I'm glad Tom was finally able to get you over, B——, she says. —He's wanted to show our life off to you for so long. He really loves you. —She coughs a little on her smoke as she sees your face go stone. —Did I embarrass you? I'm sorry. I know men don't like to hear things like that.

Uh, no, it's fine, you say. —There's a lot of stuff boys like that I don't like, or uh, vice versa.

You feel a flush of courage somehow at having asserted this, and maybe Barbara sees that; anyway, she smiles.

It's strange we never saw much of each other in high school, she says. —You were in my grade, weren't you? Or Tom's?

It's possible, you say. —I forget that kind of stuff.

School is overrated, Mona says, rapping on the table once like a medium. —Could I see my cig a second?

Barbara turns to her, frowning; Mona reaches out and plucks

her cigarette from Barbara's mouth. —Tell me about you, she asks. —What's a basic day like for you?

Barbara frowns. —Tom'll be back out soon, she says. —Maybe we shouldn't be smoking.

I mean like, what do you do all day, Mona clarifies. —Walk me through it. I want to know what married life feels like to you.

Barbara sits back in her chair. —That's—a little presumptuous, she says, carefully laughing to dilute this. —I'm sure we're very different people.

I hope we are, says Mona; you flinch. —For example, I do all kinds of things. I write songs. For my band. We just had a show.

Much as a dog can be trained to shrink from a bell when the sound has been associated with pain, you recognize this as the point in the conversation when the person Mona's being nasty to sees an opportunity to be reciprocally nasty to her, and you want to hide under the table before the crosscurrents between them shred you. But instead, Barbara's eyes get wide.

That's *great*, she says. —I didn't know you had a band.

I do, Mona says, wary.

I'm really happy for you, Barbara says. —I used to act, you know. It might have been nice to continue doing that.

Her face gets sad, and she shifts in her chair. Mona, after a moment, offers her the cigarette again; she takes it and breathes in.

And then the patio door opens and Tom Happy comes through, four glasses docked in his arms. Barbara's sadness evaporates from her face, disappearing upward to seed the heavy clouds over the backyard. She gets up from her chair, stands on her toes, waves.

Hi, Tom! she calls.

The cigarette, though, is still between her fingers, and it's the first thing Tom sees, its trail of smoke circling his wife like a troubled plane. In long strides he's at the table, the drinks set neatly on its surface. His cheeks red, he grabs Barbara's waving wrist. Her smile gutters and blows out. His emerges when he turns to you.

Drinks on the table, *amigos* and *amigas*, he says. —Scuse us a minute, though.

He begins to march Barbara away from the house, across the yard. Mona gets up from the table and steps forward, as if she's going to follow them, but something makes her stop. She stands there, three feet away from the table, her hands tensed oddly at the end of her arms, hanging at her side. You stay in your chair and try to look only at Mona. You will her: *calm down. Please calm down. Please let's don't make a scene.*

Tom and Barbara stop by the edge of the water at the far side of the pool. Tom talks; Barbara stands stiff and listens. Her wrist is still in his hand, the cigarette stub still smoking, until he jerks her hand up, takes the cigarette, and shows it to her as if it's a pet's mess. Her eyes narrow; she puts her hands on her hips; she leans toward him. She is speaking furiously. He watches her a moment, and then he puts his wide, red hand on her chest, the place just below where her collarbone and neck meet, and applies pressure. The soles of her feet lose traction; her arms flail, and her eyes, even across the water, look scared to you, B——: primal fear, balance gone, and the certainty, prior to words, that when she hits, it will hurt. But she just falls, terrified and without control, into the still, cold water instead of splitting her chin or twisting her ankle on the stone, as he could just as easily have caused to happen. She surfaces, hair in her eyes and blowing water out of her nose, hyperventilating. He flicks the lit cigarette at her, aiming carefully so that it hits the water and goes out just a few inches before her face.

Bet you don't think it's warm enough for swimming now, he says, and he begins his meditative return across the yard to the house. Mona starts to move; you imagine her springing on velvet limbs over short-mowed grass, leaping to tear Tom Happy into tiny shreds. But she avoids him altogether, moves in short, stiff strides to the place where Barbara is working to get out of the water. You're about to follow her, but here Tom is, looking at you.

Could you come help me in the kitchen a minute, he asks, and you don't know how to say no.

IN THE KITCHEN, TOM GOES to the rack of drying dishes, inspects one, and transfers the whole rack one by one into the sink, which he fills with water and soap.

She never does these right either, he says. He scrubs at the plainly clean dishes, red auras of raw tension wafting from his pores and staining the white kitchen pink. You settle on a spot next to the kitchen island.

So your pool is really nice, you say.

He sighs. —Yeah, B——, it's great, he says.

Your fingers drum against the tile as you wait for the anger to drain from him; somehow, through your presence, you know it will. And eventually he sighs and tosses the washcloth into the sink.

You know, I don't want her smoking because I don't want that stuff killing her, he says. —When I see her with a cigarette, it's like I see her dead on the ground. Like my baby dead inside her.

That sounds bad, you say.

And that's why I made a rule about it, Tom says. —Cause I can't stand to see it. And when I see her just—just deliberately *ignoring* me, like I made that rule for no reason, I just—I see red.

Wow, you say.

He lets the dish slide slowly into the water, and then he braces his hands against the side of the sink, bearing down on the counter as if he's a magnificent palace and it must bear his weight. —It's just there's this whole way things oughta be, he begins. —From the caveman on up.

Sure yeah, you say. If you say anything to dispute him, this conversation will have to continue, and there will be more conversations like it. —I guess I can see what you mean.

He nods at the dishes as if he's divining the future in bubbles of soap. You shift against the kitchen island.

Uh, I'm going to go see if Mona's okay, you say.

Sure, says Tom. —Hey, tell her I don't blame her for what Barbara's done. I really like her. I don't want her to get the wrong idea about me. —He looks up at you. —Thanks for talking to me about this. You're a good friend, cousin.

Thanks for not being angry anymore, you say, carefully.

NO ONE'S ON THE PATIO when you go out there; a pair of wet, bare footprints trail from the pool to the door. All but one of the cocktail glasses is empty. You pick it up, sip it—a terrible vodka Manhattan with ingredients you don't recognize—and look around the yard for Mona as your heart rate slowly drops. The wind is picking up for a storm and blows your chestnut hair around. It blows the walls of the shed behind you, its door slightly loose and rattling. You turn to frown at it.

Mona? you call.

There's no answer. So you go to the door, drink clacking in your hand, and open it slowly. Mona is sitting inside on a long, rolled-up rug, the butts of two cigarettes crushed at her feet. She stares right at you.

You step inside the shed and close the door. The overcast sky is coming in through the cracks in the shed walls, holes where rivets used to be, and in the pale light Mona's arms are two long, cold blue stripes. She lights another cigarette for herself and comes into red focus. This close in, the smoke mixes with the two, three vodkas on her breath.

Is Barbara here also? you ask.

She waits. —I guess Barbara slapped me in the face when I asked her if she was all right, she finally says. —I guess she thought it was my fault she got in trouble.

You don't know what to say at first. —Tom said he doesn't think it was your fault, you finally explain.

She starts to cry. You walk closer, but she looks up at you, eyes open like the mouth of a panicked cat, ready to bite.

Don't sit next to me, she says. —Sit over there.

She points to a spot on the floor of the shed; hastily, you go to sit on it. Again you feel your heart rate rising; someone is angry with you and you are no longer safe here. But you stay where she bade you go, shivering, and she watches you.

I don't know what to do, she says finally, her voice strained. —I don't know where to go. I keep thinking he'll smell the smoke and come in here, and—

I thought he was going to hurt me too, you say.

She looks at you. —Why would he hurt you? she asks. And when you don't answer: —What'd you talk about with him in there?

You don't want to tell her. —He felt bad for what happened, kinda, you say.

Good for him, she says; her voice is speeding up. —Good for all of you.

Her cigarette tip is shaking. You want to say something so she will not worry so much, but you're too afraid to say anything; you make a kind of whimper echoing off your hard palate, like a cat beeping at birds.

There's nowhere I can run to, she is saying, —absolutely nowhere in the world I can run. You're everywhere. You're fifty percent of the population.

You keep uselessly praying to cry. —Hey, you manage.

Don't make me any *offers* again, she snaps. —You're the same as any of them, you know it? Think I haven't gotten offers? What if I just refuse all of them, die on my parents' couch stinking and reeking so my sister and whoever her husband turns out to be have to pack me in a garbage can and roll me off a hill into the sea to get rid of me—

You reach out, B——, forgetting yourself; she smashes her

cigarette down on the floor of the shed in front of you. You sit on your hands.

You're exactly the *same*, she says. —You're a *man*; you're going to *hurt* me like a man. You already *have*. You can't *help it*.

You close your eyes, listening to the word sizzling in the front of your brain like a branding iron. And something about the inner contortions of a conch shell, B——, replicates the sound of the sea, as if some divine husbandry, a million pascals of pressure, has crushed the entire ocean to fit without cracking into a tiny, gleaming space that shines pink rainbows and pearls. That's what I think your voice sounds like as you say what you say to her: —M-maybe that isn't true. Exactly.

What do you mean, exactly, she asks, voice flat.

And now you can cry, and you do. You sit on the floor of the shed, and you let the ocean run out of your eyes, and you can do this because you have committed the ultimate unpardonable sin— you've told the truth where people can hear you—and they've heard you, Diane. And suddenly everything hurts a lot more, feels a lot more: the air in the shed, the smoke in your nose, the salt on your cheeks, the water massing in the sky. *Oh my. Oh gosh. Oh gee.*

Mona is watching you cry. She is looking down at you, perched smoking and thinking on her rolled up rug. Slowly, your tears stop; you wipe them away, you leave the fouled hand on the cement foundation.

Hey, she begins, and you look up. Her eyes are on you again like animals' mouths, but now the bite is a testing one, seeing how far in the teeth can push before they hurt. And you wonder just how far she understood the truth you told; just how far she heard it, specifically, at all. You wonder why she looks so tired, looking at you.

Outside, the overcast sky has erupted at last with black malignance, fat impacted celestial swirls. The wind is smashing through the trees, wrenching branches aside in cracks; the wind chimes scream; the sundial has gone out. The pool seethes, flat gusts moving like tectonic apocalypse over the surface. Then, one by one, the drops begin to fall; splashes like charges exploding from deep within the chlorine. A drop falls on you, bullseye, through your loose rivet in the ceiling. You are breathing like a girl. You have always breathed like a girl. You try to conceal this so she won't notice, so you'll be safe, but suddenly you don't want to be safe: or it doesn't matter whether you are, because something else matters more than safety.

Keep breathing like a girl in the dark—keep watching as Mona's mouth opens, preparing to ask you a question—keep watching her fingers flex, open, shut, forming a fist, then not. She looks very tired; you wonder why. And outside the place where Mona smokes, an ocean is building: waves of raindrops that break against the metal that surrounds you, Diane, Diane.

Love, Gala

# November 1, 2009

Dear Diane,

So much magic old footage of you still endures online, a spiritual stalker's dream. Sometimes Caroline and I watched it together: early concert footage and awkward local interviews where Eddie, Tom, and Adam stammer while they try not to look into the interviewer's cleavage, bizarre lip-synch setpieces—five of you posed in striped shirts, five of you posed in convertible cars, big hamburgers on trays attached to your windows, slender bikini waitresses on car-hop gravity skates blinking anxiously at the key light as they glide all Bubsy Berkeley in the background, guitars echoing out of the studio monitors. You watch it all, presumed prince surveying your subjects.

To hear a lot of people tell it—to hear me tell it, I worry—you seem avoidant, ingrown, vanishing. But on the tapes, where you're present, something else is happening. It projects from you like a force field, touching all the people in the tiny YouTube frame with you. Tom Happy in 1964, clean-cut and pumping his foot as he sings your songs to a crowd, looks back at you every four measures, smiles: do you see him? And do you think he's good? You look ahead and keep playing your bass; sometimes you remember to smile, something your father instructed you to do, a way you and your customers can build rapport.

You have more power than you believe, Diane; your inability to understand that doesn't make people less subject to it.

CAROLINE WORKED AT MY TRAILER, editing sound and curating clips from each day's backlog of raw footage, posting and feeding videos out to social media drops, liking and sharing the work of people she knew according to karmic principles of threefold return. She answered fan mail, too, *really* answered it with long letters that asked a lot of counter-questions, except in the case of obvious creeps like the guy who tracked her location based on the upload time of each video and different stuff in the backgrounds, and who kept sending emails saying he was coincidentally going to be in the same town as her next stop, or he could be, and they should have a real meeting of the minds finally. She didn't respond all the time—just sometimes, as one might train a rat in a Skinner box—but when she did, it was by hand, in her handwriting built from big swimming blobs with stub ascenders and descenders, curlicue serifs, a vacuole to accommodate any reader. (Let's not discuss my own trans girl handwriting, which you have by now experienced plenty of.) She wrote her letters and then she walked out, jacket zipped against fall winds, to the post office just before the highway access to mail them. To mail a letter you write someone: imagine that.

It was abstract to me that she had fans, that anyone I actually knew might be worthy of fans: that it was possible to give out love, to get it back. What does it feel like to have faith that your actions are worth doing?

PERHAPS YOU ARE WONDERING ABOUT the secrets of what *a trans woman and a cis woman do in bed*. A fair question, given your own mysterious circumstances! Here is how I will try to answer you. Before, my memories of sex mostly involved not wanting to exist during it: to be a presence, a little hot circle of disembodied light that moved over my interlocutor, giving something without wanting to get. If the other person wanted to give, I would let them do or have whatever they wanted: because sex is not about wanting, it is about something else. It is about wanting to be seen, in conditions where, because of my body, it was not possible to be seen. So we hid in spaces, me and my partners, where dysphoria smoked into every corner of the room like incense in cathedral corners long after a ritual has stopped.

I think it is still essentially like this, except I don't let the other person do whatever they want anymore. This is because a hand on my shoulder will make all of me reorient to that touch. Because there is hope, and I'm bashful in the face of hope. All of this is still very theoretical, something I am working out when we touch, sometimes, which we do less and less: and it was a relief, Diane, when I grew familiar enough to her to grow uninteresting, when she stopped asking me for that.

WE TALKED — ONE DAY LYING ON my sweating bed after the incident at the spaceport, a rare time she stayed with me rather than in the dorm, air thick with palo santo from the crystal shop and double estrogen sweat—about exactly how we would manage the sale of my trailer and everything in it that I'd built, when we went north to find Mona Slinks, and you somewhere beyond her.

I mean, we're gonna need money, aren't we? she asked. —As soon as we figure out the right direction to go in. Or earlier, you know. There's nothing holding us back here.

There's my friends, I said.

She laughed. —Ronda's not your friend, she said. —You don't even like her.

I didn't look at her. —It's just—suppose we like, hang out here for a year, I said. —Save up some money, keep soaking and researching. Really get it right. Then we could even buy a truck or something, you know? Outfit it with a hitch, maybe, so we could take the whole trailer up with us. We could live in it, you know, when times get bad.

She made a face. —I don't want to carry a trailer with me for the rest of my life, she said. —We could sell it now and get a car. One can totally live in a car.

*You* could live in a car, I said to her. —Or you could take the bus. She looked back at me. —*We* could take the bus, she said. —What am I going to say to B——, Diane, whatever, without you?

I'm glad you value me as a translator, I said.

Look, did I actually do something wrong? she asked.

I put my head down again. —I feel pressure from you, I said.

What pressure? she asked.

To live in a car, I pleaded. —Or, I don't know. To run off on this adventure, and to translate for your family, and to form a band with you? And maybe right this second, maybe that isn't what I need? Maybe I need to keep hold of what I have? Maybe you don't understand why I'd need that?

No, I don't, she said, and I looked up. Her eyes were level; all feeling was suddenly gone. —I also didn't say we should start a band.

I guess I made that up, I said.

It's a *great* idea, she said.

*No, I know it is*, I agreed.

We looked at one another, and I knew we were deciding what instruments each of us might play.

LATER, AFTER FIGHTING AGAIN, APOLOGIZING again, working it out between us again, Caroline lay down beside me, set her hand on my back. She petted my back like you'd pet a dog whom the thunder has startled: slowly unknotting it, whether I wanted that or not. What did I want?

As she touched my back, she whispered to me: *I've let things go too, it's okay, I've let things go too.* It made me furious, furious even as I lay there too relaxed to move. As if I haven't. As if I have no idea what comes of throwing everything you know on the gravel lawns, turning out all your lights, locking the door on your life. As if nothing might have been worth keeping.

THIS IS HOW WE LIVED — CAROLINE at work watching Mona Slinks's profile while she arranged her footage—desert skies, aisles of endless meats for grilling and broiling, gleaming incomplete towers of spaceports, my face, awkward and winking into the lens. She stitched it into weird trash mosaics, let the online tide flow out, let it bring love back in kelp garlands that she threw around her shoulders.

And I worked too: I swept up; I ran reservations; I washed and distributed towels; I prayed. And I soaked in a private bath on the clock watching the unanimous Rio Grande, my spine steeping in heat like a noodle losing its semolina brittleness, becoming supple, digestible. It was on one of those days, praying to become digestible, that I realized I no longer wanted to find you, Diane. I no longer wanted a vector for escape. What I wanted was for you somehow to find me and Caroline, here, to join us, here, in the still and quiet and safe place I had found: what I wanted was for none of this to stop.

Love, Gala

# November 2, 2009

Dear Diane,

In the studio—a day in 1965, shortly after your engagement to Mona Slinks—your family sings the melodies you assign them. (The band has remained stably a family act, save for the guitarist Charley Brushfire, a tractable bluegrass player and neighbor whom you poached from his band following an early gig, and your handpicked session musicians, Midnight Automotive, whom you can count on to perform when your brothers and cousin do not.) They flat, they miss takes, they lapse into laughter; you push, nudge, argue, cajole, sometimes just sing louder than them, your falsetto soaring above and around theirs like a hawk circling prey in slow flight. Yet slowly, wordlessly, they get better, syllables melting like fudge over the cold, carved scoop of mono production you and Midnight Automotive have put to tape, their voices, ungrounded by Tom's nasal bass, fluttering from track to track, spreading their wings in color sunburst at the peak of ascending strings, a staccato series of *ahhhhs* that ride a wave of cushioning harmonica foam, moaning midrange ecstasies as honor guard for the drums and guitars trading off as they move down in fifths to the outro of track eight. You're proud of yourself, bringing this thing through: you find yourself even believing a little in what you're doing.

It's in this elated state that you turn around at the conclusion of a take to see Tom Happy walking into the booth, your father's arm around his shoulder, the whites of your father's eyes alive on either side of his insane blue irises. It has been months, you realize, since you've encountered your father as anything but a voice on the phone: in that time, it's as if the armies of his flesh have retreated, his skin hanging looser than it had like an unprotected border. You haven't previously conceived of your father as *old*. You also haven't told him at any point over the past year that he's been fired.

Tom, you say, as your cousin leaves your father in the booth and approaches the microphones. —Glad you could make it. Why'd you bring my dad to a recording session?

He swallows. —He *is* our manager, he says. And, uh, he *was* waiting for me in the parking lot. He said you'd invited him but he'd lost his key. —He swallows. —I'm guessing now that this wasn't true.

Your dad has turned the PA volume up to Angel-of-Gomorrah levels. —All right. Test, one, two. Get Happies Recording Session. Let's go. Let's get this going. Break up that conversation. We're making an album here.

Trying to smile—trying to cheer you up, you realize—Tom takes out the lyrics and hands them to you. —On the brighter side, I got 'em all done after we talked the other day, he says.

You page through the lyrics—mostly about women, all written in Tom's awful knifelike handwriting—while your father's voice crackles and the image of cigarettes floating like longboats around Barbara's face swims in your blurry eyes. Then you think of Lana on the bed, clouds of green smoke around her, telling you how much she wants you to love Harry Corot. You imagine Tom's lyrics playing in her room, singing to her through you and your family's voices.

Eddie, shouts your dad. —Your shirt. It's not the best shirt, or in the best condition. But even the homeliest shirt, son, can look good if the person wearing it wears it well. And that isn't you right now, son.

Excuse me, you say, and you hand the lyrics back to Tom, without your verdict.

Your father has locked the door of the recording booth against you. Swallowing, you knock; the engineer opens the door, and you enter. Your dad is sitting at your console, head propped in his hands like a weary Kriegspiel player, eyes on the four Get Happies remaining around the mic.

Players aren't supposed to come up to the booth during a session, B——, he says. —Sergio, don't open the door for him next time.

Uh, Dad, so this is a session I'm kind of producing, you say. —Maybe you didn't realize that; I should have like, communicated better about that. And that's why you're sitting in my chair and all.

Your dad ignores you. He looks down at the controls; he moves one slider all the way up, taps his finger on it as if considering; he moves it back down to where it started.

What do you think about moving chairs, Dad, you say, trying to sound like a mean robot who can't be contradicted.

B——, what I need from you right now is for you to get ready to sing your part, your dad says. —You're too old to interfere with a session like this.

See, interfering, it kind of means getting in the middle of something that you're not supposed to be in the middle of, you say.

He sighs, rattlesnake-drumming his fingers on the board. —Let's just get through this together, buddy, without making this all about whatever feelings you've got today, he says, speaking slowly. —What do you say?

What songs are we recording? you ask. —At this session. What songs of mine are we planning to record? I'm just curious. What are the names of the songs?

B——, he says.

What songs did I write, you demand; your voice cracks.

He turns in his chair—no, *your* chair—and he looks up at you. His eyes are weary, patient, suffering things, as if he's a fire in a cloud, and to unburden the full splendor of his mind to you could only destroy you.

Instead, he speaks: —I can leave right now, if you want me to, B——.

I don't *want* you to, you reply quickly.

I want him to, mutters the engineer.

You shoot the engineer a look: *leave my dad alone.* And then you turn back. —Dad, I'm sorry. Come on. You can stay, but we really need to work today, okay?

Your dad looks down, deflates somehow. It makes you feel tender.

You're a good worker, B——, he says. —And I recognize top gear stuff when I hear it. You forget that. It's from me that you get a lot of your best commercial instincts.

He closes his mouth, moved to momentary silence; you let him, folding your arms. You are being very mature, a very good son. You fired him, you remind yourself, even if he doesn't know it. The thought helps you keep yourself from punching him.

What I'm concerned with, B——, is a thing you might not be as facile with, your dad says. —I mean the human heart, B——.

You think my heart's busted or something? you ask sharply.

He raises his hands. —There's no need to speak with anger in your voice, he says. —We're not enemies. We're not fighting.

You lean against the back wall. —Sorry for speaking with anger in my voice, you say.

He looks at you, cracking his knuckles over the board. —No one denies you've got talent, son, he begins. —But I built this band, together with all you boys. Let's go back to the beginning. That's all I'm trying to do. No more big business dealings with the likes of Harry Corot. No more hot shot egos. Just you boys bringing the product, and me handling the business. We could start our own record label. Why not? Any business I touch, it's just hard work. One day Harry Corot—he'll be working for *me*, B——.

You need to keep your back against the wall, and you need to not cry, and you need to not hurt him. You need to stay very still, focus on the pity for him you feel, keep all emotion from your face. This interaction will be done soon.

It'll be like passing GO again, your father continues. —A fresh start. —He keeps staring into your eyes, hesitantly, like a nervous cat: like he's convinced you're going to hurt him, but he needs you to reach out anyway so that he can safely hurt you first. No, this is unfair. No, anything you think about this person is unfair. No, the room is not spinning, fading white.

Let's go on break, Dad, you say. —A quick little ten minute break so everyone can cool down. Then you can help us record, okay?

Your dad looks at you, eyes blank.

I believe that Harry Corot is a homosexual, B——, he says. —Keep away from him. He may attempt to offer you drugs to buy your affections. You need to protect yourself. Do you understand me?

Call the break, Dad, you say.

He glowers, then touches the PA. —Everyone, B——'s called for an eight-minute break, he says. Report back to work in exactly eight minutes. Seven forty five, now. We've wasted enough time today already. —He takes his finger off the PA button; he twitches.

Cool, you say, faintly. —I'm going to go out and get some air.

He eyes the hair at your collar with naked suspicion.

One day you're going to realize who was really looking out for you, B——, he says.

IN THE STUDIO'S EXECUTIVE BATHROOM, on the men's side, you roll a joint using the drugs that Harry Corot has, as prophesized, provided for you. You sit on the edge of the tall trash can and stare ahead at the sinks, the soaps, the mirror. This is how your brother Eddie finds you.

B——? he asks. —Are you okay? Wait—holy cow, are you smoking dope in here? Can I have some?

We'll share, you say, and you pass your little brother the joint. He sucks on it, coughs, smiles, is loath to give it back to you until you proactively hold your hand out to receive it.

What was Dad even saying to you in there? Eddie asks, hoarse, half dancing from side to side like a crab. —We were all trying to figure it out. He's not pissed at me about anything, is he?

No, you say. —Just me. He thinks our A&R man is a homosexual, I guess.

Eddie giggles at this word. —For serious? he asks. —I mean, uh, I haven't talked to the guy a lot, but don't fags tend to look a lot more fruity? Like little mustaches and ball gowns and stuff.

You stare at yourself in the mirror. —I guess they look all kinds of ways, you say.

Did you tell Dad to beat it? Eddie asks. —Cause I kinda want to take off early today, but if you're letting him be in charge of sessions again, I'm not gonna be able to do that, and so maybe I'm gonna have to take off now, you know. So did you tell him?

Tell him what, you ask, closing your eyes.

That he had to go, Eddie says. —Or did you tell him he could *stay*?

Oh, yeah, he can stay, you say. —For today, or a week or so, until he gets bored of it. He probably will. He has to.

Eddie stomps his foot against the speckled tile. —A whole *week*? he asks.

He isn't hurting anyone, you say. —I mean, he means well.

That's all he *does* is hurt people, Eddie says; as soon as he says it, he giggles, and you open your mouth on reflex to laugh too, but just croak. —He's sure saying some evil shit to *you*, Eddie says.

You open your eyes. —He means well, you say, the person in the mirror says. You are somewhere outside yourself as you watch your reflection say it, old and hairy and evil. —He isn't hurting anyone.

And this reflection, B——, Diane, he, she, is so cowardly, so miserable and cowardly and craven and false and ugly and vile, and the sludge in your veins is heating up, turning the backside of your skin to bubbles and pustules and char, and it's so hot that now it has to go somewhere else outside of your skin or it will kill you, and so you stand up, you walk forward, you punch your reflection as hard as you can right in her, his, ugly face, and the mirror shatters but it doesn't shatter *enough* the damage isn't *enough* and so you punch it again more gingerly this time because your knuckles are suddenly spotlit in massive halogen pain, and you can still see your reflection, so you grind your hand around splintering even more glass shards into your skin, spreading blood on the silver, and your hand hurts but it doesn't hurt *enough* and sure you are humiliating yourself but that just gives you the anger and the strength to turn and slam your already broken finger into the opposite wall and now the pain is hotter than halogen, so bright it blinds you to what damage you're even doing, good, opportunity knocks, starlight twinkles in your nerves, and there is blood on the wall, your contaminated blood, and it's red over the white wall because the sludge is still deeper beneath you, *what is inside must come outside*, and you wish you could paint all the walls of this bathroom, every bathroom in poison blood, and if your hand isn't broken already you will break it; you raise it, glittering and studded with red mirror dust, and every part of you raises your hand back to break as many bones as you can against the wall, and then your stupid little brother *fucks up everything* by tackling you to the ground and sitting on your chest and holding your hands against the tile.

Let me go, you command, struggling.

Eddie grabs the joint, forces it between your lips, struggles to hold both your arms down with one hand while working the lighter with the other. At last he succeeds; the back of your throat scorches blue and you go limp on the floor of the bathroom, your arms at your side, your little brother's hand steadying the joint just above your lips.

After some time, you manage to reach out and take stewardship of the joint yourself. He goes to roll another one, flexing his fingers. You try to flex yours, but the pain is awful.

Gee, I think I busted my hand, you say.

Can you move your fingers, Eddie asks; he sounds suddenly afraid. The pain of having made your little brother afraid of you registers somewhere in you, a siren passing on a parallel block.

Hurts too much, you say.

He's quiet then, and you continue to smoke the joint, feeling your hand throb, enjoying the endorphins as if they're some kind of self-harm runner's high, a reward. No one has really ever seen you hurt yourself before, not Mona or any other members of your family or anyone, and you're not sure what the protocol is for this kind of thing. What do you talk about? What is appropriate to put into words, and what is better to leave in treasured, ornate silence? If only it were someone other than Eddie this had happened with—someone outside the family, someone to whom emotions are not also foreign coin.

I fired him, you tell your little brother. —I fired him and I didn't even tell him.

Eddie laughs, but he doesn't say anything. And after a while you start to worry that the mirror pieces stuck in your flesh are giving you an infection, and you turn to wash your hands. Relieved, Eddie starts dancing with his shadow.

ON THE WAY DOWN THE hallway back to the recording session, you suddenly feel an intrusive thought, a question: *should I marry Mona?* You only understand one of the words in that sentence now, and that word only halfway as yet.

She asked you, once, shortly after the incident at Tom's house. You didn't understand why; you still don't; she sounded resigned, and do you want to marry someone who feels resigned? And yet she insisted: *I really do like you. You're a truly weird person. If I wanted to get married to anyone, it'd be to you. Do you understand that?* You didn't: why would she tell you she doesn't want to marry you even as she asks you to do it?

But suddenly you think you do understand—that there is something she's more afraid of than you—and now you find yourself scared for her. You never want her to be in this place you just found yourself. Somehow, you want to put yourself between her and this place. And for a moment, you feel your foot brushing something solid in the deep: the floor of the ocean, a passing being, its blood still hot.

WHEN YOU AND EDDIE GET back to the session, your dad is making your littlest brother Adam sing scales.

You're consistently flatting your fourths and sixths, he's saying as you walk onto the floor. —Adam. You're a much better musician than this. I know that. Is there some guilt in your heart, son? Something you feel bad about that's making you want to sabotage your own brother's song this way?

I can't think of anything, Adam says, blinking fast as he stands next to the mic, holding one wrist tightly in his hand behind his back.

Dad, you call out, waving your mangled hand so he can see it. You hear Tom suck in a gasp; Eddie laughs. —Break's over. I'm back. We're doing track one now.

Nice of you to join us, B——, your dad says. —You'll notice I got the guys all warmed up for you. Eddie, I'm docking you a quarter hour's pay for being back to the session late.

But B—— was also, Eddie begins, and then he glances at your hand; his mouth shuts.

Tom, do you have the words? you ask.

He does, and you take the lyric sheet with your bad hand. Everyone stares as you move your fingers down the stanzas, humming it. You are acting like a baby, you tell yourself. You need to stop. You don't.

We're going to do the same parts, you say. —Tom, you lead. Rest of us come in under you or over you as needed. Let's try it. One, two and—

The producer counts off, your dad says. —Not the performer.

Your hand throbs. —Start singing, you command your brothers.

They follow your lead, and the voices blend perfectly the first time, rain sweet notes down over Tom's words. You feel stupid, and you sing louder and sweeter to make this less the case.

Great, you say when the voices stop. —Really nice. Tom, way to pick up with everyone. Dad, could you play it back for me?

I didn't bother turning the tape on, your dad says wearily. —Let's get something straight between us, B——.

Why didn't you record it, you shout.

Everyone gets silent, except your dad, who moves closer to the mic, unhooking his jaw to swallow it.

B——, he asks. —Are you going to act your age? Because this session's over right now, if you don't. If you're going to be a child who's out of control. You're on drugs, B——. I'm in control here. And the sooner you start listening to someone who's in control, the better things are going to be for everyone.

o   o   o

AND MAYBE IT IS THE pain in your hand, the beginnings of
fevers or blood infections, or maybe it is the drugs or maybe it
is that being a woman makes you gay, or straight, or maybe it's
that Mona Slinks asked you to marry her. You don't know what
it is. But right now, as your dad looks down on you with eyes like
poison pools spawning evil life, as you look up at him, you can
feel it: the sun is boiling away all the waves of water crashing in
your stomach, revealing a message someone scratched in sand:
YOUR LIFE HAS VALUE. YOUR LIFE IS WORTH HURTING
SOMEONE VERY BADLY FOR. Dug deep into the sand, six-
foot letters that you hope—I hope—the tide won't erase. And the
whole point of telling you this long and boring story, Diane, is to
remind you of this sentence, to scratch it into your brain again
and again, whatever damage that might cause.

And I wish I could just say that sentence and we'd be done
with all this, but everything else has to be here to convince you to
maybe take it seriously. So I'm sorry for existing. But I'll tell you
this much: You look at your father, Diane, and you know that you will
beat him. He's beaten already.

DAD, YOU SAY, AND YOU step up to the glass of the booth
and press your bloody hand to it. —It's time to turn on the tape and
record.

He raises his eyebrow at your hand distastefully; it's a mess; it's
just the kind of mess you'd make. —A little bit of humility from
you, B——, he says, just a *tiny* pinch to offset that *massive* ego—

Turn on the tape, you say. —We're in a recording session.
You're the one with the ego. You're the *child*. Do it. Turn on the
tape so we can record.

Slowly he rises from the chair.

B——, he says, —you think you can turn like this on the guy

who's done nothing but sacrifice for you, given you *everything you are*—

I fired you, you say.

And then your hand moves down the glass, raising screams as the mirror shards cut in and break molecule bonds in its surface; you open your mouth, Diane, and your voice harmonizes with the screaming. You scream new scales, new semitones prior to music, the ground of music, and when your hand reaches the bottom of its arc you move it back up to the top and start screaming again.

Your dad screams too. He screams until his face is purple and his throat is raw and his veins are pulsing and his eyes are bloodshot and wild, his face pressed to the soundproof glass so he can hear you but you can not hear him, his lips opening and shutting like a bottom-feeder cast up on the sand by victorious waves. Eye to eye you scream with the glass between you absorbing your breath. He will have a heart attack. You are killing him. You should stop, you're a child, you should stop. But you don't stop because something evil is loose in you. So you keep screaming, drag your destroyed knife hand over your father's face; you scream, Diane, you sing.

When his breath has long since given out and you feel that yours may be getting close to it, you slow your voice down and you turn and you run into the hall. Your foot slips on the linoleum and you come down, hard, and you can't get up again. Instead you huddle by the water fountain, feeling the warmth come through the motors that the company you worked for paid to install just here, for this moment, for you.

AFTER A WHILE, THE ENGINEER emerges with your father in tow. Your father has been crying. He looks down at you, sitting on the floor in the hall, bloodstains on your slacks and your fingers crushed and broken. He's still breathing heavily.

I'm leaving, he says, if you can't be mature.

You nod. —Okay, you say.

You boys won't have the benefit of my help any longer, he says. —You've ruined that. It hurts me to see you ruin it like that; you have no idea.

I'm sorry, you say.

One day, you'll need me, he says. —You'll need me, and I won't be there. You can't keep this up forever, B——. You don't have what it takes.

I'm sorry, you say again.

One day, buddy, you're gonna fail, he says.

He straightens his tie, and then he's gone. *I'm sorry,* you scream to the hallway when you're sure he's in the parking lot, but your voice is too raw for it to carry much.

WHEN YOU WALK BACK IN the room, everyone applauds. Adam is clapping too, even him. Even your baby brother betrayed your dad in the end. It makes you sick to hear.

Knock it off, you say. —We've got like—like two and a half days now. Come on. Track one.

The track starts; your brothers and cousins and Charley sing; you close your eyes.

And slowly—as your voices go into the wires, onto the master, onto the record and into a million teenage ears—you realize, wondering, that it's a good song. And slowly you feel the pain of waking up, the reverse hangover in your mind. *You've wasted so much time. He's made you waste so much time.*

You sing loud enough to drown out these thoughts; you sing and the dots of your voice, each of your family's voices, assemble into a new constellation, starlight figures reflecting in every LA pool, shining up at you as you watch from the edge with equal parts horror, vertigo, euphoria: there is now no one in your path but you. And you are the one who hangs the stars, Diane. You decide where they'll go.

Love, Gala

# PART FOUR

10

THE GET
HAPPIES
PRESENT:

## SPACE·GIRLS

# November 3, 2009

Dear Diane,

There is no point in waiting to get married, Mona decides, and neither of you want your families around when you do it. So on the appointed morning you rise from the comforter on the carpet and look at yourself in the mirror. Your incipient gut spills over the hem of your briefs; your hair is lank against your forehead; blue nightshade veins bloom beneath the outermost layer of your vermicelli skin. It's your wedding day. Did Tom feel like this on his wedding day? Is there something wrong with you?

You put on a pair of pinstripe slacks that belonged to a suit, slick your hair back (wincing as the Wildroot Cream-Oil leaches into the mirror-glass scars on your fingers), throw some identical shirts and jeans into a duffel bag, and call around to the Slinks house. Mona, in brilliant red with a forest green ribbon unevenly holding back her hair, slips out the front door and hustles to the car, keeping her head down.

Let's move our asses, she hisses.

SO YOU CRUISE UP I-10 to the municipal ziggurat where you'll meet Harry Corot's elopement guy, your fiancée you guess's right hand smoking and her left holding on her ribbon against the convertible wind. You merge in and out of traffic, the radio playing static but both of you unwilling for the moment to change it. Ashes strike your windshield and the sucking Doppler sound of the city traffic passing surrounds your ears. For a moment you pretend that you're an alien, someone to whom what you're doing seems promising, seems new.

You, uh, look real nice, you say.

Thanks, she says, and she lets her cigarette filter flick out the back.

You keep driving.

Take this exit here, she suddenly says. —Stop the car.

You comply immediately, gliding across two lanes of traffic to do so, spiraling around the off-ramp to come to rest against the curb at the foot of a high cemetery hill. You breathe, she breathes, the engine hums.

Behind the cemetery fence, sedans circle, and mourners stop to visit different gravestones. After a moment, a car tools by on the access road. It's stuffed with spectral teenage arms that grope from the windows, one of your songs blaring from its booming treble radio as it jeers and honks away. Mona's cigarette case is on her lap. She turns to look away from you out the window and toward the highway that shadows the necropolis.

Is there something we need to do in the cemetery, you ask.

She laughs. —One day, there's something we'll all need to do in the cemetery, she says. She keeps laughing for a while, and you smile, hoping you'll find it in yourself to join her, but you don't, and eventually she grows quiet.

Let's go home, she says. —Just let's forget this whole thing.

You look at the dash controls, the cars circling the cemetery hill just over your left shoulder.

Sure, okay, you say.

She takes in a huge breath—fills her lungs—and lets it out as she sits up, like a balloon inflating in reverse, like the less air she has, the stronger she somehow becomes.

No, I was being weak, she says. —Just kidding. Let's go get married.

SO YOU CONTINUE TO THE great ziggurat of City Hall. It takes about an hour, in and out, with time to find parking. You stand beside her and you watch a judge certify the decision you have both made. The judge calls her *this woman* and you *this man*. Mona doesn't look at you while he's speaking—she thinks separate things—and you both close your eyes when you kiss. Marriage has happened to you.

YOU'VE GOT RESERVATIONS AND A check-in time to make that evening in Lake Arrowhead, so you've got to get on the road out of town, barring a quick wrong-way stop at your connection's place in Venice for honeymoon supplies. Then, not speaking to this woman who is now your wife, you drive, and the county slowly lapses into desert and beyond it the wide, scratchy valley. You've been outside the county before—furious tours promoting early singles chauffeured by your dad while Eddie punches Tom, Adam closes his eyes in proto-Zen isolation, Charley Brushfire reads a guidebook with an ice pack pressed to his forehead. But this is different: this time you're alone, or anyway with Mona, who is okay with a total silence between you that is close to alone. (Advantages: with her along, you can't turn the wheel and enter the desert, the car's hoverstripes smashing against burning rocks, fuselage tearing as the car loses altitude, life bleeding out in one last futile scream. *Happy honeymoon.*) Now you've chosen it: the Joshua trees shifting in the wind like crucified bandits, killing fields of fat black cows in long white rows whose meat-stink smears against the windows like physical grease spattering, distant vistas stippled with king snakes and scorpions, slowly rising in the distance the great purple mountains that your grandfather crossed long ago to find the treasure that was his manifest destiny: and here you are, Diane, returning with it. Here even the lakes of spilled gasoline have rainbows in them when you stop to fill up; here even the convenience store where you buy a bag of pork rinds is playing your song through its frayed PA.

Back in the car, chewing your pork rinds, Mona looks out the window.

Mrs. B—— of the Get Happies, she says. —Tax papers and things will come to the place where we'll live, looking for someone named that.

Uh, sorry, you say.

She holds up a calendar with a picture of a pin-up girl in a flour sack bikini who's just burned her butt cadmium red on a Franklin stove. —I stole this from the convenience store, she says. —I want it to be our first decoration.

Gosh, definitely, you say, pleased, suddenly, that she's pleased. —We'd be liars if it wasn't.

Total liars, she agrees.


WHAT IS THE MEANING OF marriage, Diane? It occurs to you to ask yourself as you float east with your wife, the rite of marriage now complete. To your father: a key gate of achievement through which one must pass. To Lana Corot: a place to hide. To Tom: an adornment, a source of labor. To Mona: harm reduction. To your mother: it has never occurred to you to ask. To yourself?


IF ANYONE ACTUALLY LIVES IN Lake Arrowhead, Diane, they're unknown to you, their homes occluded by resorts, restaurants, tour companies, convention halls. The place you've booked is wide and Tudorish and jammed right up to the edge of the lake, its lobby filled with fresh flowers brought in by truck from a neighboring biome. The room they give you is huge, gold leaf set off by thick timber rafters and paintings of Colonial leaders enduring privations. The cavernous wardrobe and dressers easily swallow Mona's tiny duffel and your Old Touring Pro-efficient garment bag, which is stuffed mostly with identical crumpled T-shirts and jeans. The bed will easily dwarf you too; you try not to look at it. Instead you each split up to check out one of the escape routes: Mona goes into the bathroom to the west while you walk north to the patio.

A private staircase, thick black railroad ties set down like piano keys against the white sand, descends past into the needles of imported conifers, a winding two-lane road and a few rocky feet of lake beach. The lake shines dull as a quarter in the California sun, and you elbow up to the railing a while to watch it. Voices murmur from somewhere beneath you; a senior housekeeper scolds a junior; two red sails move over the silver surface of the water, tacking and jibing in tandem as the wind requires. It's nothing like the beaches you know, thick with burger smoke, suntan oil, teenage sand sex. This is a more exclusive kind of escape. The lake is far enough away that you can't see your reflection in the surface.

Oh my God, Mona cries. —You have to see this. It's obscene.

You hurry to the bathroom to find her contemplating the vast wedding cake of porcelain rising from the tile: a deco-iced toilet, sink, shower, bidet. Most in-room hot tubs would tend, you guess, to be set into the ground; this one rises in layers, a cream-cheese staircase allowing access to the top, where Jacuzzi jets bubble. You're only barely tall enough to see over the edge to the sculpted steps within; Mona, being way too short, has already climbed them and sits on the edge with her legs slung over the side like a beaming pirate queen showing off a prize.

Can we never leave this tub, she asks. —Please. Can we fill it up and lock the room door and forget our old lives and learn to breathe water. Look at it. It has bubble jets.

Gee okay, you say. —Maybe we could order some dinner first in the town.

No, we're ordering room service, Mona says. —In the tub. Where we live now.

I'm not sure this hotel has room service, you say.

Then *you* can go and feed your *body*, she says. —While *I* will stay and feed my *soul*.

Saying this, she begins to unbutton the red dress. You flush, turn the sink quickly on and off, turn to go.

Uh, I'll give you some privacy, you mumble.

From behind, a cleared throat. —B——.

You turn. Her dress is half unbuttoned, hangs open in a V beneath her throat that she doesn't try to disguise, shows the lace-less edge of her peaches-and-cream bra. She has a strange look in her eyes, like she's tending to an extraterrestrial puppy.

We're married, she explains. —You don't have to go in the other room.

I mean if you're cool with that, you say.

She rotates into profile. —I'm very cool with it. Because there's this one button. —She points to the back of the dress, high at the nape of her neck.

You nod; you climb the frosting stairs. Careful not to touch her, you work the button as best you can with your ruined hand. She sits, straight and still, patient with you. After a while she turns. Your finger brushes her shoulder; you flinch.

Are you okay? she asks you. —How's your hand? You still won't tell me what happened?

I told you, you say. —I dropped an amp on it. At the session. Ask Eddie if you don't believe me. There.

You get the button. The neck of her dress comes apart.

Yeah, Eddie's clearly who I should believe, she says. Then she takes your mangled hand between both of hers, holds it warm for a moment. You sit still; you do not want to breathe. The back of her head faces you; in the mirror you can see her eyes; she smiles; she is watching your face in the mirror as well.

You're so messed up, she says.

She guides your hand to the clasp of her bra, and you unhook her. She lets her clothes fall away, wads them, and tosses them like a volleyball into the sink. She leaves her underwear on.

Eventually you join her, strip down as far as briefs and T-shirt. Before you get in, you order hamburgers (of course the hotel has room service, Diane; you're stupid) along with French fries and a bottle of wine. It feels weird to order food in your underwear. Mona splashes in the next room. You pull the hem of your briefs away from your skin, hold it open like a funnel while the clerk describes the salt and spices you can expect to find on the meat and bun.

Gee, okay, you say. —Medium rare.

You hang up the phone, roll a joint, and climb the stairs to the tub. Mona paddles over and reaches out to take your pot from you. —Gimme, she says, and the room fills with smoke. You turn the bubbles on; they run, massaging the small of your back. Mona floats, contemplating the ceiling. She contemplates you.

You look very elegant, she tells you.

You blush. Thank you, you say.

This is nice, she asserts. —Marriage is nice. I could see us doing this for a while.

Sure, I guess that's the idea of it, you say.

You can feel her watching you.

B——, she says finally. —You like girls, right? Like—it's okay if you don't. It's really, really okay.

Of course I like girls, you say, splashing in alarm.

Okay, Jesus, she says; suddenly she's angry and you're not sure why. —You don't have to bite my head off about it. I figured you did probably. I was just asking.

I do, you say. Sorry—you just, just surprised me.

It's totally fine to like boys, she says. —There's nothing wrong with boys liking boys.

But I hate boys, you say.

There's *nothing at all wrong with it*, she insists.

No, I agree, you say. —I mean, totally. I mean, I feel like my life would make more sense if I liked boys, sometimes. It'd be this more efficient kind of thing.

She goes quiet at this, watching the bubbles. When she speaks again it takes a moment for her voice to rise to a normal speaking volume, like she's wandered down the radio dial to follow some strange pirate signal of her own, and now she has to tune back in to talk to you.

I mean, we understand one another, she says finally.

Sure, we understand one another, you say, and you hold your breath and dive underwater, pushing air out of your lungs so you can stay down as long as is possible.

WHEN YOU COME UP, MONA isn't in the water anymore. You turn your head; she glowers from the commode.

Yeah, get used to it, she says.

All you are thinking is: *She even gets to pee in a cooler way than you.*

I think the food guy's here, she says, returning your stare with narrowed eyes.

Dripping and mortified, you put on one of the two bathrobes hanging by the sink and answer the door. An older bellhop holds the steaming metal tray while you sign your name a twelfth time for the desk clerk; you're in your underwear within the untied robe, gross contours of your body clearly visible; it makes you mad and embarrassed and you take extra time signing your name so the bellhop burns his hands worse.

When you get back to the bathroom with the burgers and wine, Mona's in the spa again, gazing over the edge at you, chin resting soft in the crook of her wrists. When you climb the stairs with your burger, you can see that she's put her red wedding dress back on. The fabric floats around her bare hips, bleeding at the edges where the chemicals in the hotel spa water are breaking down the dyes of her fabric. She rises like a red naiad, blood dress pooled around her knees; she comes toward you and takes your fries.

I like the idea of being married to you, she says, in a way that doesn't brook follow-up.

You eat your food together on the linoleum of your honeymoon suite like lucky dogs, dirty water mixing with the grease and salt on your fingers, and she talks about recording and her music and what she wants to do with her future, and you sit and drip and listen to her, saying nothing.

AND LATER SHE'S FALLEN ASLEEP across the bed perpendicular to the pillows, floating on the lake of water that's slowly drained from her dress. You try to sleep on the floor beside her, but you can't quite get away from consciousness. Every time you shut your eyes and imagine yourself moving closer to sleep, you start to think about your dad.

You spend a few more minutes thinking, and then you get up. You put on one of the bathrobes and dig through your bag for the supply of pot you picked up this morning. Looking for it, you find a second bag stuffed into the first: mushrooms. *Honeymoon bonus*, reads the bad handwriting of the note in the bag. You spread four or five thin-pounded caps and stems evenly between cold hamburger meat and bun.

Mona murmurs, says something incoherent, turns on her side. Her red dress is twisted, hiked up over her thighs. You chew your drug burger and watch her.

Waking, she blinks at you, and then she swings her legs to the side of the bed. —What time is it even, she asks. —How long was I even sleeping.

I don't know, you say. —Uh, do you want to do some of these drugs with me?

A wedding night comes only once, she says solemnly.

THE BEACH OF LAKE ARROWHEAD contains no nature, its horizon replaced by the lights of other hotels peeping like raccoon eyes from the crooks of rolling hills. Picnic umbrellas rise from discarded crab shells like white necrotic deathcaps; lifeguard chairs sit nailed into the earth at regular intervals; discarded towels and chaises cover the combed and even dunes like the squares of a comfortable quilt. Even the water feels different as you and Mona walk barefoot through packed mud, water that can't support your weight. You can sink into it, go deep.

Your bathrobe says *Hers*, Mona says.

You stop. —Oh wow, you say.

Mine must logically say *His*, she continues. —Keep walking.

You follow orders, thinking about the robe, trying not to. You are beginning to worry more and more about what effect the drugs might have had on you; you are trying, as best you can, to keep it together. You must resolve to keep it together. You're alone in a strange city, window eyes of every house on you, a known celebrity at risk of radical exposure as a drug fiend and sex pervert. You have to remember to see things as they really are. You focus on this goal as you walk, muscles in your legs slowly knotting as you step on the sand, coil of nerves at the base of your spine slowly getting hot until the ice of you finally melts, and you are crawling, dizzy, along the strand.

Ahead of you, in a heap, is a castle children made. But these were uncommonly dedicated children: as you crawl toward it, your knees beginning to ache from glittering sand and holding your mangled fingers up as best you can where the belt of the *Hers* bathrobe comes undone, the thing seems to tower over you, a fat Berlin Wall capped by a tall, cylindrical tower made of pail upon pail of wet, stacked silica. You sit at its feet, imagining the kids working to build it: chain gang of boys and girls stacking sand as quickly as they can before the sun comes down and their parents call them home, hoping to build up something that the water— lake water, even, its tides rising with the moon and nothing else, no violence to it at all—can't take away.

You laugh, Diane, there on the shore, because the crappy castle reminds you of your father. He shines, every granular curve of his chubby cheek, the vein that stands out on his temple, the squint lit white by a sun that only you can see. He stands, daring the water to knock him down. And you wonder where your dad is now, whether he's okay.

YOU MUST REMEMBER THAT EVERYTHING you're seeing is caused by a drug you've taken. It isn't real at all. And yet the drug's real. The doorway it unlocked is real. Everything you're seeing you're seeing for a real and historical reason. You aren't doing a good job of keeping it together, but maybe you shouldn't be. Why are these things you're seeing somehow not the world? What if you're really right about everything?

YOU DROP ONTO YOUR BACK in the sand, your arms spread, your legs spread. Suddenly, in the absence of sun, the sand is cool. The sun has shed its skin, and deep at the center of the fruit, the cool stone pit of the moon glitters and drips with secret glassy juice. Your father's statue glows, holds together in the softer light. Then the pit cracks open and the radiation of the sun screams out again, shadows the world. It makes you warm, makes you want to get up and run into the water, alive.

You move your arms and legs in tight circles, form dark mud arcs of wings and robes, your red-brown hair spilling out like tentacle nets that gather in spectral jewels of sand. Before your eyes, the moon becomes the sun becomes the moon, each phase birthing the one beyond it in infinite *matryoshka* excess, until you can't tell the light of one from the other.

Sinusoidal motion is real: everything broken will be healed, every dissonance will become a rhythm, if you only work, if you only wait. And the voices of women come down to you from space, explaining what will happen to you next. You are an angel. This explains everything. Dumb angel sent to bring a message to the world.

YOU AREN'T SURE HOW LONG you lie there, digging a celestial pattern into the surface of the vacationers' beach. But eventually the good feeling stops in your spine, and you feel the tiny bites of ants on your soft, white skin. You walk into the lake. It's cold; it's silver; tiny fish in secret colors slip around your bare legs and hips until all the sand that's stuck to you drifts away, leaving you slimy and smooth.

Robe under your arm, you walk to find Mona. She lies on the ground, still wearing the *His* robe, huddled fetal against the packed sand. You sit down next to her, spoon up against her, draw the *Hers* robe across you both like a blanket. She shakes in her sleep, breathes, draws closer.

Wendy, she whispers. —I had the shittiest dream.

I'm not Wendy, you whisper back. —I'm Diane.

She nods. —I'm a coward, she says. Then she wipes her wet and sandy fingers on your chest in what can only be a mystic design, shakes again, closes her eyes.

You watch her breathe, your arms around her.

WHEN YOU WAKE UP, MONA is awake too, squatting beside you and hitting you again and again on your shoulder.

Come on, come on, she says, panicked. —They can't find us out here. We're wearing *robes*. Come *on*.

The sun rises pink over the green globe hills as you stand up and belt the robe over your waist, the gilt cursive *Hers* on your back glittering. Mona had her cigs and lighter in the pocket of her robe the whole time. She slept on them; the water got in and bled holes in the white paper. She smokes them anyway, holding her fingers over the slits and cracks. That's how you return to the hotel together, Diane: one flesh, waking up.

Love, Gala

# November 7, 2009

Dear Diane,

On Harry's advice, you and Mona move into a new house on Laurel Way, up in the hills. It has history: its previous owner was a silent-era stuntman known for having broken every bone in his body at least once in the line of duty, and none of the staircases or balconies have any railings. The upstairs of your new house is gorgeous: there's a built-in bookcase with a sliding ladder, and there's a wall made of thick, solid glass that fills up with the sun, and just beyond the glass a massive backyard pool with a chlorine fountain in the shape of a swollen star. Downstairs is less nice: essentially the entire bottom floor is a long, lightless corridor that runs the whole perimeter of the house, the only bathroom at one end of it by the stairs, the large studio room and master bedroom at the other end, a thin, totally acoustically permeable wall the only thing separating them. But the downstairs is fine: it's only you and Mona who'll have to see it.

In short order a waterbed arrives, a long feudal dining table, a TV and couches that face one of the great glass windows. You buy a grand piano, paint it magenta, and install it in a shaft of sunlight. You also pick up some books for the shelves—thick, lawyerly ones purchased by the foot, for dignity—but they make you uncomfortable in the space, so you end up replacing the most imposing of them with lava lamps in every color. Blue, green, red, fuchsia, egg-yolk orange, all of them in a line, bulbs bright and slag rushing in jet formations in the glass.

You hire workers to construct a recording studio downstairs. Wendy comes over to help you organize the lamps while Mona works downstairs, unpacking and learning to assemble the crates of mixing equipment, screwing in the soundproof baffles. You keep an eye on Wendy as she works side by side with you, her white wrists stretching out of her plaid blouse. Together you watch wax melt and reshape itself between leatherbound volumes of torts. Mona, when you meet her eyes, can only hold your (or anyone's) gaze for a couple of seconds before she has to look away, addressing her conversation to the floorboards. But Wendy meets your eyes, waits for you to look away first.

THE PIN UP DOLLIES BARELY exist these days: Mona's sister dropped out, already engaged to a boy who was moving to Bakersfield to implement some kind of new agricultural ideas, and to your knowledge Mona hasn't spoken with her in months. (Does Sherry even know that you and she are sisters-in-law now? Probably she doesn't exactly know that.) Wendy's around regularly, but Mona hasn't booked any concerts since the wedding. She's pivoted to songwriting for a while, she says, and all outward evidence of her activities since you've started cohabiting bears that out: her time, when not working at the record store, is spent researching songs, getting deep into songs, inviting Wendy over at weird hours to listen to songs. Her music has changed: rather than the knifelike three chords with maximum attack, she mostly plays acoustic these days: open chords in minor progressions that never quite come home to the root. She can play these progressions for hours sometimes, Wendy either accompanying her with slow bass lines or sitting cross-legged on the floor, watching your wife strum with her eyes closed. There are no words to these songs, or if there are, Mona never sings them out loud.

You are not always invited to hear them play. Sometimes, while they're alone in the studio, you hang out on your waterbed and try to hear them, but the door is solid and the soundproofing is flawless. Just outside, the pool filter is going; just through the wall you can imagine Mona and Wendy singing, voices wrapping around one another like thorny roses, puncturing one another in scratchy harmony. You listen, the ceiling fan blowing the stalactite of chestnut hair that slowly expands up your hidden midriff. *Where the deer and the antelope play*, you sing.

THE PERIOD OF YOUR LIFE when you lived alone was so short, relatively speaking, that you figured it wouldn't be hard to adjust to living with someone new. But Mona is different from your brothers, different even from the idea of her you had before. Now, legally bound, you barely see her; she moves through the house like a hummingbird, one room, two rooms ahead of you at almost all times, like the judge at the wedding has made the gravity between you too strong and she needs distance to compensate for it.

You barely use the downstairs studio; she uses it all the time, bringing her records down there to listen, sometimes a guitar that you can't hear through the soundproofed door. This is fine; Valley Forge wants to keep paying you to make records at the studio on Sunset, and you'd be hard pressed to fit the session musicians in Midnight Automotive in your basement, capacious though the studio may be. And after your housewarming party—during which Midnight Automotive jets through some John Black Zero covers, gathered around the new piano, the ancient Wollensak soaking everything in—it's the living room upstairs that seems blessed with good magic radiation, the place you prefer to be. You don't invite your family.

SOMETIMES YOU AND MONA FUMBLE for each other half asleep in the night. Mona's somnambulist voice asks you to hold her, says that someone needs to hold her. You press your cheek into her shoulder—black wires of stubble sprouting, their growth uncheckable—and you hold on.

WHEN MONA WORKS AT THE record store, she wears a wedding ring you gave her; puts it on like armor in the morning and takes it off as soon as she walks in the door at night. She brings home a lot of John Black Zero records, whatever she can find by Joan Baez and Nina Simone, Ken Nordine recordings you don't understand, strange country albums sung by trios of Christian sisters. She sits by the jukebox in the living room for long hours listening to these records.

Did you know I sell your picture all day? she tells you once while listening to it. —You and Tom and your brothers. All these men I know, on record covers and posters. It's like Soviet Russia.

You consider this. —I mean I probably couldn't have anyone killed or anything like that.

Nigel from Los Paranoias might be able to have some people killed, Mona muses. —I bet he's actually killed someone before.

Is Nigel the smart one or the quiet one, you ask.

Nigel's the cute one, Mona says. —No one suspects the cute one. The cute one is always a murder machine.

Who do you think is the cute one in the Get Happies, you ask after a moment.

She smiles, considers this. —If I tell you it's you, then effectively I'm accusing you of murder.

I haven't killed anyone, you say.

It must not be you, then, she says.

o   o   o

YOU'VE GOT SOME TIME OFF. Your hand's destroyed, Diane, and as the manager and chief songwriter, it starts to seem ridiculous to tour in support of the new album with the rest of the group. Charley can play bass just as well as you can, and you've never particularly liked playing live with everyone, not since those early shows at the drive-in, holding together your vomit over donuts and coffee and unwise A.M. drinks. You're pretty sure you're not going to miss the time spent crushed together with other people, the discord you bring to your interactions. Why should those people then miss you?

In the end, arrangements are made, and you see them all off at the airport—Charley, Tom, Adam, Eddie, your public band, your family. You wave goodbye, bandages coming loose from your destroyed hand in the background suck of silver engines.

Be good, you say. —Uh, play real sharp. Call me if you need anything.

You watch the plane go, weightless, out of sight.

SO YOU'RE ALONE TO EXPLORE the dimensions of your vision. This, as alluded to, involves going into the bathroom one day soon after moving in and locking the door, although there's no one you really expect to find at home. You fill the long tub full, take your clothes off without looking at yourself in the mirror, slide beneath the hot surface of the water. Above you a pale incandescent bulb burns; you imagine sparks falling from the socket and setting your skin on fire in a jolt. You float, trying to work up the nerve, and then you take the razor and apply it, latherless, to a single square inch of skin on your chest.

The first transgression, you find, is the hardest; after that, like two profiles becoming a vase, the disruption is no longer the shaved area but the hair growing around it. And so you set to work, leaving a dark chestnut ring like a bloodstain around the new white tub.

You study your body in the mirror. You can see the slight swell of hips, smoothness of skin, curves you couldn't see before, like a wedding veil has fallen from you. And you spend the rest of your afternoon after that first day in the pool, sunburn and chlorine aggravating the razor burn on your legs and chest and face, wrinkling your toes and scouring your skin, and you wonder who—if anyone—is watching you. What they will think when they see you. How long it will take the word to spread, house to house, teen to teen, reporter to reporter, magazine to magazine. It excites you because it's unthinkable. And so you begin to kick; you begin to move.

LATER, IN THE UPSTAIRS MUSIC room, under its massive glass window, you sit in the *Hers* robe plundered from the honeymoon motel, your smooth feet on the cold brass pedals of the piano. You play, and even the chords your fingers find are different.

ONE AFTERNOON YOUR SECRETARY CALLS you at home, insisting you return your brother Adam's call from a mysterious London number. The operator connects you.

Oh, hi Adam, you answer; you're wearing nothing but a woman's bathrobe; you are conscious of your low voice. —Is everything cool?

B——, says Adam. —Have you not been to the office lately? Your secretary kept telling me she'd have you call me back when you got in.

No, I've been at home mostly, you say.

See, I tried calling your apartment, too, Adam says tentatively.

Oh, that's the problem, you say, relieved. —I moved to a new house a few weeks ago. Mona and I got married.

There's expensive silence and radio static over the line; somewhere the breathing of the operator.

That's great, B——, Adam finally says. —Uh, give my regards to Mona. From the whole band, I guess.

Cool, she'll appreciate that, you say. —So is there some reason you called? Otherwise, I should get back to work.

The sound of your baby brother scratching his widow's peak is transmitted with ideal fidelity across the Atlantic. —I guess there was—sort of a crisis where Tom and Eddie got real sick in Germany and, you know, had to go to the hospital, and me and Charley had to divide up the vocal parts and instrument duties real quick so that we wouldn't miss a show. Or, uh, four shows, as ended up happening.

Wow, you say.

And I kinda wanted your advice on how to do that, Adam continues. —But I guess it's worked itself out now. So don't worry about us, is my message. It was kinda a funny situation, uh, after the fact.

Guess you had to be there, you say.

Exactly, Adam says. He kind of laughs.

You're silent. The transatlantic radio operator, distant, clears her throat.

Good talking to you, you finally say.

Of course, no, that's fine, Adam apologizes.

After a moment of gunfighter hesitation, you both hang up at the same time. Then you let the robe slip from your shoulders, split ends hanging against your neck, and go downstairs to fill a bath for inspiration. You hope Tom and Eddie are okay. You should try to give them a call, maybe. But probably Adam has you covered.

THINGS ARE CHANGING. ONE NIGHT you and Mona go out to a club, a pink tower at the long end of a wide street, its windows boarded up and blacked in while their tall arches still hold up the roof of the place like the ribs supporting the body of the whale that's swallowed you. Its interior is dominated by dancing bodies—men in suits, women in dresses, jeans, slacks, boots, anything—writhing side to side, pumping fists, moving hips close to one another in terrible tight synchronization. They are dancing in ways you haven't seen before. The band on stage— a tall specter in sunglasses on organ, a pimpled drummer with a pubescent goatee wisping from his chin, a sullen white man under a fat shag of sandy hair slicing space with guitar strings, a smiling black man with a crisp black suit and a necklace of shells who flutters his hands around a harmonica while the people on the floor jerk and contort. Hanging opposite the stage is a glass and metal cage containing three women wearing short skirts, tall boots, and can-do smiles. Someone has affixed cardboard dove wings to their shoulders, and they're being careful to dance without smashing into one another. You are afraid, Mona leading you by the fingers through the gauntlet of bodies that open and close like worms circulating through caverns of soil, warm and generative. Sweat and pheromones pour from necks and cheeks and armpits as they dance, filling up the floor, a slow salt lake that gathers around the cuffs of your pants, penetrating your socks, wrinkling your skin. They are the future; you're afraid of them; you are watching the women dance in ways you will never get to do.

THAT NIGHT, YOU GET OUT of bed; you put on a windbreaker with giant gashes in the lining; you walk the hilly streets with your ears burning cold red at their tips and your heart beating. You walk and think about all the different things your new album must cover—the kinds of things neighbors have on their porches and in their windows, brief scowling moments of eye contact with crewcut homeowners, the fear of sitting in the bathtub floating in a private lake shaped like a coffin and imagining you can never crawl out of it, every idea that Tom Happy will hate, and they circle like sucrose-glutted hummingbirds around your skull all night until you get home, your knees locked with chills, an hour or two before LA sunrise, and you fall into bed.

And later, when you wake up, you play the new music you've been playing since Lake Arrowhead. You revise half steps to wholes; you imagine the earth revolving around the sun, spooky space choirs crackling.

MONA ARRIVES ONE NIGHT WITH Wendy, burgers, and a record with a picture of women in gingham dresses and tight braids standing in front of a leering goat devil: *The Brenner Sisters Know It's a Wide Road to H—ll.* She sets the burger she's brought for you on the record player and frog-marches Wendy downstairs to the studio. Twanging banjoes echo down the hall, crinkling white paper, and then the soundproof door slams shut.

From the burger bag, onions, cheddar, ketchup, and taco sauce rise in mysterious mélange. You set it in the kitchen for later and return to the keys, where you play chords of transfigured failure, the melodies you've charted through them. You try to hear the choir you've been hearing—cosmic crackle of cymbals, pizzicato strings, what? Some kind of percussion, signals caught from outer stars. But no—you're the one in the outer stars, floating disconnected; the signals are coming from earth, light years away in the direction of your foot on the pedal. So you pump the pedal—you play the chords—you try to generate all the thrust you can, drive the piano down like a chisel to crack open the section of floor that divides you from Mona, to release the hidden planet sounds of the Brenner Sisters into the vacuum that surrounds you, and you play a moebius shuffle of chords as fast as you can, as if you're stabbing a knife between your spread fingers.

An angel of gender: your vision at the lake told you this is what you are. Do you agree? You imagine the kids at the drive-in parked beneath this tree of yours, your music leading them into the back seat of your Impala, and you drive them away to some anxious heaven.

YOU'RE STILL PLAYING THE PIANO, late, when you hear the door shut downstairs, and Wendy comes up. You keep playing, then turn. She's leaning against a kitchen island, watching you.

I had to come up for some air, she says.

Okay, you say, but you don't turn back to the piano, just watch her, unsure of what you should be doing. It's been a while since you heard Wendy speak—now that you think about it, have you ever? It's been a while, you realize, since you've spoken to anyone other than Mona or your band.

You and Mona seem to be having a good time together, you say finally.

Sure, Wendy says.

Some time passes. —She seems happy, I guess, you say.

Wendy gives a strange smile, wraps her arms tighter around her ribs, looks up at your very high ceiling. —She talked about how we should put on a concert soon, she said. —Just the two of us.

A concert is a good way to promote a band's new material, you say.

She hasn't wanted to leave the house except to work in months, Wendy says. —Since. —She pauses for a long time, then continues. —And now suddenly she wants to set up this everyday practice schedule, to bring the band back. We haven't been a band in at least a year. She asks if I think she can fit into her old tight pants, if I want to see if she can do it. I *can't* practice every day. I have work in the morning.

Wow, you say, lost in thought: could you fit into tight pants like the ones Mona had? The question starts to consume you: what *could* you fit into? What size even are you? You follow the spiral of these thoughts down to somewhere, before you realize that you haven't said anything in a while, that Wendy is looking at you, and you remember to look back at her. —Work in the morning, I can't imagine that.

No, guess not, Wendy says.

Mona has a job, though, you say. —Oh, but you said that.

Wendy sighs, looks around at your wide glass walls. —Look, I have to go? Could you tell Mona? Tell her I'll see her, I don't know, later this week. I just have to leave.

She doesn't wait for you to show her out, leaves you sitting at the bench of your piano. You hesitate for a moment, then start playing again.

AFTER A DAY MORE OF speculating about your size, you buy yourself a bathing suit, operating through an auxiliary, claiming it's for your wife. As the day slowly shifts into gear, sun modulating behind clouds through the heavy curtains, you figure out all the dumb tricks—how do you get it on *behind your back*, how do you fold yourself up into yourself just so—and venture the hallway, alone with your smeary reflection in the mirror. Bare feet hasty on the stone and towel wrapped tight around yourself, you slough that skin off too and dive into the pool, and the sun breaks through, shines a golden eye on you. You backpedal and kick, glittering water and poison chlorine everywhere, something to push against at last, and your hair floats around you when you dive under. Clean water enters your brain and the chords you've listened to before this bend, distort, grow. And later you find that the water has stayed in your ear, Diane; the chords have changed. You couldn't play them now the old way if you tried.

WEEKS PASS; YOU WRITE SONGS and make charts; your brothers and cousin campaign through faraway nations. You heat up canned children's spaghetti for dinner for both of you and eat in silence. Mona, over her bowl of irradiated tomato, looks far-away, lost in thoughts you can't discern.

Uh, hey, you say, and she looks up.

What, she says.

Nothing, you say. —I was going to ask, uh—are you and Wendy gonna book any more shows anytime soon?

She looks at her bowl, sets it down, picks up and lights a cigarette. She wiggles her bare toes as she sucks on its end. She does this for some time before you realize she has no intention of answering you. And you wonder how much of the truth you owe her, how much of the truth she owes you, what the contours of your arrangement with each other even are. It doesn't occur to you to ask her, but then it doesn't occur to her to ask you.

You're at a department store for plausible deniability, plus you've cased the place first, taking account of customer flow at time of day, traffic patterns for fast getaway, general spawn points for police, clergymen, angry elders, etc. On the second day you actually go in, after close to an hour of parked hyper-ventilation. Furtive steps—you tell yourself you're psyched, you're stoked, you've got it—and you put your sunglasses on and slide through the revolving doors, scales from spy movies arpeggiating through your head as you ride the escalator up. Make no excuses; keep your face expressionless: you wave to a saleslady, ask her for the misses section, tall and broad.

For your wife, the saleslady volunteers. And she leads you to the racks, whole moment thick like maple syrup, and you feel safe, Diane, a vampire on Halloween.

Humming chords, heart tangibly beating, you're trying to decide between a midnight blue dress and an orange one—every-thing's so small; it's destabilizing—when you realize that Harry Corot is browsing the clothes on the other side of your rack. Immediately you hang up the sinful clothes you've been touching, but this is a mistake; the hanging cotton, silk, mystery synthetics shake and sway, and Harry looks up.

B——, he exclaims. And you realize that he's just as terrified to see you here.

Hey, you say, gripping the hangers loosely in your fingers. —What's happening, Harry?

His attention is focused on your eyes, afraid, seeing that you're afraid, more afraid because you're afraid. Slowly, you watch him decide to smile and implement the tactic.

Nothing, he smiles. —Better halves, huh? What'd we do without them? But you know, B——, you're an important guy. Your wife should be doing her own shopping.

Oh no, you're much more important than me, you say. —I'm just working for an angel.

You try to make your eyes look ethereal and mysterious, as well as waggle your eyebrows. He laughs uncertainly. The dress on the hanger gingerly gripped between his own hands is tall and nuclear lime, its sleeves loose about the shoulders and its darts shallow. You imagine Lana trying it on in her windowless room, bright green rippling from her body and echoing from the sun-free walls.

When your attention comes back to him, he's saying something about a new album he expects you to deliver soon. —Look, I believe in you, he says, almost tenderly. —You write hits. The kids love you. The industry knows who you are. Don't worry about Los Paranoias. You're getting better and better, okay? And as long as you keep getting better and better, forever, they're going to keep loving you more and more.

You grip the hanger, sunbeam dust on your shoulder still disturbed where he touched you. —Gee, it sounds like a love story, you say.

It is. —Harry beams.

As he speaks, he waves his hands as if he's casting a magic spell, the lime green dress in his hand. On impulse, you choose the tropical orange print for yourself, secret sisterly counterpart to Lana's lime.

Okay well, I'm gonna go work on the album more, you say. —Good runnin' into you.

An undisputed pleasure, Harry says. —That'll look very nice on your wife, by the way.

You stop to look at it. —Yeah, I guess you're right, you say.

How much you realize your error varies directly with the visible diameter of his eyes. He looks at your twitching face; you try to calm it with the strength that the angel, you pray, has loaned you. He starts again to reach across the rack to pat your shoulder, but this time he stops halfway, sets his hand on the rack, drums his fingers against it. You watch them carefully drumming. He drums intentionally, meditatively: pinky, middle, ring, index, repeat.

Take care of yourself, B——, he finally tells you, his voice more sincere than you've ever heard it.

YOU HOTBOX THE CAR BLUE the moment you get back with the shopping bag and return receipt. (As long as there's no damage, says the saleslady.) You consider the situation. Harry Corot knows, he must, yet he remained kind. He's with Lana—he loves her—of course he was kind. Of course he'll protect you, just as he protected her. He even likes your dress. He even likes your album.

It makes you cry—slow eruption of realization that yeah, at last you're crying—until your resin-sticky fingers burn at the end of the joint. You passed the test the angel set for you. And not even the fact that your new dress doesn't fit you at all stops your good mood: hem too short at midthigh and a gaping pink hole at armpit, yet the printed orange sun shining, undimmed, out of your chest.

AND SOON THE MUSIC FOR the album is done. You play it through on the piano to be sure, nine quick cuts, the instrumentation Midnight Automotive will render for you approximated in your head as your fingers follow the melody, as yet in its native asemic Enochian, your falsetto accompanied in your imagination by specters of your wayward brothers and bandmates. You play them all, and then you take a victory lap of B-flat augmented arpeggios up and down the length of the keys, singing wordlessly, wondering just what text Tom will write for your music, what this thing you've done will come to mean.

IT'S FIVE OR SIX DAYS before Mona has time to listen. —So let's hear it, she says, beer in hand and plaid socks propped on the end of the couch facing the plate glass skyline, clutching the sun between her toes. —The Greatest Rock Album of All Time.

You play the angel's songs for her on the piano, accompanying yourself with voice and approximate instrumentation. You go through it all—the old classic shuffle here transfigured into something bright and unnameable, rumbling places where instruments you can imagine are to go, bubbling like a blood waterfall buoyed by lily-pad chords—major, minor, diminished, augmented, dreadful bass circling among the rocks and ferns just below sight—the treble buzz of mosquitos and no-see-ums like hemolymph roux to thicken the air around your skin as you float. Even flattened out, compressed to piano bandwidth, you think it sounds okay. You hope it sounds okay, heard outside your skull for the first time. If it sounds okay, then you will know you weren't deceived about anything else the angel told you. You'll have certainty, not just assertion: you'll have, for the first time in months or years or ever, peace. You're certain of that.

At first, Mona taps her foot against the arm of the sofa; she listens; she snickers when your approximate instrumentation is too obviously approximate. Then she stops doing that. Behind you there's only silence. You stop and turn. She's looking at her shoes. She looks up at you, eyes unreadable, until you can tell she's asking you without asking you why you aren't playing, and so you continue until the end.

So uh, all that's finished, you say, turning to Mona. —I mean it's not final. There's no words, right, and it'll get changed around in the studio and everything. What do you think, uh, in terms of what to say about it?

You should get rid of that thing with the triplets in the outro, she says hollowly. —It messes up everything.

Oh cool, that could work, you nod.

I know it could, she says, and then she sighs. —It's beautiful, B——. It's really good.

And this is all you wanted her to say, except she said too much: that name, tied to this work. You should ignore that. Ignore it, you order yourself; she heard it; she loves it; she's happy. She said your name; that will always be your name. Stop thinking about this. Mona's still talking—all the records she's been listening to, the echoes of some of them she hears in what you've been doing, the places where you depart, finding where you fit on the map she's building, staking out its borders—you can't hear what she's saying if you're thinking about your name, and it's very important to listen to her, what she's saying is very important, she is saying things that are important to her—she said it was really good, too—you put your arms on the keys, a big smear of sound, rest your head on top of it. You try to will yourself to hear what she said—*it's beautiful*—without the name. It's not a big deal. You should not let it be a big deal. You should force yourself to be happy.

Are you listening to me, she asks. —Are you okay?

Yeah definitely, you say, to the keys.

Listen, she says, and then she stops for a moment. —Listen, I think I should be honest with you.

o   o   o

AND NOW IS THE MOMENT to make things clear to her at last, Diane, because if you do that, she will be free from you and every evil you bring.

YOU LOOK DOWN AT THE carpet. You feel like you've carried a great weight up a long, spiraling staircase, and now you must let it go to release all the destructive energy it's stored, to smash the coils of staircase itself. Mona is watching you carefully; you realize suddenly that she's seen this expression on you before. —I didn't mean—are you okay? B——? Are you okay?

I'm sorry, you say. —Geez, I'm really sorry.

She swallows, knot of whatever weight she's carrying disappearing down her throat like the bulge of a cartoon rabbit down a pipe. She almost seems relieved: the time for whatever confession she was planning to make has passed. You have removed the opportunity. You exist far too much, you think.

It's fine, she says. —Breathe, okay? Breathe. Don't worry. Just breathe.

You shake your head, trying to breathe. Mona is looking at you, concern on her face. You look at the black streaks on the carpet, the ghost light of halogen ripples that move askew across it from the pool outside.

I mean uh, you say. —I mean gee. You had something you wanted to say.

No, she insists. —Go on.

I mean I don't know where I'd start, you say. —I mean I don't know how I wouldn't get it wrong.

How would you get it wrong, she says.

You close your eyes; your face goes numb; something like blood is pushing itself through the plaster of your skin from behind. —I mean it's what I said that time, by the pool, you begin.

What time, by the pool? she asks. —What are you even talking about?

This is not working; begin again. —I mean it's just—if I were a girl, I'd be you.

I can't even hear you, she says.

If I were a girl, I'd be you, you say, loud enough to shake the windows, to shiver the hammers on the piano strings. And you feel as if you've thrown up on the floor.

She stops, raises her eyes. You've filled the space between you. She has something to look at now. And now it's her turn, Diane, to make of it what she's capable of making.

THAT'S HILARIOUS, SHE SAYS. —THAT'S seriously funny stuff.

You laugh on instinct, a knee struck with a hammer, the room's air suddenly thick.

If you were a girl, you wouldn't be me, Mona says. —You wouldn't be *you*, either. You'd never have learned to play the guitar, or had friends tell you you were good enough to write songs, or had anyone with money want to *pay* you for your songs, or fucking kids, fucking kids in the music store dragging their girlfriends, their wives in by the fucking *wrists*, fingers red tight around their fucking *wrists,* who come up to the counter to buy an album with your *face* on it—

The weight within you is falling very fast now, smashing railings as it descends. —Can we, can we maybe calm down, you whimper, —or—

If you were a girl, you'd be *that* girl, Mona shouts, —the girl-friend in the store, getting your wrist crushed. No one would care that you could write songs that make me want to break my guitar. No one would want to know about it. No one would let you make mistakes. You'd *die* with that still inside of you. You know why you have the temerity to say that to me? Because you're nothing like me. —Her voice shakes. —You'd be happily married. You'd be laughing at someone's jokes. But congratulations, because you're not a woman, so you get to do all these great things, and people will care about your beautiful songs. And I'm elated for you, B——. I really am. I really, really, really, am.

I am, you say, suddenly also crying.

She laughs, sucks up snot; this time you don't laugh with her.

AFTER A LONG MOMENT, SHE grows quiet, and you can hear voices around you. *Stop crying*, they say. *This emotion is upsetting someone.*

Like Pavlov's dogs, you start to obey. If you could go back in time, if you could unsay it, you would, you tell yourself. You wish you could go back in time. You're not sure you're wishing it hard enough; you're too stupid and awful to go back in time. You look at Mona. You swallow again.

It's really true, you say. —An angel told me, you know?

What's true, she demands. —Say it.

I'm a, you begin, but you can't finish it, close your mouth instead.

A moment passes. —Are you on drugs? she asks.

You make yourself laugh; she doesn't. —No, you say. —I mean, I was when I came up with the idea.

She gets up, sighing. —Can we maybe take a break for a while? I don't have the energy for this right now.

Sure no problem, you say, and you make laughing sounds again. You're sitting on the floor, not sure how you got here.

Great, she says, and she wipes sawdust from the guitar up with her hand. She looks at you. She sucks in breath, bites her lip, carries the guitar carefully across to the stairs—passing in front of you, sitting with cheeks wet and shaking like a priest at a vigil—to the stairs, socks padding down on the wood into the deeps of your house.

After a minute, you lie on your back and watch the ghost light of the pool move over your ceiling. Moonlight is reflected sunlight;

the sun is where all angels come from; they drift over you, bless you with their liquid hands. And you realize that no part of you wishes you could go back in time, unsay what you've said. You feel clean, Diane, clean like chlorine.

YOU FEEL CLEAN UNTIL THE shout, the fast soft steps down the jailor's hall, the rush up the stairs, Mona, your wife, in her *His* robe, shoving your black swimsuit at you, its crotch distended by malignancy. You left it in the bathroom to dry, Diane, and then you forgot to hide it.

What the fuck? she says. —Is this yours?

No, you say immediately, voice breaking into a chirp.

She stares at you, panic and frustration in her eyes. For some time, she stares at you, and you look at her ankles, unable to meet her eyes. After a while, you roll onto your side, pretending to be already dead.

Get up, she says, her voice terrified; —Get, get off the floor, okay? Jesus Christ, get off the floor—

The swimsuit in her hand looks like a dirty diaper; you get on all fours, tie of your robe dusting the floor like a slinking tail, and you try to crawl away from it. She steps in front of you, blocks you.

Get up, she says again. —Have a grown-up conversation with me. Get up, please; this isn't funny; this is terrifying, B——, okay?

You try to circle around her, to make it to the stairs, but she cuts you off again and again, circling easily on her grown-up legs to block you, to shove the evidence at you, until you finally decide to stand up and run past her, like a human; you guess that maybe this will make her happier, calmer, to see you being a human, that this will solve your problems, but nope: she grabs the tie of your robe. And it catches around your shoulders, it comes open, it pulls you backward and makes you smash into the floor. You lie there, spine aching. She steps around you, stands between your legs to keep you from closing them, her own legs vanishing safely into the *His* robe, the swimsuit in her arms, dangling at you. She looks down at you, false halo of the living room track light burning around her head. She is what you will see, you think, when you die.

Are you shaving your legs? she asks. Then, her voice quiet, like she's looking into a spider's nest: —Who *are* you?

There's no point in moving; there's no point in trying to wriggle free. You lie there, pinned and hairless and naked before her gaze, and your muscles flood with endorphins all laying down their swords and shields at once. It is a feeling of great euphoria. All your blood vessels, your heart, your skin tingles and pulses with it, the great euphoria of being pinned, naked, hurt, invisible, blood singing harmonies as you endure the stare of someone who—you know it, in this moment you are sure of it—despises you, who always has.

And you know why she despises you: because she is real and you are not. Why did you seriously expect she might take this any other way? Why did you seriously think anyone other than the devil was telling you what you'd become?

So all you can move is your neck, and so you lift it, and you smash it backward into the cracks in the floor, soft and tentative and babyish at first and then harder and harder with the rhythm, until you see stars, until your eyeballs shake and lose orientation with the impact, until your mind and your female soul and your fears and your power to make music and perceive the mind of God all just *SHUT UP* and are all just *SMASHED OUT OF YOU* for once, until your head will crack, it will crack open like an egg and some new you, screaming and pink, will be born from it, will fly to freedom, a second chance, a girl this time.

But you don't get your second chance, because Mona drops and sits on your chest and screams at you, grabs your skull and shields it with her fingers, so you're smashing her fingers and not your skull, and this horrifies you; you stop immediately, but she doesn't stop. She keeps screaming at you, and then she hits you in the cheek, first one and then the other, and then she strikes your chin, and once, you think by mistake, your mouth. Salt and copper is what you taste, after that. She is no longer screaming; her own mouth is closed, tight. And then she gets up and stares down at you from above again. Her eyes are furious and afraid, and you want to hurt yourself again, imagine her thinking about kicking you in the ribs; you want to hurt yourself first, before she will.

But she doesn't anymore: she only stares down at you. You stare up at the ceiling. Streaks of light from the pool—what were you calling them—you can't remember—pool angels?—they move over everything. Perhaps they are the force that's protecting you right now.

MONA EVENTUALLY GOES DOWNSTAIRS, WATCHING you out of the corner of her eyes as she backs away. She's still holding the bathing suit slightly away from herself, flexing the hand she's hit you with as if she's not sure she can trust herself with it, or maybe because she is thinking of hitting you again? It's very confusing, imagining what other people may want or do. You think about this as you lie there, alone, your head aching; you think about this, and maybe about whether you have a concussion. You're not sure what you're thinking about, where the borders around thoughts are supposed to fall.

She comes back up after some time wearing a peacoat, her hair choked up in a ponytail, an overnight bag on her shoulder.

I'm going to Wendy's, she mumbles, and she exits through the front door.

You lie there a while, and then you put on the swimsuit and go out to the pool to float under the stars. You can think of nothing; the Lady of the Lake has blessed you with a vast bleed of damage into your brain.

o    o    o

AND SUDDENLY, FLOATING THERE, IT feels as if everything stuffed into you, so impacted into your spiritual sinuses that you've forgotten what forests smell like, is released all at once, the pressure suddenly changing to the motion of a vacuum. You start to cry in the pool, sniffing, real sinuses emptying as well and becoming antiseptic in chlorine. And this time you don't want to shut it off, spilling disease into the lake, watching it transform into something clean.

THERE, CLEAN AND DRIFTING IN water perfumed with secret bodily salts, your thoughts arc, blissed out, to Mona— Mona, her progress seeming to be projected in eerie visions on the reflecting bands of light and chlorine that surround you like amniotic fluid, Mona's choking ponytail tossing against her shoulders in time with her unbelted body in its seat as she glides, untrained, down the road in your stolen Impala, its hovergyros caroming from curb to curb in a quest for the straight and narrow that pretty soon she ditches, fuck it, and she wants the radio on and all the way up, newscast or jingles or drums and guitars blasting through speaker mesh or eardrums and squashing all thoughts shy of destination; but she can't turn on the radio; the odds are too much in her favor that she will hear your voice like the walls of a cage she's sealed herself in, here in your flying car, here in your life. So she smashes fenders and scrapes paint and sings "Daydream Believer" until her vocal chords peel.

She pulls up to Wendy's, smashes your door against a fire hydrant on the way out. Her heel cracks off on the staircase; her sole slips and brings her to her knees; she thinks—I am a dog—she decides to embrace it, on her knees she climbs with her peacoat shucking off her shoulders; she growls and snarls before Wendy's door, scratching it with short bitten nails and howling and barking, until Wendy fumbles with the chain and opens up, night-gown half knotted in front of her stomach—*Mona?*—she asks, and then she screams as your wife leaps forward at her, and continues to bite the air and sob half-in-half-out of the neon evening until Wendy grabs her ponytail and forces her to the carpet, forces her to lie still, leads her inside—Mona presses her cheek harder into the hooks and fibers, feels Wendy's arm holding her, Wendy's cheek against her body, and she closes her eyes and breathes in strange dust; she smiles; there is nowhere at last that's lower to go.

You see it all, Diane, as you float alone in the lake your money has bought you. So much money buoys you up as you float, as you think: even if you are not real, you have been of use to someone. And you ask yourself if it hurts. And you don't have an answer, either because it hurts too little to register, or because it hurts too much.

LATER YOU ARE ASLEEP ON the couch, still in your swimsuit, with the shreds of sunrise moving over your aching, chlorine-steeped arms, your pounding skull.

The key turns in the lock; the front door creaks open. Your arm aches, but you keep it still and close your eyes and try to match your breathing to that of sleeping people. The sun burns atomic stencils into your eyelids and you watch them, feigning rest, until you're aware of a shadow over you, a foreign planet eclipsing your sun. She stands, watching you; you can feel her mind, another mind, moving over your face. You go on breathing.

B——, says Mona.

You keep your eyes closed.

B——, she repeats. And then, voice tired: —Is there something else I should call you.

You open your eyes. She's standing there, her ponytail hacked off with what looks to be kitchen scissors. You can see her eyes scanning your pupils, looking for signs of dilation, concussion.

You do not want her to be worried. You wonder if she would be happier going somewhere else for a while.

I guess Diane is okay, you say to her.

We should tell each other things, Mona says. —We should tell each other all kinds of things. We never have before. It could be fun.

You are lying in a halo of bleach and chlorine, etched into your couch in chemical burn, like evidence of lightning. And Mona kneels there beside you, crying, and begins telling you how in love she is with someone who is not and never could be you.

Love, Gala

# PART FIVE

the GET HAPPIES' new no. 1 HIT!

PSYCHIC ATTRACTION

# November 21, 2009

Dear Diane,

Everyone knows how it begins: your brother Eddie's voice, low and young, scratching like a cat trying to get through curtains. Adam joins him, matching and doubling his tone, difficult to perceive as anything other than an echo effect (except to us True Fans, Diane), a recording artifact. Next, the pincers: Charley moving in from the top, his voice as high as yours but soapier, a pink prom date at your door, Tom's bass rising from below: sneer of a Cadillac hoodlum who wants to spit tobacco juice on your dress in the backseat. You join them, falsetto buzzing the top of your palate, fighting your testosterone-poisoned vocal cords, seeking the purity of the vision you received.

A LOT OF PEOPLE KNOW that you didn't write the lyrics to the songs on *Space-Girls*, Diane, but take the official and public credit line (the band *en masse*) at face value. A lot of people are willing to overlook the fact that you and your band never quite produced anything of that particular quality again: what Tom Happy was to call *music for drowning yourself to* in later interviews.

I imagine you writing it like this: piano and pen fade out to conversation—you and Mona, no microphones, no one can know what you say. All we have are the letters you both produce: letters to Wendy that you and your brothers' and cousin's and neighbor's voices would carry to her over the radio, long after you're dead and she's dead: confessed feelings, confessions of disbelief, confessions of betrayal, married to music that forgives it.

It's the only time it happened. It's the reason Caroline is rich: the publishing royalties for those songs, source of the blue fiscal blood flowing into her accounts.

The follow-up single—"Psychic Attraction"—was an attempt to work according to the same system, to follow intentionally what emerged by chance. There are the original, in retrospect valedictory lyrics, which as far as anyone knows were never officially published. True Fans have reconstructed them from studio bootlegs, concert fuck-ups during the bad 1980s years, conjecture based on established tic and rhyming patterns from the *Space-Girls* tracks. The lyrics everyone knows are a Tom Happy gloss, prepared hastily for the single release, mostly about how a girl with psychic powers is good to have sex with. Yet vestiges of the original glitter through. You can hear them glittering, now, in Tom Happy's nasal yawp in the recording booth.

As you record—somewhere, blearily, in hour forty-seven of spooling tape and overdubs that True Fans will later memorize and disseminate in shadowy forums—Charley plunks the five-string banjo he's waited for years to use on a real Get Happies recording. You don't know if you have the heart to tell him his instrumental mic isn't live, that his performance, whether it's good or not, will be overdubbed by Midnight Automotive. This can't be helped; the recording needs to be perfect; the vision demands it. And it is perfect, engraved in every American heart like Martian canals. "Psychic Attraction": your last number one hit.

o  o  o

IT'S GOOD THAT YOU HAVE a number one hit, because *Space-Girls* is a failure, selling mere tens of thousands.

You tried to stretch, Harry Corot tells you at a meeting. —It's admirable to try that. It's worth losing some sales for a little while, to do that. Really, I believe that, B——. There are a lot of easier businesses to make money in than producing records for teenagers.

Gee, you say. —The company's going to be okay, right?

Harry smiles at you, as you imagine a kind parent might do. —Let's not do this again, he says. —But yes, I think we'll make it through.

The new album's going to be better, you say. —It's going to teach people how to appreciate the last one, you know? It's going to teach people how to appreciate a lot of things.

Then I'll look forward to hearing it as soon as possible, Harry says.

You'll hear everything, you say, your third eye beaming secret context at him.

He smiles, and you have faith that you've succeeded in transmitting.

AT A BAND MEETING TO discuss the new album, you draw a triangle on the studio chalkboard.

One of these points, we'll call them, you explain, —that means the moon. Another one represents the sun, see. And so this moon is constantly sending its energies, in the form of *light*, to the *sun*, and vice versa.

You generate a series of rapid scribbles back and forth between the two points, an expressionist sketch of people on an escalator or a furry arm. —See, this is light going back and forth from the sun to the moon. And when light goes from the moon to *this* point of the triangle, that's money. —You draw a line to a point obtusely far from the other two, pressing so hard your chalk breaks. —And see, between these two points, that's male energy and female energy, so that represents sex, or gender.

You said gender, giggles Eddie.

You're fired, you say automatically. —So the sun and moon generate the genders, but then the sun beams *money* to the third point, and that's not complete without *magic*. So that's what the album's going to cover. The tracks are kind of connected according to that.

Tom raises his hand, and you point to him. —None of this makes any fucking sense, he says. —Are you on drugs, B——?

Yes, you say carefully. —But that's where the teen market is going now.

Tom straightens his back. —You know where we play a lot of shows? he asks. —Kansas. Right in the middle of this country, the place least like California. And part of the reason we sell so good there is because parents in Kansas aren't building huge bonfires of our records, like they are lately with Los Paranoias.

They've got to *buy* them to *burn* them, says Eddie, but Adam shushes him.

I wonder, says Charley, raising his hand first. —We've got a really squeaky clean image, you know, and it could be good in the market place for us to get a little *je ne sais quoi* to our image.

Yeah well *parley voo no one asked you*, Tom says.

It doesn't matter what anyone thinks, you say. —This is the album we're doing.

Soon they'll be touring again, you remind yourself; soon, without your family, you can really accomplish something.

AT HOME MONA IS ALMOST always in the studio while you're upstairs watching *Lost in Space* reruns, or floating in the star-shaped pool, or at the piano bench. She leaves the door cracked sometimes, and you can hear her working when you're lying in bed alone, working through the wall: her strange chord progressions, dreamy fields of fingerpicking, quiet singing. You can never make out the words to her new songs.

Sometimes she keeps working long after you're asleep. Sometimes she cuts it off early and joins you, making the waterbed tilt and sway beneath you.

Do I ever get to hear what you're working on, you ask her.

When it's finished, sure, she says.

You always get to hear what I'm working on, you tell her.

Me and the whole world, she says. —So whose work is worth more?

I still want you to write the new album with me, you say, suddenly, too loudly, you're sure.

She sits up, gets up, walks to the bedroom door. —I'm sorry, you say.

It's fine, she says, hesitating before sitting, cross-legged, on the hardwood floor. And she watches you, covers over your face, until you fall asleep.

THERE'S ANOTHER NIGHT, ONE OF the ones when you both stay in the same room: she's turned away from you, murmuring strange oneiric visions into the crook of the pillow, and you put your ear close so you can listen to them. And then you slide out of bed and put on your *Hers* robe. The months, chlorine, and cheap construction have all rebalanced its color: all the white has remained at the neckline while all the red's pooled around ankle height, like you're surrounded by a slow, lazy fire while you wear it. It hangs small on your broad shoulders. You slip it on now, pull it as tight as you can over your front, stand in profile in the mirror looking at your chest. Imagine Mona's head pillowed on your chest.

You sit at the piano with a taper candle burning in an old bottle of wine and your bathrobe burning around your bare ankles as they make cool sliding contact with the varnished black wood of the pedal mount. You press the pedals down, soles of your feet shocked by brief brass ice. You play strange melodies you aren't sure whether you've played before. Your voice is wordless, high, clear.

Mona sleepwalks. You keep singing, telling yourself that she probably won't hear you, that you're just being paranoid again. But you know inside that you want to wake her up. You want her to come and find you here, Diane, bathrobe around your shoulders, playing melodies with the candle flame reflected in the French glass and the still surface of the blue pool beyond. You want to play them, pretending that you're not observed, while she watches you leaning on the hallway wall. And when you can't think of any melodies anymore you can turn around and pretend to jump with surprise. *Oh, it's you!* you'll yelp. Maybe she'll smile.

She doesn't come. Instead you eat some whipped cream on Wonder Bread in the kitchen, chewing sugar as you keep watching the candle flame burn down. It looks beautiful, melting: the wax firming up as it falls from the flame, castles hanging from the sky. Then you go back to bed. Mona has the pillow over her head. You take the *Hers* bathrobe off, take off everything else, quickly slide under the sheets with her. Her body under the pillow faces the ceiling, still like a statue holding a cold sword, and you're afraid to touch her.

WENDY HAS STARTED DATING YOUR little brother Adam. You found out during one session to record radio promos when she accompanied him to the studio, and he admitted it when you pressed. Wendy's style is femmeing out crazily, like a time lapse photo set. She never speaks to you, and Mona never speaks about her. You wonder if she ever hears tracks from *Space-Girls*, maybe over the radio late one night while she's asleep in her apartment, asleep in your brother's arms: Mona singing to her through your falsetto, sending astral letters to her, cut by cut. But the album was not a hit, and the radio is a rural post office that one day stops delivering.

SUMMER FUN BEGINS WITH "BEAUTIFUL Dreamer," a spooky Stephen Foster cover—nighttime music, stars coming out, patterns from above to below—that opens up at its conclusion into a glissando of piano scales, the settled surface of a river in the flat sunlight. Banjos twinkle and buzz; a washboard scrapes; snare drums slap like a paddle wheel and a chorus of voices provide a cushiony throne for a goofy stentorian lead vocal—destined for Eddie, you decide—introducing the river and introducing the journey, "Mark Two Twain." You accompany the boat you've crafted along with the current to the first port of call: horns, death, lyrics speaking through skulls in the jazz funeral of "Frenchman Street Blues." Slavery is discussed via the tack piano and holy harmonica/clavichord glamour of "Auction Block Rock"; a rain of pizzicato strings and harps delivers the ecological force of "Grow Forest Grow"; a solid hour looking up Old Indian Legends at the library in books with neat illustrations yields the phonetic chant chorus of "Trail of Tears." You anticipate Tom being skeptical about the plan to record the actual hellish industrial sounds of an auto plant in "Merrie Machine Melodies," but you predict Mona will like it.

The next song, starting the album's second side, tells the story of a nebulous narrator who decides to grow a girl in the backyard. (The implication is that this seedpod was already extant, that it tumbled down a Jacob's ladder of moonbeams to land on the doorstep.) Via artful watering and management of sun exposure, including some worrisomely exact descriptions of just how deep to plant the pod, whether nitrogen powder and potassium ought to be added to the soil, etc.—a sprout emerges one day, growing a thick, fleshy fruit that slowly unpeels to reveal a girl who falls splayed to the soil. She is a cis girl. In the final stanza, she slowly arranges her legs, trying to stand against the bark of a tree, some shade of meaning in the chords indicating that she's somehow new; she must learn to walk again; the birth caul flesh dries like papaya from the skin of her shoulders. "Girls Grow in the Sun" is its title. It is a legend and I love it, Diane.

But after some connecting pieces—harps, ghostly voices, ethereal textures et al—our journey across America brings us at last to "Donner Pass," a feel-good saga of cannibal surf rock action. "God's a Girl" is a power ballad about sentiments made pretty clear by the title; you see it as the single. "Little House on the Moon" is a kind of country number, the girl from "Girls Grow in the Sun" building a home for herself in space, a lot of pedal steel. "The Highway West" is a classic Get Happies car song gussied up with a bunch of eerie drum treatments and lyrics telling the story of a woody station wagon launching itself off its cloud of hoversteam and rising higher, higher, slowly driving into the sky. Manifest destiny ends in heaven far above Hawaii; the band returns to earth via rain and the thunk of ukuleles.

THE INAUGURATION OF ANY MYSTICAL work is the most vital factor determining that work's ultimate spiritual nature. You dress for it, soon after your band departs again on tour (for Europe, for Japan, for points beyond) in the dark of your bathroom, standing naked but for red underwear, a green thread stitched into the hem, before the mirror, where you apply an athame to select sites—sternum, navel, pad of flesh and hair that shields your pubic bone, very lightly—you close your eyes and hold your breath—in the hollow of your neck. Four tiny drops of bright red blood stick to your skin, vivid as ladybugs. The remainder of the garb goes on over the scabs: silver gown, neckline cut to below the navel to form two vast shining suspenders that crinkle like leaves. A golden belt with a clasp shaped like a waxing crescent moon holds it snug around your waist, and you wear two green bracelets, wood and gold and jade, for accents. The moon motif is repeated in a kind of crown or garland on your head, your red-brown hair spilling out around it. Fringed chamois boots and a gold pentagram around your neck complete the ensemble. You watch yourself transforming thus in the mirror, try to make your face placid, to look through your eyes at what you imagine, within your skull, to be a smoky nebula full of glimmering stars.

MIDNIGHT AUTOMOTIVE SITS ASSEMBLED BEFORE you in the studio. Some of their instrument cases are open and some are closed, everything frozen in the state it was in the moment you stood on the chair at the front of the session room and everyone realized it was you there, dressed like a lunar goddess and hovering above them. You smile to put them at ease as you prepare to explain what you will all be doing for the next weeks and months, the degree to which you believe in them.

Is this a joke? asks the bassist.

You stare back at her, mystical glitter settling to the base of your neck like butterfly wing dust. —This is the plan now, you say, your voice you hope not too low.

THE FIRST SESSION IS GOOD. One by one you teach everyone their parts, clear up any obvious errors, and start to tighten and polish. Once the focus is squarely on the music, stuff gets faster; everyone has something safe to concentrate on. You end up with a good day's allotment of takes and variants, maybe halfway through the track. (Good: at this rate maybe you'll be done by September, prime for a Christmas release.) You don't even care, exactly, when they call you B——, or he, or when you can tell that as they talk to you they are speaking with real respect to the *inner* you—i.e., the competent, male you—and ignoring your freakish and troubling female exterior in the name of tolerance and getting the job done. You're grateful to them.

ON THE WAY OUT OF the studio, you start, on instinct, to walk to the men's, and then you go in anyway out of spite, squat in a cold and spattered stall with your gold leaf dress dragging on the tile. The same mirror that was watching you on the day you smashed your hand is here—or its replacement, which Harry Corot paid the studio for—but your reflection is different: older, rounder, a garland of moonlight on your brow, your fingers right now still and numb. If you squint the dark shadows on your cheeks blur and smear away beneath your makeup. And on your dress, just below the belt, is a horrible dark blood stain, a blotch in the shape of Texas. You yelp and investigate; the scab from the knife has come loose, and for a long time you look in the glass at the place where your white flesh is covered with old blood, the place where you opened it.

A QUIET DINNER THAT NIGHT: watery fettuccini and broccoli, and your thoughts stay occupied while Mona goes below to plug at her guitar, goes to the freezer for late night ice cream, goes to bed, gets up and goes in her robe (a new one, blue and scarlet, such as a casino kingpin might wear) to the edge of the pool. You can see her out the glass of the living room window, watching black waxing-crescent moonlight and thinking thoughts that remain her own.

WHEN YOU'RE NOT IN THE studio, you're still recording. To connect the songs, you don't want some boring blank space and hiss of the needle; you want everything to flow into everything else, same way the music doesn't stop when you shift back and forth from waking to dream. Fresh Wollensak at your side, you convert the world into tape. A day at an auto demolition yard gets you some good clanging timbre for "Merrie Machine Melodies," as well as miscellaneous screams and shouts from workers carrying torches and the susurrating shift of garbage piles underfoot. Fake radio static mixed with seagull cries over Redondo Beach give you the opening of "The Highway West." Honking horns, waves, birdsong in the park around the Getty, guttering of a candle recorded in a bathroom, a lawn, a closet with only the flame and the edge of the Wollensak mic and the sunburned fat of your fingers visible in the dark. Whatever you record, the spiritual energy is transcribed too, so you must be careful, Diane, only to record the good things in the world.

YOU SPEND HOURS AND HOURS of studio time after most of the session players have gone, mixing everything you've recorded until it sounds nothing like itself, blending with instrumental textures and a capella floating vocals. Often you discard it, sometimes use it to thicken a piano or a bass line: little paintings that you *whack whack whack* with paint and knife, microscopic flecks of spirit swimming like plankton over the canvas, nutrition for whales too large to perceive. It feels like falling over a cliff, like wanting to drive toward one, glide over the side and fly for real. Fly toward the place where Lana waits for you, Lana and all the new, good people who are better than the old people you've outgrown, like your new band eclipsed your old one, like being a girl eclipsed being a boy. These are the voices you heard during your vision on the beach: other women like you. A whole nation rising out of the sand, a signal that only you can hear, that now you've got to articulate.

It occurs to you that when you release this album, your father will see it too. Or no: you never want that; never let that happen. Maybe he'll give this one a miss. Maybe he doesn't want to hear what some whatever you are, some boy-who-thinks-she's-a-girl produces. A signal to the Moon: and when it's released, Lana and all the moon women will come to see you and take you up to the moon in a cloud, and your father, your brothers, your band will not be able to hurt you ever again. The new women will protect you from them. They'll want to make you their queen, of course, but you'll refuse. Oh, you don't want to be queen, you'll tell them; you'll blush.

AND SLOWLY, SLOWLY THE TRACKS come together: four fat monophonic cords of ideas adjusted and mixed down, glossed and mixed down, glutinous psychedelic impasto. You sign time-cards, and master tape spools collect in fat columns.

We'll slow this take down, you punch in. Then: —We'll slow this take down again. —After you're down to maybe three seconds per beat, the band, at your direction, generates new melodies to fit into the void spaces between notes, sound squiggles like patches of grass between railroad ties. Sped up again, they resolve into texture, thickness.

Suppose you do this on every track? You resolve to come back to this idea. In the meantime, you try speeding all the tracks up instead, writing new slow melodies around the surrounding insectoid buzz. You arrange strange clusters of instruments around mic bulbs, buzz viola strings into bass pickups, loop a member of Midnight Automotive on a clarinet over himself into a thick layer cake of woodwinds iced with peppery tack piano. All the time you shout ideas back to the booth: —Right here, when we have lyrics and can do the vocal parts, see we've built this real tight top end, but we'll need Tom for the lows, he'll be like the lava, so you should make a note right here that this is what we're doing—

SOMETIMES, IN BED AT NIGHT with your legs curled beside you and the day's work crunching through your skull, you can hear Mona's guitar echoing down the hallway: rough chucks, rainstorm strums, fingerpick trials that start slow and get faster, cleaner, surer as she goes, fingers curling and flexing like they're stroking a cat's throat. You feel, listening to her, like you're stalled behind another car, watching its signals blink in time with your wipers for one brilliant moment before the lapse into counterpoint.

By day, the white sun burns through the picture window of your living room, watching your pool, watching you. One day you work a can of paint open with a screwdriver tip, prop it against the back of the couch, stare at the smear of white around the sun. Sticking your finger into the surface of the paint, you draw a cheery orange face over the sun, translucent like a juicy fruit. The whole color of the room changes—the lava lamps glow warmer, melting and changing in the space where books should be, magical action.

You spend the rest of the afternoon tracing emanations down, one by one, big halos of color that represent the vibrations that fall from the light to different spots on the wall, the space between the paths filled with rainbow bursts. You smear over pinhole after pinhole until there's a fat diamond form, a splayed gecko crawling up your window, the white light stopped and filtered at the source. Paint dries on your hands, stretches the ridges of your fingerprints. Your heart is going very fast, and the colors are vivid, absorbing raw sun force that makes them seem to smoke.

Mona is into the paint on the windows. —It's so fucked up, she says. —No one can see us in here now. I love it. Keep going in this direction.

Mona knows about a bar in North Hollywood, gets a gig there one night to play the new songs she's writing: a squat brick building with a dented roof and no windows, and only women inside: blazers, ties, crew cuts, sunglasses perched on bangs, nervous expressions, hands stuffed in pockets and eyes circumambulating. (Women and you, Diane, and where do you count in this calculation, changing in a bathroom stall into a blouse that you hope yet don't hope will be mistaken for a fancy men's shirt.) This is the first time that you've seen her perform since the days before your marriage when she opened for you, Wendy at her side and smoke, black leather, and lipstick coating her like a chrysalis. Now she's molted: hair cropped, glasses hooked into the neck of her blouse. She prefers not to wear them while playing: without them, she can't see the crowd, only a vague peach blur, white faces like a shoreline she's throwing bottles at. She stands up straighter under the guitar strap, sniffs loudly, opens her eyes to stare. Behind her, the hot bar lights melt her shadow like an oil slick climbing the wall.

This is a song about a girl who broke my heart and whom I wish all the best, she announces.

And the crowd laughs and hoots and claps before she's even started singing, when her wrist starts chucking at the strings in old, good three-chord agitation, her index finger curved against her thumb as she pinches, twists the pick.

The crowd loves her, applauds more and more with each new song—and she keeps having new songs, reconfigurations of chords and melodies and progressions hung like fairy lights on bramble forests of words that describe other people, other rooms, other lives than your own—not the furious songs she sang before, but a new music, the ghost of something that haunted *Space-Girls* and then moved on, leaving only a silent grove of wet grass, bare moonlight. Each song is a letter to someone, and Mona folds them into planes, bare fingers strumming up a wind with her new, whole guitar; she flies them into the crowd, and the crowd catches them while you try to find reasons that the words she sings might describe you, at least a trace of you. And you think of something she said to you in a dream: *our story looks very different depending on which of us you think is more culpable.* Is one of you more culpable, Diane? Is culpable the right word? And when Mona finishes and bows, the women push toward her, circle her; their eyes light up.

WHO DO YOU IMAGINE APPEARING at your concerts, Diane, when *Summer Fun* appears? I mean, I will. Lana Corot will. The two of us sitting in an empty auditorium, applauding you as you play on the piano. Who else will be there, specifically? You had imagined the same faceless teens who are always there. It hadn't even occurred to you to consider other possibilities, or to consider that although this room is full, it is small compared to the places you and your band of men have performed. Considering that, you start to hear a tiny whistle of escaping air in your mind, a puncture in the balloon you've spent the past year since your night on the beach slowly filling with your breath.

OKAY, YOU SAY TO YOUR family on the phone across the gap of time zones, the cloud of transatlantic relay static. —Okay, a rough playthrough. Just—you know, try to realize that it's not going to be this terrible when it's done. Okay. Here goes. The spiritual sound of 1967.

You hold the receiver up to the console, set up the playback. The backing tracks stream in. A wild bass flaps, imagined Gabrielino and Chumash natives chant, kettle fill drums march forward angrily accented by fast guitars that feed back into themselves in reverse like storm clouds. The take grinds, repeats, swells for a good ninety seconds, all of it galloping across America from relay point to relay point, like a blood-glutted worm writhing in cool desert. You imagine your brother and cousin receiving it in their ears nine time zones away. You imagine your dad listening to it, the cherry of his cigarette floating somewhere right of his fat cheekbone like a misaligned third eye, bobbing in tune with the chords. His other eyes squint. His teeth grind. The take ends.

See without the voices on the top it has kind of a temperature and sonority issue, you say over the phone. —You maybe noticed. But that will take care of itself.

A horrible delay follows, which you ascribe to the operator.

We believe in what you're doing, B——, Adam says, gently.

Panicking, you set the receiver down.

YOUR MOTHER, WHEN YOU CONTACT her, suggests you wear what she calls normal clothing for lunch, to make it easier for her. She suggests the place for lunch, too, a café bored into a quilt of storefronts in Playa Del Rey, a sidewalk island between stoplights full of cruising cars in all hues. The walls of the café are painted a teal so dark as to be almost navy, and each white-clothed table is stocked with salt, pepper, ketchup, and its own painting. More than one painting, sometimes; paintings crowded into the spaces between paintings, crushed in, sunbursts and moonlit gardens, wheat fields and beaches, spooky abstract connect-the-dots over splotches of primaries, each in its own shadowbox frame. The only light, beyond a tea candle on each table and some City Code-mandated sconces, is the sun, funneled in through a single wide window that rattles every time a car passes outside, and the sun doesn't reach all the way to the back wall.

Your mom orders a salad laden with pink shrimp and orange wedges. She looks down at it, faint, pinched smile reflecting in her coral lipstick. She's gotten very old, you realize, since last you've noticed, like her own shrimp's shell wouldn't take much anymore to crack. You order a burger and feel too sick to eat it, hair hanging around your ears over a red headband with tennis dress and sandals, which you figure is pretty normal for a lunch and beach outing with one's mother. She doesn't confirm this or deny it.

So—so the doctors are sure, she asks you after a while.

Gee, I never thought of asking any doctors, you say. —What kind would you even ask?

I don't know, she says. —A hypnotist, maybe? It's an interesting question.

You both sit there, chins in hands, pondering the question.

How'd you find out about this place? you ask her after a while. —It's kinda spooky.

I know, she says happily. —It's been my little secret for years and years, ever since Adam started going to school. Get up, get the wash in, put away the breakfast dishes, sweep the deck and make sure the beds are made and your father's ashtrays cleared and the bathroom's spic and span, and if you do it fast enough, you get to zip down here for a nice, long late lunch. Sometimes I bring a book, sometimes I do some drawing, sometimes I just chat with the owner. He's a nice Japanese man. He knows all kinds of interesting things.

She doesn't elaborate on these.

I didn't know you drew, you say after a while. —We can make one of them part of the album art, maybe?

You look at her, almost hungrily, but she bites her lip. —They're only on napkins and things, she says carefully. —I don't save them.

Can we get a napkin right now, you ask, but you know she won't show you this piece of her world.

Your dad doesn't want me to meddle, she says. —He says we need to keep out of your affairs, that you don't want us around. Other things too. —She pauses. —He really misses you, B——, she says, and she claps her hand over her mouth. —Oh no, she says. What do you want to be called now? Do I need to think of something?

Diane, you say. —I don't want to talk about Dad.

This last part feels dangerous to assert, but she may have only heard the first part: she may not want to talk about him either. But it's so rare that you and she have ever talked about anything else: there are not many paths that feel correct.

Di-ann, she says, nodding her head deliberately on each syllable. —Okay. Got it. Okay. We don't have to talk about him. Hello, Diane. I promise I'll get better at that.

You look down at your plate. —I mean, just if you remember.

You watch the tea light for a while, and then you lift your head. She is looking back at you, a shrimp balanced in her fingers. What is her expression? You see fear, certainly, but you don't know if it's of you or if it's of herself: maybe she will say the wrong thing. Maybe she will disappoint you. It's suddenly very important that you communicate to her that she is okay, that she is safe, that any sadness you feel about how she is handling this, you will make it your responsibility to correct. So you smile, and soon she smiles too. The old agreements still hold.

Do you want to go for a drive? you ask her.

You need to go to work, don't you? she asks nervously. —I don't want to ruin your work.

I don't, no, you lie.

A QUICK CALL TO THE studio sends Midnight Automotive et al home for the day, with full pay for the never-held session. You take your car, leaving your mother's hovering in the tiny angled lot adjoining the restaurant block. And off you tear to the highway, floating over the roads through chugging dotted lines of traffic and around the wild jasmine orbits of the off-ramps, windows down and knocking you and your mom's hair down in split end tangles, both of you in sunglasses and looking ahead in parallel streams of thought, and one of your songs comes on the radio, Diane, but you turn it off.

She wants to take you, she says, to Venice, so that you can see the house where you were born. It's hard to find; the Venice she remembered is covered in strip malls now, bubble letters advertising two-for-ones and daily specials and bright blue and pink paint covering every surface. The beach is covered in green glass Coke bottles, and the air stinks of burger meat fried in canola and cooking suntan butter beneath bikini straps, every wave lousy with surfers. Again your songs are playing on different radios; this time there's no way to shut them down. No one is looking at you; the sight of a weird gross-faced tall lady walking with her mother apparently does not register among the teens.

This is just awful, she says after the third circuit around a stretch of fenced-off beach, hunting for some sign of your former backyard. Finally she sits and sulks on a seawall. —This is just the pits.

Gee, I'm sorry, you say.

It isn't your fault, she says. She pulls out a skinny cigarette and struggles to light it in the sea wind.

I wonder whose fault it is, you say.

Some other person's, she says.

You sit next to her and breathe in smoke and salt, ignoring the choruses of your songs. After a while, you pull a joint out of your pocketbook. —Can I light this off you? you ask.

She lifts her sunglasses. —Is that drugs? she asks, wonderingly.

Sure, you say. —Want to try some?

She hesitates, eyes sparkling, but ultimately nods. You get the joint lit and show her how to smoke it; she coughs. —Too rich for my blood, she says.

You take it back, and side by side, you generate rival clouds of smoke, each slowly dissipating and converging in the air's secret convections.

I just remember the way it used to be out here, she says. —Wake up and cook the coffee—drink it looking out at the water— seagulls on the patio—and at night, sometimes, the girls sneaking out here with beers or gin, drinking them on the beach. I used to watch them out the window; I tried to stay low so that they couldn't see much of anything of my face.

I used to do that, you say. —When you and Dad were at dinner. When I didn't want anyone to see me. I'd hide under the porch.

It used to feel so desolate here, your mother continues, not seeming to have heard you. —Like the very end of the world, especially when your father was away, and I was just here, working, with you. I used to come out here and feel so alone. And now it's just *spoiled*. —She exhales. —You used to love it here, too, she says. As soon as you could walk, you went running for the water. Just charging, like you had no fear of it at all, like it wasn't real. I had to pull you back in before you drowned.

Dad didn't come after me? you ask.

Your dad wasn't much for swimming, she says. —Her cigarette is nearly gone; she puts it out on the seawall, holding the butt carefully like a marble she's afraid to lose in the sand. —Your father—Diane—you can't tell him what you've told me, she says.

I know that, you say quickly. —Don't worry, I know.

He can't know about it, Sue pleads. —For one, he's old—his heart—it could be a real shock.

Gee, I sure wouldn't want who I am to murder him, you say.

Also, you don't know him like I do, she says. —He doesn't let things go. You don't know how much trouble he can make for you.

You turn to look at her. —Why do you think I don't know about the trouble Dad can make, you ask.

I guess you probably do, don't you, she says, behind her sunglasses.

You look at the sand, letting your joint slowly go out in your fingers, red hem moving across legs. You should apologize; you feel very strongly that you should do this. This is what she needs, and you need. Why can't you do that? Instead, you listen to her open her bag, take out a tissue; she sniffs twice, three times, tightly. You can hear her take her sunglasses off, dab her eyes, put her sunglasses back on. She lights another cigarette; smoke bleeds like a ghost around her cheeks. When you look at her full on again, she's looking at the sea.

What's he gonna do, anyway, you say after a moment. —He can't touch the business anymore. He can't change the album.

He could have you put in jail, she says, voice dreamy.

They can't put me in jail for releasing an interesting album, you say.

They used to do it with movie stars, sometimes, she says. —You'd read about it in the papers.

Times are changing, you say to the ocean.

It's a while before your mother speaks again. —Are you sure this is what will make you happy?

You don't have any answer to this.

Being a woman, she says. —It's kind of a—a cruddy thing to be, Diane.

You still don't know how to answer, but you guess she's not really expecting an answer from you. After a while, you stand up to stretch; she stands too.

I don't know how I'm going to explain this tan, she says to herself.

TOGETHER YOU WALK BACK ACROSS the green glass beach to the car and take the freeway back to her secret restaurant, where you find her car missing, towed.

Don't worry about it, she says. She writes the phone number of the towing company in a notebook for tomorrow. —Now I just need to figure out where the bus stop is, and I'll be all set.

I could drive you, you say.

She smiles. —Well, goodness, then he'd see you, she says.

We should just tell him, you say angrily. —We should just tell him everything.

She laughs, a high panic laugh, and you laugh too. Then she passes you a cigarette from her pack. It's slimmer than the ones you're used to, like sucking a drinking straw until your head gets light.

You drop her six blocks from the house and around a corner, so that it's unlikely she'll be observed. —Be careful, she tells you, and she begins to walk down the sidewalk at an even pace. You watch her, bag swinging as she disappears in your mirror. When you think about it, Diane, you've never seen her smoking before; her skinny filters have always been absent from your father's ashtrays.

THE STACKS OF TAPE GET higher as you bounce multiple tracks down to single ones and start new tapes from those seeds, pitch shift up and down and call back performers for overdubs, spend whole fat days marinating in chants and rhythms and harmonies destined to be chopped to four quick bars' worth of transition between cuts. You smoke a lot; you order in a lot of food; you get to the sessions early and you stay late; at night you can't sleep and so you light candles and sing in your bathrobe to strange gods filtered through your painted moonlight and Lava lamps.

It's some combination of these elements that gives you the idea for recording "Donner Pass."

The plan, when you start to lay it out, is pretty feasible in every way except financial, and you're long past letting that stand in your way. The musicians are understanding, though there are questions about the overtime fees involved; agreements are brokered; an engineer is dispatched to negotiate with the studio manager for equipment loans. Phone calls are made; carpool assignments are struck. It doesn't occur to you to call Mona until you're already bound north on I-5, refueling the hovercar flotilla en route through Bakersfield.

Oh gee how are you, you tell her via pay phone. —So I'm not

gonna be home tonight or maybe for a couple nights because I've gotta take the band into the mountains to do some recording, if that's cool. To the Donner Pass.

Part of you, you realize, hopes she's disappointed that you won't be home.

Have fun, she says brightly. —Don't eat anybody.

LATER, AT A STOP IN the Bay Area to buy extra clothes, jackets, rain gear for the musicians, along with a gas generator and a camping store, you suddenly want very badly to talk to her—suddenly you remember sitting in her bedroom listening to records, long ago, when you were a man and you were cold—and the conversation no longer seems to suit you. So you call back on another pay phone, but the line to your house is busy. And you make yourself smile at that, make yourself whisper a prayer for her success, whatever that means to her.

YOUR INITIAL IDEA IS TO use the tents and Colemans purchased in San Francisco to camp out at the intended recording site, just where the Donner Lake breaks off via a stretch of creek into the Truckee River, but the engineer insists you find a real hotel.

The recording equipment can't get wet, he explains. —Plus we have a full day of recording tomorrow and we're not going to be able to keep the whole band out here to get a good take.

We're not gonna play well if we stay in a hotel, though, is the thing, you explain. —The whole point is to play as if we've been destroyed from staying outside in the weather because that's the power of the weather, which we have to get on tape.

The equipment is on loan from the company, though, and the engineer insists he'll lose his job if it's destroyed by the power of the weather, so you suck down a compromise to your vision and find a hotel. This is harder than you'd thought it would be; the ski season is out and most places you stop at are locked up until next winter. By the time you find a place, it's near sundown and there's nothing for it but to jump on the opportunity sight unseen. The rooms are plush enough, dark billiards-green carpets and mahogany furniture with skimpy white lace curtains that barely filter sunlight, like a powdered sugar dusting over a stiff zucchini bread crust. A candied cherry painting of either a Madonna or a burning/weeping saint hangs above every bed. You stare at the painting, trace the garish holy fire in printed oils around its hyperbolic active edges.

We need this painting for the album, you say. —I'm stealing this painting.

This done, you round up everyone for dinner in the luxe, louche restaurant grafted onto the hotel's edge. "In the Wee Small Hours" pipes over the PA while a waiter comes to the cluster of tables you've all commandeered, patiently gathering orders and qualifications, and you wolf complimentary garlic bread and duck and weave your head to the *ring-a-ding-ding* horns and strings.

We need this for the album too, you insist.

Maybe we need this garlic bread on the album, says the marimba player, and Midnight Automotive laughs at you. But you consider it. Wheat, milk, healing. You are wearing a silver blouse with a necklace you bought because it looked magical to you in the window of a store, and waiters are staring at you, refusing to believe that you are what you are. You miss your wife who will not be your wife forever: here, in the mountains, you realize for the first time that this is true. But your album will be forever. And so you stare at the bread, and so you think about what you need from it.

No one knows what to do about your room assignment at all. It seems obvious to you: you and your bassist are the only ladies. You wait for people to understand that, or to be willing to understand that, you guess, before you suggest it tentatively. Everyone agrees because you're paying them. They seem embarrassed somehow, and you wish you hadn't given them cause.

Your changes of clothes put away for the night in the dresser, you and the bassist settle in side by side in the twin beds, unfamiliar Westerns playing in black and white on the TV. She carries teabags and brews a pot using aluminum foil and hotel matches, and you each carry a hot cup in your hand like it's Christmas wassail.

This is nice, you say. —I'd never have quit touring if it was always this nice.

She nods furtively, and you realize that she has no desire to speak to you. On the tube, a young cowboy explains a plan involving the entrapment and murder of rustlers. You try to involve yourself in it.

You're very brave, she says to you, just as the cowboy is shot in the back. —The things you endure I can't even imagine.

She says this and she looks at you, smiles faintly, and you make sure to smile back at her so she'll feel normal and not afraid.

YOU GO TO USE DRUGS on the balcony. It's cold up here in the mountains, colder than you'd have expected for the high summer, and you shiver in the melting wind. There are stars, and you imagine drifting between their waypoints in a woven raft. From some balcony below you, you can hear the male members of your entourage laughing, loud and bass. And you drop ashes on the snow heaps below you, looking out at the river. No new snow is falling, Diane; all of it just sits here crystal and preserved, safe from summer melt by grace of altitude, nothing else.

SO YOU GO DOWN TO the river, you and Midnight Automotive and your friends, you in white and blue with a lunar crown at the head of a delta like the smallboss of all the geese, everyone hauling instrument cases and folding chairs and your old Wollensak recorder. It's a state park, ill-attended on a weekday at this time of year, and although the engineer has insisted that you have a story worked out for whatever park ranger intercepts you, you encounter no one on your way down the slopes of grass and trees that lead you to the river itself: framed by spiral mountains, wide as a lake in places, tightly funneled into white rapids like wet, braided lightning in others, yet constantly moving forward. You have no clue about directions up here, but clearly it's flowing west; everything is. Anyone who tries to go crosswise to the river must go under, a team of horses and wagons sucked out of existence.

Does anyone know the exact spot where everyone started to eat everyone else, you ask loudly. —It's real important that we get those psychic resonances on the tapes, okay?

Ghosts are a thing you believe in now, says the engineer, but you ignore him. Physical resonances are a more immediate problem, is the thing: the musicians obviously need to be set up in their folding chairs as close to the water surge as possible, but the crash and roar over the stones produces sound waves that outright cancel anything your instruments may produce. Everyone waits patiently in his or her chair, tuning, as you take your trusty Wollensak to different spots, attaching different meshes and filters to the pickups. A couple of times, sweating, your hands touch; he jerks his away.

This is useless, he finally says.

No, we can't give up on this, you say. —Try moving it maybe three inches this way, right. And we can use this chair to make a kind of a baffle, which should filter out a lot of the high pass and keep the low end loose—

We need to go home, B——, says the engineer.

You ignore this, squat on your heels and poke at the recorder, thinking about rotation, mesh pieces you might attach, every possible variable. You look out at the river, pressing forward, crashing and rolling down from the Continental Divide until it reaches the ocean to become waves for surfers to ride, and you imagine that your anger is rolling out with it. If you hurt or disappoint anyone, you know, you'll be like your father was, and that can never happen.

Patiently, you try to explain. —If you're like making a painting or something, you say, —you can just make up whatever you want to. Because people are just seeing like red and purple stone dust and oil, right? And the pattern of the stone dust is fooling them. But if you're taking a photo, then people are seeing the real thing. You're sucking up light, right? So you've got to suck up the right light. It has to be on the *tapes*. And it's the same principle here? We've got to haunt the tapes. Otherwise the album will fail.

You think you can hear one of the band members mutter the word *Diane*, maybe in reproach, or maybe this is just a ghost hallucination. And you realize that your engineer—no, that all of them—are receiving hourly wages to be here, hourly wages that your soul first generated for them and is now jeopardizing for them. That's all that's keeping them here now; that's possibly not enough.

Your band watches you. You watch the river. Silver current, leaf boats rushing downstream to oblivion, hidden fish spouting enough foam where the rapids stop for you to float on. A whole island of bubbles you might build.

All right, you call, turning about and clapping your hands. —There's only one way out. We all need to go into the water.

THUS YOUR BASSIST PUTS HER hand on the small of your back and slowly lowers you into the river where the settlers died. The hem of your skirt flares in the current and silver drops bead on the leading edge of the crescent moon strapped to your forehead. Then rise, sputter, baptized Diane forever in the eyes of your congregation.

Everyone, c'mon, get in, you shout, —this is it, this is what we were missing—

The bassist is the first to follow you; the drummer strips off his shirt to reveal a salt-and-pepper Iron Eagle of chest hair that mats to his pectorals in the instant his cannonball strikes; everyone else follows. Clothes soak, drag, disappear piece by piece, rush into the rapids as everyone circles and splashes and chuckles, all of them on the clock. Smiling, the vibes player forms his hands into a steeple and shoves a controlled burst of water into your face, sending you down. You splash back in a wild spiraling flail, and he laughs and lets the current drag him further along. And your moon crown is gone, Diane, washed away into some estuary where the wolves go and no one besides.

The only one left on the bank is your engineer, alone with an expression you can't read among a skeleton scrub forest of empty folding chairs stacked with instruments and cases. —*Record this*, you command. And he is on the clock; he takes the Wollensak and points it at you and the band and the ghost water vibrations that waft from your bodies as the water kills everything bad in you, and all of you are only good now.

AND WHEN YOU COME DOWN from the mountain, Diane— when you and your collaborators put your clothes back on, pack up the cars, let the asphalt river carry you back west to the last outpost of civilization—you'll take this entire recording and crop it to a tight ten seconds, mixing it behind an urgent bass-and-organ fill, a glaze of joy and river scum to provide texture that all but the most expensive stereo equipment will miss. But it will be there; you know that. It *is* there: joy haunts the recording, every detail of it present in the waves, your half-naked laugh as you dive and your legs kick up and disappear, the cannibal ghosts of the river roaring in the natal surf that rocks against you. You paid for all of it.

But the microphone sucked this into the tapes as well, Diane: the silver jet that tears the sky open as it streams across the mountains, high above you and heading west as well, a jet just like the one that will soon bring your family home to you. You can hear their voices singing now, more beautiful in your head, more good to you than anything microphones can record. Soon you will help them, too.

Love, Gala

# November 22, 2009

Dear Diane,

It was Caroline and her obsessive willingness to survey YouTube panopticon footage, her power to squint at compression artifacts until they resolved into auras, that finally brought us to Mona Slinks. Caroline had been looking for studio clips from the sessions around the *Space-Girls* era, alternates of the famous photos from "Psychic Attraction" (you at the piano, your family circling your shoulders like a congregation), some shadow of Mona in the corner of a frame. Instead, she found a café open mic that someone had filmed, maybe without the knowledge of the participants. The grainy video had seventy-two views, a mic placement that sucked up every crowd chuckle or clinked mug, the stage and performers squeezed into a spatial dungeon in the lower left of the frame. From the applause, even compensating for echo, there couldn't have been more than fifteen, twenty people watching each performance. In the corner, a blocky camcorder timestamp gave the year: 1998. We watched it while we were in our underwear, the space heater on us against November chill, a plate of canned spaghetti I'd made split between us on the bedspread.

It was hard to make out the exact appearance of the woman who was performing: Agness Underwood, said the description. Her body glowed in a compression artifact aura—did she have short hair? tank top? glasses? wrinkles cut deep in suntan skin?— and room tone hiss and tape degradation had largely swallowed up her chucking guitar strings. But we could hear what she was singing: "Psychic Attraction," with the original lyrics.

Thanks, she says, voice rasping at the conclusion of the performance, which earns hoots and whoops. —I wrote the words to that one.

There's good-natured laughter, and the performer laughs along with it.

FROM THERE, IT WAS AUTOMATIC. The coffee shop in the video was still in business; it still had a legal address listed with the Montana secretary of state. The ZIP code was adjacent to the PO Box for Lipstick Killer Recordings. And as Caroline pulled up a copy of the local phone book, hunting Agness Underwood's address, I found myself praying: don't let there be anything. Let this trail be dry. But there her address was, plain as the ocean. Caroline plugged it into the map search, rubbed her hands together as the street view began to load.

A COUPLE OF WEEKS BEFORE, me, Caroline, and Ronda were all together in the bar in Elephant Butte, a social outing, a queer takeover. There was nothing to take over; the vacationers were mostly gone for the coming winter, the town people holed up at home, just us and the bartender reading a book on real estate investment between fill-ups. Ronda and I were laughing meanly about someone she'd once known, an older trans woman from a support group with a sense of paranoia about people, a habit of lecturing Ronda about her makeup and clothes choices with a haughty smile—*real ladies don't use reds that bright, real ladies don't blot*—and we sat there coming up with other things real ladies didn't do, *defecate during anal sex* being Ronda's best and *transmute food into bodily nutrients* being mine, while Caroline sat between us at the bar sketching storyboards in her notebook. After ten minutes of transsexual banter, she got up and went outdoors, and the conversation between Ronda and I became one-sided, then petered out. Ronda didn't even seem to mind when this happened anymore while the three of us spoke: she accepted the way the conversation faded when I began to worry about what Caroline thought. That upset me enough that I excused myself and went out as well to find her somewhere in the dark.

I circled the building, but Caroline was nowhere I could see in the parking lot. Where had she gone? How far away had she wanted to go from us? Circling the bar, I suddenly wished for her to be very far away: somewhere she didn't have to hear trans-sexual women talking, somewhere she didn't have to see us or think about us or feel the sadness about us that it seemed in that halogen parking lot moment as if there was no way for her not to feel, because we are poison women, Diane, because our bodies do all turn what enters them into poison, and we make poison and spread poison, because we are sadness itself. There is no way for us not to be that.

This is what I was thinking when Caroline came back from the convenience store across the street, smiling and camera moving, holding out the knife she had just bought: a six-inch switchblade, its handle carved from an alligator, cheap fake rubies its eyes. She hadn't been thinking about us at all: if our being mean to the older trans woman had upset her, she had quickly forgotten it.

I'VE GOTTA GO INTO WORK tonight, I said, getting dressed. —I'll leave you and your grandmother alone together.

You're joking? she said. —Come look at her house with me. Don't be a doof.

I'd made it onto my bike before she appeared on the porch, buttoning a pair of jeans against the cold.

What the fuck is wrong with you? she asked me. —This is my grandmother, finally! We've been trying to find her for like months! Can you not take like fifteen minutes to be late to work? It's not like you do anything! You change water for people!

I looked at the cis woman I'd summoned, standing there in the afternoon light, her roots now almost totally exposed beneath her fading purple fringe.

I should not have to take care of you, she said from the porch, and her voice was different. I couldn't make out her expression: I imagined it angry.

I'll be back late, I repeated, trying to keep quiet: I didn't want to be angry back. —You know—help yourself to anything in the fridge. Or anything you want, okay? Just help yourself to anything.

With that, her hazel eyes resting on me, I biked into the desert, leaving my trailer and the bare sand space beside it behind, before I could see what Agness Underwood's Montana house looked like.

I DIDN'T ACTUALLY HAVE WORK that night. I passed houses behind chain link fences, land on which nothing but death brush could ever grow, gas stations shuttered with plastic bag fossils hanging loose over the pumps and no gas anymore. At one of these I stopped, smoked a cigarette, and cried. I was crying a lot these days. For a long time, when I was younger, I couldn't cry at all, so I never really take an instance of crying for granted when it comes. It will take me a long time, I know, to get sick of it, to want something else.

THE BATHS WERE ALL CLEAN, but I skimmed them anyway, walking along the stone edges in bare feet and sequin dress with my long net moving around two bathers, some young hippie couple here to photograph abandoned boomtowns. When I was done, I looked out at the mountain where I'd first seen Caroline's red eye watching me, and then I went into the third bath, took off everything I was wearing, sank and soaked beneath the water and the stars.

What was the purpose of this, actually? Cleaning sacred springs of dust, suntan slicks, little wet wads of toilet paper? What was actually the purpose of my life, except as a brackish pond where bills and wages exchanged places? Nothing I'd done in the past year had obvious market value. I'd grown some plants—I'd stretched some muscles—I'd paid some rents—I'd learned how to summon the archangels to my aid. I'd listened to my favorite band. In magic you summon the angels to create a clean space from which you can work; over time, that space becomes wider, cleaner, easier to attain. Emptier of anything but what you bring to it.

Caroline was offering me a real place in her story, in yours. That's what I'd summoned her to do. And the only magical error you can make is to lack the courage of your convictions, not to believe, absolutely, that what you desire is good and not wrong. The only magical error you can make is not to follow the advice the angels give. One time I followed that advice, and it brought me here: a desert where I skimmed spa water and wrote letters to you in the dark. And one time you followed it, and it brought you *Summer Fun.*

I sat back, floated with arms and legs spread like a star inscribed in a circle, my head up and then my head down with the heat of the earth bubbling beneath me and the stars washing down from above.

WE WOULD GO, TONIGHT IF possible; we would drive north into the Continental Divide. We would plunge in—race the chthonic spirits of America's cannibal soul to the bottom—and we would bounce, roar up out of the canyon like a bald eagle bursting into flames, on tire tracks of fire we'd fly north and west in the car we'd trade my life in for, drive as high as the mountains could take us all the way to Montana and Mona Slinks's door. I'd stand there at Caroline's side as she bowed, finally, to accept the anointing blessings of her proto-punk rock queen. Mona would teach us the songs she'd written—do away with Caroline's false inheritance, teach us the true one, the one not bound to the world, to *money*. We'd learn to play instruments, to manipulate new forms of video. The two of them would resurrect the Pin Up Dollies, multigenerational, forge anew the band that should've played by your side all along. They would let me play with them, perhaps bass or tambourine. You would join us too. *We would become the greatest band in America at last.*

That's where we were going to now. It was going to happen tonight, once everything I'd bought, everything I owned was abandoned to the red desert sands. It was what every rock song had told me to do.

I STOOD UP—WET, COLD, SHIVERING—FROM my geothermal womb, and I made the Sign of the Enterer, as best as I could without back strain, at the moon in the sky. I put my clothes on and went to tell my boss that I was quitting, effective immediately, to help my cool cis gal pal achieve her dreams. I made it as far as the office, which is where I called Ronda.

Come pick me up, I said. —I need to crash with you for a while, okay?

Love, Gala

# November 26, 2009

Dear Diane,

I'd forgotten how miserable it is to live with other people: the way you wake up in a strange house and are immediately subject to other eyes, the politics of spending as long as you can under a blanket trying to stay warm and nonexistent before you have to get up and invent some kind of plausible pretext for being awake.

It must have been just as bad for Ronda to have me around. On the first night it seemed okay: she came to pick me up at work, lingering with me in the hot tubs for a while first as I told her I was having some trouble with Caroline and no I didn't want to talk about it and no I couldn't go home, and she sat and soaked and exuded smugness from her pores, having told me so. In her truck we were silent, and at the trailer I feigned exhaustion and went to bed on the couch early with the musty back-of-the-closet blankets she found for me, lying awake in the darkness wondering which stars I was seeing smudged through the glass of her window.

RONDA AND I DIDN'T TALK that whole first day. The second day she cleaned up around me while I sat writing to you on the couch: filled the sink with detergent and mopped around me, a furious shuffle-boarder. I raised my legs to let her slop water just beneath me, set my bare feet down in the space where the mop had been.

Do you need some help or anything, I asked.

No it's fine, she said in a cloying, suspicious voice. But she started mopping less angrily after that, and soon she put the mop away and went to sit on the porch.

Sometimes she took a shower while I was working, and I thought: a poison woman is in the next room. A woman like me is there, becoming clean.

ONE NIGHT RONDA HAD TO work. She wrote an address and a phone number on a piece of paper and handed it to me.

Text reception fucking sucks in this whole state, she said. —So it should take about three and a half hours to get out there, work, and come back, okay? If I don't come back or call by then to tell you I'm running late, first thing I want you to do is to try to call me on the land line. Try four times, spacing it out by a minute.

If you don't pick up? I asked.

Call the police, she said. —Give them that address.

I must have looked alarmed, because she gave me a strange, tight smile and patted me on the head. And I thought about Caroline and the money in her bank account, how I should have found a way to take some from her. A big stack of dollar bills I could divide up with Ronda, to keep her from going wherever she was going. I didn't tell her this was what I wanted to do.

The hours passed, and I couldn't concentrate well enough with the sun down to write to you anymore. So I sat by the phone, hand on the receiver, and I tried to meditate and kept losing my count, kept dozing off and snapping myself awake. If I fell asleep I might miss Ronda's call; Ronda might die. I told myself this was unlikely, but I had no grounds to tell what was likely from what wasn't.

At last, delirious, I picked up the phone receiver from its cradle—hours of charge left—and crept with it into her bedroom. I climbed into her bunk bed, surrounded by the smell of her cherry blossom body wash and her body, and wrapped myself in the sheets—my back was aching, after the days on the couch; it was so good to have a real mattress under me; it was so good to have a human smell—and curled myself up around the phone, my cell next to me leaving the lights on, staring at its blue light to make sure it stayed charged and active. If the blue light stayed lit, I told myself, Ronda was alive.

I had dozed off by the time my cell buzzed: *All clear coming home <3*. And I dozed off again sometime between then and her arrival, woke for a moment to find the room dark but for a votive candle atop the ancient NES, her in bed with me: hair damp from the shower, body warm. I nestled in closer to her and fell asleep for a long time.

AFTER I'D JUDGED IT SAFE, I began to go to work again. Work had piled up in my absence—guest registrations, contractor invoices to hassle for cash—and I tried to get in early to make some dent in it, please my boss enough that I wouldn't have to explain where I'd been. He apologized when paying me that week, having docked me for one of the three days I'd deserted him. I couldn't bring myself to give him the rest of his money back too.

I stayed at the dorms too, some nights, when I was feeling too good after the spa to want to take the long bike hike back to Ronda's. The room Caroline had been in was safe: her guest registration was waiting in the office, red stamp across her face: *PAID IN FULL*. I slept in the bed where we'd first been asleep together, and I tried, as my breathing slowed, to work out where she might be given her unknown date of departure, given her unknown rate of speed, her destination unknown. Was she gone from New Mexico altogether at this point, or just staying at my trailer, a lamp burning in my plexiglass window? I imagined my altar smashed, or maybe the trailer was simply dark, candles unlit. Or maybe boxed up and sold on Craigslist for a lump sum, along with everything else of mine: clothes, books, plants, dishes, empty orange prescription bottles that now held cheap plastic earrings, letters. The whole trailer hauled away by the bumper cross of a tow truck, pink slip swapped for a fat check and a plane ticket. All these fantasies of her caring enough to want to hurt me, and of a flat space in the sand where my life had been, the wind blowing over it and over it again until the flat space was smooth.

I lay in the dark and thought about that, and then I texted Ronda: *you okay?*

She texted back—*yeah why?*—but I'd already fallen asleep in the women's dorm, any guest's eyes able to fall on me as they wished.

RONDA INVITED ME TO THANKSGIVING at her father's place, further east, close to the Mescalero Apache reservation. I assembled a Nice Date outfit from some of the clothes deep in her pile: black sheath cocktail dress, weird mesh shawl, bracelets carved from bones, striped scarf, Oldie but Goodie tube of mascara. Ronda went in another direction, kind of a 1980s TV vision: blush-contoured cheeks faded hyperbolically into scumbled blue-black shadow and sticky whorls of mascara, lips blood red with attention paid to their vertical grain, sincerely awful Xmas sweater and skirt-with-stockings below it, hair teased out to intense effect. Her brother Dino rode in with us in the back seat of Ronda's truck, looking at the ground; he'd shaved and dressed as if for a piano recital in khaki Dockers, blue tie-less polo shirt, boat shoes without socks.

Fuckup brigade assemble, Ronda said, and we set off.

WE CRUISED SOUTH AND EAST, meeting few cars as we weaved around the San Andres mountains and the White Sands

Missile Range. I kept my eyes open for incoming nuclear rockets or outgoing creepy government false UFOs, but no dice on either: just red soil, red adobe guardrails, *GUSTY WINDS MAY EXIST*, and sky that the winter morning had washed out to gray. She hesitated to tell me her father's name. —Redacted, she finally offered, and I reminded myself not to say this name around her again.

SHE TOLD ME SOME ABOUT her life as we drove. Ronda and her older brother, Desi—Dino, she clarified, was only her half-brother, a product of her dad's distinctly ill-fated second marriage—had been the progeny of an idealistic middle-class white anthropology student and her husband Redacted, a sound engineer and 3.125 percent descended from members of the Mescalero Apache nation, a fact Redacted liked to highlight, though he never seemed to go to any tribal events or know anyone else. Ronda allowed that there were maybe good reasons that her parents had come together in the first place, but by the time she and Desi had been born, eighteen months apart, the bloom had pretty much been yanked from the rose, crushed into an ashtray, and left to steep in a mixture of rainwater, beer-spill, and Ibuprofen dust, its surface regularly disturbed by the T-rex ripples of the arguments Ronda and Desi watched from their shared bedroom.

Much later, Ronda's mother would blame herself for having run off to Texas with her kids: she'd denied them a strong male role model, strong male rituals of *becoming*. Ronda offered counterarguments—why was Freudian psychology even credible on transness; why hadn't Desi also been affected; why was Ronda's soul alone being described as an awful personal tragedy? Ronda hadn't spoken to her mom for years.

Desi tried to be extra solicitous, enterprising, and cheerful whenever his mom was down, and thus he was honored; Ronda, whose main accomplishment was learning how to fold a note into a perfectly self-sealing triangle, as the girls did, wasn't. She spent most of her years being either ignored or scapegoated, an exhaust valve for all the bad energy the family could muster. She spent a lot of her time in the family computer room, playing *Descent* or listening to girl music and fantasizing about ways she could be hired as a backup singer.

Everyone but Desi told Ronda college wasn't really on the table for her. Desi always tried to be nice to his sister, even when he clearly felt she was maybe kind of a mope, someone who needed to suck it up and like join the army or something. Out of spite she started cosmetology school, failed out, started work at a warehouse instead, got promoted, got promoted again, read a lot of websites, transitioned on the job, got fired. On the day she got fired, she drove to Desi's apartment. Ronda knocked on his door, shaking on his welcome mat with her wet hair hanging over her waterproof-foundation cheeks like serpents coursing over eggshells, cheap dye from the patches on her warehouse supervisor uniform shirt, which she guessed she'd now technically stolen, seeping into the skin of her shivering stomach. Desi's door opened; the floor of the apartment foyer had been waxed recently and smelled like pine, like a forest was springing up at Ronda's feet. Her brother stood waiting. And she waited for him to invite her in; he didn't. So she drove back through the dwindling rain—over as soon as it began, as is the Texas way—to her mother's house.

Six days later she'd packed or sold whatever she had, and she was pointed west for New Mexico, where the birthday cards from her father arrived every one to three years. As her car left the city's orbit—as before her the Southwest began to rise in sudden mountains and canyon sweeps of red desert, tiny town squares and scrub brush that polka-dotted the sand as far as you could see, that foamed up beneath you when you squatted to pee from too much energy drink and coffee along stretches of badlands highway—Ronda sang along with the radio and felt like a mermaid in a net, slowly being winched from the trench depths of the ocean toward the light, low pressure and deliverance. I imagined her that way for the first time as we drove.

WE RODE IN SILENCE FOR a while. —So, I finally said, —like have you seen your dad in the past year, or anything?

He hasn't really wanted to see me, Ronda said, biting her lip. —The forty-eight hours we spent together were not great. Like he told me never to see him again not great.

Oh, I said. —I guess I can't help but notice we're driving to his house, though.

Well, maybe he forgot he told me that by now, Ronda said.

We kept driving. —Does—does your family know we're coming? I asked.

She pulled the truck over to the shoulder and stared at me.

They're my family, she said. —They can't keep me away.

After a moment she started the car again, and I looked out the windshield, thinking about other landscapes, ones I hadn't looked at in some time.

REDACTED'S HOUSE SAT ON A little bed of crushed quartz gravel, a squat ranch-style up on blocks and surrounded by a sprawling wooden porch. The place was in okay repair, a little tool cabinet on the front porch and some box planters empty for fall. One corner of the wood exterior siding was bright white, a tight rectangle of clean lines surrounded by the general soot-and-dust color of the rest of the house, like an improperly concluded flood fill in a paint program. Plastic drop cloths sat beneath the rectangle, neatly folded.

Ronda left me with Dino and went to knock on the front door. She stood there on the porch—biting her lip and squinting her eyes against overcast desert glare with her Aquanetted hair flickering like film grain—and then a brunette, darkish cis woman in yoga pants and sports bra opened up. She flinched when she saw

Ronda, flinched again when she looked over and saw me. I waved, sweating. Beside me, Dino weakly raised his hand and waved as well. The woman crossed her arms.

Your dad is very sick, Redacted, she said. —This is not a good time, okay?

Is my brother here? Ronda asked, stepping past her. I don't know if the woman—Desi's wife Lynda, I guessed—was too startled to keep Ronda out, but she'd regrouped by the time Dino and I had made it to the porch. She maintained perfect *tadasana* in the doorway, her furious intention keeping us out. I waved at her.

Hi, Lynda, I said to her. —I'm Gala. It's nice to meet you! You have a lovely sister-in-law!

She bit her lip at the tone of my voice as she gave me the quick cis appraisal once-over. I could watch the battle in her eyes between (1) throwing me out as a gross, unexpected guest who could not but ruin Thanksgivings, and (2) the possibility that I or God might think of her as unprogressive. I exhaled, waiting it out.

Dino, Lynda said at last. —Why don't you and Ronda's friend Gala come in, okay?

Dino began to move toward the door; I waited for him to pass before following. —Thank you, I said to her as I entered.

IN THE AIR OF THE single massive living room—off which extended a tiny hallway and a kitchenette, maybe fifteen square feet of floor space—sour, waxy menthol tobacco clashed for territory with the waft of roast turkey and corn stuffing. A single complex recliner opposite an old UHF/VHF TV set with a satellite dish cable deftly hand-spliced into it was the major option for seating, along with a wooden kitchen chair and what looked like an outdoor porch swing with ancient mud still caked onto a couple of the legs. The floor was covered in boot prints, though Dino immediately slipped his shoes off, and I squatted to unlace mine too. Every table and shelf was covered with the kind of debris that gathers in the houses of lonely men with technical prowess: coils of wire and loose nuts and screws, sometimes collected in plastic tubs and sometimes not, dogeared volumes of history or biography with black and red spines and solid fonts, big polyethylene hunks of empty computer cases and parts, a stack of speaker cones with too many cracks to justifiably install, but not so many cracks that you could comfortably throw them out. Tapes and DVDs surrounded the TV, mostly Westerns and Martin Scorsese movies, and a Willie Nelson album jacket had been nailed into a wall stud and crowned with the skull of a mule. The only softening touch was the card table stacked with foil-covered food just by the door, the shadow of a coat rack bisecting it.

I finished taking off my shoes and put my clean stockings on the unevenly muddy floor while Dino sat silently on the swing, balancing on the edge of the seat as if he might topple and break were he to relax either forward or backward. Lynda, keeping her arms folded, turned to him and smiled more warmly.

How are you feeling, Dino? she asked. —Are you okay today? Can I get you anything?

No, ma'am, Dino said.

Do you need any water? she asked. —I can get you some water.

No, ma'am, Dino said, pressing his hands to his face as if he was making eyeball wine.

Lynda nodded encouragingly. I could watch her relaxing, drawing some kind of etheric energy from this other Normal Person in the room. Her left foot crept up her right calf.

Oh hey, you're doing tree pose, I said happily. —I'm bad at that one.

Maybe because you're tall, she said. —You should practice more.

I practice all the time, I said. —I was just practicing for like, four hours this morning. Sometimes I practice so hard I see Lord Shiva in neon, just screaming at me.

Excuse me, Lynda said.

She stepped into the tiny kitchen, leaving me with Dino, serene on his couch. I thought about talking to him for a moment, and then I started for the back of the house in search of the others. Ronda was coming in the other direction; we collided, hard.

Can I have a cigarette, she said.

As soon as we got outside to the car, where my smokes were, she opened the backseat door and started to throw stuff from the seat onto the cold quartz: crushed cups, gum wrappers and empty matchbooks, an important-looking binder. I sat down on the trunk and watched her cover the pavement in trash until she finally sat on the ground and whimpered. I tried to put my hand on her shoulder, and she swiped at me like an angry cat. After a moment, I picked up the pack of cigarettes from where she'd thrown them and lit one. Eventually, she joined me.

Your sister-in-law is terrible, I told her, by way of icebreaker.

She always was, Ronda said, in reverie. —She's a financial planner. Stability is their couple thing they do together. —She swallowed some more smoke. —Desi said they want me to move Dino in here with them.

I smoked a moment. —You support him, though, I said.

Yeah, well, they don't want me to, Ronda said. —While my life's in *upheaval*, they say. While I'm still *figuring things out*. They want him to go to treatment.

I bit my lip.

They want him living in Texas, under their power, Ronda continued. —They want my dad under their power too. Get everyone back to Texas, where things are *reasonable*. Where people make *smart decisions*. —She swallowed. —Get everyone away from the black sheep tranny.

Girl, I said, helplessly, and she seemed to feel a little better for this.

I'm glad you're here, she said, and it surprised me: the idea that I might be a positive force for another trans person was something

I hadn't considered. I felt strange, like there was open space inside me, like this was how normal people must feel all the time.

Do you want to just go? I asked her suddenly. —I mean, we could do that. We could get Dino and just take off, have our own Thanksgiving somewhere. We can get good omelets.

She looked at me. —We can't do that, she said. —It's my *family*, she said, as if that should mean something specific to me.

I looked at her for a long time, my cigarette ash getting long, and then I looked away. And after a while, she got down on her knees and started to replace all the trash in her car, piece by piece, leaving no trace.

INSIDE, RONDA'S BROTHER DESI WAS by the kitchen, nodding and listening to Lynda complain about something. As soon as we entered, they got quiet.

Desi looked almost nothing like his sister or his half-brother; short hair gelled up and a permanent part in his lips, revealing solicitous, musteline teeth. His T-shirt promoted a public radio station, maybe a pledge reward.

Hi, he said. —You must be Ronda's friend Gaga.

Gala, I said.

Right, he said; he repeated it a few times. —Gala. Gala. It's nice to meet you, Gala. I'm Desi. Ronda's brother.

He extended his hand for a hearty shake, which I returned.

So are we gonna do this? Ronda asked. —Y'all need help in the kitchen or anything?

I've got it, Lynda said. —Everything's done. Why don't we all just sit down?

There aren't enough chairs though, Ronda said, slapping her palms against her thighs.

Suddenly the kitchen felt crowded, roasting turkey odor overpowering. —I can go buy some chairs, I said. —From like a yard furniture store. Or I can sit on the floor.

It was a little hard for us to plan, is the thing, without knowing you were coming, Lynda said tightly to Ronda.

Honey, said Desi; he put his hand on her neck as if he was scruffing a cat. —I'm sure Dad has folding chairs in the shed or something?

Lynda stepped forward, away from his massaging fingers, and walked to the back of the house. Desi waited a moment before letting his arm drop to his side. He shot a kind of shy, conspiratorial smirk at Ronda, who was sulking. After a moment, he allowed it to arc over to me. On instinct, I returned it, feeling slightly better: in only two hours, maybe three, Ronda and I could leave.

RONDA AND DESI WENT TO get their dad ready for the table, and Dino seemed too peaceful on the couch to disturb, so I spent a minute peeking at the food beneath the foil before I went to find the bathroom, makeup satchel in hand. As with the exterior, big *yang* patches of rust and mold on the tub were fighting *yin* swathes of clean void, and there was a neatly organized plastic shower basket stocked with essential oil shampoos and organic shell scrubs—I assumed brought in from suburban Texas—which sat next to a sad straight razor with a rusty blade, a shaving soap still partially in a wrapper bearing the profile of a cruel cowboy, a dusty bottle of witch hazel, and a patchwork soap bar assembled from many-colored ruined soap slivers. Little bags of supplies labeled *D & L* in Sharpie were everywhere, their zippered edges tufting up like flags, and I tried to count them as I sat on the toilet half-reading a roach-spotted and waterlogged Lew Shiner novel that seemed from the dust patterns to be a permanent sentry atop the tank.

In the corner was a stack of promo CDs. Your name on one of them, Diane, caught my eye.

Making sure the door was locked, trying not to make any sound with my breath, I slid the CD out of its bag: *Get Happies*

*Reunion—Promo Single MY CAR IS AN ANGEL—Not for Distribution.*

The proof of occult power is in its manifestation.

I sat there on the toilet with the promo CD for some time, and Caroline ran through my head—I imagined her disappearing into violet vapors—and I listened to the sound of footsteps, slamming oven doors, metal chairs unfolding bleeding through the walls around me like rainfall. And before I left the bathroom, I put the promo CD in my purse.

WHEN I CAME OUT INTO the hallway, a very large, very old man blocked my way, Ronda and Desi flanking him to either side like a color guard. With every step, the man drove a cane with four prongs covered in tennis ball halves into the parquet like a softcore battering ram. Exhaling, he turned to me in the bathroom door frame. His white hair was buzzed short on a dry brown scalp, and the long, mean line of his mouth looked wilted, like a pole bean at either extreme. He scowled at my chest.

Wait your damn turn, he said, and he slowly turned back and continued his clomping.

After a couple of minutes' work—Desi on point, saying encouragements; Ronda walking behind in sorrow like a pallbearer—Redacted made it to the living room, where he collapsed slowly into his recliner, ratcheted it back with rusty clicks. I had no idea how he'd get it back up again, but the problem was mostly sidestepped by Ronda and Desi lifting the card table full of food and carefully hauling it over to him, like A&W carhops attaching a tray to his car window. At the last minute, a corner wobbled, threatening to pitch the stuffed turkey and its scalding grease into Dino's lap, but I was able to catch it.

Thanks—Gala, Desi said.

No prob, I said, and Redacted started at the sound of my voice.

You a boy too? he asked.

I froze; Ronda slumped against the side of the couch; Dino stared straight ahead, undisturbed.

Dad, Desi said carefully. —This is Gala. She's Ronda's friend, and she's also chosen to identify as female.

Redacted's pole bean mouth twisted and curdled. —I'm gonna be dead soon, he said.

Setting my jaw, I knelt down in front of his chair. —Hello, I said. —I'm Gala. It's a very beautiful experience to meet you, sir.

He reached into the pocket of his shirt. There was a little plastic box inside, studded with buttons like a pineapple. A tube extending from the bottom of it tethered it to something beneath his clothes, perhaps beneath his skin. —Insulin, he clarified.

Oh cool, I said.

He pressed a button on its side; the box beeped like a Game Boy and some substance hissed within the tube. —Keep talking to me, he dared. —I've got as much of this as I need.

LYNDA HAD CHANGED FROM HER yoga outfit into an eggplant cocktail dress and a lot of jewelry in silver and turquoise. She looked at Ronda; she looked at me; she looked at the serpent bracelet twining up her wrist. She smiled.

What's this sorry bunch of nothings done to deserve this? said Redacted.

You look great, honey, said Desi. Dino didn't speak, just closed his eyes tighter. As I looked at the floor, I caught a glimpse of Ronda also looking at the floor: the weird solidarity of kids being caught at something.

Thanks, Lynda said. —I wasn't going to dress up, but then I thought—it's the holidays, why not? —She turned to me and smiled. —I couldn't find any other chairs in the shed, Gala, she said, but you're more than welcome to take mine.

I sat immediately on the arm of the couch next to Dino; my

head and shoulders towered over the table like an awful crow. I set a plate in my lap.

This'll be fine, I said.

LYNDA HAD DONE AN INTENSE job on the spread, especially given the not-great state of Redacted's oven. There was turkey, which Desi carved inexpertly but assiduously; there were complexly scalloped potatoes, corn soufflé, yams baked with pecans, yams baked with marshmallows, fresh cloverleaf rolls, and a pumpkin pie that I was assured was sugar-free cooling on a black metal burner. Redacted ate as heartily as the rest of us, every so often hitting a button on his insulin pump to top off, like it was a gas tank. Dino took very little, and Lynda kept putting food on his plate. The cis people all talked: Redacted and Desi about their work in radio and their bizarre audio engineering experiences, Lynda and Dino about whether Dino was comfortable, Redacted and Lynda about the quality of her food, Desi and Dino about the latter's financial situation and what he was doing, or might do, to improve it. Ronda kept gazing at them, looking for some scrap of silence in which to speak. I felt angry, either with her or for her or both.

Redacted beeped his insulin computer. —Hey, he called, nodding to Ronda, avoiding her name. —Pass me one of those rolls, *por favor.*

Lissomely, Ronda lifted the plate of rolls and handed them to her father.

Gala's all into radio and shit, Des, she said suddenly, and the table fell silent and turned to her. —Why don't you ask her about the Get Happies or Los Paranoias or one of those old person bands? She knows all kinds of facts about them.

I don't know about Los Paranoias, I said, and now the cis people were staring at me. Redacted was the one to break the silence.

The Get Happies, he said. —What is it you like about them?

They have this spiritual quality, I said, blinking as I looked at the table. —I guess they sound like America to me?

You know, I saw the Get Happies one time, said Redacted.

Why don't you tell us about it, Dad, Lynda said, disassembling a roll on her father-in-law's plate.

It was 1982, maybe '83, he began. —Big show in Washington, DC, big deal show, Fourth of July. They had a bad problem with one of their stacks, nobody could fix it, but I knew a guy on their road crew who knew I was staying there a while, and he said, hey, you know Redacted, that bastard, he can fix *anything*. And I *could*. So I got the work done; it wasn't anything, and they invited me backstage. —He paused to swallow another fork's worth of potatoes. —They were terrible, he said. —It was the worst show I ever saw, and I've seen plenty. Meaning no offense to your band.

Well, yeah, 1983, that *would* be terrible, I said. —Like Di—or B——, I mean—wouldn't have even been with the group then, there was that thing with Adam, and Charley was going through—

I don't know about any of that, interrupted Redacted. —I just know they couldn't play for shit. Famous band like that—I was thinking, what'd I even fix their speaker for? I met them, too. I meet a lot of bands, working, and I like most of them more often than not. I didn't like these men. Nasty people. Something real sick about them.

If you like the Get Happies, Gala, Desi suddenly said to me, —you've got to be pretty excited about the reunion tour, right?

I hadn't heard about it, I lied.

Redacted coughed again, and Desi abruptly went back to cutting his meat. Dino had his hands resting in his lap, fork and knife crossed before the shuddering gem of cranberry sauce Lynda had just set on his plate. She looked at me, twisted her bracelet.

Gala, what is it you do for a living? she asked.

I work in a hostel, I said. —Just over in T or C.

How interesting, she said. —Are you doing that while you're going to school?

I'm not going to school, I said. —Just hard to employ in other work?

Redacted looked at me then, and his gaze, I was able to meet.

You're working, he said. —You're happy?

I had no idea how to answer that, sat there in silence feeling everything in my stomach—a thick wash of melted butter, cream, evaporated milk, brown sugar, gourds and sprouts—all that had been given to me, freely, to keep me alive.

If you're not happy, he said to me, —get happy, okay? —And then he laughed until I joined him.

THE CONVERSATION TURNED TO SOME construction project Lynda was involved in back in Texas, the complex details of which Redacted happily engaged with while Desi rested his hand on his wife's turquoise necklace. Dino dozed, and Ronda kept watching the conversation, smiling and sometimes jumping in.

I went to the bathroom again, where I considered putting back the promo CD I'd stolen—suppose Desi got it into his head to play it for me, some kind of special treat, and then he couldn't find it? But in the end, I kept it. When I left the bathroom, Ronda was waiting for me in the hall, her hands disappearing into the sleeves of her sweater, like a little girl.

It's going well, she said, keeping her voice down. —It's going so well.

Congratulations, I whispered.

We both stood there smiling at each other in the hallway, both caught in the planet gravity of the people around the holiday table in the next room, fucked-up elliptical moons free-falling together somehow.

o   o   o

DISALLOWED FROM HELPING WITH DISHES or cleanup, I haunted the foyer like a coat rack while Lynda washed, Desi dried, and Dino lay on the couch under a blanket. Ronda and her dad held court in the main room, Ronda sitting in a kitchen chair next to Redacted's recliner. If Redacted still felt as he had on the day he'd kicked her out, he wasn't showing it, at least not for today, and it was up to him and her, I guessed, to decide tomorrow. Both of them faced the TV on the wall to which Ronda had wired up her NES. She mapped dungeons while her dad powered through the early game.

Is this the place with the fuckin' knights, he growled, sailing to an island dungeon on a log raft.

This is the place with the wizards, Ronda said. —You always forget the order and you didn't even get the white sword. What's wrong with you?

You got your way of playing, I got mine, Redacted said. —I don't need the white sword to bring the pain.

I watched them play, invisible, imagining Hyrule draining off the TV in a whirlpool of pixels and color, watching Redacted's hand do double duty between the controller and his insulin pump like a chess player using a tournament clock.

AS THE SUN BEGAN TO go down, no one felt like waking Dino or raising the question of whether or not he'd return to Ronda's or return to Texas, where the people with good lives dwelled. So in the end it was just Ronda and I who got back into her car with our Tupperwares of leftovers. Ronda hugged her dad goodbye in his chair; he returned it warmly while I watched them from the door. When they were done, he nodded to me.

Get happy, okay? he said, poking my sternum where my bra cups joined. —Remember?

It was nice to meet you, Gala, Desi said to me.

Good night, said Lynda, curling her serpent braceleted arm into her husband's. —Real pleasure.

Dino breathed, dreamed, apart.

WE MADE IT, I CHEERED at Ronda once we were in the car, speeding back to Truth or Consequences and safety. —Congratulations! Now I need to buy two packs of cigarettes and a bottle of wine immediately.

Ronda drove for a little while in silence. —That was nice, she finally said. —I was expecting that to go so shitty, and it turned out to be really okay.

It did, I said. —I mean, don't count your chickens, but it seemed like you and your dad had a really nice time.

What do you mean, don't count your chickens, she said.

I mean, everyone's nice once in a while, I said.

She frowned so hard she swerved a little onto the shoulder. —Are you talking about my family? she asked. —Or maybe are you just talking about how you are?

Stung, I leaned back.

So which is it, Ronda challenged.

I tried to focus enough to answer her; it was difficult to know what to say that wouldn't make the situation worse. —Why would you say that to me, I finally asked.

Why'd you say that about my family? she asked. —In fact, why are you saying anything?

You're right, I nodded. —Let's call a moratorium on human speech right now.

With this, I made the zip-lips motion, and I drew out the promo CD I'd stolen and shoved it into Ronda's car stereo. A moment of glorious vocal harmony—I blinked; weird aged voices; this was unexpected—and then Ronda pushed eject. She snatched the CD, squinted at the print on the label.

What the fuck, she said. —Where did this come from?

I don't know, I said. —I maybe, uh, found it? In your brother's bag in the bathroom?

Ronda pushed on the brake: the aging discs clamped and squealed against the tires, and the car dragged itself to a stop. We were just alongside White Sands; over the ridge, crossing floodlights washed over the sky in a man-made aurora, painting out the campfires of the stars.

We have to take this back to Desi right now, she said, her jaw firmly set.

No we don't, I said. —Why would that even occur to you?

She put her key, fluorescent anime princess chain dangling, into the ignition, but I grabbed her knuckles and kept her from turning it.

You fucking bitch, let me go, she said viciously. —I can't believe you stole from my *family*.

Desi's a jerk, I shouted. —I mean, he seems nice and all; they all do; that's what I'm *saying*. But like—girl, they kicked you out! They're planning to steal your brother away to some rehab facility! They could barely even call you by your *name*—

I want them to fucking love me, okay, she shouted, almost wailed.

And I started laughing; I don't know why. At this, Ronda got silent, wrapped up in herself like a flesh straitjacket, staring at the asphalt and the floodlights.

I let go of her hand; the keychain dangled freely against the car. Her emotions flickered against me, drying out all the moisture inside me, curling me up into leather, into ash.

Families tear you up, little by little, I told her. —For years. And it'd be so easy to get free. Just push on the gas; just keep driving this way. Everything'll get really clear, like a big sheet of paper.

She didn't say anything, and I reached out to touch her on the shoulder.

Don't touch me right now, she said.

God, whatever you say, I said, slumping into my seat.

After a moment, she spoke again. —You never talk about your family.

And I never will, I laughed, but I stopped quickly, and there was another period of silence.

So do you just leave people who aren't as cool as you or who make you sad? she asked. —Is that what you're gonna do to me sometime?

I recoiled. —That's not fair, I said. We're not even dating or anything.

What the fuck does it have to do with anything whether we're dating? she shouted. —Where did that even come from? Just because we're not dating we're not *connected*?

I opened the door lock, swung my legs out, hesitated. Then I hit eject on the promo CD, grabbed its silver-rainbow tongue from the dashboard, and shoved it into my purse before getting out of Ronda's sedan and beginning to walk.

I WALKED ALONE IN THE shadow of a vast military installation, only desert, floodlights, a chain fence to keep me out, a distant unseen flag that protected me from infinite dirt, carnivores, and silence. I took comfort from that presence, from that and the CD in my purse. For a moment, they seemed to be one and the same.

Ronda pulled alongside me. She leaned on the horn and rolled down her window at me.

What are you even doing, she shouted.

I'm confiscating the CD, I shouted back. —You can't be trusted with it.

You can't walk back from here, she shouted. —It's a million miles of desert.

You don't know anything about geography, I shouted. —It's maybe a hundred or so miles of desert is all. Have fun with your stupid life.

I kept walking, but she kept driving behind me, close enough for me to feel heat on the back of my leggings from her lamps. *Take my advice*, I kept praying. *Take my advice and leave me alone*. Finally I turned and glared at her, the sedan bearing down on me.

Go away, I said.

Please get back in the car, she said.

This is how you disconnect from toxic people, I said. —I'm modeling good behavior for you.

I'm not going to leave you in the desert alone, she said.

I don't even *like* you, I shouted.

I don't like you *either*, she shouted back; she sounded as if she was crying again.

This stopped me. I stood there, facing the blinding high beams that hid another person behind them, the desert haloing out. And I thought about her sitting on the arm of her dying father's recliner, telling him he was bad at Zelda. Two faces getting stupider together over video games in a wash of cathode light. This is what did it. I tried to keep walking, but it seemed pointless to go anywhere, or to stay upright. Carefully, I sat down in the sand and brush at the shoulder of the road, abandoning my purse beside me to darkness and scorpions. I sat there, staring into the headlights, until Ronda's shadow crossed and broke them. She sat beside me and put a hand on my shoulder this time, carefully, like I might suddenly scratch her hard enough to break her skin. Or maybe it was just me who was afraid of that.

Love, Gala

# December 21, 2009

Dear Diane,

*Summer Fun* still lacks lyrics as of the first vocal session. This isn't Tom's fault; you know he'd be elated if you asked him to write them. You can't work up the nerve to insist, again, that Mona write them. And how could you write them? For the time being, you decide to record all the vocals wordlessly: just sounds, harmonies, chants, howls. You can go back in and fix them up with a second recording later. It's a terrifying method of working, profligate even, but you feel you're equal to it. You've done so much already, and if you do it once, obviously you can and must do it again.

The morning's howling harmonies go as well as they might be expected to. In the afternoon, you hold a conference with Tom in the booth.

You gotta call me Diane, you say to him. —You gotta get used to it. If you don't, everyone else starts saying, you know, the other name, and *him* and stuff. It makes a problem.

What, you can't say your own name now, B——? Tom asks. —No one can say it? What are you, Stalin?

Aw, c'mon, I'm not like Stalin, you say. —Leave Stalin out of this, okay?

This is literally what Stalin did, Tom says. —This is America, where we use *real names*. Quit being so sensitive about it—meet us halfway instead of pushing us around.

You'd never thought of it this way, that you're pushing all of them around. You turn the idea over and over, sitting in your chair, looking wistfully at the sticky ashtray.

How about this? Tom says. —I can just call you by your initials. I'll call you D, but I can make it stand for David in my mind. That's fair.

The D has to stand for Diane, you say.

It can in *your* mind, is the beauty of this, Tom says. —You can't control what's in *my* mind.

Maybe I can, you say, widening your eyes and making them spooky.

He puts his fingers to his temples. —So tell me what I'm thinking right now, he challenges.

You can not do this: you can only tell him what he was thinking when you told him about yourself, what he said to you after looking at the floor, grinding his teeth: *why would you do that to yourself? Why would you be one of those people?* And his eyes move over your body, widening in fear, imagining the ways it will be surgically transformed, imagining the parts that signify *woman* to him grafted onto it: once you are attached to these parts, will he desire you, by way of commutativity? Does he want to? In 1962, you came to his house at night because he was someone who was a little bit afraid of you. Now he's afraid of you in a different way altogether. Now he is kind of dancing from one foot to the other, working to move past the fight, working to get over that fear: working toward professionalism. This is, suddenly, all that you want too.

Let's all try to be professional, you say on the mic, and your family laughs.

o   o   o

OVER THE NEXT DAYS, WEEKS—WHENEVER you can work up the willpower to roll your car down the hill to the studio for sessions—you draw the band through vocal arrangements, much as you'd draw livestock across the mud of a riverbed. They follow your lead: they pretend to be slave choirs, gears, whistles, plucked-cheek clicks of industrial machines, chipmunk-shifted children who line the unbent highway, skeletons, cannibals. For inspiration, you buy raw meat from a quality butcher and lay it out on the lunch table at the edge of the room.

You don't really have to eat it for the recording, you offer. —I mean you can just chew it so that we can get the take and then spit it out.

All it takes is one egg, B——, says Tom fretfully. —One egg and one worm.

I bet Valley Forge Records will pay to get the worm removed, you say quietly. You don't correct him about the B——: if you did that consistently, you would only be doing that. —Here, you can spit it out into this ashtray, okay? Come on, we're on the clock.

Maybe we could chew on cooked meat, Charley says thoughtfully.

Eddie slowly covers his bare arms with meat, drapes of pork links like deconstructed bracelets, shoulder pads of ribs, a half chicken for a hat that falls off when he leans back to drape a thin flank steak over his face like a death mask. He grips it in his teeth and shakes it like a Rottweiler, atomizing drops of congealed fat and blood, and then he drops it into his hands and laughs.

Later you throw the meat away, uncooked save for a cigarette burn marking the side of a lamb chop, the meat sizzled, popped, dried.

DID YOU RECORD YOUR FIRST album in a week only four, five years ago now? Heedless folly! A week on *Summer Fun* gets you four, five minutes of viable takes, each achieved after hours of agonized indecision and variations, each thrown into the archives, you claim for later use. Sometimes even the finished songs start to become less finished; do you need these vocals there, wouldn't that section of "Frenchman Street" go better in the middle of "Mark Twain"; should Midnight Automotive come back in to write transition parts? You spend twelve hours with a flashlight, stepladder, and drill, trying to find and neutralize the sound of dripping water; then, missing its echoey presence on the tracks, you spend another three working in vain to restore it.

A RARE DAY THAT WEEKEND with Mona home, no lunches or dinners with new friends, no day trips up or down the coast, phone calls late from motels telling you not to wait up. You accompany her while she waters her plants, the whole secret enclave of them out by the pool, in the nook by the pump and the diatomaceous earth storage where you never have good cause to go. Most of them are dead or getting there, and she curses as she waters them from a dented rain barrel.

There aren't any *seasons* here, she grouses.

She stares with earnest hate at her charges, their gray putre-fying roots growing from cracked black soil from which you can almost see the summer steam rise.

While she tends to her plants, you float by the steps of the pool, watching her. When she's finished, she strips down, tucks her hair behind her ears and sets her glasses on a chaise, dives in with her arms stretched to her sides like an aquatic superheroine surveying her chlorine city. You watch her, buoyant, her clear chemical waves sluicing over your razor-burned legs, amniotic water making the tiles at the rim dark.

After a while, she notices you looking at her. She fixes her face in a rictus grin and waves, and then she swims over to join you, sits on the step next to you, elbows you so hard it hurts. And for a moment you wish she was your sister, so she could be in your band.

IN THE MUSIC ROOM SHE plays you her new material, guitar-nylon jungles of three-chord strum, no accompaniment required. You know there are lyrics, pages and pages of lyrics she writes and types and collects in binders when she finishes them. She sings them for you, so many you can't keep up. The melodies are the same arrangement of chords; the lyrics are what matters. She's playing with other people now, a group of women she met at one of her shows who live together in a private house in Torrance. You dropped her off there once after a session, met three or four of them who play instruments: you didn't linger; they seemed nice. Mona goes there a few times a week, sits in the living room with them and plays music that grows, one voice at a time, swells, and finally, when everyone's tired, stops. You wonder how someone would go about selling music like that.

I think one of them wants to sleep with me, Mona says.

You look at her; you laugh nervously. —Gee, you say. —How can you tell something like that? I've always wondered.

It was pretty easy, since she asked me, Mona says.

She looks at you, her long chin raised like a bayonet, and you don't ask how she answered.

ONE FRIDAY, YOU BUY A football from a department store toy section and get to the parking lot of the studio half an hour early to intercept your band when they arrive. The pitcher of lemonade you've assembled sparkles, resting on a rolling chair you've taken from the reception desk.

We need to have a strict policy of joy from here on in, you explain.

Tom doesn't want to play football with you while you're wearing a dress, but Eddie tackles him, and you snap the ball to

Adam, who responds to the gesture, makes a game effort to race out to meet your bad hand's throw. With rules to shape his aggression like a potter's wheel shapes clay to a hand, Tom slowly gets into it, goes out for passes and makes fanatic end runs to the mint green sedan that both sides agree is the goal. In one sense there are teams and in one sense there are not; you fire a pass to Tom on the sidewalk and Tom tackles you, brings you to the ground where you roll from side to side to escape him, skirt twisting around your ankles as you giggle furiously, and later the boys circle the microphone right where you tell them to and sing from throats bright with citrus and white sugar, and you congratulate yourself: for a while, they forget you are what you are.

You KNOCK OUT A SOLID nine takes of the middle eight chant on "Mark Twain" before the lemonade hits your bladder. Sitting in the stall, sugar and acid pouring out of you as you worry about the album, there's a knock on the bathroom door.

Diane, says the engineer. —The man from the record label— Mr. Corot—he's here to see you.

You think about this a moment, and then you flush the toilet, suction wind on your inner thighs, and you begin to apply makeup, trying to repair the damage sweat, asphalt, and citrus have done to your morning foundation.

Harry is waiting by the men's room door for you. When he turns to see you emerging from the women's, his face passes through three stages: he is startled; he is smiling; he is slowly turning pale as his eyes follow the seam of your dress up toward your face.

B——, he says.

Oh hey Harry, you say, forcing residual citrus brightness into your voice. It's up to you not to make this weird.

He doesn't move. —I knew you were recording today, he says. —So I decided to swing by to find out what you've been doing, B——. With the album. How is the album.

It's Diane, you say helpfully. —Guess I should've reminded the guys to tell you, huh? But yeah, Diane. And the album—I don't know how to explain it. Do you want to hear any of it?

No, your band didn't tell me, Harry says. —What a look. Very nice. Is there somewhere private where we can talk for a minute?

How about the bathroom? you ask.

Why don't we go to studio B, he suggests. —No one's using it today.

Studio B is the same room in which you and the guys, under your dad's hand at the boards, cut your first professional recording in a handful of billable hours. The synchronicity appeals. Today the place is vacant: a wide live room, a clear buffet table, a disused trapset, a metal skeleton forest of mic stands. A lone mic stands in the isolation booth beneath a bare, dark bulb.

Gosh, it feels great in here, you say, your voice echoing back to you from the emptiness. —Do you think it'd make sense to start recording in here instead? That's maybe what we've been doing wrong. Being too much in the present time, you know.

The door to the hallway closes, and Harry rolls his shoulders in his coat.

B——, Harry says. —I'd like you to tell me exactly what's going on. So that I'm sure I understand what you think you're doing.

You blink. —I'm bad at explaining it, you tell him. —You really have to listen to the tracks.

Tom called me, Harry says. —He said there were things that concerned him about the recording process.

I mean I know we're probably spending a lot of money, you say; maybe he will be happy if you just talk about money instead of the things he wants to talk about. —But see, we're going to end up *making*—

And I know, B——, what I should say, Harry replies. —I know what, as an executive of Valley Forge Records, I'm *supposed* to say. I'm supposed to be the fogey who comes in and tells you no, B——, stop spending so many hours on these tracks. *Stop creating, B——!* Creativity costs money! And you know, all these terrible ogrish things that your record company man is supposed to say to you, right?

He pauses, grinds his shoulders in their sockets like the gears in a nutcracker.

In another life I might've been up there with you guys, he says. —You've got me wrong. I know creativity isn't a waste of money. It's *good business*. I'm right up there with your vision of things. If we really respect and cultivate those creative elements in your formula, we're all going to do good business together. Not everyone will understand that, but as a fellow creative person, I do.

Right, exactly, you say, wary.

But honestly, B——, Harry breaks in. —Speaking for a moment as a business type. There are elements of these recording sessions that are of concern.

Let's go listen to the masters now, you say. —They can all be singles.

Something in his eyes goes soft. —B——, he cautions.

I'm serious, you say, standing up straighter. —I know no one thinks I can do that, but I can. The first album with 100 percent A-side material.

I'm a creative guy, B——, Harry says. —I understand where you're coming from. I just want you to think about a few other things, too. —You can see his brow flexing, thinking. —Heinz Telstar, in London, he says. —John Black Zero. Crazy Thomas Edison himself—the man tested the recording purity of his phonograph cabinets by gripping them with his *teeth*, B——. He thought he could record ghosts.

Why do you think he couldn't, you say.

There's something about recording audio—that makes men unsound, Harry says. —I don't know what it is, but this whole

industry is built on that unsoundness. The special energetic qualities it produces.

I'm not crazy, you say. —Also I'm not *men*.

B——, he warns.

It's actually *Diane*, you say. —That'll be the name on the back
cover of the album, you know, as its composer. It'll be a hit.
There'll be all kinds of publicity angles. Transsexual women—
women who were men once, according to doctors—will be the
hottest commodity going one day. No fooling, Harry.

At this point he exhales; the shoulder he's been priming
slouches to his side. He leans against the wall of the isolation
booth, his neck, peeping from the sudden gap in his collar, dark in
the shadow of the mic.

I'm going to tell you what will happen to you, he says. His
voice has gotten tight, as if he's been stung by a bee, an anaphy-
lactic spiral starting up.

FIRST, HE BEGINS, —EVERY ACCOUNT we wholesale to—
all of them—will refuse to stock the album.

Aw, c'mon, you laugh, but Harry doesn't share in it.

There will be business for this album, he says. —Professors interested in psychological curiosities. Novelty labels. Sounds of the
circus. This is not the kind of business Valley Forge wants. Think
about what's going to happen in the South, in the Midwest. Those
are your *markets*, B——. We've built those markets together.

That sounds like a really tough challenge for you, you say.

The next thing that's going to happen to you is the movie
magazines, Harry says. —This may have happened already, if you
haven't been careful. Remember Monty Clift? No reputable paper
will stand up for you. You and your family's reputations will be
ruined. B——, I'm not sure why I have to *explain* this to you.
—His voice breaks. —You'll be left holding thousands—tens of
thousands, maybe—in album production costs that you'll never

be able to make back. Valley Forge will sue you, and I will be fired, and a lot of people, including everyone in your family, will lose their only source of income, which will be transmuted into debt. Record stores will close; tax bases will collapse. What part of what I'm saying is wrong?

Maybe your height is upsetting him; you sit down on a chair beneath the mic revolving from the ceiling, looking at him across the space. Frightened, you try to relax your spine, uncross your arms, put on a smile: but in the end, you do none of those things. You just stare up at him, your anxiety rising every second.

You, and I, he says, —and all the good people we know, we live in the suburbs. We worked hard to get there. I've met your father—he gave up a lot for you. And you're going to throw everyone out. Everyone will have to live in the slums, on the street, on the beach. Nowhere. This is America, B——. That's not how people live here.

Don't talk about my father, you suddenly snap, and Harry Corot seems to shrink.

LISTEN, HE SAYS FINALLY. —HOW many of the lyrics have to do with, with sex stuff like this? Let's compromise, okay? We can fix it up together. I can structure your words for you. Make it obscure, *poetic*, like folk songs, so no one really knows what you're trying to say. So the wrong people aren't listening in. How does that sound, B——? I'm sorry, *Diane*.

You exhale, acid in the back of your throat, and you look him in the eyes.

I want Lana to hear it, you say that to him. —And she needs to hear it the way it is.

AND YOU'RE ABOUT TO KEEP explaining what you mean by that, Diane, but he swells up suddenly, starts to stalk toward you like a robot—*oh shit what does he think tell him it's not like that tell him about the world you and she and the women will build—* but he isn't concerned with what you mean; he is breathing far too heavily now to be concerned with what you mean. What he's concerned with—you realize, once it's too late—is that you know exactly how the name Lana Corot relates to this discussion, how it relates to him.

HIS FOOT LEAVES THE GROUND and smashes into your chin, and you feel your throat start to strain like it's being stretched beyond the point where it can endure, front teeth slotting between two lower incisors as the blow forces your chin up. When you drop to your side and curl your limbs into yourself it's more out of terror than out of any Newtonian force he's inflicting on your body. He steps to your side and kicks you in the ribs, taking careful aim; you hear a sound like a snare, a shock like a cool shower, and then pain. He circles you one or two more times, kicks you while you lie there flat and whimpering; he kicks your knee, kicks your shoulder so your arm snaps back.

In a way he is being careful; he is taking care not to hurt you too badly; this is what you tell yourself, along with: *Do not fight, do not resist, he will hurt you more if you try to stop him. Accept what he's willing to give. Make space for him.* Kick drums, toms, maracas, the microphone glittering about you like mistletoe. You wish you had this on tape for the album. You start laughing, and he kicks you hard in the stomach, and you stop.

And here is a secret, Diane: your whole life you have waited to feel like this. You're home at last, like you can set your luggage down. Maybe he'll kill you. You lie on the floor, your manager very precisely beating the shit out of you to prevent you from speaking anymore, and you finally feel innocent of all of it.

FINALLY HARRY COROT IS DONE kicking you. He squats on the floor next to your face. You try to bury your mouth in your arm, but he grabs your hair and yanks it, exposing your ear, to which he draws close and whispers.

Listen, he says. —I want you to understand this. You are never going to tell anyone. I've worked very, very hard for what I have. If you take away what I've worked very, very hard for, I'll take away everything from you, too. Do you understand that, *Diane?*

You pretend to be dead, the ache in your ribs sharp.

You can't call the police, he says. —They'll put you in jail. And when you're in jail, they can make you do whatever they want. They do it every day. So don't think about it.

You start laughing again to yourself, but you try to stifle it. It's too late; he puts his shoe on your neck. It's smooth and cold and smells like polish.

You don't do anything to violate my privacy, he says. —Nothing. All right?

Yeah of course, you say agreeably.

He squints at you in the dark of the isolation booth, and then he takes his shoe off your neck. He squats down next to you. His breath is on your ear, hot and fluoridated.

Did you fuck her, Diane, he whispers. —Is that how you knew?

Your name is worse than the kicks. You start to hyperventilate; you need to get your breath back under control; every short breath is making him angrier, but you can't breathe normally; what is wrong with you? After a while, he gets up and straightens his jacket. An erection tents his pants. He stands in place and bites his lip, exhaling until by force of will it descends. You manage to breathe normally again, like a good kid, face dried salty in the air conditioning like a sugar glaze on a pie.

Wait ten minutes before you follow me, he insists, and then he leaves you along with the recorded ghosts.

IT TAKES FIVE MINUTES BEFORE you realize that he has no way of knowing exactly how long you've waited, but you give it another five anyway before you start to clean yourself up. One of your teeth hurts and feels like it's moving when you run your tongue over it, and it still feels bad to breathe, like you're sucking sparks through a tube. Your knee and shoulder feel mostly fine, though, even kind of warm and good when you flex them. You can't tell whether the tooth has affected your singing voice in any way; you're scared right now to test it.

This is how Lana feels after Harry hurts her, you realize. The thought comes just as you remember that your recording session is still in progress. Your band is expecting you.

YOU SNEAK OUT THE BACK door, imagining your band waiting, pacing back and forth within the soundproof walls, wondering just how much longer, just how flakey you can manage to be. *Good old B——*, they will sigh as they pack up their belongings and instruments and travel together to get dinner. *From another world.* On the way out of the building, you pass the empty jar of lemonade; you never bothered to collect it.

IT'S A WEEK BEFORE YOU can face the band again, a week during which your rib mostly knits, you think, and your tooth fails to fall out. Your voice, lucky you, is fine. Maybe nothing bad really happened, you find yourself thinking: you complain so much about everything.

It's a week during which you think a lot about the record, lying on your back, Mona in and out to her music group or to gigs. You try to stay in dark rooms, not to bother her with the purple-yellow sight of the injuries your record executive inflicted on you. It gives you a weirdly good feeling to conceal how injured you are from her, like you are making savvy investments in a bank of secret pain, investments that will one day compound. If you tell no one, you're secretly the strongest person of all.

You think about this a lot, lying and aching on the bed, snatches of *Summer Fun* flying like wasps around your head. You try to think about the songs instead, but it's hard for you to do so in a constructive way. It feels like everything connects to everything else, LA municipal sewers that conduct every decision you make down occult waterways to the river and then the ocean, where they dissolve in the immensity of other thoughts. All the borders are breaking down. It feels great. You've never been more creative.

Other things you think about: the last moment you saw Lana, the sight of her as Harry Corot's bedroom door closed over her face, her pot smoke fading from your nose. When you think of Harry's voice your brain shuts down, winks out like a match being pinched. You don't want to think about Lana anymore. You don't want to write a record for her. Neither do you want to exist anymore yourself. Or no, I'm sorry: that's too strong, isn't it? Say it this way: you don't want to be trans anymore. You want to be a cis person. It's the same.

AFTER A WEEK, YOU DON'T feel better, but you schedule a session anyway and come in to work. Somehow you keep expecting Mona, Tom, your brothers, *someone* to notice the bruises on you and to ask about them, or to ask you if Harry Corot said anything bad to you, or to ask about the weird echo of pain that you know is in your face, the hollowness in your voice as you call for yet another take of yet another harmony that you know you have to record because a happier you wrote it down once on a schedule, and you'd better do what that happier you planned if you want to one day be happy again. But if they notice, they don't ask. You guess that even if they knew about your being beaten up, they wouldn't need to ask the reason. The miracle is that no one's tried it already.

SHOULD WE MAYBE COVER THE pool? Mona asks you one day. —Last year we didn't when fall came around, and it got all empty and sad.

I dunno, you say. You are lying on the couch of your painted living room in your bathrobe in the dark, spooky wall of sound waves echoing from the John Black Zero record on your turntable, caroming off the beads and bubbles in your mystic diagrams of paint, which you are slowly forgetting how to read. —We can do it later maybe.

Yeah, fuck the pool, she says. —Let it shatter. —She looks nice, wearing a black dress she's stitched with cobwebby lace at its sleeves, gold birthstone pendant at her neck.

Are you going out to play music? you ask.

No, she says; she sits on the floor by the piano, in your usual spot. —I see my music group a lot. I wanted to stay in tonight, if that's okay.

Okay, you say.

So what's going on tonight, she asks.

Not much, you say. —Listening to some records.

One record, she says. —Haven't you listened to this record a lot lately?

Sure, you say, staring at the ceiling. *You turned me onto this record*, you think, but maybe she will be angry if you say it. She sits on the floor near you; the record loops back on itself, drowns you in oceans of evil sound.

How are you lately, she asks suddenly. —Are you like, okay?

Yeah, I'm fine, you say. —Why, aren't you fine?

You could maybe cook something for me, she says. —Or we could go out to Sal Angel's if you want. Is that what you want?

Sure, let's go, you say automatically. But something about the way you say it must be wrong, because she doesn't get up from the floor, and neither do you, like the John Black Zero record is hardening to amber around you, preserving you within it. Her friends can make her happier than you can—this is what you keep thinking—and if this is true, there is no reason anymore for you to try. But that can't be correct either—you need to try, you want to try—and you try to think of how to go about trying until she finally gets up, stretches, walks downstairs to go to sleep.

ONE DAY YOU PSYCHE YOURSELF up to listen to your old albums in reverse order: start from *Space-Girls* and work back. The harmonies and Midnight Automotive chime together, churn together gloriously. How were you so good before? Why can't you be that good now? It's like there's a doppelgänger leading your life, some phantom Diane who's worked her way into all of your photos, smiling at everyone you know, and the maddening part is that no one but you understands how fundamentally deceived they've all been. How deceived you yourself were, even: because you remember being that Diane, you remember how you felt then; you did not feel as happy as your lying face would indicate.

ON THE DAY OF THE next overdub session with Midnight Automotive, your Impala won't start. You spend a solid two hours trying to fix it, shivering in the fifty-degree October chill of the driveway, the car up on blocks so you can replace the burned-out hoverstrips, the sky full of yellow clouds that threaten rain that never ultimately comes, mandala wheels of engine parts arranged around you on an old beach towel. Finally you give up and call the studio.

Diane! your bassist says. —We were just about to give up on you!

You close your eyes and bite your lip hard to punish yourself. —Hey, you say quietly. —Can you drive over and pick me up? My car—something's wrong.

She arrives to find you waiting beside it, hood up and parts scattered. —I maybe see your problem, she says.

Yeah sorry, you say, blushing.

She's willing to wait for you to put the parts away in the garage, but there's no time; people have already been waiting on you. So you get into her car—nicotine smell, echo of dog, broken heater—and you shiver on the seats covered by old blankets as you float down the hill toward the session.

I bet people are worried, you say to her. —About whether the album is coming out at all.

She looks at you and waves her hand. —Why would people be worried? she asks. —You're just taking your time with it. It's a good problem for a producer to have. Everyone understands that, Diane.

A lot of people are expecting me to fail, you say. —I mean, I don't blame them. I mean—you don't think I'm taking up too much time, do you?

No, she says, and you're sure she's lying. So you ride down Sunset with her, stopping at traffic lights, covered in grease, worrying you haven't shaved well enough. Everyone on the street is clearly looking at you. Some of them want to hurt you; you can see it in the smears of their eyes. You imagine a studio full of musicians whose eyes look the same.

At the studio, she gets out of the car. You stay inside until she opens the door and smiles at you.

Everything's okay, she says, maybe asks.

Yeah, you say. —Actually, uh. Maybe today's not the best day for recording. I'm not feeling it today.

She hesitates, nods. —Okay, she says. —It's just that everyone's already here, with our gear set up, you know. It'd be pretty easy to start today.

Everyone'll get paid, you say carefully. —I'm really sorry. I don't know why I feel like this today.

She sets her jaw. —Diane, some of us canceled other sessions to do this for you, she says. —It's not about the money. You have to get out of the car, okay?

You sit there, swallowing spit; this only makes you feel more upset. It's good that you're upset, you think; if she sees that you're hurt, then she'll understand that she should leave you alone.

I'll come to the session in just one minute, okay? Just give me one minute, you tell her. —One minute to y'know, to get myself together.

Sure, she says. And then she watches you for a minute, and then another minute, and then she gets up and closes the door, you guess to give you some privacy. You sit in the car and breathe in, breathe out, watching the street lights change, until finally she gets back into the car with you.

I'm really sorry, you say. —We'll schedule another time. I'll pay for that too.

Her face is hard for you to understand and adjust to. —Sure, she says. —It's not a problem. Just try not to worry too much about anything, okay. Just—get yourself well.

This is impossible advice for you to follow, at least on the silent glide back up the hill to your house, the cars all around you filling the sky with white smoke, everyone bound for real destinations somewhere in the city. You keep wanting your bassist to turn the radio on, but she doesn't, and you can't either, sitting on your hands and trying to take up as little space as possible. And many of the engine parts are gone from your driveway when you arrive: another problem you should probably take care of at some point.

EVERY MORNING YOU TOY WITH the idea of scheduling a makeup session. *Later*, you think. *When I'm rested. When I'm well. When I'm able not to waste anyone's time.*

You work hard to get well. It's a little difficult without a car, but you work out an arrangement with the grocer to deliver to you. You cook a lot of things with vegetables in them, watching Mona's dead plants on the deck. Without proper nutrition—sun, water, nitrogen-phosphorous-potassium—any plant, cut off from the earth, is going to die, is not strong enough to live alone. You've got to make yourself strong enough. The album will wait for you. It's only music. You have time.

You wish Mona would help write lyrics for you, because you don't think you can write them on your own. She's real—you think, listening to your acetates in a different running order every night—and you're not. Only real people get language to write in.

BUT YOU STILL KNOW THAT you will get better, Diane, until the day you know that you won't.

MONA'S AWAY IN TORRANCE, PLAYING music with her friends. You're at the piano, trying to figure out the chords to the latest Los Paranoias single, when the doorbell rings. You play louder, hoping to convince whoever's there that you're hard at work, not to be disturbed. But the ring doesn't stop, however loud you get.

When you finally go to the door, your father is standing there.

You pull the lapels of your robe tighter over your chest; your long hair matted to your forehead; your lipstick you hope not too smeared.

B——, he says, and his voice is just the same as it was two years ago, when you last heard it: some great scratch has thrown the needle altogether out of the groove while leaving the record spinning, and by sheer force of will the needle has held itself in position in outer darkness, controlled its descent, fallen right back into its place.

The last thing he said to you: *You can't keep this up forever, B——. You don't have what it takes. One day, buddy, you're going to fail.* Now he says to you: —B——. Come with me. We don't have much time.

HEY, DAD, YOU MURMUR. —WHAT'S happening. What's going on.

You press your bare feet tighter against the porch of your house—the house you *own*, the house you bought with your *own songs*. The house is lined with dead plants, full of food dirt and napkins and empty bottle pyramids, its windows slathered in meaningless paint. You see it as he sees it. That's his great power: in his presence, your own eyes stop working as they should.

We're leaving immediately, he says. —Put your coat on, if you even own one anymore.

You stand up straighter, the familiar sting of his contempt registering on your brain as you feel yourself adjust to his presence, aspic firming up with the temperature drop.

Hey Dad, you say. —Come listen to something a second. I want to play you a record.

He sighs. —Are you going to be a child who runs from his problems, B——? he asks. —Or a man who confronts them?

You want to say to him: *I'm a woman.* But this is the one person to whom you can never say this. It would destroy one of you, you're pretty sure, and it's intolerable, unthinkable, that either of you should cease to exist.

This'll just take a second, you say. —C'mon, you've never been over to visit before.

You bring him into your living room; he says nothing about its condition, the paint cobwebbing the windows. Surprisingly, his terrible vibrations do not tear apart everything you own. You sit on the floor in front of the turntable, at his feet, and you put on the acetate of the latest session for "Girls Grow in the Sun." Your head resting on the speaker cabinet, you watch his face as he listens to it. His shoe taps slightly with its beat, like he's grading you. Behind him, one of your lava lamps has burned out, its shifting forms stilled. When did that happen? You should fix it, you think, eyes registering the taps of his foot.

The music finally stops, and you switch the cabinet off. The acetate, fragile, rests beneath the needle.

It's a very pretty melody, he says, nodding. —The recording—there are a thousand things I want to say about the recording, B——, and I know you don't want to hear any of them.

Maybe later, you say.

Okay, he says. —But to lay it on so thick—destroy a pretty tune like that under all that garbage—

Dad, why are you here, you say.

He sighs, luxuriantly. —Don't question me, B——. We're going to do what needs to be done.

And you know you've already won the one fight you're capable of winning.

You do own a coat, a ridiculous mink mantle you picked up during the good days of recording. He doesn't make any comment. There are two blue Impalas in the driveway, his and yours, the one that works and the one that doesn't. He ushers you into his. You're sitting again in the front seat, the one your mother used to occupy. The car interior smells musty, leathery, preserved, and there's a glass bottle of white powder on the dash. DESPUTAL, it reads. Your dad shakes some of it onto his hand, snorts, and offers the bottle to you.

It's for my weight, he says. —You might see the benefit of it.

Where are we going, you ask, to which he responds by turning on the engine. The hoverstrips whistle; the car lifts slowly into the air, bobbing from your mutual weight. Your dad lurches into reverse motion, pulls onto Laurel Way, narrowly misses the rear bumper of a neighbor's car parked at the curb.

We're going to save your marriage, B——, he finally says.

You stare at your neighborhood as he sends you both rushing downhill. From your perspective, it looks like his car is the only still point; he turns the wheel and whole boulevards swing across your gaze.

How'd you know I was married, you finally ask him.

Don't be an ass, he says, sniffing. —I know plenty about you
and what you've been up to. A young man's rebellion, cutting the
old man out of the picture. It's understandable. Darwinian. I did
the same.

Cool, you say, shutting your eyes as mink tickles your cheeks.

But I let you cut me out, B——, he says. —I gave you the space
you needed. I let you make an honest try of it. I knew you needed
that in order to grow. But I'm coming back into the picture now,
B——, because I know you need me to do that. Don't argue with
me. You can't stand on your own right now. You need my help.

His voice is too fast, too angry. —Did Mom put you up to this,
you ask, lying back in the seat and letting the relative G-forces
keep you in place.

Your mother lives in a fantasy world, he says. —A world where
everything's handed to her. I should have worked harder against
her influence, but I let you down. —He closes his eyes without
braking; you wonder if he is imagining you thanking him.

Please tell me where we're going again, you say, pressing your
hands against your temples as he U-turns onto La Brea.

We're going to find your wife, he says. —So you can bring her
home.

You cover your face, groaning slowly, letting a monstrous
snake of air pass through the falsetto gate of your throat. He
drums his fingers on the dash, and Desbutal grains float like snow
globe glitter.

Toughen up, he says. —It's the mark of a man to have an honest
conversation with the woman you've welded to your life.

I'm not a man, you laugh.

He says nothing at first. —I understand that you kids feel as if
you're reinventing the entire world, he begins. —I read the papers,
I understand the score.

You don't understand *anything*, you shout suddenly.

I understand that you're in pain, he says, licking his lips.

You stare at him. It feels like pepper is flooding your sinuses. Your hand, your rib, your shoulder, the knit splinters in your brain, all the damage you've done to yourself, you've taken it on yourself so that you wouldn't have to hurt him. And you understand that he understands this, somehow, in knowledge prior to words. And you understand that he wants it this way, and always has.

Or maybe this isn't fair. Maybe your father is not evil. Maybe he's just someone who's very good at protecting himself, and what he's offering you is the best power he has. And he is half of what makes up you.

Your spine spasms; you twist up the handle of the door.

B——, he warns, voice breaking.

Let me out of the car, you scream.

Adults don't shout, he yells. —We *reason*.

Slow down and let me out, you yell. —Please!

He speeds up, drives through a red light.

The key to reason, B——, he says, licking his lips and punching in the car's cigarette lighter, —is to recognize when a *reasonable man* is talking, and to respect—

OH MY FUCKING GOD SHUT UP, you scream. —JUST SHUT UP SHUT UP SHUT UP. SHUT. UP. SHUT THE FUCK UP.

He begins to open his mouth. —SHUT UP, you scream, and then you breathe. He watches you breathe.

First of all, he says, and then you press your fingers against your eyes, leaving perfect speaker-cone space for your lips to amplify your scream as you scream and scream and scream until your voice goes out altogether. Scream until there's nothing left to scream, no signal left, just pink noise, room tone, the cars that pass the Impala, which you realize, as your ears adjust to the sonorities of relative speed all around, has stopped. Your father has stopped.

You open your eyes. He's sitting at the wheel, licking his lips, hands drumming unstoppably. His eyes are dry, evaporated entirely; you've never seen them otherwise.

I'm sorry, he says, and you can tell he is trying to be kind.

YOU GET OUT OF THE car, stand on a sidewalk near Pink's, hot dog patrons pointing at you and laughing or muttering, worried, and you stand still with your lit-up desert city spinning around you. You have no idea what direction you should go in. You try to breathe. After some time, you return to the car.

Are you all right now, your father says.

I'm fine, you say, throat shredded. —Sorry for raising my voice.

He straightens up. —You're under a lot of stress, B——, he says. —I understand that. It can happen to anyone who's not vigilant. We've just got to work extra hard to make sure we don't *stay* in that position.

SO YOU ELECT TO FORGIVE him. You elect not to interfere in his errand, to accompany him with humility and grace. Already you feel comfortable, sleepy, as if it's already Christmas, and you're back home.

NUMB, YOU WATCH YOUR DAD park his car in front of the Slinks house. Mr. and Mrs. Slinks are waiting on the front porch. Your father-in-law is wearing a black turtleneck and a knit cap. He's carrying a long case meant to hold a telescope. He embraces his wife and younger daughter as if he's not sure he's ever going to see them again.

Exactly what are we doing here, you ask your father, but Mr. Slinks has already slid into the back seat with his long case.

Richard Slinks, he says, extending his hand to your dad. —I appreciate your call.

Just call me Bill, your dad says. —My son, B——, I gather you already know. Throw your case in the back if you like. You can slot it in right beneath.

Mr. Slinks elects to keep his case with him. He doesn't even look at you or your pink coat. And you know you should run from the car again, Diane, obviously you should. But without you, where will these two dads go? You are very cold, and you pull your ratty mink collar tighter around yourself, keep yourself as safe as you can.

EN ROUTE TO TORRANCE, BILL goes over the strategy. Things have fallen apart; the center has snapped. According to informants, Mona is falling in with a crowd of Sapphic vampires. You, possibly as a result of marijuana use or wicked Hollywood influence, are now confused, infected with a false belief that you have the right to usurp a female identity that can only lower you. The symptom of this evil is your inability, due to immaturity and failure to absorb reasonable lessons, to submit yourself in good faith to the yoke of heterosexual marriage. Like you, your father is good at seeing the secret connections between things. But Mr. Slinks seems less comfortable now that he is in the car with the two of you, listening to your father explain his theories as the bottle of Desbutal on the dashboard steadily drains, proportionate to the hoverfuel in the tank.

I thought you said that Mona was in some kind of trouble, Mr. Slinks says. —That she was being held against her will.

She may not understand that yet, your father says. —The question, as I see it, is whether we park out front or take a stealthy approach. We should also decide—and I understand that there may be some debate on this question, and I'm prepared for it— whether these women's status as inverts means that we should feel free to, as they say, take the gloves off this operation.

What do you mean by that, asks Mr. Slinks.

Your father doesn't answer, only nods. You try to unfocus

your eyes so that the lights streaking around you look like space worms, emissaries from some better world in the skies. You suppose that Mr. Slinks is going along with this because he doesn't seriously believe that your father will do anything but ask Mona to come with you, and that once asked, she'll accept. You experiment with the idea of believing that as well: this gives you comfort, right up to the moment when the Impala pulls up in front of the house, a cheerful ranch-style with a ring of wooden chairs under a spreading tree. One chair contains a stuffed pumpkinhead scarecrow, the other an ashtray filled with roach ends, toothpicks, and olive pits.

Before Mr. Slinks can react, your father reaches into the duffel bag and removes the rifle. He steps out of the car, applying the child locks first to seal you and Mr. Slinks in.

B——, you'll wait here, he says. —Be ready to start talking as soon as I bring her in. She won't be coming willingly, and soothing words may help the situation. Think up a lullaby.

Hold on, Mr. Slinks says, laughing.

I'm sorry for deceiving you, Richard, your dad says, not laughing. —You're a decent person. More people should be like you.

Dad, you say. —Let's go home, okay?

He looks at you, eyes hurt, and then he turns and walks toward the house.

Mr. Slinks is fumbling with the child-proof locks. But you're in the passenger seat, Diane: your own lock is free.

You scrabble the door open and chase your dad through the dark yard, coat flapping open over the cinch of your bathrobe. Seeing you, Bill turns. He crosses the rifle stock in front of his body to ward you off, like he's holding a halberd, or a flag.

Get back in the car, B——, he growls.

You grab the gun barrel; on instinct, he moves his hand to adjust his grip, clamps it down on your damaged palm. You reinforce with the other and hold on, wincing. —Dad, come on, you can't just do stuff like this—let's go—

*You can't just do stuff*, your father repeats, sweating, growling. —It's not as if it's loaded—I asked Richard not to load it—you're acting hysterical—I need you to let go—

Lights are coming on in the house. The sound of guitars strumming, room tone you'd barely noticed: it all cuts off, replaced by shouts, confusion.

I'm not gonna fail, you say, —I'm not, you were wrong about everything—

And as you say it, the fact that you're twenty-four and he isn't prevails. You press through—you twist the gun out of his hands— he falls to the ground. He twists, writhes, shakes, snorts Desbutal grains out of his aging, cartilaginous nose.

You've won, Diane.

And then you set the rifle down and it goes off, discharging a blank round and powder and smoke just past your face, potential from infinite to zero in a single exhausting second.

SUDDENLY THE PORCH IS FULL of shouting women. Your father has rolled away and gotten to his feet; he is sprinting, wheezing and limping, for the car, where Richard Slinks still struggles with the child lock. Your dad is faster with the keys; he scrambles in, guns the engine, tachs it up, tachs it up, power stroke, here he goes; he is gone. You are alone in the yard of the lesbian music collective house in a mink coat and bathrobe, a smoking rifle at your feet.

In a trance, you pick it up. You're holding it when Mona crosses the yard to you, guitar pick tucked behind her ear, eyes sealed against you like the door on a pyramid.

What the exact fuck are you doing, B——, she demands.

You don't know what to say. After a moment, slowly, you hand her the rifle. She doesn't take it, steps back as if you're opposite poles of a magnet. You sit on the grass at the feet of the scarecrow, and she steps back again.

It was my dad, you say. —He surprised me.

You brought your father, Mona says in her alto stage growl. —To the house where my friends, who are gay, live, you brought your father, along with my father, and a gun.

He apologized to me, you explain.

She closes her eyes, and white pain blooms on her lip behind her teeth. She looks down at you, your coat drawing moisture from the grass, the long hair she watched you grow. She looks at your dad's gun in your lap. She looks for a long time. You smile at her, watching as the last ties that connect you fall away one by one; you smile at her because you want her to know you forgive her for it. Of course you understand. And then she turns around and goes inside, leaving you on the grass.

You walk home, the gun abandoned on the musicians' lawn. If you keep heading west, you will strike a freeway or an ocean or both, and your brain is a vast purple aspic of old airless blood in which your focus floats suspended, and all you want to do is find a space to stop, sit down, sleep. But someone else owns every piece of land you cross, and soon the sky is heating up, cerulean, daylight.

There's a man in a throwback Pendleton shirt at the corner. He stops and stares at your face, your pink coat, as you hustle past.

Hey, he shouts. —What's your hurry? Hey. I want to ask you something.

You speed up, huffing; get into a side street, lungs cashed, sedentary heart jostling for position in your knitting ribcage; hide flattened against the recessed metal shutter of a loading dock, praying it's recessed enough to shield you from his eyes.

But he never comes. How important do you think you are, Diane? You think you owe this man an apology, too.

o    o    o

You finally sleep in a dry culvert of the LA River, a place where the water has receded long since but remains close by, cool against your sun-cracking cheeks. And you think, falling asleep on damp, hot concrete: *this isn't so bad. There is plenty lower you might go.*

Somehow you're able to talk a cab into taking you back home on spec. When you get home and hustle inside for the money, there are grains of rice on your front porch. A whole trail of rice extends from your kitchen, whose cupboard doors are all sitting open.

As soon as the cab is paid, tipped 100 percent, and gone, you inspect the house. Different dishes are gone, a copper pot, a set of highball glasses with pebbled accents, a cereal bowl Mona always liked. On the stove, a pot simmers over a low flame. You turn it off; the pattern of the burner has stained the metal base black; the interior is full of rice cooked so long it's as if it was never cooked at all, fat white seeds steeped in so much water that they dried up and burst free, leaving the pot full of dry husks like molt from cicadas.

All the makeup is gone from the bathroom. All the clothes that aren't yours, some that are, are gone from the drawers; all the guitars are gone from the studio. Its light is off, its door ajar, its shelves bare. All tape has been removed. And upstairs, all the acetates of *Summer Fun*—the records you have been listening to, nights, trying to find some way in—have been removed from the cabinet beneath the record player. The house is silent, robbed of sound.

You sit at the piano, crack your fingers, begin to play "Diner Girl." You do this initially because it was a hit, and it makes you feel happy. But soon your fingers, good hand and bad, are shaking too much to play it.

o   o   o

THE FIRST STEP IN RECOVERING is to leave the house. After a few days of lying in bed, you split this task into manageable chunks. You manage to get to the porch to sweep up the remaining disassembled parts of your car and throw them away. The day after that you pull up the dead brown stalks of vegetables in the yard. The day after that you put spoiled food in the black kitchen trash, and the next you take it outside. On the fifth day you manage to think about the album for a while. You're healing, Diane. You will be better in no time. The important thing, until you're better, is to keep yourself away from anyone who'll hurt you and anyone you might hurt.

MEETING MONA, YOU DECIDE, WAS the true actual moment of your birth. Without her, what are you going to do? But exactly what did you do while she was here? Were you ever anything to each other beyond weird novitiates, using each other to get at *female* in opposed ways, purposes crossing at the center? No, you don't know what you were to her because you don't know anything about her. You never will.

You hope you haven't let her down, and becoming certain you've let her down, you hit your jaw hard enough to knock you down the top two stairs. There are flashes of light when you do it, like cameras, so you can always remember this moment. She took your acetates to break them, to shoot them to pieces with her father's rifle like musique concrete clay pigeons while the strum circle laughs. You lie on the floor with your robe spread around your legs like fat leaking from a split beached whale. *Why are you so weak. Why can't you work on the album. Get up and work on the album.* You lie there instead feeling tender toward yourself, because if you do, you think, at least there will be some tenderness somewhere.

Why can't you work on the album, Diane?

*Summer Fun*, up close: a warm texture of takes, sliders, mic placements, session fees, like a blanket of tawny fur you could bury yourself in. From where you're at, distant from it, it is obviously a tiger. It wants you to die.

You lie in bed. *Kill yourself*, you think. *Kill yourself. Die immediately. Take a knife and cut your throat.* You beg for mercy from yourself. If you're dead you can't finish the album, and that's all that makes your life worthwhile. The album is the only marketable value you retain. This last prayer is the only one that makes the tiger pause.

TWO PIECES OF MAIL COME for you in this time. One is a cardboard box on your stoop, spade sign of ketchup packets from Sal Angel's taped to the glass. In the box are your acetates. There's a sheet of hotel stationery taped to each—a hotel someplace in Utah—the letterforms of each line, organized into stanzas, jaywalking across the implicit baselines with their ascenders like the tails of comets. Letters to you. You imagine what one of them must say: *You didn't hurt me like a man. You hurt me worse.* You hide the box in the corner of the studio, out of sight.

The second piece of mail comes from Valley Forge Records, skinny and certified, and you know what it says without opening it.

ONE DAY ADAM INVITES YOU over to his house for Christmas dinner.

Today's really not a great time, you say. —There's a lot of stuff on the album I've got to consider. Can we do like—a makeup Christmas?

I think you ought to come by, he says. —Everyone's already here.

o   o   o

YOU CALL A CAB, PUT on a white blouse, skirt, knee socks, and then your robe on top. Adam's house in Silver Lake is almost unchanged from months before, when you sat here teaching him how to say your new name. The same guitars are in the kitchen, the same uninflected furniture, bare walls. But this time, it isn't just the two of you: most of your family is already here. Adam and Wendy, Eddie, Tom, Charley. Your mom sits, flustered, on an ottoman. Your father is absent.

We asked Dad not to come for this first conversation, Adam says.

Smart, you say. —Is he going to be here for the second conversation?

He feels really bad, B——, Adam says.

Gee, that's rough, you say, your eyes for a moment losing focus.

No one speaks. Wendy holds onto Adam's shoulder, looks at you like she doesn't know you. You remember Mona's arm around her, the two of them sharing vocals on a single mic at Sal Angel's. No one seems to miss Mona, you realize. No one mentions her.

So except Mona, you're all here, you say. —That's cool. Uh, do you need any help in the kitchen? I can probably do that kind of thing for you.

They don't say anything: Eddie fidgeting, Tom scowling, Charley looking at his feet. Wendy, arm around Adam's shoulder, looks at Adam; Adam looks up at you with an angel's mercy and compassion.

I guess you're all mad about the album not being done on time, you tell them, voice louder than you intend. —Listen, I'm really sorry, but okay, I'll say it: we're not gonna be done on time. That's it. Because I've been considering what we've gotta do, okay? —You swallow, try to hook up the thoughts that swirl like earthworms in your mind's drying soil. —We haven't been able to do *Summer Fun* because we haven't been equal to *Summer Fun*, you finally explain. —We've got to go back to the beginning and do it right this time, everything right this time.

They all watch you.

See, I get why you're all wary of me, you say. —Cause it hasn't always been this formula, you know. That's why you're all having a hard time adjusting, right? To the new sound, and to the new, uh, band dynamic, gender-wise. So I figured out a solution. We'll fix all the problems before we even *create* them. There never was a Get Happies. There never was a B——. Just two brothers— a cousin—a neighbor—and the big sister of the family, Diane, a lady from Hawthorne, CA. Like I was always there. It'll work, that way.

Still, they're silent.

We'll think of a new name for the band, you continue. —We'll rerecord everything, each track, hit or no hit. We'll do it using all the skills we have now, like—making sure we don't cheat any song of its, uh, lyrical or harmonic possibilities. We'll get it *right* this time. I mean we're only five, six years into this band. That's nothing; that's zero time. And when we cycle all the way through—when we get back to *Summer Fun*—it'll be waiting for us. Its arms will be open.

B——, says Adam. —Are you done?

Our first track was "Drivin'," you say, raising your voice over his. —Are we still married to that title? We still remember how it goes, right? One, two, three, four—

B——, says Adam again, and this time you stop talking.

The semicircle is watching you, except for your mother, who looks out the window frame to elsewhere.

We want you to get help, B——, Adam says gently. —This is an intervention.

He has a look of great moral sobriety on his face. You look back at him, your baby brother, anger rising in your throat that you try to choke down, re-digest.

Maybe I'm too stupid to get what you mean here, you say. —Are you intervening in the album? Me too, that's why we're having this meeting. So let's go. Let's get recording again.

Adam sighs—Tom cracks his knuckles and shakes his head, furious—but it's your little brother Eddie who speaks.

Who even cares about the album, he shouts. —B——, you're blowing it for us here, okay? And you're getting scary, and you, you've gotta cut it out!

We do have to care a little about the album, Adam says.

I meant to call you Diane, Eddie says. —I meant to. Everyone was all *no you gotta call him B——, assert a sense of reality*, but fuck everyone on that! Right?

Cool thanks Eddie, you say. —You guys had a meeting? Gee, I wish I'd have been invited to that meeting, since it's about me and all, and I have opinions.

You barely came to *this* meeting, Tom says. —You barely see us anymore. I asked you to pick up the new lyrics, to go over them with me. You didn't even care to return the message.

What lyrics, you ask, but Adam cuts you off.

We just don't want you to be unhappy, he says. —And you seem, I don't know. Kind of unhappy.

Staring at your brother, you wonder if you should hit yourself in front of him and then ask him, *Gee what do you mean?* Also: when did you ask Tom to write lyrics? You asked for nothing from any of these people. You stand, looking at your feet, imagining that quicksand is opening beneath them. You wish it would hurry up, wonder if it will be cool there under the ground, away from the sun.

I started this band, you say. —I mean, all of us have money now because I started this band. —Suddenly you remember your father at dinner, a glass hitting a wall, and you stop speaking; if you continue to get angry, where will anger stop.

We're grateful you started it, Adam says.

Sure, Eddie says. —Jeez, B——, we want you to keep running the band forever and ever, okay? We just—

What we want is for you to stop pretending that your being sick is somehow normal, Tom says. He stares at you, his eyes their same range blue, the blue that makes you suspect he's planning to hit you. But as you keep watching him, he starts crying. —This irresponsible magic shit. This I'm-a-woman shit. This avoiding us, this—this hurting yourself—your hand, and—it's all exactly one and the same thing. It's all from the same sick root. Don't try to tell me it isn't.

No one tries.

I want you to be okay, like you used to be, Tom says.

I mean no one wants you to give up anything cold, Adam says. —You, y'know, you can wait until you're seeing a competent therapist, who can give you relief. We picked some out. No one's talking about anything crazy, like going to the hospital, or getting shock treatments, or anything like that yet. I mean—and, also, B——, we can help you out with the recording stuff. We're your employees, B——. We're your *family*. It'll be okay.

You keep thinking of you and Tom, holding hands and singing spirituals to calm the dog.

But it's never been okay, you say.

That's bullshit, Tom says, eyes still wet; manfully, he refuses to wipe them. —It seemed pretty okay. —His face is very close to yours, leaning forward into the semicircle; for the first time in a decade maybe you can smell the bright toothpaste and almond-spit aura of his breath. —I mean what is it, B——? he asks hotly. —Are you lying now, or were you lying then?

Aaaaaa, screams Charley Brushfire.

Everyone stops and looks at Charley, and in a panic, he stands up. —Aaaaaaaaaaa, he screams, louder, turning to look into each of your eyes one by one, spending equal time on each. —Aaaaaaaaaaaaaaaaaaa! —And then, snapping his jaw shut, he walks to the front door, exits to the street, slams it behind him.

All of you look at one another. Eddie's face is painted with a fantastic, wax-jester grin.

And then your mother whispers: —Stop fighting. —And the room full of your family gets even more silent.

SHE STANDS, COMES CLOSER TO you. She stops about five feet apart, stops short, as if she's hit a wall. She looks at you, and you look at her. And you can feel yourself shrinking before her, Diane: shrinking into a child.

Honey, your mother says. —Aren't you tired?

No, you lie, and you close your eyes and sit down.

To do what you're doing, she says. —I've never heard of anyone else who's done it, ever. Just tabloid stories—no one real.

She laughs, hyperventilates a little, like her throat is a vacuum sucking her laugh back up into itself, like joy is limited and has to be carefully conserved.

Listen to Mom, Adam says. —Do what she's saying.

I'm not saying anything, she says. —I'm saying—look, honey, I'm saying that whatever you tell me, I'll believe.

Your eyes are closed, golden bands of sunlight washing over your hidden corneas like tide over beach sand.

If you really believe, deep down, your mother says, —that if you do this, you'll be safe, that you'll be happy like we all are. If you believe that, 100 percent, that you have the power to do that, then I'll believe you. Okay? And everyone else will too.

And she gets silent, waiting for you to tell her what you believe.

YOU FANTASIZE ABOUT FIRING THEM all, all your family, and replacing them with Midnight Automotive. And then you dismiss the fantasy. It isn't real. Neither are you. If you were, someone would say it: you do not have the power to say those words yourself. This is because you're afraid every time you go outside. You're afraid of every passing car. You're afraid of magic. You're afraid of mirrors. You're afraid of record executives. You're afraid of losing the things you never thought you could build for yourself, that you built in spite of yourself, that being mistaken for male when you set out in 1962 have allowed you to build. Or no, not mistaken for being male, that can't be right: not being able to go back in time, far back in time to the moment of your birth, so you can make yourself a girl for real. Something other than these unjust gains that you hold now and want to keep. Some law they'd accept.

You're afraid of silence. Isolation. Nonexistence. You're afraid of yourself most of all. You know that. So what do you do about it? What you do is, you open your eyes, or else you close them.

YOUR FATHER BELIEVED THAT THERE was only one way to succeed. When he saw you diverging from that path, he told you that you'd fail. And then you did, though you've got to say that you tried. You will pat yourself on the back for that.

And it doesn't even feel bad, at first, when you answer your family's request of you. It feels like falling asleep when you have a headache, like admitting you're sick and going to bed at last, like relief.

I'm going to continue to call you Diane. Please don't think of it as a sign of disrespect toward your capitulation, even though it kind of is.

ADAM ISN'T EVEN THAT DISPLEASED, ultimately, to find the letter from Valley Forge, the one suing the band for breach of contract following a failure to deliver *Summer Fun* in a *mutually acceptable form.*

Don't worry about it, B——, he sighs. —Tom and I can sort it out, okay?

You nod to your little brother, not meeting his eyes; you're grateful.

Your bathtub is full of waves of red-brown hair dusted by spumes of stubble from a medium setting of the electric clippers Tom loaned you. Your clothes are boxed for anonymous donation; your Lava Lamps removed as hazards. Charley and Eddie are here to get rid of the mystic gibberish painted across your windows. You watch them work, your hands alternating between two chords on the piano over and over in a drone shuffle while they hack whole sephira out of existence, leave crude Vitruvian arcs and pentacles hanging in sheets in the void.

My goodness, Tom says, observing. —It'd be easier just to replace the whole *window*.

So they do that: Eddie shatters the glass with a hammer, and they peel the clear pie pieces back one by one. Sheets of gummy, layered paint hang in the vacancy like a terrible occult Charlotte's Web, devil sigils that fill like sails until Eddie slices them down the center, laughing, and they luff to rest. Now there's nothing but clean light and wind coming in on you, Diane, blowing the arms of your brand new pinstriped robe. The boys picked it up just for you.

Wendy and Barbara Happy are rolling in the chlorine lake below you, margarita glasses in their hands, while the men work. You watch them, the city wind blowing stubble from your bare skull, and the boys sing along with your drone, finding the harmonies you taught them.

Love, Gala

# PART SIX

# December 25, 2009

Dear Diane,

How much else do you even want to know about me anyway? Ronda hasn't spoken to me since she dropped me off at my trailer, all the belongings I'd brought to her house in my hands. I was still wearing the black cocktail dress I'd borrowed for the holidays: she never asked for it back, and I didn't volunteer.

The trailer was still there, everything in it untouched. I put the promo CD I'd stolen into my clock radio and let it play, steeping the room in the mysterious vibrations of a bunch of old people singing together, letting the altar drink in some sense of magical accomplishment. It had done good work. The world you'd built for us four decades ago felt solid and clean, as did, I hope, the world we built for you.

There was a ring of purple hair dye around my bathtub, and above it, hanging from the faucet and forgotten, Caroline's bathing suit: purple and metal, like the shed scales of the dragon who will end the world. I touched it, hoping it was still wet, that she'd only left recently and that some hope of a vector of passage still remained. But it was dry, and I sat on the edge of the dry tub for some time reminding myself again and again of that fact, as from the other room your promo track played on repeat: your voice winding around your cousin Tom's, both of you, as all of us, old.

AND HERE YOU ARE AGAIN; it's 1971; you're still young, or more young.

You don't do much driving these days, Diane, even though it hurts to walk down the sidewalk in your sandals alone—city grit and sand glass between your toes the whole way and panting, legs straining to move your frame, fifteen pounds per year heavier now than you were before your history ended. You have a beard now, long and straight and red-brown as your hair. *Take that,* you thought as you watched the hairs grow in, long and thick as Morgellon's wires.

You revised the *Summer Fun* tracks into their ultimately released form on your return from your involuntary weeks at the desistance-focused hospital your family found for you. In the interest of speed, you elected to ditch the previous masters and redo the whole thing in Mona's former studio with just piano and backing harmonies. Three or four of the new, leaner *Summer Fun* cuts, coupled with some solid new numbers from the classic team of you and Tom—"Feeling Empty," "Musta Been Lies," "Scary Spiral," others—were assembled, sans lyrics for the most part, into an album you personally named *Dead Summer Fun.* Your band was initially okay with this name—*anything that makes you feel comfortable, B——,* Adam said—but Tom and Adam managed to pick up a new deal with Keen Beat Records, who felt the title was negative. They changed it to *Summer Fun Alive.*

There were two groups of people who bought *Summer Fun Alive*: people who expected a live album, and people who expected some credible follow-up to the "Psychic Attraction" single. Neither group, you are pretty sure, bought the subsequent music products you offered them. Commercial and reputation problems aside, you were glad the mutilated tracks were out there, that the whole embarrassing *Summer Fun* chapter of your life was neatly buried. Cool—you tried elevating yourself to a new gender via a teen surf band. It didn't work out. It never could have, could it? So this was fine. So now you had the rest of your life to learn to be a good person in a way that did not feel right or comfortable to you, but that you guessed would be worth it. Yet you had to learn fast, Diane—clearly your bandmates were ahead of you. Clearly your fellow men had learned to exterminate their own drug delusions about being the wrong gender *years* ago, so efficiently that you hadn't even noticed them doing it.

So you carried on making albums as fast as you could, digging your way out of the debt of studio fees and cis life experience frantically, like you were digging a hole in the desert, trying not to let it fill with fresh sandslide. Album after album: *Happy Mountain. Family. Number Fourteen* (your thirteenth full-length album, counting *Summer Fun*, but you're superstitious.) *Live Album No Joke. Another One. Music. More. Fillin' Time. Here You Go.* The songs are mostly instrumentals or covers (of your songs and of other people's songs, leaning heavily on Los Paranoias and John Black Zero), none of them topping three minutes in length. You kept using Mona's old studio in your house, where you could work fast and at whim—3 A.M. shuffles, bossa novas at seven on a Friday, whole evenings recording and re-recording nonverbal chants. A few times you use the studio as a kind of diary, free-associative confessions over triadic vamps of chords, but you knock it off when you wake to find Adam and Eddie in the studio listening to tapes of you describing what it must feel like to be a ghost, subject to updrafts from Santa Ana winds, as if you have no body at all. After this, your brothers start to show up more and more, asking you nervously what you want, what you need.

o   o   o

YOUR FATHER EXPLAINS THE FACTS to you while the session musicians—two men from Midnight Automotive, plus a few of the people Adam likes to call in these days when he's recording—sit in the studio room and try not to pay too close attention to what's happening. You don't let their judgment trouble you. You've asked your father to be here, because you know now that you need him.

Now listen, B——, you're too tense today, your dad is saying. —You've got to loosen it up, son—not so loose that you go spinning out of control—but not so tight that *heart* doesn't come through either. Heart—spirit—that's what music *is*, son. You have to play from your *heart*, son, always. To lay it on so thick, all that garbage you were putting in over those pretty melodies back in 1966, 1967—that destroyed me, son. We're not going that direction anymore. We're being *sincere*, yet commercial with ourselves.

He looks different following the infarctions that kept him out of commission during most of the late 1960s; his frame, swelled a few belt-notches during your early success, seems to have imploded, and now his shirts hang loose on him, stretched skin peeking out to double his cuffs. It's as if his gravity and yours have somehow swapped polarities, as if your body is a great, inert planet devouring his mass. Only his eyes are the same, or close: where once all you could see in them was terrible, present fear, as if he was dodging an avalanche every moment, now his eyes are blank. The worst things that could happen to him are behind him. And here you both are, you and your dad, alone on a flat, sandy plain, and he looks at you as if he knows he's failed you in some terrible way that time has locked away from him now, that, no matter how well he charts his profits and losses for any given year, is beyond his power to manage or correct.

Basically he's happy you and the gang called him in today to work on the new single. It gives him a feeling that he can fix things. You like to give him that feeling; it's good for him to have it. You guess that you must feel good when your dad is around.

The song you asked your dad to write for you to sing and produce is called "Anything I Want (I Get)." You gave him carte blanche in terms of theme and approach—on your own you've already sunk the band twice—and this is what he decided would best represent your work when in *fighting condition*, as he says.

You sit in the booth, singing the words your father has written for you, and you take your headphones off as soon as the light goes out. —Is that a take? you shout. —Can we move on?

Do you think it's a take, B——? he asks you. —Music is about what *you* want. Not what *I* want.

Sure okay, you say, guessing that this means it isn't a take. —I'm thinking, though, let's change up the instrumentation?

He nods vigorously, happy like a dog who's been fed. You have guessed correctly. Smiling, you close your eyes, replace the phones, and sing.

THE SESSION WRAPS AT EIGHT so your dad can get home and get to bed. He hasn't been sleeping well lately, he insists. You walk him out to his car.

Are you happy with the tune, he asks.

Of course, you say quickly.

Don't lie, he says, voice a dust bloom on an attic shelf. —I can tell when you're lying, B——. It's important to me that you're happy.

You look back at him, wary. —Yeah I'm definitely happy, you say in as reassuring a tone as you can muster. You make sure your body language is open, your tone modulated and bright. —Of course I'm happy, Dad. Everything's gonna be totally okay.

And then—automatically, like some demon puppeteer is doing it—you offer him your destroyed hand to shake goodbye.

He looks you in your eye, his old mouth a grim line, as he shakes. Close of a business deal: he's aware of the terms you're offering, and he's satisfied.

SOMETIMES WENDY WILL CALL YOU up, or the other way around. Invariably she comes over to your place. Your whole thing started you don't know—1968, 1969, after she and Adam split up, whenever the live album came out. You'd asked her to do backup overdubs (nothing's live, Diane), and she came over to record them. You hadn't seen her for years; she'd cut her hair short and grown her bangs out, and she wore a ring you didn't ask her about.

Do you still talk to Mona ever, Wendy asked at one point, a few months after your thing had started, after a long lacuna in conversation. —I don't. I haven't in years.

No, you said. —I haven't. Uh, I guess we're still married legally. So there's that.

You smiled, some retrograde, depreciated part of you wondering whether it was a guy smile or a smile among female friends. She didn't react either way, so you guessed it was fine.

There's that, she replied.

Somehow this led to you leading her down the dark downstairs hall to the studio where she and Mona used to talk and listen to creepy gospel and play guitars; somehow this led to her flattening you against the wall and biting your lip hard when she kissed it, like she was trying to draw out some long-ago mingled blood.

Now she comes over whenever it's convenient for both of you. For the most part you just lie back and try to relax while she mounts and grinds herself off against you, though sometimes she asks you to penetrate her and you try as best as you can. She used to let you go down on her more often, which you liked because it meant you existed less, but since you've grown the beard she's less into this, and you're afraid of what might happen to you if you shave it off.

Best of all is when she falls asleep for a few hours before she's expected somewhere and you hold her, dusting your fingers over her hip, nothing more expected of you and your body: you are grateful she's stopped here for a while, that this is a place everyone can be still and safe for a while.

You never talk anymore about Mona, though you know this is at the core of what's happening. It's important, you know, that both of you know this and never speak about it. You never talk about the music that, as months turn into years, begins to bleed more and more through the walls of the studio while your brothers are here, nights, recording tracks, sound that brushes over your spooning bodies like tails of feral animals. And you never talk as you get dressed in the morning—you in your robe, her in her smart pantsuits and secret ring, bound for her life on the surface.

Sometimes she runs into Adam while they're both here. Wendy is awkward about it, but Adam never seems upset. He seems professional.

TOM AND ADAM COME OUT of your house to find you lying at the bottom of the empty pool next to a bucket of chlorine, reading a *TV Guide* and imagining what the programs would be like to watch. This is better than what you were doing before, which is lying on the floor of your studio with the voice that you now recognize speaks for your father coming upon you.

It's like he's written a play for you, to commemorate your relationship. *You should die*, read the lines of the play. *You're a waste of good food and water that other people paid for. You're worse than other people because you think you're better than them.* The stage directions call for you to hit yourself, and part of the excitement of the drama is whether you'll be able to resist them or not. It never gets old, and you are careful not to do any permanent damage, and you're careful not to do anything strenuous for the rest of the day whenever it happens. That way he won't come back. You are still working really hard, Diane, to get well again, to forget about your poisonous delusions: once you forget them, you can start to work on everything else. Then maybe you can make some records, and people will like you once more.

But today Tom and Adam are interfering with your plan to be healthy. They get between you and your light. Pissed off, you stub out your cigarette on the gunite.

You getting your beauty tan? Tom asks.

Adam shoots him a warning look. His new mustache hangs to his lower lip, brushing off whatever dust is to be found there. —Did you take the water out of the pool? he asks. —I thought that the weight of the water was what kept the pool from, you know, cracking into pieces.

Weird theory, you say, lighting another cigarette. —Is that all you want?

We listened to your song, Adam says. —The one you and Dad did for the new album. It's, uh. The melody is really interesting. The lyrics are positive, which is good.

It's shit, he means, Tom says. —You're not even trying, B——. What the fuck's wrong with you?

Let's cool down, Adam says. —Let's be positive for B——.

Tom crosses his arms. He's wearing a tie-dyed rainbow poncho that makes him look like a sherbet cone with his arms crossed. His hair now is as long as yours once was, like a lion's mane, sweat dripping down his neck like sugar melting. Since the restraining order from Barbara came through, he's been on the dating scene, and you guess that the women he's interested in are into this kind of thing. You wonder if you would be into it, were you still a woman, but this is a dangerous path to go down, and you try to straighten up your thinking before he notices.

It's cool if you don't like the song, you say. —I mean, you don't have to use it. You guys did a good job on the last album. You'll do a great job on this one.

We really like your songs, Adam says. —The kind you used to write.

So just put those songs on the album, you recommend. —Greatest Hits Number Three, I think.

We need *new* songs that are *like* those songs, Adam says.

I dunno, you say. —I've been feeling really tired lately.

Tom snorts and picks up a pebble from the deck, which he tosses down on you. It bounces off your chest.

He don't wanna help, he don't wanna help, Tom says. —He can lie in a hole forever feeling sorry for himself if he wants. Let him.

B——, Adam says firmly. —You have to come out of the pool if you want to talk to us, okay?

Okay, you say, and you remain in the pool. You roll onto your stomach, carefully balancing the cigarette as you pick up your *TV Guide*. The sun burns the backs of your thighs just under the hem of the striped robe. You can hear Tom pace and mutter, and you adjust your arm to ash your cigarette. You wish you'd thought to bring an ashtray down here. It's another failure, but you tell yourself you'll do better the next time.

We're going to finish recording "Girls Grow in the Sun," Adam says. —We need you to be a part of it.

You roll onto your back again, ashing on yourself in alarm. —I don't want you to do that, you say.

I'll explain why we're going to do it, he says, —if you come out of the pool.

You glower at him, but you slowly get up and slink to the edge: sun-blind, the world around you washed out to blue.

Gosh, you say. —I thought Valley Forge kind of owned those tapes. So maybe it's tricky, legally speaking, to finish that song. I don't want you to finish that song.

Keen Beat paid off the studio fees, Adam says. —On a trial basis. They were, ah, disappointed in how the last one sold. But there have been bootlegs—rumors circulating, people talking. About, you know, the tracks from, well, the 1967 album.

You don't say anything, just frown as the colors return to your vision.

THE NEXT ALBUM FROM THE Get Happies, Adam explains to you, tentatively to be released in 1972, will be called *Broken Treaty.* It'll be the first rock album dedicated to the support of the Indian Rights movement (Charley's idea, but everyone else likes the media possibilities and karmic glamour of it.) The rest of the band has been writing lots of material: Tom's got a toe-tapper called "The Red Man Was First," detailing different American inventions that were humorously anticipated by his notions of First Nations technology. Charley has a long instrumental piece about the magic practices of shamans. Adam's contributing a soulful guitar-driven suite called "Rain Dance." Eddie has a series of ballads about what it might be like to be exterminated, expropriated, and have one's culture stolen for profit, titles TBD.

We're gonna maybe cut those, Adam explains. —I mean, you know Eddie.

They are planning to record this album on tribal land, or as close to it as they can get. Keen Beat's worked out a deal with a place in New Mexico; they'll ship the studio gear over and everything. It will be a real adventure, with a social message, too. Social messages are what the public wants these days, and the Get Happies, Adam and Tom explain to you, intend to deliver.

They have already bought your plane ticket east, where you will go to help them deliver it.

ANOTHER TIME THAT YEAR—OR ANOTHER year, it doesn't even matter. You're walking down the sidewalk in Sunset Junction on some drug errand or other for your brother Eddie, your robe on your back, your feet bare against the asphalt. That's when you see her shadow, a profile against the bricks of the diner just across from the Black Cat Tavern: a woman as tall as you.

You duck into the shadows as best as you can and circle to the other side. There are three of them loitering against the wall, just across the street from the bar. Two tall and one as short as any cis woman, eyes shaded and lipstick bright. They're playing Los Paranoias songs on a transistor radio, sipping Cokes, one beach bag between them and fast food wrappers peeking from a paper sack. They are not white, like you are.

One of them notices you and taps another on her shoulder. They're all looking at you now, Diane, the bearded white person in a bathrobe watching them. Their radio plays; the hem of their beach towel rustles. You can see other people in the park start to slow down, noticing you noticing them. There's a traffic cop within your field of vision who may notice soon.

Can we help you, one of the women calls out. The other two laugh.

You think about them a lot, Diane, the ones who built the moon world you thought you could build alone, who did it without your help.

# December 26, 2009

Dear Diane,

The first stage in completing the sure-to-be-a-top-40-LP *Broken Treaty* is to dismantle the studio in your house. It's the most cost-effective option, for reasons that Adam and your new A&R man try to explain and that you don't care enough to contradict. You watch movers cart away the consoles that Mona used to record on. You hate it, but you guess there's nothing you can do to stop them. Technically, the band owns that equipment, and it's not as if you've used that studio for some time.

They rent other equipment as well: a new sixty-four-track mixer, a Moog, new amps for everyone, baffles and monitors and concert toms and all the capital investment necessary to craft a hit, you guess. The plane is dry, tiny nozzles above each first-class seat sucking away your air. Every time the drinks cart comes by, you order a Bloody Mary with extra pepper. A hot towel sucks sweat from your forehead, and the alcohol dehydrates you further until you are all dust and liquor held together like a gelatin mold by your dirty bathrobe belted to your chest, cigarette halo around your eyebrows.

Through the window you can see the red mountains of the

Continental Divide, strange circles of green irrigation as if the land's been plotted by compass, and on the PA the captain tells the passengers he's happy a musician of your caliber has chosen to fly with Hughes Aircraft today, and the cheerleader stewardesses clap for you in their chartreuse miniskirts. Your beard is coated in olive flesh and ashes. And the plane carries you down, Diane, down into the land of enchantments.

A CAR CARAVAN FROM THE regional airport in Albuquerque is organized to bring the company south to Truth or Consequences. You and Adam go in one car, Tom and Charley in another, Eddie, a flight risk, securely embedded in the car of dour technical personnel. The sedans and trucks carrying your disassembled home studio shoot like flagellant sperm down I–25, the canyon walls rising alternately around you to hem you in. Where there's no canyon wall, there's desert that you stare at through the sedan window, weird stillborn sprouts of brush cracking the shell of the flat land, the space that will one day bear the spaceport where this woman who's in some slightly-more-than-symbolic way your granddaughter and I will argue in a dream someone has yet to dream.

The cars have real tires now: hovering days are done.

YOU AREN'T INTERESTED IN TALKING, and Adam is congenitally uninterested in talking, and the radio is broken. But three hours is a long time to be silent, and Adam cracks first.

The place we're going has a river, he says. —The Rio Grande, I think?

You watch the wind roll dead brush into flashfire tumbleweeds out the window. —Yeah, cool, you say.

There's a hot spring too, he says. —It's a sacred site. The ghosts of Indian ancestors.

Oh slick, you say. —You'll probably get some good recordings done.

We all will, he reminds you.

He keeps driving in silence for a while, sucking on the end of his mustache to clear the sweat from it. It makes you sad.

A break in the canyon walls approaches. You point at it. —Let's turn off, you say. —You and me and maybe Eddie. Maybe even Charley, or Tom. Maybe everybody. Let's go back to LA or anywhere. We can buy property in the badlands, maybe start a new band. I mean we've got money. We've got enough for a while, you know?

Adam keeps driving in a straight line. He nods. —Sure, B——, he says. —For right now, let's just focus on getting this album done, okay? We owe it to people.

You keep silent for a moment. —I'm tired of owing things to people, you say.

We all are, your baby brother says.

The desert curves, Elephant Butte coming into view ahead of you, the Rio Grande like a silver choker around it.

I just wanna see you do it again, he says suddenly, sounding like a child, but then he falls silent.

MONA'S STUDIO IS REASSEMBLED IN the room that will one day become the women's dorm. You watch from the shade of the small office hutch while the technicians haul amps and equipment, and you try to follow the conversation your family has over cans of supermarket beer around the long table in the center of the space: roommates are assigned, schedules are laid out. It's hard to follow; for years now they've toured together, worn new grooves of relationships with one another that you can't access: Eddie goading Adam, Tom and Adam disagreeing over copy and cover art, Tom and Eddie cold-shouldering where necessary, Charley drinking beer with the engineers and discussing Lead Belly records until they excuse themselves. Everyone stops talking and turns to you hopefully when you speak, so you try not to speak.

And when you can't sleep, when you rise from the dorm room they've assigned you to share with Adam and two other men—their testosterone snores battling the leaves that scrape the corrugated metal of the shed—you walk to the side of the river just beyond the docks. Charley is still out there, a guitar at his side, watching the top of the dark hill where I will first see Caroline, as if at any moment he expects the pink sun to break through. You watch him for a long time; he never notices you.

YOU TRY. YOU REALLY DO, Diane! When the studio's set up and the band begins in earnest to write, rehearse, and record following each morning's spirit circle and quasi-sweat lodge, topless in the teepee and led by Adam and Tom in partnership, you fake it: rearrange old riffs into new ones, elaborate on them, take your Wollensak out to record natural sounds, as you did when you were young—back to the beginning. You present your efforts to Adam like a cat offering dead gifts. He receives them in the same spirit, says the group will try to fit them into the material they've already written. You harmonize, corkscrewing your nicotine voice back into its old range as well as you can; you nod along, ready to step in where needed as they record songs you had no part in writing. They work in ways you can't understand anymore. You hold yourself up next to them, a limb whose connection you've cauterized without knowing when, and you pretend as best as you can that it's alive, because if you pretend well enough then maybe it will become true.

You don't know what else to do.

AND THEN IT'S TIME TO work on "Girls Grow in the Sun." The moment they put the tapes in the playback machine, all five Get Happies crowded around it as if it's a space heater on a sub-zero night, you start to run away, but Tom holds your shoulders down.

Just listen, Adam says softly.

So you make yourself listen. It makes you remember how things were: floating on your back in a swimming pool with straps of swimsuit loose on your shoulders, summer skirt hanging from your hips, directing a room full of musicians who believed in you. You can't believe you ever felt like that: so unconscious of yourself, so heedless, like you might do anything. It's mortifying.

It's junk, you say when the tape begins to click on the end of its spool. —I'm sorry we all wasted our time on this one.

Jesus, B——, it's beautiful, says Eddie.

It's something, says Tom, and you glance at him suspiciously, but he's nodding, moved.

Adam is the first to break the silence. —So how do we complete it? he asks. —Everyone, input?

Charley strokes his chin. —This is a case where pedal steel might be appropriate.

Lyrics, says Tom. —I wrote some a while back, but I forgot them. I bet I could recollect if I had to.

Were there ever lyrics, B——? Adam asks.

You blink, and you look around the studio from your house, resembled here a thousand miles away. The amplifiers—the cabinets—the spare guitars. For a moment, you're relieved to think that they haven't brought it, but there it is: the box buried for years in the corner of your studio, its Utah hotel stationery faded but still affixed. The workers shipped it here too: who knew what piece of the detritus of your life might end up being important?

Think carefully, Adam says. —We really need you to be a part of this production.

You remember his face as it had been in the car. It isn't that way now, but it might be again.

Mona may have written some lyrics for it, you mumble.

Tom scratches his long hair. —Your crazy ex-wife? he asks. —Christ, that's *all* we need.

You have a restraining order against you, Eddie says, giggling.

Adam clicks his tongue at them, silencing his troops. —Do you have them? he asks, an edge in his voice. —Think really carefully, B——. Do you remember what they were?

Eight bright eyes blink at you, the never-completed track lying ploughed up before you, waiting here to be filled under the desert air.

You're about to give them what they want when the knock comes, and a voice. —Sorry, but there's a telephone call, for that one?

IN THE OFFICE WHERE ONE day I will work—no computers, no radio, just you and a telephone and a calendar marked JULY 1971, some subsilicate property of the window glass making the moving river, which bends like an ouroboros, look still—you take the long-distance call from your mom in California.

Hi, you say. —We're recording; I can't talk so long.

Her voice is strange, weightless. —Oh gosh, okay, I'm sorry to bother you, she begins. —Well.

Well, you repeat.

Well, she says. —Your father's had a stroke.

Her voice is moving like an unanchored moth in a closet full of coats, rising toward a false sun somewhere above.

Okay, you tell her, the blood in your own brain now building up.

Do you—could you maybe get Eddie and Adam? she asks. —I guess I should tell them, right? —She laughs, a bright sound like a picture frame snapping.

I'll tell them, you say. —It's cool.

She keeps laughing, and then suddenly she starts to sob. —Who am I going to take care of now?

You listen to the sound of her voice wailing, volume dropping as her breath runs out, until you finally hang up.

o   o   o

WHEN YOU GET BACK TO the studio, pieces of equipment arranged around the room like cooked brains in a busted skull, your family—your neighbor, your cousin, your newly orphaned brothers—gathers around you, hands full of coffee from the craft table in the corner.

B——, Adam says. —Is everything okay? You've got those lyrics for us, right?

You do not look at the box in the corner, which you've had yet to open. Instead you close your eyes, and seeing your family still there watching, you speak: —You don't get to touch me anymore, you say. And before your band can stop you, you've pushed the white button on the console to erase the master tape.

YOU HAVE A BODY, DIANE, and suddenly it hurts.

So you go to the third bath. You take off your clothes, article by article, fold them neatly on the side of the stone. The mountainside where Caroline will walk by one day, seeing me or not seeing me, is watching you. It's old, thousands of years old, and it watches you just as much as it's ever watched me.

In the water—in the end, just a tiny plug of water left to you, a fat cylinder big enough for one, maybe two at most—you gaze down at yourself. Unshaved legs. Disaster of genitals. Belly hanging over them, its dire red stripe of fur an arrow pointing to your face. The chest whose breasts—creatures suggested by weight alone—are scuffed with yet more fur. Broad shoulders. Beard. Hair clipped short. Eyes that are somewhere emotion can not get to, eyes that want to shut, that blink a message to the outside in Morse code: OKAY. GEE. IT'S COOL.

Next to your reflection, my reflection stands up, sucked by a time gate shaped like a pentacle into the past.

You look up, startled, as I'm looking at you. We look at each other, mountain and whirlpool our witnesses, for a long time. I know what I'm thinking about this, whether I tell you or not. I don't know what you're thinking about this at all. I don't know what you think when you shout at the sight of me, when you turn and fall backward, strike your head on the way down, slide beneath the bubbling water. And maybe you're trying at last to die, Diane, there beneath the mineral pocket ocean, or maybe you're only trying to go to sleep and dream of some way to swim back through the time gate, here to the future you glimpsed once in a vision, the future where I live. Maybe this is a place where you can live, too.

But in the end, whatever you're trying to do doesn't matter, because your family has heard you shouting, and they are here to save you instead. They pull you out, slap you, force you to breathe their air: there's plenty of money to be made from you yet.

Love, Forever, Gala

# PART SEVEN

# December 31, 2009

Dear Diane,

I have to imagine that Caroline didn't hesitate. I have to imagine her excellent at leaving, efficient at jimmying her wadded clothes and the grainy maps she'd printed on the office inkjet into the big camping frame backpack she'd relied on for years, charging her spare camera batteries overnight like eager crock pots, cleaning her boots, filling up on salad bar at the cruddy diner for times when no fresh vegetables lay ahead, for the stoic seasons.

I wish we had touched, hugged or shook hands or shared blood or something, when we'd said goodbye—I wish I'd said goodbye. If we had, then I'd have been able to feel both parts of her, the uncertainty and the fear, the quiet will that ran through her like iron rails toward the promised end of her story. I envied her those rails.

What must it be like to have something at your center, Diane?

I LIT ALL MY INCENSE, and I drew a pentagram starting from the top, lay prostrate with the smoke billowing to the trailer ceiling. What I projected into that smoke was not a recording: it was something better.

I could see Caroline, rocketing north in her seat on the bus next to the bathroom, reviewing footage and marking timecodes in her notebook as a conversation maybe strikes up—maybe a cishet couple in their twenties, tattooed and striking north to Denver to rejoin their families for the holidays; happily she talks to them, interviews them about their lives and lyrics, shares cigs with them at long cold rest stops outside of Santa Fe and Pueblo while big shadows of trucks—carrying logs or mystery sewer parts or who knows what they are carrying—downshift and rumble, the December snow on the mountains fluttering in cold off the Continental Divide, without which she'd be able to see clear to California—and then her new best friends are saying goodbye to her, gathering their bags and walking into the stern wanting arms of a mother, father, toddler maybe left behind for safekeeping months before, and not so many people are getting on the bus anymore, and Caroline is riding alone, nothing to film but the bus window and what's outside it, poison ridges and dead brush spines of badlands covered in snow. As she rides, she writes a long letter: filling sheets of notebook paper, crossing out lines, wadding them up and beginning again.

She thinks about buying a car. She thinks about it even more when the bus stops at Fort Collins, the route further north pre-empted for weather advisory; she is the only one booked through to Montana. She thinks about it as she humps her stuff through the drifts, cash refund in her hand, looking for a net café (or a Starbucks if she *has* to), somewhere with Internet and food so that she can find a rideshare and a hostel or a sublease or anyway something to get her out of the cold.

She could hell of buy a car; she could. Just a little used one. She pictures herself in it while she eats stumpy Mission-style burritos in a student café with furniture chiseled out of varnish-slick redwood and bad art on every wall, while she edits and uploads her interview with the metal couple and adds a noodling and aspirational Popol Vuh soundtrack that she appropriates from a defunct Myspace. If she only had a car she wouldn't have to wait; she could be moving, driving north through the snow to her goal. She wouldn't have to stop for anything. She has no idea how much money she even has, how much interest has compounded and accrued, untouched, above her like birthday confetti ready to rain down the moment she stabs the piñata. But she won't do it, she decides. It's not the first time she has to work to decide this. Every day she makes the decision, a little, to stay pure, to leave the money where it's at. Purity is important.

And sometimes—now, in the café, in fact—she wonders how long she's going to be able to stay pure. Soon the mystery that's been building up since her tenth birthday—since longer, since the unremembered, unrecorded moment when Dahlia Slinks walked out on her father—will be solved. She is very close to the end of the rails. What will she do after that? Maybe she will make a documentary of the people she's met, punk and queer in its sensibilities. She has great footage of weirdos from all parts of the country. A lot of people, she's certain, could relate to a story like that.

The vision informs me that Caroline totally finds a rideshare. He is awful at conversation and argues about politics in a voice thick with reasoned condescension while she watches out the window, the flat snow and fog plains, distant purple mountains, stark black fences topped with twists of sharp wire. They pull forward through Wyoming, across the borders of the Crow Reservation and into Montana; she asks if she can check her email on his fancy phone, gambling, fruitfully, that he owns one. Already her creepy fan has commented on her latest video, congratulating her on making it to Colorado, speculating about whether they could meet when she made it to her destination. She stares at the comment while the reasonable voice lectures her about historical materialism.

He drops her off, late at night, at the truck stop in Billings, the place where her journey will end. She films a map of local attractions—the cave, the reservation, the Little Big Horn memorial, the river—and then she shuts the camera off. And while my vision lasts, Diane, she won't turn it on again.

She's so close now—the morning sun is burning off the fog—she trudges through slush drifts marked by paw prints, boot tracks, yellow-rimmed holes in the snow, her camping frame on her back. She passes SUVs, quad motorcycles on trailers in garages, outsize American flags hanging from porches, bumper stickers reading NOBAMA or NOT IN MY TOWN that peel from the backs of sensible sedans. The house is the same as any other; she half expected it to be dark purple inlaid with silver spiderwebs and coffin-shaped moldings, surrounded by chairs and painted in anarchy As. But it's a boring blue, and there are boots stacked up on a wooden rack by a welcome mat with a picture of a cool black cat, one such as a witch might have. Caroline wants very badly to film the house, stands outside it for fifteen minutes instead while suspicious commuters wave at her from car windows.

There's a mailbox by the door. She sets her letter in the box and walks away.

She has time to kill, so she walks to the river, a glorious hour passing warehouses, trucks hauling loads of dirt for uncertain reasons, wild rock mushrooms in tectonic bloom just off the capillaries of the interstate. She cuts behind the Phillips 66 over the hill, stands there on a rock beach, pine tree spears covered in snow at attention all around, their tall shadows reflecting in reverse. There are no hikers; she's alone. She looks at herself in the mirror; she sees herself; she's young and dirty and loved. She is recording nothing. None of it can be sold. And if the season weren't winter and the river weren't awful, she would bathe in it, wash the grease out of her hair, let it float her away west to the ocean or wherever it goes. Instead she sits and looks at it and thinks about people she's met along the way and how she misses them all, misses how real she felt when she spoke to them, like different colored stage lights were lighting her up. She makes a vow to get back in touch with all of them, when she has the time.

She is a real and separate person who can bathe in a real and separate river whenever she likes.

When she gets back to the house, her letter is gone from the mailbox.

Her heart engages. There's a light in the window, and someone inside is playing a guitar, a song she hasn't heard before. The person is playing very loud, as if for an audience. Caroline starts to cry, hot tears on cold cheeks. She is very ready to come inside. So she climbs the steps of the porch—the song gets louder, and a white-and-gray cat is in the window, its eyes owl-like, watching her as she advances—and she knows that she will find the door unlocked. She opens it. Palace light surrounds her, envelops her, and she steps inside, out of our sight. She will live happily ever after, Diane. I don't think any of us doubted that such would be Caroline Wormwood's fate.

Love, Gala

# January 6, 2010

Dear Diane,

The knowledge that the Get Happies were preparing to mount a national reunion tour in the twenty-first century—and that you, yourself, would be a part of it—blindsided the whole sizable community who still found spiritual importance in 1960s pop music careers. I don't think anyone else may have noticed the reunion of a band who, for years and years following the *Broken Treaty* sessions and your subsequent total retreat from the world, had been putting out work that—despite everyone's best efforts and more heroic work than I have time and space to fairly record— was steadily more forgotten, a last entropic expenditure following the great nova of a collapsed band: a singularity containing all starlight, invisible unless you got close enough to notice its suck. Your band had gone wherever music went when people had no use for it anymore.

It's not like the band was getting worse in that time since 1972. Under Adam's direction, it was perpetually getting better, crisper, more professional. Whenever musicians hung out, they talked about the Get Happies' tour chops, stamina, keen timing, efficient logistics chain. They talked about the arrangements: stages

stacked with triple drum kits, six guitars, backup choirs, all of
it precisely conducted by Adam and his guitar at the center, a
weight of instrumental force that drowned out Eddie, Charley,
and the stiffly gyrating Tom at the corner of the stage. If any of
the original members resented being drowned out, they didn't say
anything; they were the ones, in the end, who got the applause.
Why play, really? Why record new music when you could release
greatest hits? Money told you what people wanted from you, and
the money, in the end, was just as good this way; actually, better.
So you sang about the time when heteronormativity was king and
cars could fly.

Then, a few months into 1982, your baby brother Adam drove
his car to the marina, abandoned it with his vintage Fender in
the trunk, bought a sailboat with a suitcase of cash, and sailed
it west out of Sausalito Harbor. Eyewitnesses said they could see
him balancing on the boom, hanging against the tilt of the head-
wind—counteracting the keel with his own insufficient weight—as
he headed into the ocean. Whether he made it safely to some fair
harbor or not, no one knows, though many speculate.

Without Adam to mediate, Tom and Eddie's working relationship lasted four weeks. Formally expelled from the group, Eddie
spent two or three years turning up drunk or coked-out, depending
on the planets, to concerts, sometimes sweet-talking security or
promoters into letting him play: as the only surviving brother of
the great elusive genius B——, Diane, no one really had the heart
or promotional recklessness to refuse him. He spent most of these
shows screaming abuse at Tom from his drum throne or soaking
up adulation from the crowd as the familiar refrains began—
"Suntime Funtime," "King of the Drags," "If We're Married,"
"Diner Girl," "Psychic Attraction." But soon enough, security
got smarter; Eddie turned up less and less and looked more and
more hollow-eyed every time he did appear. At last, the inevitable
call came that summoned police and paramedics, too late, to the

rental house he'd claimed over in Venice, the mark of a knife still dragged into the old, warped plaster of the walls with an apron hanging in it, spent bullet casing on the floor beside your brother's head. John Black Zero was also there, also shot, beeswax candles burning throughout the room and a Qlipoth tree drawn in blood of uncertain origin on the wall. Amphetamine and psilocybin caps were everywhere, both musical heroes were wearing red robes (each robe sized to fit the other man). A storage space he'd leased years before turned out to contain boxes and boxes of tapes, gorgeous melodies he'd paid to record and shared with no one.

Charley Brushfire never left the band so much as faded out, his one contribution to the group as producer—*The Get Happies Say God Bless America to Our Musical Heritage*—justly forgotten. Instead, he began to play with various contemporary bands, filling out a rhythm section for a new wave sensation here, adding his tenor to a backup chorus there. Slowly, he became known as a session musician of great patience, skill, and professional discretion; he was someone who took his job seriously, someone you'd always be pleased to hire to finish a complicated piece of work when your more charismatic bandmates had flamed out, someone who knew lots of lore about American music that he'd be happy to tell you if you cared to listen. Look through liner notes; you'll find him. He moved into his parents' house when they died, sat on the porch nights and played guitar for the power-walkers who coursed by him at sunrise en route to work. And when he died—struck, while onstage with Ricky Fataar of Los Paranoias during a 2003 All-Star benefit concert to distribute malaria nets to sub-Saharan Africa, by a burning gamma-irradiated rivet from an exploded government space shuttle, a tragedy which led, via a strange chain of tech investments, to the florescence of the spaceport just down the highway from me—the few notices that appeared in the music press were gracious. His friends simply missed him, felt his lack.

Tom Happy alone survived. Tom Happy was built to survive.

Now, on his own, he worked to save the band he'd inherited. He tore out the complex, costly arrangements Adam had put into place, replaced them with guitar-bass-drums-synth versions, and hired a rotating skeleton crew of twenty-something enthusiastic up-and-comers and dabbling celebrities to perform them: the new, fiscally responsible Get Happies. He sought gigs at baseball stadiums, county fairs, casinos, drive-in theaters, anywhere controlled by someone excited by the power of a famous name, famous memories; he chased lawyers for Valley Forge who'd been withholding residual income for decades; he hired a series of savvy managers to pursue, on commission, soundtrack and endorsement deals, putting his lyrical talents to work on putting a new and lucrative twist on old standards.

And every penny he saved, every penny he earned, he invested. He bought shares in big box corporations, tech firms, military contractors, oil futures, private space-exploration ventures, media conglomerates that licensed your hits as theme songs for conservative talk hosts whose angry white male listeners remembered you fondly from the days when you were all young together. Tom funded Republican education initiatives, compassionate conservative welfare-to-work programs, a national campaign to teach a new generation about the power of compound interest. Some of the money went to keep all the records in print, to reconfigure and recirculate the greatest hits collections, to keep the musical stock in the project high. He kept the band alive. *Healthier than ever,* he liked to say. *I'm a big believer in health.*

SOME OF THE MONEY WENT, at regular intervals, to a mysterious address, sequestered in some tiny inlet of Atlantic coast, in the shadow of stone beaches.

You survived, too. Unseen beneath the surface of the ocean, you survived, the swells of mystery volcanism beneath you sometimes propagating to the surface as whitecap rumors. Sometimes people said they'd seen you at rallies for some hermetic group or time cult, sometimes in deep conversion therapy at an undisclosed location, sometimes dirty and wrapped in windbreakers, beard full of food scraps down to your heart, screaming at the ocean. Or maybe you slipped away like Mona did, shed yourself entirely, reemerging as some aging instrumental virtuoso, industrial music pioneer, shadow producer on obscure labels far across the Atlantic Ocean. People heard traces of you in everything.

We trafficked in rumors like these, me and my post-high school pals; we played our *Summer Fun* bootlegs—assembled, lyricless, from smuggled acetates and undemolished masters; we wrote out key changes and melody lines from variant arrangements, tried to glean secret messages in the progressions: CAGE, BABBAGE, EGAD A# BABE. It was very important to us—to me—to know where you were, what you were doing, that you were okay. It was more important to me, sometimes, than knowing I was okay. It's possible I conflated the two.

REMEMBER WHEN I SAID I wasn't going to tell you anything about my life story? But I will tell you this: I'm an American. Exactly how much of my story can I realistically separate from yours, Diane, from the stories you make me listen to every time FM Radio has a retrospective weekend? From my memories of every car trip of my childhood, roller rink bound in a minivan with school friends, someone's mom singing "Psychic Attraction" at the top of her lungs? Exactly why should I abstract myself out of the dream inheritance all of us drag around? Why is it classy or pure to do that?

LITTLE IS LEFT TO TELL—EXCEPT, oh jeez, for the reunion concert that all this ceremonial witchcraft mumbo jumbo brought about in the first place! How did *that* go, you are asking?

First, you should know that I have a ticket. Two tickets, one for me, one for Ronda, courtesy of her brother and the radio empire he works for. *As a fan of the Get Happies,* he wrote to me, *I fig-ured you'd be interested in these. Have fun!*

Second, you probably know already that this tour is being billed as the first time in history that *Summer Fun* will be played live for general audiences. You know about the interviews, music press retrospectives, statements from figures throughout musical history past and present—Travis Dark, the surviving Los Paranoias, Harry Corot, old and stuttering and billed on the news as LEGENDARY HITMAKER FROM VALLEY FORGE RECORDS. *We always believed in the Get Happies,* Harry manages, his grin lightened by fabulous ivory dentures. *Even when circumstances forced us to be apart.* And of course you know that Tom Happy is making the rounds as well, his hair shock-white beneath a trucker's cap labeled BRING JOY TO SPACE, his face shifting between legalistic scowl and thin-jowled grin, a new engagement ring shining on his fourth finger. His skin looks really good; he looks the way he did that night long ago when his girlfriend made sandwiches and neither of you could sleep, like he knows how lucky he is to be present at something that he can't wait to see happen: it is his winter, this is his Christmas. You are no longer letting him down.

Third, you probably know how much money you are making with this tour. The amount of money this tour will generate is fre-quently speculated on. It's a lot of money, is the consensus; it is a whole new planet full of money. Get Happies fans whose message board posts I still follow, when the computer in the office works and everything, have already published a whole PDF denouncing it. *The whole point of Summer Fun is that it doesn't exist,* they assert. *There could never be any Summer Fun.* This is the kind of idea I used to believe in a lot.

But okay, this last thing for sure you know: there are three things that the promoters of the concert have *not* announced:

(1) The reason why, after years of personal silence following the abortive 1972 recordings, you're now reemerging with your infamously lost album that infamously lacked any known lyrics,

(2) The reason why the first stop on this tour is slated to be a hastily constructed amphitheater on the property of a yet-to-be-built spaceport, and

(3) The name, anywhere in the official press releases or promo materials, of *B*——.

You know that this concert is your personal gift to me. We *all* know it.

HERE, BELATEDLY, ARE THE RULES of magic: you draw the signs. You clear the space. You invite in the archangels, you summon the powers you must summon. You ask them for what you want. You listen to what they ask of you, in return. And then you decide what you can offer, and what you can accept. And then, finally, it is time for you to thank them, to allow them to go: to return to the world you have left, the one that you aren't at the center of, the one that moves whether you leave it or not.

IMAGINE THIS CONCERT. SERPENTINE LINES of rabid fans flown over from the UK, wealthy nostalgic couples south from Taos, north from Las Cruces and Texas, east from California, west from everywhere, LA and NYC journalists converging in the mountains as fast as expense accounts can get them there. Bootleg merch hawked to thousands of people waiting, sweating in the heat (the original, never-pressed album art, beer cozies and model hovercars and surfboards with the sun stenciled across them, your face screened on black tees.) And there's legit merch sold inside by tired-looking kids who stand behind official tables with big jugs of water, security guards with earpieces and tats hired in biker bars in Albuquerque who scream at everyone to get in line and have their IDs out, the Westboro protestors, the spatter of urinal troughs and excretory footprints in the sand, murmurs of speculation about the soundcheck's bleats of bass guitar—

Everyone eats, pees, takes their seats—the stage is empty, save for a drum labeled with the leering mystical face of a medieval moon—time clicks on past the appointed hour—fifteen, thirty, an hour past—the sun has long since gone down, maybe it's a mirage, maybe this reunion is a fake just like all the other chimeric reunions were over the years, maybe there never was a *Summer Fun*, maybe there never were cars that flew, *maybe there never was a band*—the hideous aporia where people have yet to be entertained—even the hit parade PA system has gone silent; there is no music; there are only confused and lonely people corralled into uncomfortable seats and lawns in a freezing and unpleasant desert, full epiphanic moon hanging overhead emitting selenic death rays, no food, no buildings to speak of, just fake-looking conquistador gear shoved to the side in boxes—

And then the altar lights up. Roadies, then musicians emerge, cross to guitars—young ones and old ones, surviving members of Midnight Automotive called into service nearly fifty years later for one last duty, the bassist setting aside her cane, strapping her bass across her seated legs, smiling. Thousands of people whose brains tell them to believe in the same idea begin to roar, and it echoes around the canyon as the band raises hands in cheers and blessings and signs. Tom Happy emerges, old arms waving, limping imperceptibly as he crosses to the mic at center, his beard grown in long like a goat's. He points to women in the crowd, capers, mocks deafness to increase the cheers. On a platform at the center of the stage, just between Tom and the drummer, is the same piano that sat in your house. Spotlights cast from materials as expensive as moon rocks trace it in lights. Tom spins, leaps—and then the spotlights pirouette, slide to stage left, where someone is emerging—they catch, first, the splash of silver sequins as if from a crown in the shape of a moon—and then it is happening—you are coming onstage—and the applause is fighting with the silence of a thousand sudden gasps, silence that you will have to find a way to fill.

Polite society has advanced to meet you, Diane; the time to make money from your secrets has arrived at last.

I MEAN THIS IS HOW I have to imagine it, because it's not like I actually *went* to that concert. I mean seriously I have so much better shit to do than that. I don't want to be healthy on those terms; I want to be healthy on mine.

The purpose of any magical action, Diane, is to perform the Great Work: to transform those heaps of dirt and money that surround us into something true. To perform it, though, they say you must work as hard as you can to divest yourself—shave your head, let go of your ego, lay down all your possessions at the gate, make yourself light enough to walk through. You failed for so many years in your Great Work because you couldn't bear to divest yourself. That's one narrative, and it's nice to believe that you could have done that. It makes it easier on everyone if we can find concrete ways in which you have done the wrong thing.

I wish I knew how to divest myself, too. But I know—or have been taught—that there is no excuse for not trying. And I know that we don't always divest ourselves by letting go of what we've been given.

Therefore, here I am, watching the smoke that used to be our concert tickets, all these pages of all these letters I've written: what a mess I was, to do that! What a mess I am! The letters commit themselves to the air, curl into smoke sigils over the altarpiece that sits between Ronda and I in the desert (if she trusted me enough to join me), here in the ghost town we've walked to, the place we got to after walking from our doorstep as far east as we could. Here

we walk the circle—we draw the pentagrams—we banish everything evil from our hearts, for today, for right now. We swear we
will work really hard to keep it all from coming back in. And we
draw a card: The World, a woman entering at a door. It is a pretty
good omen, I think! We talk about The World. We clean up our
campfire mess. And then—turning ourselves west, we think—we
are maybe lost and don't want to admit it, but Ronda swears she
can see lights at the horizon, it could be California—we walk,
single file, through the desert, dragging our inheritances behind
us, toward the home we are building. And you can come and join
us there, Diane, if you are willing to travel light, if you are willing
to be kind to yourself, if you are willing to try—

2009–2019

# Acknowledgments

Thanks need to start with Peter Ames Carlin for writing his excellent biography *Catch a Wave*, which started me thinking about these times in music history. Good information also came from *Gay LA* by Lillian Faderman and Stuart Timmons, *On the Rez* by Ian Frazier, and *Perfecting Sound Forever* by Greg Milner. Thank you also to David Leaf, Stephen Gaines, Paul Quarrington, Lewis Shiner, the Smiley Smile forums (which I lurked for years), and whatever ghostwriter in the Landy Organization was responsible for *Wouldn't It Be Nice*. Invaluable, also, was the website "Cougartown" (cougartown.com) by Hawthorne High alumnus John Baker ('62), which the writer Joseph Mailander once described to me as having "a street-by-street intimacy" that reminded him "of the way Dante covered Florence." (Thanks also to Joseph Mailander for lots of long, good emails about bands of the 1960s, growing up in Hawthorne, and the frustrations of writing weird long books; I appreciate you a lot.)

Thank you to Dan Dzula of Squirrel Thing Recordings for his work in introducing the world, very belatedly, to the lonely genius of Connie Converse, whose story and music are also deep in the DNA of this book. I hope Connie Converse found her happy ending too. If you are not familiar with Connie Converse, please check out *How Sad, How Lovely*: "Talkin' Like You" and "One by One" are my sad faves.

So much gratitude to other friends who gave their time and energy to talk with me about this weird book and the frustrations of its long road to publication: Miracle Jones, Wren Hanks, Anton Solomonik, Kevin Carter, Casey Plett, Cat Fitzpatrick, Simon Jacobs, Emma Copley Eisenberg, Sarah Marshall, Rachel Riederer, Chavisa Woods, Brandon Taylor, Bishakh Som, Naomi Kanakia, Stephen Ira, Joseph Sachs, Amanda Spitzer, Tim Miles, Kathleen Jacques, Torrey Peters, Jackie Ess, Natalie Braginsky, Bill Cheng. Very special thanks to Todd Rawson for giving me a USB stick containing like 100 hours of bootlegs and band interviews from this time period. Inevitably I'm leaving people out.

To my Topside Press tourmates of 2014, Imogen, Casey, and Red, for conversations that deeply informed this book: I remember writing the first draft of the Donner Pass Italian restaurant scene while lying on a blanket on Brattleboro floors next to a giant dog, hoping y'all would think what I was writing was cool. Thank you to Riley MacLeod and Tom Léger for making that tour possible at a time when I really needed it.

Thank you to Riverbend Hot Springs Hostel in Truth or Consequences for being a refuge in 2002; part of me is still there. Thank you for space and time to Lambda Literary, and to the Grace Paley Project of West Virginia, where I felt flows and drew the first sketches of the album illustrations in a grass field in 2017. Thank you most especially to Genre Reassignment, the all-trans reading series in Brooklyn whose attendees got to hear many parts of this before anyone else. It's such a privilege to have shared the stage with all of you: this book is for all you weirdos first.

Thank you to Justin Torres and Sarah Schulman for believing in and advocating for my work. Thank you to Sean MacDonald and Victory Matsui for having generously given me their thoughts on this book; I took it to heart and I hope it shows. Thank you to Lauren Hook and Jamia Wilson: it mattered and matters to me a lot that you gave me the time you did, and I'm still thinking over things you said. Thank you to Marcos Martinez for early enthusiasm and belief. Thank you to Kevin Killian for having been excited to read this one day; I wish I had been faster and that you could have.

To Jin Auh, a tireless advocate who once told me, after we'd received some really unexpected bad news on the book, that you would continue to believe in me: thank you for doing that, and for not minding too much when I told you about rambling band facts.

Thank you so much to Soho Press folks, including freelancer Sophia Babai for brilliant copy edits that called me on all my weird little word decisions, Alexa Wejko for thoughtful and thorough publicity plans, and to Rachel Kowal for careful identification of what is a song and what is not. Thank you especially to Mark Doten for a fantastic editorial eye, and for seeing the potential in this decisively strange book. A global pandemic creates maybe the worst conditions for editing a book, but I appreciate the care with which you treated this.

Thank you to my family, who are good folks whom I love very much. Special thanks to my father for having been convinced for like eleven years that this book was on the cusp of being published any day now. I'm glad this finally came true, and I appreciate your faith. And again, thank you to Wren for being there for most of the years of writing this book, including very difficult times, and for believing in it so many times when I didn't.

Last but far from least: thank you to Van Dyke Parks for writing an impeccable note declining to read the manuscript of this book. Thank you to Connie Converse, wherever she is, and to American Spring, and Darian Sahanaja, David Marks, Blondie Chaplin, and Ricky Fataar. Thank you to Bruce Johnston, Al Jardine, Carl and Dennis Wilson, and Mike Love. And thank you to Brian Wilson. I saw you perform at the New Jersey Performing Arts Center in 2017, and we gave you a standing ovation for "God Only Knows," and I will remember forever how you insisted everyone sit down and stop clapping for you before you would continue to sing. <3